Greig Beck grew up across the road from Bondi Beach in Sydney, Australia. His early days were spent surfing, sunbaking, and reading science fiction on the sand. He then went on to study computer science, immerse himself in the financial software industry, and later received an MBA.

Today, Greig spends his days writing, but still finds time to surf at his beloved Bondi Beach. He lives in Sydney, with his wife and a loopy golden retriever.

If you would like to contact Greig, his email address is greig@greigbeck.com and you can find him on the web at www.greigbeck.com.

THE SILURIAN BRIDGE

ALEX HUNTER XI

GREIG BECK

momentum

Pan Macmillan acknowledges the Traditional Custodians of Country throughout Australia and their connections to lands, waters and communities. We pay our respect to Elders past and present and extend that respect to all Aboriginal and Torres Strait Islander peoples today. We honour more than sixty thousand years of storytelling, art and culture.

First published 2024 in Momentum by Pan Macmillan Australia Pty Ltd
1 Market Street, Sydney, New South Wales, Australia, 2000

A catalogue record for this book is available from the National Library of Australia

The Silurian Bridge: Alex Hunter 11

EPUB format: 9781761561849
Print on Demand format: 9781761561115
Original cover design: SaberCore23-ArtStudio.

Macmillan Digital Australia: www.macmillandigital.com.au
To report a typographical error, please visit www.panmacmillan.com.au/contact-us/

Visit www.panmacmillan.com.au to read more about all our books and to buy books online. You will also find features, author interviews and news of any author events.

"*The Great Old Ones who lived ages before there were any men, and who came to the young world out of the sky. Those Old Ones are gone now, inside the Earth and under the sea; but their dead bodies had told their secrets in dreams to the first men . . .*"
— H.P. Lovecraft, *The Call of Cthulhu and Other Dark Tales*

The Silurian period, approximately 420 million years ago, was a time of explosive biological growth in the sea, and emergence onto the land. There had been a breathable atmosphere for 100 million years, and evolution was just beginning to flex its muscles.

However, much of this distant period remains a mystery as examples of primordial lifeforms from that time are fragmentary, difficult to interpret, and the fossil evidence of many species, large and small, may never be found.

Then there are the anomalies, things that defy description or test the bounds of reality. Things that evolution created and then cancelled. Or perhaps evolution had nothing to do with them at all, because they never originated here, and time wisely kept them hidden from us.

PROLOGUE

The Silurian period, 420 million years ago –
East coast of the super island of Laurentia, which
would one day become America

There was a crackling sound like that of an electrical discharge in the air, followed by a smell of ozone.

The atmosphere along the waterline was heavy, hot, and humid. Huge balls of pocked fungus, feathery lichens, and vines that supported sticky-looking bulbs were scorched as a ball of blue light grew from a dot to around ten feet across. It flared for a second into excruciating brilliance and then vanished.

Silence returned.

But there was something left behind.

The seated man blinked several times and then his eyes widened. "*Oh my God.*" His mouth curved into a grin as he turned slowly. "We did it."

CHAPTER 01

Present day, Saturday, July 12, 0800 hours –
Buchanan Road, Boston, Massachusetts

Alex Hunter had his back turned, preoccupied, but suddenly
spun and caught the football on its way to his head. He held it
up and laughed softly. "Yeah, nice try, buddy."

Joshua grinned. "Good reflexes, Dad. As always."

Alex threw the ball back. Hard. And Joshua *oofed* as he
caught it at belly level, and then raced back upstairs.

Aimee came bustling through, baseball cap pulled tight
over her black hair, which she'd tied back in a short ponytail.
She began putting things in her bag and listing them off as she
went. "Keys, sunglasses, phone, ah, directions . . ."

She looked up, and then to either side. "Come on, Josh,
we're late, and we don't want to have to end up parking miles
away."

Alex flipped the tea towel over his shoulder and walked
away from the kitchen sink where he'd been cleaning up. He
grinned. It was Aimee's turn to take Josh to football practice.
He loved watching his son play, or even just train, but as it
was a beautiful morning, he was going to enjoy just sitting in
the backyard, coffee in hand, the sunshine on his face.

"*Coming*," Joshua yelled.

Alex chuckled at the sound of rumbling from upstairs, but neither Josh nor Torben, their massive German shepherd, made an appearance.

He loved his life now. From time to time he missed the adventure and thrill of the HAWC missions, and also the camaraderie of being with his other Special Forces compatriots. But he now knew, home was where he belonged.

His son was growing up fast, and he didn't want to look back when Joshua was a man and wonder how or when that had happened – he was going to be here watching it, he and Aimee, together.

The other pleasure of family life was that the Other, the demon that hid deep inside his Id, was silent. The thing of violence, anger, and fury was either gone for good, or banished to some corner of his mind where it couldn't find the energy to reemerge.

Alex turned to look at Aimee standing at the door with her hands on her hips. She looked impatient as all hell, and he just couldn't resist.

"Hurry up, Josh, or Mom will end up at the back of the coffee queue. And you know how angry that makes her."

More rumbling, and then the massive German shepherd came thumping down the stairs. Tor, who was now pushing 280 pounds, leaped from halfway up and made some of the furniture jump when he landed. He immediately turned and barked back up at Joshua.

"Yeah, you tell him, big guy." Alex laughed.

"Thank you. Big help, buster." Aimee rolled her eyes and stood by the door. "Out, out, out."

Joshua raced downstairs after the dog. "See ya, Dad," he called to Alex as he headed out, Tor at his heels.

"Have a good one." Alex dried his hands on the towel,

flipped it back onto his shoulder and stood watching his wife and son from the doorstep.

Aimee rushed back to kiss Alex on the lips. "Don't forget, we've got the Jeffersons coming over this evening. You need to get ground beef for Josh's favorite."

"Burgers." Alex nodded.

"And steaks. Good ones, for them." She waited.

Alex groaned.

She smiled up at him. "Stop that. It's called being friendly to our neighbors."

Alex just groaned louder.

"C'mon, Mom," Joshua called.

She turned. "Oh right, now *I'm* the one holding everyone up."

She headed down the front path to the parked car and Alex watched her go.

He smiled; he felt so lucky. Blessed even. He had the two best people in the world as his family and wanted nothing more than to spend the rest of his life with them.

Tor came back and nudged his hand and then sat beside him, watching as well. Alex looked down at the dog. "Okay, the three best people in the world."

Alex saw Aimee and Joshua reach the car.

Then the hair on his neck lifted, and time seemed to freeze around him – a leaf falling in the garden was suspended in the air. A bee stopped mid-flight. And every sound vanished.

A wave of nausea washed over him, and alarms screamed in his head.

Danger.

Joshua spun back toward him, and their eyes met. They both knew. Something was coming. Something bad.

The high-velocity bullet entered the back of the boy's head and exited the front, taking away most of his forehead.

In that split second Alex's muscles unlocked and he began to sprint forward.

Aimee, still focused on the car, hadn't even registered what had happened.

Then the second bullet took her – in through one temple and out the other.

She simply crumpled to the ground, like a puppet whose strings had been cut.

Time resumed, sounds intruded.

The dog was howling, and Alex was screaming. He rushed first to Joshua and lifted the boy in his arms, cradling him. He dragged him over to Aimee and held her in his other arm. He said their names, over and over, but he could already feel that their spirits had left their bodies. They were gone.

Alex rocked them back and forth and threw his head back, screaming to the sky as their blood drenched his body. *"Take me. Take me."*

But the third shot never came.

* * *

Alex barely heard his former boss speaking. He wasn't even sure when he had arrived.

"Sniper," Hammerson said softly, and handed Alex a large stoneware mug of black coffee. "We found the cartridges. They were forty-eight-millimeter Whisper rounds."

Alex took the large mug, not by the handle but the cup part. He ignored the scalding heat as he continued to stare at the ground.

"That's why even you didn't hear them coming." Hammerson watched Alex for a moment before continuing. "That means it's likely that a Russian Lobaev SVL sniper rifle was used. The best, and accurate up to 1.2 miles." Alex could feel his colonel's unblinking stare but ignored it. "We've found the shooter's nest; it was a building half a mile out. They shot from an open window."

"Lobaev," Alex mumbled. "Assassin's weapon."

He sat on the couch in his living room. It was the only piece of furniture still intact. Everything else hadn't been destroyed so much as pulverized. There were even holes in the walls. He didn't remember doing that.

"Yes." Hammerson's eyes were hooded, and he spoke without emotion. "The young couple who owned the apartment were murdered. The killer shot them both and then set himself up at their window. We think he was there several days. Just stepping over the bodies, watching. Watching you, Aimee, and Joshua." He exhaled. "It looks like a professional hit."

Alex just sat there in a grimy t-shirt with the dog sitting beside him, alternately resting his head on Alex's knee, and turning to glare at Hammerson.

"A hit?" Alex slowly looked up from his fugue. "Why?" he asked. "Why them, and not me?"

"We don't know. You were probably meant to be next, but the shooter might have been interrupted. Joshua was seen as the long-range threat because of his abilities, so they took him first." Hammerson sat forward. "I give you my word we'll find who did this. I'll never stop, never rest, until we get them."

"Sir." Alex looked up with dead eyes. "When you find them, let me speak to them first."

Hammerson sat back. "I'll keep you informed, daily." He got to his feet. "Also, Sam is going to drop in on you."

"You mean to keep an eye on me." Alex's voice was low and the hand holding the coffee mug began to tremble. "I don't need anyone *keeping an eye on me*."

"He worries about you," Hammerson replied in a calm voice. "We all do." He sighed. "I can't imagine what you're going through, Alex. But what matters now—"

"*No*." Alex came upright, roaring, and the thick stone mug exploded in his hand. "*Nothing matters anymore*."

The huge dog also jumped to his feet, hackles up, his head low. His eyes were fixed on Hammerson like twin lasers.

"Easy, son." Hammerson stood his ground but knew things could go real bad in the blink of an eye. Real bad for him.

Alex's fist was clenched and his body was still vibrating from pure rage. His hand bled, but it quickly stopped, his rapid metabolism already healing the wound.

The HAWC commander went to step toward his former soldier, but the dog sensed it and advanced, getting between them, and growled low and mean. Hammerson froze.

"Sam will come around first thing tomorrow," he said.

But Alex barely heard him as he retreated back into himself again. He spoke as if in a trance. "You find the shooter. Or I will."

Hammerson grunted. "I'll be in touch."

He headed for the doorway, where he paused to look back at Alex Hunter one last time. Then he went out, shutting the door quietly behind him.

* * *

Alex sank slowly back down into the couch. And then stayed there all day. The sun went down, and he didn't notice. He did nothing but stare at the floor and wish he was dead.

It was only when Tor raked his leg that he blinked a few times and returned to a form of consciousness that allowed him to remember that the dog needed to be fed. "Okay, boy, okay. I'm sorry."

He rubbed the huge animal's head, but then stopped as a thought came to him. He stared into Tor's eyes for many seconds. "Is he . . . still in there with you?"

Tor's gaze was unwavering as their eyes locked. He came forward to bump his head into Alex's chest.

"You're all I have left now."

Alex grabbed both sides of the animal's face and leaned his own forward, resting his head against the dog's as the hot tears came.

CHAPTER 02

Twenty-two years ago – Larz Anderson Park, Brookline, Massachusetts

Jeffrey Butler jogged along the dark and damp track, blowing steam into the freezing morning air. He wore a knitted cap, gloves, and a jogging suit with leggings underneath. And still felt the cold.

Benny, his springer spaniel, came back and dropped the ball in front of him again, and Jeff paused to pick it up and toss it once more out onto an open space of dewy grass beside the track. Benny shot away in frenetic pursuit.

Jeffrey had Larz Anderson Park, or the LAP, to himself, and that was why he came so early. The LAP was a wooded and landscaped parkland with ponds, a few historic buildings, and a skating rink, and at sixty-four acres, with hills and winding tracks, it hosted cross country running competitions most weekends. It was a place that made him forget about the high-rises, traffic snarls, and an office full of shouting fund managers.

Jeffrey sucked in another deep breath of the biting, clean air, and then bent to scoop up the ball again, grinning as his manically happy dog, now with wet ears and tummy, ran backwards waiting for the throw.

"An-*nnnd*. Go!" He tossed it, and once again Benny belted away into the predawn darkness.

Jeffrey ran on, smoothly and easily, delighting in his level of fitness. He worked in structured finance, and knew how to make big deals happen, and for that his funds management firm rewarded him handsomely. That was why at just thirty-three he was already wealthy. Sure, it was stressful, but he could take it.

He jogged along the empty winding tracks, bordered by huge American beech trees, eastern hemlock, and sugar maples, whose branches joined overhead to make massive arched tunnels beneath them.

Soon he would reach the old domed-roof band rotunda marking the point where he began the final leg of his jog, passing through one of the most heavily wooded areas of the park.

Jeffrey could already taste the egg-white omelet with lightly toasted brioche bun he'd whip up when he got home to refuel and recharge, all washed down with fresh pomegranate juice. Life was good.

He turned onto the dark track past the rotunda but then slowed, frowning; a soft glow from the deeper forested side of the path drew his attention. He'd thought there was no one else for miles, and at this time of day his only companions should have been squirrels, foxes, and maybe a few eastern screech owls shooting him disdainful looks.

He whistled to Benny, who lifted his head then sprinted to join him, and he jogged on the spot for a few more moments then stopped. He squinted; there was something in the brush giving off a luminous blue glow, he was sure of it now.

Is someone camping in there and that's their lantern? he wondered.

Benny growled beside him, and Jeffrey shushed him. He checked his watch. He didn't want to hang around and cool down, but curiosity got the better of him. He reached down and picked up Benny's ball, then threw it hard back down the track, and the dog belted away.

With the nosy dog occupied, Jeffrey eased his way into the forest, pushing through the prickly bushes and trying not to snag his three-hundred-dollar jogging suit.

He saw then that the blue glow was coming from a puddle of water, almost a small pond but not quite. He sniffed; oddly, he smelled something like brine.

Jeffrey's eyes widened as he crept closer to the glow. He was right, it was the pond – or something in it – that was glowing. As he approached, he looked around and quickly grabbed up a stick about four feet in length. When he got to the pond's edge, he could clearly see a shimmering blue ball of light within the brine-smelling water – seawater – and the smell reminded him of his last holiday down on Santa Rosa Beach in Florida.

He held out the stick and poked it into the water – just a foot separated the glowing ball from the end of his stick, then inches, and then he touched it, and without warning, he was yanked forward.

Jeffrey Butler felt himself falling and tumbling; a vortex of light swirled around him, and giddiness made his stomach flip.

One minute he was on bitterly cold, dry land, and the next he was under water, and it was warm and salty. He kicked hard and spluttered to the surface, which thankfully was only a few feet above him. He came up into brilliant warm sunshine and flicked water from his face as his sodden cap floated away.

"*What the fuck?*" he yelled.

Jeffrey Butler, fund manager, financial shark, spun one way then the other. There was no one, nothing, and just an endless blue sky, water as far as the eye could see, and definitely no predawn park with all its cold, damp, and shadows.

"I can't . . ." He turned again. "What . . .?"

Was it some sort of elaborate prank? Was he hallucinating? But he could feel the sun's heat on his face and taste the seawater.

He felt his jogging suit beginning to weigh him down and he dipped his head below the surface and opened his eyes. Shafts of sunlight fell away into the depths, but it was far too deep to stand, and he knew if he didn't find some land soon, he'd tire. And then sink. And drown.

Jeffrey spotted something that broke the surface a few dozen feet from him. From sea level he thought it looked like a greenish-hued truck tire, and he took a few strokes toward it. Oddly, he closed the gap faster than he expected, making him think it was also coming toward him.

When it was just a few feet away he saw that it wasn't the soft rubber of a tire as he'd first thought but looked more shell-like. He reached out to touch it and at the same time felt the gentle caress of something against his legs. He looked down into the clear water and alarmingly saw that there were ropes, or rather, tentacles, coming from underneath the object, and they were wrapping around his legs.

"*Gah.*" He violently kicked the thing away, and it scooted off. And then submerged. "*How is this happening?*" he yelled.

He trod water, looking one way then the other. "Oh, thank God." Relief flowed through him as for the first time he noticed something that looked like a reef or low-lying island in the distance.

He could make it there and reassess what had happened. He began to swim, thinking that he had probably hit his head and was dreaming this entire thing. Yeah, that was it. He must have slipped, and he was still lying in the forest, knocked out cold.

He swam a few dozen strokes and saw that the weird island was just a featureless gray lump, with some sort of banding across it. It didn't look that big, no more than fifty feet in length. But at least it would allow him to climb from the water and rest.

As he closed in on it, he looked up again and then slowed his stroke – the island had changed shape. Or moved.

Jeffrey stopped swimming and blinked seawater from his eyes. As he watched, the island moved again, this time he was sure. And this time it moved toward him.

He stopped swimming.

What happens if you die in a dream? he wondered.

He gulped as he trod water again – the thing was definitely coming closer.

I hope you're a whale, he prayed. *One of the friendly ones.*

The island began to speed up. Coming right at him.

"*No, no, no . . .*"

Jeffrey sucked in a breath and ducked his head beneath the crystal-clear, bath-warm water, and looked ahead. Coming out of the blue gloom was a huge, cylindrical body – and then its seven-foot-long triangular head angled sideways and split open down the middle, revealing teeth as long as his forearm.

It was no whale.

Jeffrey's last thoughts were that this wasn't a dream. It was a nightmare.

* * *

Massachusetts Institute of Technology (MIT), Physics Department, R&D Room 24

"*Whoa*, what just happened?" Phillip Hanley held his hands up as he jumped to his feet, making his chair skid back across the linoleum floor.

"I think, I think . . ." Rashid Jamal shook his head as he furiously worked the controls. "I think we just had another temporal projection anomaly. Just a tiny one." He half-turned. "Jimmy, check my numbers."

"On it." Jimmy Chen's fingers worked the keyboard so fast and so expertly, he was like a concert pianist. He nodded. "Yep, confirmed, we had a projection."

"Shit-damn, another time interstice." Hanley grimaced and then turned to the lead-glass wall behind which a ten-foot-tall, spherical machine was glowing a soft blue. *"Shut it down, shut it down."*

Rashid and Jimmy tapped furiously on their keyboards and the hum and glow coming from the device faded away to nothing.

Hanley sighed and then lifted his head. "Please tell me it didn't—"

"Yeah, it did. It opened a portal and projected it." Rashid checked his console, his lips moving as he quickly read down the data and tried to find the end location of the energy pulse. He looked up, his forehead deeply creased. "Not far."

"Found it." Jimmy looked up from his bank of small screens. "It was in the park."

Hanley tilted his head back and looked skyward. "Please take me now, Jesus." He lowered his head to glare at his colleague. "And I'm betting it was back to . . .?"

"Yeah, way, way back," Rashid replied. "It's saying 420 million years – ocean world."

"A least it's consistent." Hanley sighed and leaned forward on his knuckles. "Would anyone have seen it?"

"At this time of day? I doubt it." Rashid smiled helpfully.

"Maybe just an owl or two." Jimmy shrugged.

"Fine, if no one saw it, it didn't happen." Hanley sat back down wearily and turned to his colleagues. "We need to control these rift projections." He went to face his bank of computers again but paused. "Imagine if one of these aberrant events happens to spit out a portal into a heavily populated area, during rush hour? Forget about having our funding cut, we'll all end up in freaking jail."

"I'm on it. But working with the subatomics means they're doing what they usually do; they escape, especially the tachyons." Rashid pulled his chair closer and began to open the millions of lines of code and subroutines for the gateway generator.

"First thing we need to isolate and eliminate is the tachyon stream generator's ability to project." Jimmy bobbed his head. "Obviously got to have that only occurring when and where we want it."

"Obviously." Hanley rubbed his forehead. "We've created a prototype for the first working time machine the world has ever seen. And after two years of testing, we still can't control it." He turned to the others. "It's like building a cannon that fires its shells at the target, as long as the target is only in one place. Oh, and sometimes it decides to fire them anywhere it wants."

"And that target is basically the dawn of time." Rashid lifted his eyebrows. "Hey, we knew the birth of time travel would be painful. But we've done a lot. Brought it a long way. If only we weren't short of funds, equipment, and ... fresh thinking. I'm losing control of all the code." He took his hands off the keyboard. "Maybe we should bring in—"

"No." Hanley rose to his feet. "We're not bringing in the military, investors, or anyone else." His face softened into a more benign expression. "We might lose everything. Sorry. No."

"Private equity would throw money at us." Jimmy Chen straightened. "What's wrong with making a few bucks while we build something that will change the world?"

"I said, no." Hanley glared at each of his colleagues for a moment, but then he sighed long and loud. "Guys, we're just not ready yet."

Rashid held his palms up. "Phillip, we're going broke. If we don't get more funding, we may never complete our project. Using jerry-rigged tech is the reason things are still going wrong. And if we have a serious accident, we *will* lose everything."

"He's right, Phillip," Jimmy said.

Hanley groaned. "Okay, okay, I'll look into it."

Rashid nodded, but still looked disbelieving.

"It's on my list. Promise." Hanley crossed his heart. "But for now, just stick with it; you'll get it."

He sat down and sighed. "Time is the most valuable thing in the world. And we're about to own it."

CHAPTER 03

Twenty-two years later, July 17 – The Janus Institute, Landsdowne Street, Cambridge, Massachusetts

Phillip Hanley had briefly left the office to grab a coffee and waited at the corner for the traffic lights to change.

He sipped the brew and let his mind run. It had taken them over twenty years to solve the portal projection issue, and after so many failures, near misses, and accidents, today was the day when he expected the rubber to hit the road.

He looked up at their building – the least impressive in the street – and spotted the small sign for the Janus Institute, which showed a human head with a face on both sides. This was also fitting, as in ancient Roman religion and myth, Janus was the god of duality, gateways, and time, and was usually depicted as having two faces – one looking forward, and one looking back. Hanley liked the concept and knew that was exactly what they were trying to do – and all being well, *would do* today.

The lights changed and he crossed the road, pushed backwards through the glass doors, and headed for the elevator. It glided open immediately and he rode up five floors to the offices and laboratory.

He sipped his coffee again and smiled – Rashid had been right – extra cash had made all the difference. Despite his reluctance, he had secured some funding from the Occam Foundation, a benevolent company that was set up by tech billionaire Gilliam Bates who in his will had requested that companies that showed promise could apply for funding, even significant funding, with no strings attached, as long as they were working on something for the betterment of humankind.

Hanley snorted. He'd had to do little more than deliver a brief presentation to Occam's board of fossilized men and women and was granted approval in two days – ten million dollars. He still couldn't believe his good fortune.

Once cashed up, it was easy to find several top physicists and technical professionals wanting to work with them – they could take their pick.

He drained his coffee, dumped the cup in the trash basket in the corridor and entered the Janus lab. He nodded to a few of the staff and then his business partners, Rashid Jamal and Jimmy Chen.

His friends and colleagues of over twenty years looked a little worse for wear. Rashid, now forty-eight, had lost his youthful looks, and his head of once jet-black hair was streaked with gray. Crow's feet pinched the corners of his eyes and his waist had expanded.

Jimmy still looked the best of them and could probably pass for thirty. Good genes, Hanley guessed.

Phillip Hanley knew he undoubtedly looked the worse, living on a diet of too much strong coffee, donuts, and hurried takeout meals. His hair had thinned and his glasses were thicker than ever. But he consoled himself with the fact that their three minds were still as sharp as ever.

"D-Day." Hanley sucked in a huge breath and let it out with a *whoosh*. "Let's make history, people."

Rashid beamed. "The culmination of twenty-five years' work and millions of dollars."

"Thankfully, other people's millions of dollars," Jimmy Chen added.

Rashid laughed. "And God bless America for having rich companies that want nothing but our success." He clapped his hands once, then looked back down at his console with multiple screens. "Go time. Jimmy, are you ready?"

"I was born ready." Jimmy looked up with a huge grin. "I've been waiting my entire life for the moment when I could say that."

Rashid chuckled as Hanley looked over the laboratory floor. In the center of the large gleaming lab was the tachyon drive, a sphere, roughly four feet around, now encased in a fifty-foot shield of three-inch-thick, lead-impregnated, tempered glass.

The device had been vastly improved and miniaturized from their first prototype. The previous machine had been a ten-foot ball that looked like an armored dreadnaught. But their new device was just fifty inches across, and a gleaming silver globe – it was a thing of wonder and beauty.

It had taken them their entire adult lives, from university days to now, to successfully harness tachyons, the rarest of subatomic particles that not only traveled faster than the speed of light but also back and forth through time, as if the barriers defined by physics didn't exist. And for tachyons, they didn't.

Hanley smiled at it. It sounded so simple, in theory: all they had needed to do was tap into the relevant tachyon stream, create and sustain a bridge, and ride across it.

They still had work to do, as the tricky bit was making sure they got off the time bridge at the right exit. And, as yet, that was proving elusive. So far the only bridge they had been able to cross was one stretching all the way back 420 million years. But identifying, capturing, and then crossing more recent temporal bridges should be within their grasp soon.

"My time machine," he whispered.

Beside the sphere was a pedestal, three feet around with a flat top, and what looked like the muzzle of a large gun pointed down at it. In the center of the pedestal's top was a protective waterproof case containing a small camera.

He focused. "Everyone, take your positions." He waited a few seconds. "Don glasses." He looked around the lab.

They had a team of five of the best physicists money could buy, and around the room, the group was spellbound as they waited for what they hoped was the first successful recording of, and therefore documented, there-and-back tachyon bridge event test.

They'd already sent things back and retrieved them. But this time, they were going to actually see what was back there.

"Is everybody ready – Doreen?" Hanley found the small woman and lifted his chin, waiting.

Doreen Peng was their technical group leader, a graduate of MIT, and one of the most pragmatic physicists they had ever met. She was uninspiring and methodical, but what she lacked in creativity she made up for with an encyclopedic knowledge of the scientific processes and a mind like a human computer.

She was their tiger mom, and she looked at the team, nodded to each with her usual stern gaze, placed her shaded and blast-proof goggles over her eyes and then turned to give Hanley the thumbs-up.

Hanley pulled his goggles down over his eyes. "Doctors Jamal, Chen . . . let us see what we will see."

Rashid looked from Hanley to Jimmy, who nodded, and then back to his screen. He glanced at the device, and then to the small camera. He licked dry lips, and then pressed a button that would capture all his words and actions.

"Recording," he said, and then cleared his throat and leaned a little toward the microphone. "Commencing viability test forty-two. Objective is a controlled tachyon capture, portal opening, and creating a chronological singularity via a two-way bridge, between one point on a time line and another. We will, in effect, be sending an object into our past, where it will remain for exactly thirty seconds, capturing images of the Earth during the Silurian period. We will then bring it back on another bridge." He smiled nervously. "We hope."

Hanley hoped as well, because he remembered the results of the last forty-one tests. They were able to capture tachyons and open portals, and even send things back. But there had been bugs in the return process. Their computer programming had code that considered the massive geomorphic changes, sea and land level rises, and even temperature and atmospheric differentials. But most times the objects couldn't be located, or they brought something else back, or the computer algorithms said the retrieval had been successfully completed, when there was nothing there at all.

Rashid and Jimmy had assured him these were yesterday's problems, and he had high confidence in his team. But still Hanley whispered a tiny prayer for luck.

"Camera on." Rashid walked around in front of the device, bent to check that the lights were on, and gave the small lens a fragile smile. He hurried back to his console and moved a lever, and the spherical device began to glow a soft blue again. "Particle capture. Opening portal." Rashid stared, his eyes almost bulging from the intensity of his focus.

"Identifying object," Jimmy said. "Got it."

A blue ball of light began to form around the camera device on the pedestal. The scientist rested his finger on a small button.

"Creating bridge." He drew in a breath. "And . . . *sending*." He pressed the button.

The ball of light glowed brighter for a second or two until it became blinding. And when it winked out, the camera was gone.

No one moved or made a sound.

Hanley brought his hands together under his chin as if in prayer as he counted down the seconds.

Here goes nothing, he thought.

At twenty seconds, Rashid sat forward. "Reopening portal. Collecting tachyon stream. Searching for object." He swallowed as the small ball of blue light reappeared on the pedestal.

"Come on, come on, you can do it," Jimmy Chen almost begged. And then, finally: "Found it . . . and we have locked on." He licked his lips.

"Okay, creating return bridge, a-*aaand*, bringing it back." Rashid pressed the button again.

The blue light glowed brighter, and then rose to a searing flash. And then, as the light died away, they could see that something was left behind on the pedestal.

Everyone stared, waiting for the retinal flash images to fade from their vision. Then they saw: it was the camera. But it was filthy and covered in some sort of lichen.

Hanley's smile drooped, and his brows came together. It looked almost as if the camera might have been trapped in the past for years, not just the thirty seconds they had experienced.

"Okay," he said softly as he lowered his goggles. "I want full quarantine procedures. Let's not run into any primordial bugs we aren't equipped to deal with." He turned to the others. "Guys, what happened?"

Rashid and Jimmy's hands flew over their keyboards. "I think . . . I think we were only off by a few months or years," said Rashid. He continued to type. "We can fix that. Just a little distortion." He looked up and grinned. "Yep, here we go. At our end it was gone for thirty seconds. But at its end it sat there for six months." He shrugged. "Not bad. A blip really. After all, it went back over 420 million years."

"Let's prove the hypothesis," Hanley said. "The case looks intact, so let's see what's on the disc." He looked to the assembled technicians. "Doreen, do your stuff."

Doreen Peng bustled forward and ran a check on the air in the chamber. She nodded. "Air is good, no biological contaminants other than the usual soil decomposition microbes. Also, no significant radiation." She then entered through the security shield, and slowly walked around the camera. "Device is not compromised."

"Good, good." Hanley sighed with relief. "Proceed."

Doreen lifted a cord from the pedestal and plugged it into the camera port. She smiled. "Files still viable. Accessing the internal memory." She uploaded the data to the Janus mainframe.

Hanley watched impatiently as the files were populated on their mainframe, and he was delighted to see they were of significant size – meaning the camera had most likely kept on recording for the entire length of its twenty-four-hour battery life.

He rubbed his hands together. "Let's see what we got."

He turned to Rashid and Jimmy who had both left their consoles and come to stand beside him. Hanley leaned over the master console and hesitated over the buttons, keys, and levers. There was always the chance the camera had ended up face down, filming the ground the entire time.

Please don't be blank, he prayed, then initiated the video recording and sent the images to a large wall screen in the laboratory.

The first blessing was that it worked.

The film opened with the scene in the laboratory, which to them had been only a few minutes ago. On screen was Rashid, who gave the camera a little smile. Then the screen's image glowed blue and went haywire. It was as if the camera had been dropped into a bucket of water stirred by an artist's paint-soaked brushes.

And then it suddenly cleared, and the image auto-focus corrected itself as the depth perspective altered.

Everyone held their breath.

And then they saw.

The lab was gone, the people were gone, the walls, ceiling, everything was gone, and in its place were hanging fronds of verdant green, vines covered in bulbous grape-like growths, tree trunks that were covered in papery bark like peeling mushroom skin, and a steamy-looking mist that hovered near ground level. Everything looked wet, dripping, humid; even the very air seemed a hazy green.

"Oh my God, oh my God, oh my God." Jimmy's mouth hung open in a wide grin. "*I love it!*"

"*Ho-ly* shit." Rashid stared. "Is it really there?"

"Is it there?" Hanley snorted softly. "It's there, and it's here. *Right here.* But about 420 million years ago." He felt a ball of happiness bloom in his stomach.

"The Silurian period. Long before even dinosaurs walked the Earth," Rashid whispered.

Jimmy rested his chin on his palms. "The world was mostly an ocean then." He sniffed deeply as though inhaling the scents of the scene. "I want to see it, smell it, feel it. I want to be there."

The group watched, spellbound. Unfortunately the images were at ground level and the light was muted.

Rashid tried to adjust the lighting to remove some of the shadows but all that did was alter the depth perspective. "I think . . ." He fiddled with the luminescence again and then gave up. ". . . we're either at some sort of twilight period in the day, or more likely under a heavy tree canopy. Not much light getting down to us."

"Next time, we should send something with wheels." Hanley grinned.

Rashid looked up. "We could do that." He smiled back. "Like the Mars rover."

Minutes ticked by as the first hour passed. But nothing changed. And then just as the group was becoming impatient . . .

"Hold it. Hold it." Hanley walked forward, hands up in front of him. He stopped and his eyes narrowed. "I think . . . *there.*"

He pointed to the side of the screen just as a tiny snout pushed through the ferns. And then it was followed by a head and neck.

Rashid also came slowly to his feet. "What is that thing?" He turned. "That's not a dinosaur."

"No, of course not," Jimmy scoffed softly. "We're hundreds of millions of years before them."

Hanley folded his arms. "This is something else entirely."

The group walked closer to the screen.

The animal stared a little dully, and then turned one dark eye on the camera. It slowly approached.

It was an oddity in that it looked a little like a tortoise out of its shell, with gray-green skin, a flat beak-like top lip, but also with downward-curving tusks on either side of its face. Though its nostril slits didn't twitch, Hanley bet it was inhaling the smells of the new arrival. And in its mind it probably wondered if the new thing was edible or not.

It came right up to the camera, and when the auto-focus capabilities of the device zoomed back to stop it blurring, they saw the squat, muscular arms on each side of its body, more like a lizard than a mammal.

"Looks like a deformed cross between a pig, turtle, and a reptile," Rashid said.

They could see then that it had small forearms, each finishing in tiny taloned hands. It slowly reached forward and touched the screen, quickly, and then pulled back.

When it perceived no threat, its head came forward and the beaky mouth opened. Inside the mouth they caught a glimpse of flattened teeth and a dry tongue, like a broad finger. It slithered out and probably licked the screen. Then it pulled back a little as its head tilted to the side, one single dull eye still on the camera.

Rashid observed, "Does anyone know what type of creature that is? I mean, if it's not a dinosaur."

"Something primitive, *very* primitive," Jimmy said. "There were creatures that lived long before dinosaurs that had the characteristics of both dinosaurs and mammals – wild evolution."

"Someone has been doing their homework." Hanley grinned. "We can find out later."

"This is so cool." Jimmy rubbed his hands together. "We did this. We really did this."

With a blink the creature turned and then, eyes wide, leaped at the camera and over it, sending the device tumbling and making the screen go dark.

But then the camera started to shake and bounce letting in slivers of light for a few moments.

"Is there an earthquake, or maybe volcanic activity?" Rashid asked. "Is that what scared it off?"

"Definitely high volcanic activity at that time. But I don't think so." Hanley unfolded his arms and craned forward. "Something else."

"Maybe something wanted to eat the little creature." Doreen Peng said.

"I agree; I think it just got knocked face down by whatever scared the little pigosaur away." Hanley blew air through pressed lips. "Maybe even damn buried it."

He felt frustration boiling up inside him as they had only watched around one hour, fifteen minutes out of a potential twenty-four hours.

"Thanks, you fat little bastard," he yelled at the dark screen.

"If someone was there, a human, that wouldn't happen," said Jimmy. "That's the age-old problem of using remote devices."

"That might also be why the retrieve algorithms couldn't immediately find it." Rashid scratched his chin. "I can fix that."

The trio continued watching for another ten minutes but the screen stayed dark. They fast forwarded the film to the end, hoping for more action, but it stayed mercilessly black.

They then rewound the footage and watched the beginning several more times, halting and focusing in on the minutiae of the animal, the plant life, and the surroundings.

When they were finished they all fell silent and Hanley felt his spirits lift. He turned to his friends and colleagues and smiled broadly. "We didn't get everything we wanted, but the bottom line is, we did it."

"It works." Rashid beamed back.

The team in the room erupted into applause, and even the normally brusque Doreen Peng smiled widely, and half-bowed.

Beaming, Hanley waved them down.

Rashid was already diving into the programming. "And I already know how I can code in fixes to the small displacement issue by adding a tracker, rather than a location. Easy."

Hanley straightened up, stretching his stiff back. "Mark today's date. It will go down in history as the moment working time travel became a reality." He nodded to himself, feeling self-satisfied, and turned to his partners.

"Let's get some air," Hanley said, and he, Rashid, and Jimmy walked outside together.

After a few moments he turned. "How does everyone feel after that?"

Jimmy fist-pumped the air. "Alive, energized, proud, ecstatic."

Rashid nodded and grinned at his exuberant colleague. "Yeah, it went well."

"Better than well. In fact, I think we're ready to move to the next level." Hanley waggled his eyebrows. "A live test."

"When?" Rashid asked.

"Why wait? Tomorrow," he replied.

"I'll go," Jimmy said immediately.

Hanley and Rashid turned to stare at him.

Rashid's brows came together. "Wait, you're serious?" He shook his head. "Not a chance. We've got a lot—"

"Nope, it's settled." Jimmy shrugged. "It works. I can guarantee no stranding problems or remote tech glitches. Send me back for just one minute. Or even thirty seconds. My observations and insights will be invaluable."

"I won't have solved the displacement issues or have a tracker by then," Rashid complained.

Jimmy shook his head. "I won't move a muscle. I promise. Half a minute."

Hanley began to smile. "You want to be the next Neil Armstrong."

Jimmy chuckled. "I didn't think of that. But the reality is I've loved this stuff ever since I was a kid – all those sci-fi books like *Jurassic Park*, *The Time Machine*, and *Primordia*. I want to see what it is really like."

Rashid made a strangled sound in his throat. "No way. There are so many risks that they can't even be formulated at this time. You might get lost, or stranded, or – die." Rashid spun to face Hanley. "If you let him do this, I'll . . . I'll . . . I'll walk out the door. I'll quit."

"Rashid, calm down." Hanley sighed.

"Phillip, it's my body, my risks." Jimmy's jawline was set hard. "I know what I'm getting into."

Hanley turned back to him. "No, you don't. No one does. How could they?"

"Patience." Rashid held a hand up in front of Jimmy's face and then turned away. "I'll get Doreen to prepare one of the rats."

"I'm here, ready, willing, and able, right now." Jimmy straightened.

"No. It's settled." Rashid frowned.

Hanley pinched his chin. "Wait a minute."

"What?" Rashid spun back. "You're not seriously going to go along with Jimmy's idea? It could be suicide."

"No, no – well, not yet. We do the rat tests first, okay?" He looked to Rashid. "*Okay?*"

"Good, yes." Rashid nodded.

Hanley then faced Jimmy. "We start them tomorrow. As soon as we have a successful send and receive, you're up." He lifted his brows. "Sound good?"

Jimmy grinned from ear to ear. "You bet."

Hanley clapped his hands once. "Then everybody is happy."

Rashid still scowled. "But—"

"But someone has got to do it." Hanley shrugged. "Better it be one of us, who knows what they're doing. Besides, Jimmy is right. His insights will be invaluable. And another thing; if this works, with a person, then we'll be ready to make a public announcement." Hanley smiled. "It will be the most momentous event not just in the last century, but in *all* of history." Hanley drew in a deep breath, his chest swelling. "We will have conquered time itself."

"We're being impatient." Rashid's complaint turned into a groan. "I want it on record that I object to this."

Jimmy nudged his friend. "Hey, I know you're worried about me. Don't be. This is a dream come true. Let's just see how it goes for the rats. If it's okay for them, it'll be okay for me. I promise not to ask again until the rat test is successful. Deal?"

"I guess," Rashid replied grudgingly.

"Okay, we perfect the current stream timing, and then we can work on more recent jumping-off points for the stream." Hanley glanced at Rashid. "I eventually want us to be so accurate, we can choose a date and even a time to leave the tachyon bridge."

"We're not there yet," Rashid replied. "But good to have it on the long list."

The trio walked together for another few minutes before Rashid clapped his hands once and rubbed them together. "And now, I have some coding work to get back to, so we can get the tech teams organized for tomorrow."

"And we have one more thing to do." Hanley stopped and stood in front of his friends.

"Yes?" Rashid and Jimmy stopped and looked up.

"Find a place on our bookshelves for our Nobel Prizes." Hanley grinned.

The men high-fived, and then Hanley watched his colleagues head off in different directions. He saw the slight stoop of Rashid's shoulders, compared to the bounce in Jimmy's step.

We're being impatient, Rashid had said. Hanley secretly agreed. *But without risk-taking we'll never progress*, he mentally countered.

He half-smiled. *It's all in the hands, or paws, of the rats now.*

* * *

Down in the Janus carpark, Doreen Peng crossed quickly to a waiting black BMW. She bent to the driver's side window as it slowly wound down. Inside there was a dark-suited man whose hand rose to the open window.

She handed him something and smiled. "It works."

CHAPTER 04

July 18 – The Janus Institute, Landsdowne Street, Cambridge, Massachusetts

Bert, the black laboratory rat, was inside a glass case, in a harness that rendered him immobile. There were sensors attached to his head and body, measuring his heart rate and brain waves to gauge the effects of the time displacement on his system. Every scrap of data mattered now.

Rashid and Jimmy turned to Hanley, waiting.

Hanley pulled his goggles down over his eyes and then folded his arms. "Make it happen."

Rashid turned back to his console. "Commencing."

He pressed a button on the pad, and once again the soft blue glow appeared around the spherical device.

"Selecting bridge stream. Opening portal." Rashid moved a lever and the device's glow began to increase as it built up its displacement charge.

A blue ball of light then began to form around Bert on the pedestal. Rashid drew in a breath. "Sending."

The ball of light glowed brighter and brighter for a second or two until it became blinding. And when it winked out, the case and the rat were gone.

"Good luck, little Bertie," Jimmy whispered.

The only sound in the laboratory was the soft hum of the displacement device. The entire lab team watched the small digital clock count down from thirty seconds. At five seconds remaining, they pulled their goggles down again, and the flash of blue light immediately followed.

When it dissipated, they saw that the package had returned. But the glass case was empty.

"What?" Jimmy stood.

Phillip Hanley came down the few steps from the raised platform and walked closer.

"I don't understand." Rashid frowned. "Where is he?"

Hanley looked it over for a moment. "The box is intact. Unopened." He spoke without turning. "Doreen, send the case to my lab. I'll analyze this myself."

* * *

Phillip Hanley opened the glass case and slid out the small sled that the rat's harness had been fixed on. When it was fully in the light, he saw that everything inside the box was as it had been. Except there was a fine layer of powder or dust in there with it.

He used a scalpel to scoop some up, and gently poured it into a small plastic tube. He added some distilled water and sealed it and then took it to the spectrometer.

He smiled ruefully when the results started to come in.

Yeah, they were all there; the elements of a once-living creature. Hanley got down on his elbows to peer in at the powder in the glass box. "Hello, Bert."

* * *

It took the team several hours to work out what had happened and identify the errant coding. Bottom line, Bert had aged thousands of years in seconds because the device didn't know he was alive.

Rashid and Jimmy furiously adjusted the algorithms. This time they had sampled the rat's DNA and fed the strand information into the computer so the algorithms would be able to recognize its total form. They included genetic makeup, skeletal design, mineral composition, plus cellular analysis, brain electrical activity and function, and details right down to hair strand mechanics. Basically, they described to the computer what it was to be a living rat.

By day's end they felt they were ready to try again.

"Test forty-four – three seconds only," Rashid said, and glanced at the pedestal in the control room.

"This time," Hanley said, and lowered his goggles.

Rashid nodded and looked back to the rat. "Sorry about Bert, but good luck, Ernie."

"Come back to us," Jimmy said, and crossed the fingers on both his hands.

Rashid pressed the initiation switch and the blue glow began to form around the spherical device in its sealed chamber.

"Go," Rashid whispered.

In a blink, the rat was gone. And just as the glow was receding, it brightened again, and the case returned.

The light died away. And then a cheer went up.

Ernie was still there. Alive, and, by the look of him, unharmed.

"*Yes.*" Hanley fist-pumped the air. "Well done, everyone." He laughed out loud. "We did it."

Rashid gave his colleagues and friends a small salute, and Jimmy raised both hands in the air and whooped.

Jimmy then turned to Hanley. "And?"

Hanley nodded. "And . . . you're up."

CHAPTER 05

July 20 – The Janus Institute, Landsdowne Street, Cambridge, Massachusetts

Phillip Hanley leaned forward on his knuckles, watching from the raised management level of the Janus laboratory.

He, along with Rashid, Doreen, and the entire team, were focused on Jimmy Chen, who was seated on a single wooden chair on a four-foot-wide disk inside the ionic lead-shielded glass of the tachyon chamber.

Jimmy turned to give them a thumbs-up, and tried to smile, but it crumpled quickly, and his body betrayed his nervousness as his feet jittered and jumped beneath him.

Hanley flicked open the mic. "Still not too late to change your mind." He shared a sympathetic smile, but secretly hoped Jimmy would stay the course.

Jimmy shook his head. "What, and give up show business?" He faced front. "No, I'm ready. Let's do this."

"One small step," Hanley said. He turned to Rashid and nodded.

Rashid had been watching him, and his expression was pure stone. "I want it on record that I'm—"

"Yes, yes, I know, you're against it." Hanley sighed. "But carpe diem, and all that." He tried to swallow, but his throat was bone dry; he felt he could almost taste the victory champagne.

Rashid turned away to issue last-minute instructions to Doreen, and she entered the chamber to fuss over the seated man.

Hanley watched as Doreen checked Jimmy's heart rate and looked into each of his eyes. Then she examined all the monitors and camera equipment strapped to him.

She patted Jimmy on the shoulder and then quickly exited to join the technical team, who were watching like sports fans in ringside seats at the stadium.

Rashid finished off his coding, his fingers moving in a blur over the keyboard. Hanley knew the man was a master magician, the ultimate translator, who could turn a scientific concept into a language their powerful computer could understand.

Hanley said a silent prayer – this was the first human trip, and every second of data they gathered was pure gold.

He opened his mic again. "See you soon, Jimmy. Drinks will be on me."

Jimmy turned to give him a rictus-like grin. "I'll be there. Make mine a double."

Hanley noticed Jimmy had his fingers crossed on both hands. He straightened, sucked in a lung-filling breath, and let it out slowly. "Initiate."

"Come back to us, my friend," Rashid whispered, and then, "Commencing tachyon generation and bridge selection."

The generator began to glow blue.

"Opening bridge and accessing stream." Rashid kept his eyes on his screen even as the glow reached out to touch Jimmy.

Their friend glowed brighter, and then with a flash . . . was gone.

The room was silent, and all eyes moved to the clock on the wall. The old-style foot-wide analogue clock had a second hand that counted down the thirty seconds until the preprogrammed return.

Ten seconds gone.

No one said a word and Hanley could feel his own heart beating in his chest like a drum.

"*Come on, come on, come on,*" he whispered.

He didn't know if his friend was brave or crazy. A small part of him envied the man, and another part of him knew he wouldn't have been the first to try this trip for ten million dollars.

Twenty seconds.

He looked down at Rashid and saw the man's hands poised over the keyboard. His left hand shook a little.

Ten-nine-eight . . .

Hanley straightened and folded his arms, trying to act casual, but his hands were curled into fists under his arms.

Five-four-three . . .

He pulled on his goggles and leaned forward.

Two-one . . .

"*Initiating,*" Rashid said.

* * *

Before Jimmy even opened his eyes he felt the heat and humidity pressing in on him. He inhaled, smelling the cloyingly sweet plants and damp earth.

He still felt dizzy and a little nauseous from the trip along the tachyon stream, but his stomach quickly settled when he felt gravity kick in again.

He opened sticky eyes and blinked several times to clear his vision. Then a grin split his face from ear to ear – around him was a dripping wet jungle. He slowly turned to the left and squinted, seeing the reflection of water through some prickly-looking vines that had fungal blooms like burst poppy heads all along their strands.

Turning back, he saw some broken rocks and plants that looked like heads of broccoli, or exploded mushrooms. He inhaled deeply now, and smelled things like rotten eggs, stagnant water, and something that reminded him of when he was a kid with his dad walking through the zoo's animal enclosures.

"*Oh my God.*" He turned again slowly. "We did it."

He bet his seconds were fast running out, and he knew that even though his cameras and sensors were recording, he could never hope to describe all that he was experiencing.

Jimmy looked around – he needed something – some sort of proof, or token of his visit to the Silurian age. Split seconds mattered now. Then he spotted a small plant with an orange head – it wasn't a flower, more a fungal growth. But it was weird, and unique, and the right size for him to snatch up and take back. He'd get it.

He stood, took two steps, and then froze. He heard something crashing its way through the undergrowth, something big and heavy. He looked up in time to see it.

He fell back into the chair and held up a hand. "*No.*"

* * *

"Bringing him back." Rashid initiated the tachyon bridge and opened a stream.

There was the familiar flash of blue light that quickly vanished.

Hanley flicked up his goggles.

There was a single scream, then others cried out. Rashid cursed, and Hanley gritted his teeth to hold in a mouthful of bile.

It wasn't Jimmy.

Or maybe it was.

There was a pile of viscera on the four-foot-wide floor disc. In among it was some material that was the same color as the sweater Jimmy had been wearing. There was also a single shoe, and some fragments of broken chair.

Hanley hung his head and closed his eyes. He didn't need to see Rashid's face to know the man's eyes were on him.

After another moment he lifted his head, a vein pulsing in his temple. "Clear the room." He exhaled when he heard no movement. His anger exploded. "Clear the *fucking* room!"

CHAPTER 06

Five days later – USSTRATCOM, Nebraska, Sub Level 3

Colonel Jack 'the Hammer' Hammerson sat in a large, sound-proofed meeting room with the two intelligence officers. The pair had been working furiously to quickly pull all the facts together into an intel package that made sense. Because once they briefed Hammerson, he was going to have to take it to General Marcus Chilton – who would in turn report to the Commander in Chief.

Will Benning was the manager of Asian field operations and was running an entire intelligence network, as well as high-placed operatives both at home and abroad. Also in the meeting was Bernadette Cooper – she was the chief science officer attached to the CIA, foreign department, and had degrees in physics, chemistry, and biology. Hammerson had worked with her before and knew that she was a straight shooter who knew her stuff.

The stakes were high, and so far, Hammerson didn't like what he was hearing. He tilted his head back for a moment and shut his eyes. "Okay." He opened them again and leaned forward. "Let me bullet-point what I think you're telling me, just to ensure I'm not having some sort of damn nightmare right now."

He lifted a hand and counted the items off on his fingers.

First finger. "One. Time travel is real."

Second finger. "Two. The Janus guys have been working on it for around twenty-five years, but they only just got it working in any sort of controlled way."

Third finger. "Three. Soon as they just about perfect it, they have their damn plans stolen."

Fourth finger, and his lips pulled back in a near snarl. "And four. The assholes who stole it are North Koreans. A damn adversary state."

"Five." Cooper held up her own finger. "We believe the NKs have been working day and night to create their own prototype of the device."

Hammerson ground his teeth for a moment. "Of course they have."

"Something else." Benning meshed large fingers together on the table. "We also believe the NKs are ready to make their mission jump. Somewhere in the United States."

"What? Why here?" Hammerson frowned. "What the hell could they do to us over 400 million years ago? Nothing they could leave behind would be effective after that amount of time."

"Based on what we think might be their targets, we now believe that might not be true," Bernadette Cooper said.

Hammerson cursed under his breath. "Go on."

Cooper's lips pressed together for a moment. "We can only speculate about what bad actors would do, although we can guess. What we're seeing might mean that time itself could be the most powerful and deadly weapon ever invented."

"A time bomb, in the true meaning of the term," Benning added. "Following the chatter we picked up between Pyong-yang and an employee of the very secretive Janus Institute, we performed a data lift on Janus. We found out what they were working on, and where they were up to. We then included surveillance of all the actors. They've been doing some pretty wild and high-risk stuff. In fact, unbelievable stuff." He looked up. "We know that the tachyon drive, their time machine, is finished but not perfected," he said. "They have only managed to maintain what they call a bridge between the here and now and the Silurian period, some 420 million years ago."

"Why only then?" Hammerson asked.

"Good question." Cooper half-smiled. "But we think it's the particles themselves that are the problem. The tachyons actually increase in speed the older they get. And the older ones are far more numerous, having been around since the birth of the cosmos."

"Hence, there are more bridges for longer ago," Hammerson deduced.

"Yes, we think so." She bobbed her head. "The Janus team just need to find a way to identify, select, and then harness the nearer-term ones. It's proving a challenge for them. But they'll get there soon."

Benning shrugged. "Now some good news."

"About damn time." Hammerson's eyes were half-lidded, and he doubted the news was going to be that the NKs' had managed to blow themselves up.

Benning's face still looked drained. "The device is not perfected yet, and the NKs only got to where they are on the temporal bridge technology on the backs of the stolen Janus research and development. Now we know what they are doing and have shut down their information pipeline, they have to do the work themselves. And, frankly, we don't think they're up to it. Bottom line, what they have is all they'll ever have."

"That's good, but they still have the ability to establish a bridge and travel back to the Silurian period. So that's where they'll go. And I do not want them fucking around with our country's past." Hammerson looked at each of them, his fingers drumming on the table for a moment. "There's something that's been bothering me. I thought there were some sort of rules or restrictions to do with paradoxes making time-based event alterations impossible."

"There's theoretical rules for theoretical scenarios. But then again, everything about this is theoretical." Bernadette Cooper half-smiled. "Or it was."

"Guess we'll be finding out as we go," Hammerson replied.

"Or we may not. Think about it; just how would we know if there was a time-based alteration? The new, altered timeline would be the one we are now living in. Meaning, the previous one will never happen, because it was changed. How would we know if there had ever been changes?"

"I don't like this," Hammerson replied. "If we know who stole the blueprint for the tachyon drive, and when, then why didn't we go back and stop them? And if we stopped them, and therefore the theft never happened, then why are we still having this conversation? Unless we didn't stop them."

Cooper's face was grim. "Or they stopped us."

Hammerson rubbed a hand up through his iron-gray crew cut. "Makes my head hurt." He felt they were moving away from the real threat and wanted to pull them back. "You never answered my question – how badly could they damage us? If there could be damage at all after 420 million years?"

"Well, larger transport loads are now being successfully accommodated, so think about what they could take back with them." Benning opened his hands. "Our best guess is something that would destroy all our natural oil reserves."

"How?" Hammerson frowned.

Benning turned to Cooper. "This is your area of expertize."

She nodded. "He's right. And not just destroy our oil reserves but prevent them from ever forming." She typed for a second or two on her laptop. "We war-gamed it, and this is the most likely scenario."

She turned the laptop around, and Hammerson peered at the screen, which seemed to show several large unrecognizable islands.

"This is our world during the Silurian period. It looked very different from today and was mostly a global sea with many small landmasses floating on the tectonic plates. The United States was divided into three super islands called Laurentia, Baltica, and Barrentsia. Eventually, they collided, and then millions of years later some parts broke away again. But 420 million years ago those islands were separated by the Lapetus Ocean. It was 2500 feet deep, 600 miles wide and over 2000 miles long." She smiled grimly. "Its fossilized layer of sediment is what gave us the vast petroleum reserves in our interior."

"Where much of the Midwest would be one day," Hammerson said.

"Yes." She pointed at several places on the screen. "Now imagine if it was rendered unhabitable to sea life for maybe tens of thousands of years; there'd be no animal life to leave a sedimentary layer for the creation of petroleum."

"Which could be done by using a dirty bomb," Hammerson said softly.

"Correct," Cooper replied. "One bomb by itself wouldn't do it. But they could plant a dozen, a hundred. And worse still, they could stagger the times at which those bombs detonate – they certainly have the technology to rig something to go off every decade or every century. Just as the environment is cleaning itself up, the next detonation could occur. And then in another hundred years, the next. And so on. And so on."

Hammerson whistled softly. "I used to think time travel was science fiction. Then I learn that not only is it real, but the technology, developed by a US company, has been stolen, and is about to be used against us. What a monumental fuck-up."

"That it is," Will Benning replied. "It seems the Democratic People's Republic of Korea had an agent at Janus for years. And the spy cell has already disbanded and vanished."

"But not before they got nearly everything they needed." Hammerson looked toward the man. "How long?"

"We estimate we have six months to stop them," Benning replied. "Because the action will be taken within our country, and they'll be accumulating and stockpiling fissionable material locally for their weapons. It'll take them that long to amass the required amount."

"Six months." Hammerson scowled as he drummed his fingers again on the desk, his mind working. He stopped. "Why can't we just track down and pick up all their agents if they're working in the US? You must know who they are."

Benning shook his head. "We've never seen a mission so tightly protected. They know it's an act of war, and if they're found out, it would be grounds for military retaliation. We guess they're working on the basis that they conduct their mission before we find them. And anyway, if they succeed, the US most likely won't exist anymore. Remember, these guys think they're a superpower and maybe they think without us standing in their way they'll take over the world."

"The mouse that roared." Hammerson sat back, making his chair groan. "Without proof, we can't act. And by the time we have proof, it might be all over."

"They make that mission jump, then it *will* be all over," Cooper replied. "But until they do, we won't know exactly where they are planning to bed the devices. We literally need to stop them at the moment of their jump. Which will be near impossible without better intel." She shared a flat smile. "Or we follow them and stop them there."

Hammerson sat thinking for several moments, and felt the agents watching him. He looked at the pair from under his brows.

"So, I'm going to take a report to a four-star general, who will then take it to the President, which states that we think the North Korean government are planning on not just destabilizing our country, but totally destroying it. Without firing a shot. And we don't know when, where, or who is involved. But they're already here and planning the attack soon. Oh, and one more thing, they're using a time machine – *our* time machine." Hammerson growled low and mean. "The general will rip my fucking head off. And so he should."

The agents sat and watched the brutal-looking military commander of the feared HAWCs in silence.

Hammerson bared his teeth for a moment. "If it was up to me, I'd nuke 'em right now. Today. Massive first strike – melt his damn presidential palace down to the bedrock."

He looked at the man and woman before him, and both just stared. He had been shouting, he realized, so he dialed it back a notch.

The Hammer sat forward, deciding to press them. "You guys need to squeeze your informants. You need to pay, beg, or brutalize these people until you have answers. It sounds like our clock is ticking, and I, for one, like our country exactly where it is and the way it is. Bring me something by week's end. Something we can act on."

Hammerson stood. "One more thing; we need to pay the Janus team a little surprise visit. Just to focus their attention." His chin jutted. "Dismissed."

"Yes, sir." Will Benning and Bernadette Cooper gathered their notes and began to leave.

"Cooper," Hammerson said.

The woman turned. "Sir?"

"Two minutes." He waited until the soundproof door was closed and it was just the pair of them. "You said that there's a chance we could follow them back. Stop them there. Expand on that."

She nodded. "Yes, sir. The fact is, unless we know exactly, and I mean *exactly*, where any devices have been planted, we're bound to miss some. As it is, due to geomorphic displacement we may never know where they are, or how many there are, or when they were timed to go off. We only need to miss one and it would change everything." She held up a finger. "But if a team followed the NKs back, right on their asses, we could track, locate, and destroy the devices, as well as the team that brought them, before any catastrophic changes can occur that affect the future time line. Full clean-up."

Hammerson nodded. "No mess."

"If we can't find them and stop them here, that is. Then this might be the best hope for a high-success mission. Like I mentioned, if they initiate a temporal bridge and conduct a stream jump, we can spot the tachyon energy pulse. Follow them back." She lifted her chin. "It could work."

Hammerson nodded, staring straight ahead as he thought. After a moment he remembered he had left Cooper standing there. "Thank you. Dismissed."

She stayed where she was. "Colonel?"

He turned back. "Yes?"

"I would volunteer to go." Her gaze was steadfast.

He stared back into her eyes and saw the resolve there. *We'd need someone with her knowledge and experience*, he thought.

"I'll think about it," he said.

She nodded once, and then left. Hammerson then began to prepare his report, and when done he lifted the phone.

He would need to meet with General Chilton ASAP, and he was not looking forward to it.

CHAPTER 07

The Janus Institute, Landsdowne Street, Cambridge, Massachusetts

"Morning, everyone." Phillip Hanley pushed in through the lab doors, nodded to a few of the tech staff and then his business partner, Rashid Jamal.

Rashid looked up from his bank of computer screens, his face twisted in concern, and his usually olive-skinned face looked oddly pale.

Hanley stopped. "Okay, what's up?"

"The government is here." Rashid grimaced. "And I think the military."

"Seriously?" Phillip Hanley looked skyward with an agonized expression. "And who let them in?"

Rashid Jamal shrugged. "Don't blame me, someone must have taken the call and booked them in. They're in the meeting room. And by the way, where is Doreen? She's supposed to screen this stuff. Is she still off sick?" He looked around, raising his voice. "Anyone seen Doreen?"

"Fuck the government and fuck the military," Hanley seethed. "They can cool it in the room for a while. If I decide to meet with them, I'll be there when I'm ready."

Rashid straightened. "Do we really want to piss them off? At this time?"

Hanley snorted derisively.

"No, we don't." Rashid shook his head. "We better meet with them. And there's this one guy . . ."

Hanley made a throwaway gesture. "As far as I'm concerned, we have all the funding we need and we don't need them. I'll go there when I'm ready."

"You're ready now."

The two scientists turned toward the voice.

Standing in the doorway was a man of about five-ten or -eleven, older at around fifty, but fit, tough looking, with an iron-gray crew cut and a face that looked like it had been carved from granite. His expression looked even harder.

"Um, ah . . ." Hanley composed himself, trying not to be intimidated. "How did you get in here?"

"Doesn't matter," the man said. "I'm your nine o'clock. We need to talk, Dr. Hanley." His eyes moved from Hanley to Rashid. "And you too, Dr. Jamal." His eyes burned into them like lasers. "Now." There was enough menace packed into that single word that it screamed: *Don't fuck with me.*

Rashid's voice was a few octaves higher than normal. "I think we can spare you some time." He half-turned, almost begging. "Phillip?"

"Okay, okay. *Jezus,*" Hanley cursed under his breath. "The meeting room, go, you know where it is." He made shooing motions with his hand.

* * *

Colonel Jack 'the Hammer' Hammerson entered the glass-walled meeting room and nodded to his two colleagues.

He'd brought with him Will Benning and Bernadette Cooper. Together they watched Doctors Phillip Hanley and

Rashid Jamal enter the room. Hanley had his jaw set and looked determined. Rashid Jamal looked nervous to the point of fainting.

"Take a seat," Hammerson ordered.

"In my own office? How kind of you." Hanley chuckled, sat tall, and then squared his shoulders in his seat. "I can only give you a few minutes as there are many other pressing things that need to be attended to. So excuse me if I don't offer you all a coffee as you won't be here long enough to—"

"*Shut up.*" Hammerson's roar was like a slap.

Rashid physically shrank in his seat, and just looked at a small spot on the table.

Hanley blinked twice and then began to splutter his indignation. But the words never came out.

"You have no idea of the shit you are in." Hammerson's furious, unblinking eyes were like twin gun barrels. "Tell me about Doreen Peng."

Rashid's brow creased. "Uh, she's our head of technology. Basically runs all our tech teams. But she's not in today, been off sick for a few days; flu I think she mentioned," he added.

"How did you come to employ her?" Hammerson pressed.

Hanley licked dry lips. "After we got our funding, we needed to staff up and we recruited some of the best people in the industry. As luck would have it, Doreen sent in her application and bio at the right time and her credentials spoke for themselves. So we—"

"So she approached Janus." Benning's voice was soft and measured. "How do you think she heard about you?"

Hanley shrugged. "I don't know. Professional grapevine. What's the problem? It happens a lot in the small tech world."

"Of course it does." Bernadette Cooper smiled warmly. "Dr. Hanley, tell us about your technology, where you are up to, and then tell us about your security."

Hanley held a hand up in their faces. "Sorry, what we do here is confidential. I don't have to tell you anything." He glanced at his watch. "In fact, I think we're done here." He looked up, his gaze flat. "Or do I need to call my attorney?"

"You can do that," Hammerson said. "And I'll ensure you do twenty years in jail for aiding and abetting a foreign actor to place the United States, its people and territory, at risk. I'll also ensure your company and all its technological assets are folded into our own military technology centers by the end of the day."

"What?" Hanley just stared as if he had been frozen solid.

"Oh, God." Rashid exhaled and looked ill.

Benning sat forward. "Here's the thing, gentlemen. Doreen Peng is not her real name. In fact, she is an agent of the Democratic People's Republic of Korea, and has established a direct pipeline to their local spy cells, through which she has funneled all your technological secrets, progress, data, and know-how. By now, we expect they have established a prototype device of their own."

"A prototype of their own time machine," Hammerson spelled out. "That's what you've built, right?"

Hanley's mouth opened and closed several times like a fish just hauled onto the deck of a boat.

Bernadette Cooper's warm smile remained. "Dr. Hanley . . ." Her voice was as soothing as honey. "We've been monitoring you ever since we picked up the chatter about your company and the agent intrusion. I ask again, tell us about your technology, where you are up to, and then tell us about your security."

Hanley's lips pursed.

"You better wise up, real quick," Hammerson said, far less patiently. "I suggest you work with us and save your skin. Or we'll call up some agents to escort you, and Dr. Jamal here, straight to jail."

Hanley's face began to turn red, but his lips remained pressed tight.

Hammerson turned to Cooper. "How long will it take you to break down this technology and assume control of it?"

"I have a team of programmers and physicists on stand-by. Few days, a week, maximum," she replied coolly.

"Tell them what they need to know, or I will," Rashid almost begged. "We're going to lose everything."

"You probably have already." Hammerson folded his arms.

Hanley's lips worked as though pressure was building behind them. And then he just threw his hands up. "*Fuck it.*"

"Good choice. Let's begin." Hammerson drew out a picture from one of the folders Agent Cooper had brought and slid it across the table. It showed a smiling and boyishly enthusiastic Asian man. "Do you know who this is?" His eyes were unblinking as they bored into Phillip Hanley.

Hanley and Rashid both glanced at the image, and Rashid screwed his eyes shut and turned away.

Hanley just nodded slowly, and his voice was barely above a whisper. "Yes."

"Of course you do. It's your colleague, James 'Jimmy' Chen." Hammerson placed a finger on the picture. "We can't seem to find him. He seems to have fallen off the Earth."

Hanley looked unfocusedly at the photo and his lips curved slightly on one side. "Or at least fallen off *today's* Earth."

Hammerson sat back. "Tell us everything. Start from when Peng was involved in your company. Leave nothing out."

Hammerson, Benning, and Cooper stared at the two scientists as a snake might stare at a mouse.

"Things were going so well." Hanley exhaled a long and slow sigh. "It was only a week ago, July 20. We had just developed the new temporal bridge generator to a point where it could be tested." He smiled pitiably as his vision turned inward. "Our confidence was as high as our arrogance. But we were naive."

Almost trance-like, he began to talk. "We had previously tested the device and sent a camera back and successfully retrieved it." He splayed his fingers on the table and just stared at them as he spoke. "It was a momentous occasion. So we were ready to go to the next level – a live test."

"The next level being a live test with a rat, hamster, or rabbit? And how many did you run? Six is usually the standard to confirm repeatability, correct?" Cooper raised a single eyebrow.

"Two." Hanley gave her a fragile smile.

"*Two*," Cooper repeated evenly. "Both successful?"

Rashid just stared at his hands clasped on the table and Hanley bobbed his head, his lips pursed. "There were a few minor technical hiccups on the first test, but we believed we had corrected those." He looked up and smiled. "We did correct them."

"One successful test, then?" Cooper's brows were up.

Hanley nodded.

"And then went Jimmy," Hammerson growled.

"He volunteered." Hanley looked up hopefully. "There was no stopping him. Besides, after the camera run, and successful rat trip, we were so full of confidence. And hubris. And arrogance. I see that now."

Hammerson saw Rashid's eyes slide to Hanley, and he bet he knew which one of them was full of those characteristics.

Hanley continued, but his eyes were unfocused as he began to talk in a monotone. "That was the last time we saw Jimmy."

"Alive," Rashid mumbled.

"Tell us," Cooper said soothingly.

Hanley nodded, as his hands gripped tightly together on the tabletop. He talked for an hour straight, primarily about the test procedures, the sending, and the retrieval. And then just a few minutes on the gruesome results of their rushed work.

"Poor old Jimmy," Hammerson said. "Time travel's first human guinea pig."

Hanley looked up defiantly. "He was our friend as well as our colleague. I, *we*, loved him."

"Not enough to tell anyone about his death, though," Agent Cooper replied. "Concealing a crime is a felony," she pressed.

"It wasn't a crime, it, ah, was a laboratory accident. A significant one, sure, but it was a risk, a challenge, Jimmy wanted to take." Hanley sighed. "It was—"

"*It was fucking manslaughter*," Hammerson roared, and smashed a fist down on the desk so hard it made both the scientists jump in their seats.

Hanley looked down at the table.

"And after concealing this crime, you pressed on," Benning stated. "What did Doreen Peng do?"

"Doreen?" Rashid gulped. "She was actually a big help. Cleaned up the mess and helped keep the technology staff quiet. She was well organized."

"Of course she was," Hammerson replied. "She wanted you to iron all the bugs out of the project before she took more results back to her handlers."

"I don't know anything about that. But I don't believe it. We do background checks, you know," Hanley replied, but he didn't sound so sure anymore. "And you're right, we did press on. After taking a few days off to grieve, the project drew us back. We were so close, we just had to finish."

"So, you fixed the bugs?" Hammerson asked.

Rashid shook his head. "There were no bugs. Not really. What happened to Jimmy wasn't a bug. It was a placement issue – he arrived, literally, into the jaws of a proximate threat. We just needed to improve the code."

"And you did that," Cooper asked. "And they were success-ful send and receives?"

Hanley just grunted his confirmation.

"And that was the moment you, and everyone else in the laboratory, thought that it worked." Hammerson turned to Benning. "Show him how effective his staff background checks were."

Will Benning took out a small device that might have been a phone, searched for something, found it, and turned the device around. "This was taken July 17, at 3.17 pm – after your successful run with the camera," he said.

Hanley leaned forward and watched the film, and a vein started to pulse at his temple. "That's our parking garage," he said softly.

"Keep watching your prized employee." Hammerson's eyes were on Hanley, not the film.

The film showed Doreen Peng crossing to a black BMW and bending at the driver's side window as it slowly wound down. There was a man inside and she handed him something.

Benning narrated. "We believe that was a small hard drive with the plans to your temporal device. And . . ."

Peng leaned into the car and said two words.

"She says to the driver: *It works.*" Benning's eyes went from the small screen to Hanley's face.

The man in the car held the drive in his fist for a moment and then nodded. He looked up at Doreen Peng.

Benning narrated again. "He replies: *Well done. Get back to your duties. Further instructions will be coming.*" Benning finished and sat back. "In another hour the data on your temporal device was probably being reviewed in Pyongyang. And then we expect Doreen received instructions for her next steps. Whatever they were."

"Construction of their own device would have commenced immediately. And they would have worked around the clock." Hammerson dragged in a deep breath through his nose and let it out slowly. "Like a remora attached to the side of a big fish, she's a parasite that's been feeding off you for years."

Rashid began to weep. "We've been working on this day and night for decades."

"And without knowing it, you've also been working for the Democratic People's Republic of Korea. And putting your own country and its people at risk. Well done," Hammerson said brutally.

Hanley closed his eyes. "Where is she now?"

"*Hey.*" Hammerson's voice was soft but menacing.

Hanley opened his eyes.

"She's long gone." The colonel leaned forward, his eyes pinning Phillip Hanley. "And now, you're going to help us stop whatever they are planning." He smiled without warmth. "You can you do that, can't you, gentlemen?"

Hanley looked up. "How do we do that when we don't even know what they're planning?"

"We can guess." Hammerson smiled grimly. "How about the total destruction of the United States?"

Hanley looked confused. "I don't—"

"You've created the most devastating weapon that has ever existed." Hammerson glared at them. "And its use against us is imminent."

CHAPTER 08

Utah, House Range, eastern side of Swasey Mountain

The two scientists crouch-ran out from under the helicopter blades. They then straightened and turned slowly to survey their surroundings – dry, rugged, and littered with crumbled limestone and, unlike the rest of the mountains in the area, also some broken shale. There were a few scrubby plants with spindly, sharp leaves managing to survive in an environment that was hot in summer, freezing in winter, and dry all year round.

"An ancient and desolate land," Shuchang Xi muttered. "Nothing here."

"Nothing here *now*." Soong-Li Song walked a few more paces out across the scarred and rocky surface. She put her hands on her hips and turned slowly. "But there was once."

She put a hand over her eyes. They were over 6000 feet above sea level, looking out over sharp hills spotted with juniper bushes and bristlecone pine. Lower down there were grasses of varying shades of brown with just a hint of green.

"Out there." Soong-Li pointed out over the lowlands. "Just on 420 million years ago this would have been the coast of the super island of Laurentia, just as it was becoming a continent from its collision with two other super islands. The collision created a tectonic upfolding that was the genesis of the Appalachian Mountains."

"Unbelievable." Shuchang shook his head in wonder. "Hard to imagine what the world was like then. It must have been like an alien planet."

Soong-Li nodded. "We don't even know what many of the creatures looked like, as the vast time frames destroyed most of their fossils."

Shuchang squinted off into the distance. "Only ghosts now."

"But ghosts that can be resurrected," she countered.

Right now there was nothing but an eerie silence on the mountain and Soong-Li crouched and grabbed up a handful of limestone pebbles. She held them in her palm and used a finger to sort through them.

"Right here was the edge of a swamp. The world's glaciers had melted, and most of the planet was covered by a mighty ocean. This place had been raised up by continental collision and tectonic uplifting, and the sea level dropped by hundreds of feet." She pointed. "But out there was a vast sea between the landmasses some 600 miles long and 100 miles wide."

"But this here was dry land?" Shuchang asked.

"Well, not dry. But not under water. We think." Soong-Li stood. "And this is where we will conduct our viability test." She marked a large "X" on a level part of the ground with the heel of her boot, and then waved to the huge helicopter. "Bring the prisoner."

Two Asian men in camouflage uniforms and dark glasses raced over with a three-foot-wide disc they placed on the ground over her marked spot. They retraced their steps to the helicopter and quickly returned holding another man between them.

One of the men carried a wooden chair and placed it on the disc, and they sat the third man down. He seemed groggy, and they quickly lashed his ankles to the front chair legs and his wrists to the arms.

Soong-Li approached and grabbed his hair to tilt his head back. The man's eyes blinked in sleepy confusion.

"You will make history, Mr. Jung Sun." She smiled. "And if you return, you will be absolved of your crimes." She let his head drop, and then held an arm out as she took a few steps back. "Stand clear."

She had a remote in her hand and pressed something on it, and from inside the open door of the large helicopter a blue glow emanated.

"Initiating bridge," she said as she focused on the device. She pushed up a lever, and a beam shot out of the helicopter to envelop the man and chair. "Sending."

Soong-Li's eyes were wide as she gripped a small jade amulet around her neck that had a swirling image of a sun carved into it. She rubbed it with her thumb. North Korea was an atheist state, but individuals believed in many forms of good luck and worship from Chondoism to Christianity.

Soong-Li believed in the spirits of good luck in a quasi-shamanism belief system. She didn't pray to it but called on its luck from time to time. Like now.

The glow intensified, and she clenched her jaw as her back teeth ached. When the glow dissipated, she shut down the device. She exhaled, satisfied.

Shuchang walked forward, waving his hand over the empty space. "And he's gone."

"Gone and not gone," she said. "He's actually right here. But 420 million years ago."

She checked her wristwatch. "Thirty seconds. Enough time. Initiating return bridge." She pressed more buttons on the small device.

"What will he have seen? What stories will he have from that period of our infant Earth?" Shuchang murmured.

Soong-Li felt a bubble of excitement in her chest. "Let us find out." She moved the lever up again, and a soft blue beam shot out of the chopper to touch the pad that had been left on the ground. "Got him. Returning."

The blue glow intensified to become blinding, and then it vanished, but not before a small wave of water surged out to wash over their boots.

"*Ach.*" Shuchang turned away.

Soong-Li's eyes bulged at the grisly sight.

Only half of their test subject had returned. The man's body, as well as the top half of the wooden chair, had been ripped in two. His revolting remains still sat upright and the ankles jiggled macabrely as if still trying to pull free of their restraints.

Soong-Li steeled herself and stepped forward, noting that blood still pooled around the man's shoes. But there was something else – as well as the wave they had brought back, the man's pants and shoes were drenched.

She touched them and then tasted her fingers. "Seawater," she said. "We are a little too far east."

"Did something go wrong?" Shuchang asked.

She bent to examine the remains. "I saw a man torn in half by a crocodile once. It looked like this." She straightened. "Mr. Jung Sun just had the bad luck to arrive in the ocean, I think, just as a large sea beast was swimming by."

She bent over the grisly remains, and then actually reached out to touch the still spurting mass. She reached into it and jiggled something.

Shuchang grimaced. "Horrifying. How can you?"

She laughed softly as she turned and Shuchang saw she was holding up a three-inch conical tooth. "Yes and no – horrifying and satisfying. Because this tells me nothing went wrong with the send and return. Nothing alive today has teeth like this. So he just went somewhere where the owner of this tooth lives. And that means the device works." She held the tooth high. "Proof of concept."

"Time travel is real," Shuchang whispered.

"It will change . . . everything," Soong-Li said softly as she clutched the tooth in her fist and closed her eyes. It cut her, blood ran, but she didn't care. "Our time of ascension is here, and the age of hegemony will be eradicated once and for all."

"There are so many unknowns." Shuchang sighed. "Are we . . . doing the right thing?"

Soong-Li's eyes flicked open. Irritation rose inside her and she turned her full gaze on him, her near-black eyes unreadable. "Be of no doubt, Shuchang." She took a step closer to him. "Remember, from the result of our actions, no one will die or be killed. Some people may never be born, but that doesn't matter. What matters is that our country, our people, and our Dear Leader, will be allowed to have their time in the sun. No more Western hegemonic oppression. No more jumping to American, Chinese, or European demands. And no more starvation brought about by global sanctions."

She sucked in a deep breath, her chest swelling with both pride and anger. "The rise of the Democratic People's Republic of Korea is inevitable." She smiled and reached out to grip his forearm. "Or it will be soon."

She squeezed the tooth. "Praise the Dear Leader."

"Yes, yes, all praise to the Dear Leader." He nodded, but kept his gaze averted.

Soong-Li turned away, feeling she could spin in a dance of happiness. But a small gust of wind brought the smell of the fresh meat of the half-carcass into her nostrils.

She turned to the helicopter to yell, "Bag that mess and bring it."

Shuchang turned away as the men scraped and shoveled Mr. Jung Sun's remains into a large plastic sack. Beside him Soong-Li twirled her finger in the air.

The pilot nodded, and the huge helicopter's blades began to slowly turn. The pair quickly climbed in, and in seconds they were being whisked away, leaving the plateau to the ghosts of the past once again.

CHAPTER 09

USSTRATCOM, Nebraska, Sub Level 3

Four-star General Marcus Chilton let the report drop on the desk, meshed his fingers together on its top and exhaled loudly. "Jesus, Jack, this is a nightmare. How the hell did this tech fall into the wrong hands?"

"Quite easily, unfortunately, Marcus. One of the Janus company founders, Phillip Hanley, needed a capital injection and approached what he thought was an American philanthropic funding company by the name of Occam's Foundation."

Chilton shook his head. "And surprise, surprise, they weren't American."

"Nope, North Korean Communist Party front. They gave Hanley and his team ten million dollars, for what the Janus guys thought was nothing more than well-intentioned seed funding. But in reality, they sent in a sleeper agent by the name of Doreen Peng, who secretly copied and supplied all the data to Pyongyang. And we believe they've recreated the device."

"Our naivety is still the gift that keeps on giving," Chilton growled.

"It gets worse. They either manufactured the device right here or transported it to the United States. Because that's where they plan to use it," Hammerson added. "Currently, the device can send people or objects back and forth in time. But to the exact spot they occupied here, just in a different time period. It means if they want to disrupt or destroy our country, they need to do it from inside its geographic boundaries."

"So they're here somewhere. Do we have any leads?" Chilton's eyes narrowed.

Hammerson shook his head. "We can't find them unless they actually use the device. When they do, the tachyon stream gives off a particle energy burst, a signature, that we can see and home in on."

"But by then they've already used it. And come back," Chilton mused. "So we can only shut the gate after the horse has bolted."

"Correct." Hammerson sat forward. "And we've just had information that they've already completed a test run."

Chilton made a rumbling sound deep in his chest and steepled his fingers. "Can't let them succeed. Not even a little bit." He looked up, his eyes half-lidded. "Right now, I see only two options. Our destruction – or war. Neither is acceptable. Give me another option, Jack."

"Agreed. There's a chance we can send a small team after them. Clean up the mess before it's made."

"Back 420 million years?" Chilton raised his eyebrows.

"Yes, and as we can only send a small team that can move fast and strike hard," Hammerson said, "it would need to be the best of the best."

Chilton's gaze was flat. "And your best just retired." He rubbed his chin.

"I might be able to bring him back in. But it won't be easy." Hammerson looked at Chilton.

After a moment, the general nodded. "This overrides everything else. Make it happen."

"One more thing," Hammerson said, and saw Chilton's brows go up, waiting. "We think the NKs will try and stop us from following them. So may take a run at the Janus Institute in Boston. If they do, we'll be waiting for them, but it might mean there'll be blood in the streets."

Chilton snorted softly. "Everyone wants to be the beast until it's time to do what beasts do." He continued to stare. "Be the beast, Jack."

"Leave it with me, sir." Hammerson stood, saluted, and exited the room.

CHAPTER 10

Four months later – USSTRATCOM, Nebraska – Hammerson's office

Hammerson pulled the briefing report toward him and flipped it open – another Russian with criminal links had been beaten to death in the Massachusetts area. He sighed and turned to the autopsy page and looked at some of the images.

"*Jesus Christ,*" he whispered.

They were as gruesome as the notes suggested. Beaten to death was an understatement. The man in the picture had been pulverized, his face flattened as the front of his skull was crushed in on itself. The report said that the impacts were indicative of a high-speed vehicle collision. But it also mentioned that the skull-bone fragmentation pattern suggested it was done by a single blow from a blunt object – impossibly, it was shaped like a fist.

Hammerson knew injuries. And he knew a skull crush would require 520 pounds of direct force. That was roughly twice as much force as human hands could generate. Unless it was a very unique pair of human hands from a very unique human being.

He read on and saw that, in addition, the Russian's rib cage had been splintered, the neck broken, and arms dislocated. Hammerson could picture what had happened – after, or perhaps during the beating, the dead man had been flung around by one of his arms and smashed into the ground like someone was beating the dust out of an old rug.

The HAWC commander wondered if that had happened after he'd had his face caved in. He closed the report and sat back. This was the fifth of these type of deaths in the last ten days. The police were classing it as some sort of Russian mob turf war, but Hammerson knew differently – his man, Alex Hunter, was out there searching for his family's killer. And the Russian sniper rifle was enough to send him working his way through the Russian underworld demanding answers he would never get.

He knew he needed the Arcadian back in the fold, and he had conjured a mad idea of how to achieve that objective. It would either work, or it would detonate in his face.

"Win, or die trying," Hammerson said to the empty room. He stood and looked down at his desk. He edged open the top drawer and saw the large black Desert Eagle sitting there. He took it but knew that if he was ever put in a position where he had to pull it on Alex, he'd be as good as dead before he could even fire a shot.

Jack Hammerson's Frankenstein monster, Aimee Weir had called Alex Hunter one day. And Hammerson knew that her death, and Joshua's, made him more of a monster every day.

He drew in a deep breath. *Time to pay the ghost a visit*, he thought as he headed out the door.

* * *

It was still early morning when Jack Hammerson walked up to Alex's front door and paused. The door was ajar. He pushed it open but stayed where he was.

"Alex?"

He waited, letting his eyes adjust to the gloom inside.

"Son, you in there?"

He took a breath and stepped inside.

Alex hadn't been answering his calls, and though Sam Reid, the closest thing Alex had to a friend, had been checking in on him, the feedback was he'd been like a hollow shell.

But Hammerson knew the man wasn't hollow. There was a demon living inside him, called *the Other*, an entity of violence and hate, and the last thing he wanted was for that creature to be released any more. Already it seemed the local Russian mafia had been meeting that entity several times a week. None of them had survived that encounter.

"Alex, it's Jack Hammerson."

Hammerson's eyes began to adjust. Sam had also said the damned dog gave him the same reception he routinely gave Hammerson – distrustful, dangerous, and mean as hell. Hammerson was always armed, but he knew if he was forced to defend himself against a near 300-pound genetically modified German shepherd with above average intelligence who had once had a psychic link to Joshua Hunter, he wouldn't be the winner. And if he somehow managed to take it down, then what would Alex's response be to the guy who killed the last link he had to his murdered family?

Hammerson knew he wouldn't just end up dead, he'd probably finish like one of those obliterated Russians.

He moved through the house, ignoring the mess, and in the kitchen he saw plates piled with gnawed bones – did the dog eat that? Or Alex?

"Alex?" he called again.

He heard a low growl coming from out in the backyard and crossed to the window. There was Alex, just standing there, facing away from the house. Beside him sat Tor.

They were two monsters together, but both ripped apart by

a fathomless grief. Hammerson knew that made for a volatile and dangerous mix.

Alex was in jeans, bare feet, and a dirty t-shirt. It was cold outside, not quite freezing, but the man had been trained to ignore discomfort, pain, and even torture as a HAWC. Plus, his rapid-healing metabolism could easily deal with any trauma to his flesh.

His body looked strong and fit, but it was his mind that concerned Hammerson. Would he still be mentally intact? Or would the psychological demon inside him have been allowed to take over?

Hammerson stared for a moment more, steeling himself. *No one lives forever*, he thought, and pushed the back door open.

He crossed the wet lawn and stopped about a dozen feet behind Alex. The dog, Tor, was sitting but now straightened – even sitting it came close to the colonel's chest. Its head was lowered and jutted forward in obvious distrust.

Hammerson knew that the boy, Joshua, and the dog had shared a psychic link. He wondered what would have happened to the animal when the boy was killed, and if some part of Joshua was still in there.

"He told me you'd come," Alex said without turning.

Who told him? Sam or the inner demon whispering to him? Hammerson wondered.

"I don't want to speak to anyone," Alex said softly.

"Yes, you do," Hammerson said.

"Everything I had is gone. I have nothing left." Alex's voice was low.

Hammerson waited. "You have a lot. People who still care about you. Friends."

"I only want one thing." He snorted softly. "No, two. I want them back. And I also want to know who did this." Alex turned to face him. "Can you give me that, Jack?"

Hammerson was surprised by the way he looked. His eyes were red-rimmed, telling of very little sleep, and the dark semicircles under them made them seem almost luminescent. Or was it the usual silver sheen that showed up in the darkness? He also had a black beard, and his face was streaked with grime.

Here goes, he thought.

"What if I said I *could* give you not just one of those things, but both?"

Time seemed to stop as Alex became absolutely motionless.

"What if I said I could put you in front of the shooter?" Hammerson took a few steps toward him.

Alex's eyes lifted to his, and the silver glow seemed to intensify.

"What if I said I could put you there, *before* the shots were even fired?" Hammerson's eyes narrowed as he watched his young protégé.

Before he could even blink, Alex had crossed the ten feet of lawn and had Hammerson by the throat. He lifted the brawny senior officer off the ground.

Hammerson had a gun and a knife, but ignored both and just used his own hands to hang on to Alex's wrists and take some pressure off his neck.

He would weather the storm, and just hope he didn't end up like those Russians.

Alex pulled Hammerson's face close to his own. "Don't say those . . . *things* to me," he hissed through clenched teeth.

"You could save them," Hammerson croaked. "And I can help."

Alex tossed Hammerson to the side, and the older man hit the ground, rolled, and came to his feet.

The huge dog was immediately in front of the colonel, finger-length teeth bared and a low growl emanating from deep in his chest as Alex walked away, his hands to his head.

"Call off the dog, Alex. We need to go inside and talk," Hammerson said. "This is serious."

Alex half-turned and the dog immediately quietened and walked back to his side.

Perhaps Joshua wasn't the only one who had a link with the animal, Hammerson thought.

Alex continued to stand with his back to the HAWC commander.

"Time travel is real, Alex," he said softly. "It's newly developed and has some limitations, but it works."

Alex turned and unleashed a penetrating gaze on Hammerson that made him feel like he was being x-rayed. And in a way he was. The man could tell if he was lying or if there was subterfuge simply by the speed of a heartbeat, or perspiration on the brow, or even one's pupils being dilated.

After a moment, Alex walked toward the house. "Tell me everything."

An hour later Hammerson had brought Alex up to where they were with the Janus Institute. Now came the hard part.

"The Janus technologists are working on creating bridges to other parts of the time line." Hammerson watched Alex, who stared straight ahead. "We believe, and they believe, they can choose a destination – a time and a place – and return there. Think about what that could mean."

Alex turned. "We know where the shooter was. And what time they were there." His voice was deep and measured. "I could return to that place before they opened fire." He stared and the intensity of his gaze was scalding.

Hammerson nodded once. "Yes."

"When will it be ready?" Alex asked.

"There's a complication," Hammerson replied.

Alex looked away. "Of course there is."

Hammerson continued. "The reason we even know about the Janus temporal displacement device is that their offices and technology were compromised by the North Koreans. They've stolen the know-how and by now have constructed their own device. The complication is that we expect they will try and destroy the United States from within."

"You said they only have a bridge back to 420 million years ago." Alex frowned. "How could they—?"

"By planting one or more dirty bombs in the inland sea of that time," Hammerson cut in. "Rendering it toxic and unhabitable for many thousands of years. Long enough to prevent the creation of the petroleum beds. Our country would be altered forever. Weakened. Destroyed, maybe."

Alex stared.

"We now know they've been acquiring significant amounts of fissionable material. We believe they've got everything they need." Hammerson sat forward. "Think about what it could mean if they succeed; maybe none of us would even exist. Certainly there'd be no going back for Joshua and Aimee."

Alex's eyes narrowed. "Where are the North Koreans now?"

"We don't know," Hammerson replied. "We're using all our best resources to try and find them, but we're coming up empty. If they make the jump back and detonate those bombs, it will be too late. For everyone." He sat forward. "We won't know when they've gone, or where from, until they depart. When they do, we will get a signal on our sensors."

"And once you know that?" Alex turned, his eyes now glowing intensely silver in the dark room.

"Then that gives us one option for stopping them. Because, if they cannot be detected or stopped here—"

"Then we go back. And we stop them there." Alex turned. "Right?"

Hammerson nodded slowly. "That's right, son."

"And you want me to go." Alex's eyes narrowed and he looked down at the dog as if sharing a thought for a moment. He then looked up at Hammerson. "I will, on one condition."

"Name it," Hammerson replied.

"You look after Tor."

Hammerson's eyes slid across to the huge animal with the pale, unblinking gaze. "Come on, Alex, the thing hates me."

Alex turned to the dog, stared for a moment, and then the dog softened its gaze and went and sat by Hammerson's side.

"Not anymore."

Hammerson looked from the dog to Alex. "You can link? I thought only . . ." He didn't want to say Joshua's name.

Alex nodded. "I can now. I see what he sees. And vice versa."

Hammerson grunted as he nodded. "You're on." He stood. "We've got to be ready to jump any time. Training starts tomorrow. I'll send a car. Be ready."

CHAPTER 11

USSTRATCOM, Nebraska, Sub Basement 4 –
Weapons Research and Development

"Are you sure?" Dr. Andrew Quartermain paused, holding his instruments in the air while the brawny female HAWC sat with the stump end of her arm on the operating bench. "To say this will be painful—" he looked up into her face, "—is an understatement."

"Pain nourishes your courage." Casey continued to look down at her arm.

"*Hmm*, I like that. Who said it, Jung?" Quartermain's brows went up.

Casey scoffed. "No, Mary Tyler Moore. Now come on, Doc, hurry up. Got things to do."

"Okay." Quartermain grimaced. "I need to attach the electrodes directly into the bone matrix and nerve endings. Then I need to use a biological adhesive to bond it, permanently."

She clicked her tongue. "Ready when you are, kid."

Quartermain was now the head of WRD, Weapons Research and Development, for offensive and defensive weaponry for the US military Special Forces. But much of the newly developed equipment was first given over for field-of-fire testing to the HAWCs – the secretive, effective, and brutal Hotzone All Warfare Commandos.

In turn, the HAWCs simply called his division the Toy Box, and Quartermain supplied everything from ballistic armor, explosives, combat lasers, robotics, and too many penetrative projectile armaments to count.

He also supplied internal and external combat chassis and enhancement prosthetics, like the limb he was about to graft onto Lieutenant Casey Franks' right arm stump.

"Okay, Casey, enjoy the ride." He exhaled. "It's going to be a rough one."

He held on to her arm and pressed along the muscle bunching. He wore a visor that amplified the work he was doing while also allowing him to see below the epidermal layers of the flesh. He could see the bones, arteries, muscle striations, even the branching nerve endings.

On the table there were half a dozen needle-like probes that needed to be embedded in the nerve clusters of Casey's forearm, and also two quarter-inch-thick spikes that would then be forced into the sheared-off ends of her radius and ulna bones.

Casey should have been given a general anesthetic and be out cold. But she had only allowed him to supply a local pain deferral gel and a mild narcotic – she was high, but he knew the pain would still be excruciating. More than most people could bear. He expected her to black out – it would be a mercy – before he was finished.

He drew in a breath. "Nerve endings first."

He took the first of the needles and carefully inserted it into the stump, turning it slightly so he could pierce the tough flesh. It was hard going as the muscles automatically contracted from the trauma, making it like trying to penetrate gristle. At least there was minimal blood.

Casey let out a small groan but kept a tight smile on her face. "Dealing with pain, trains you to deal with pain," she whispered.

It was the same for the other five spikes. The female HAWC, with her white crew cut and scarred cheek that made her seem like she was permanently sneering, just nodded and smiled.

Quartermain knew this was why the HAWCs were so tough – not just their physicality, expertize, and intelligence, but their ability to absorb pain, and keep coming back.

He finished the nerve implants. "First round done. How you doing?"

Casey grinned up at him. "That all you got?"

"Unbelievable." He shook his head. "And unfortunately, no."

Quartermain checked the screen of sensors and was satisfied to see all the implants registering nerve connectivity. He then focused on the two sheared bone ends.

"This is the big one. I ask one more time, Lieutenant; can I please give you something to numb the pain?"

She shook her head. "I can take it." She began to take big breaths and looked away.

The scientist exhaled. "Better you than me."

Quartermain picked up the first knitting needle–sized spike and held it up, twirling it slightly as he examined its tip. On completion of full depth insertion, small barbs would extrude into the bone to lock it in place. It should be functional immediately, but a rest period of at least a week was recommended, or better yet, a month. But looking at Casey's bulging muscles, he doubted he'd get two days' rest out of the HAWC before she hit the gym again.

He sighted the ulna's bone ends under the skin, positioned the spike, and then began to push it into Casey's flesh. It was hard going.

Casey exhaled loudly through pressed lips, but Quartermain kept going, met the bone, and then inserted and forced the spike up into the open marrow end. He locked it in place.

Casey had her head down and he saw that her shoulders were making small jerking movements. *Is she crying?* he wondered.

"Hey, you okay there?" He laid a hand softly on her upper arm. "We can stop for a while if you want."

She looked up, grinning. She had been laughing.

"You're right, Doc; *fuck, that hurts.*" She blew it off and nodded to her now bleeding stump end. "Final round; I'm ready." She made a tight fist with her other hand.

Quartermain shook his head in disbelief and picked up the second spike, slowly repeating the procedure. Casey banged her clenched fist against her thigh as the spike met the end of the radius and slid in. He locked it in place.

"Done," he said.

Casey tilted her head back and nodded slowly. He saw that her face was pale. "Man oh man, wouldn't want to do that every day."

"I wouldn't want to do that *any* day," he replied. "But when done, your new hand will have perfect dexterity, be extremely powerful, near indestructible, and have a range of different functions. Going to be very useful as a HAWC."

"Load me up then, Quarter-dick," she replied.

"Very funny." Quartermain picked up the gauntlet. It looked like a human hand but was a black metallic structure and a little more skeletal-looking than normal. It had been matched to the size of Casey's other hand. Its attaching end had several sockets waiting to receive the node ends he had just implanted.

"Here goes," he said, and gently slid it onto the waiting spikes, with the sleeve end covering her stump. He then locked it in place with an audible *click*. He felt along her forearm.

"Swollen now, obviously, but that will recede. "How's the pain?"

Casey lifted the arm and flexed the fingers, one at a time, and then made them ripple like she was playing a piano. "Wow, man." She smiled as she reached across to Quartermain's instrument table and picked up a steel beaker. She lifted it, holding it in her fingertips for a second, before gripping it and then crushing it in her fist as if it was paper. "How's the pain?" she asked. "Worth every damn second."

"Now, remember, this is still an attached prosthetic. You'll need to undergo controls education, repetitive drills, and bimanual functional skills training. It shouldn't take more than a few weeks, as I can see that the nerves and prosthesis have already developed a strong biomedical handshake."

"Yeah, yeah," she replied dismissively.

Quartermain took hold of her arm and ran his fingers up from the steel to her flesh. "I can fit you with a synthetic sleeve, if you like. Looks like real flesh and will match your other arm." He let go of her hand and waggled his eyebrows. "Even add your tattoos back. I have all the designs in your file."

"Nope." She raised the black skeletal arm and made a fist. "This is badass as all hell. I like it just the way it is."

There was a small *blip* that came from the wrist communicator Casey wore on the other arm and she glanced at it.

"It's the big boss." Her brows knitted together as she read the message. "Okay, Doc, weapons training starts now. I've been called up for a mission – tomorrow." She looked up, her eyes luminous. "With the Arcadian."

"The Arcadian?" Quartermain straightened. "Alex Hunter . . . he's back?" His eyes were wide. "Oh my God."

CHAPTER 12

USSTRATCOM, Nebraska – Administration Center, Briefing Room 1

Colonel Jack Hammerson entered the room with Agent Bernadette Cooper. Several of the HAWCs were already there, some seated, some standing.

No one needed to jump to their feet and yell: *ten-hut*, as they weren't that sort of soldier. But they all knew who was in charge.

Hammerson glanced at them. "Soldiers."

The enormously fit men and woman already seated straightened in their chairs, and the few standing sat down.

Hammerson looked over their group. He nodded to Sam Reid in the front seat, the oldest in the team at thirty-nine.

Just behind him sat Casey Franks, the female HAWC who at five-ten was the shortest, but who was basically a human battering ram. She would always be the first through any door, first into the field of fire, and first to break a head. He tried not to smile at her as she nodded to him and gave a small salute with her newly attached skeletal black hand.

There were also some new HAWCs, all elevated to the 'A' team because of their required skill set for the potential mission: Bill 'Beast' Brandt, ex-Ranger, like himself. A specialist in electrical engineering and hand-to-hand combat. The man was big, raw, and had a granite chin that looked like a cash register with the drawer open.

Sitting next to Bill was Eric Gonzalez. Only a hair's-breadth taller than Casey, what he lacked in height he made up for in his expertize in explosives. He was their team MacGyver – give him a rubber band and a popsicle stick and he was the guy who could make an airplane or a bazooka with his bare hands.

Finally, sitting off to the side was Ito Yamada, heavily decorated, ex-SOG, the Japanese Special Operations Group, and one of the few HAWCs with more dragon tattoos than Casey Franks. His specialty was weapons, all of them, but mainly knives, and he was one of the most accurate marksmen they had ever had on their books.

All the HAWCs looked alert, and impatient. And Hammerson knew why. Word had already spread as to who would be joining them to lead the mission – the Arcadian, Alex Hunter – the man who couldn't be killed.

But they might have also been slightly wary, as they knew Alex had a volatile demon inside him, especially Casey and Sam who had worked most closely with him. And they also knew what had happened to his family. The guy might be the deadliest time bomb to ever walk on two legs, a time bomb that could detonate and destroy them all.

The HAWCs' eyes slid across to the woman Hammerson had brought with him. But he wasn't ready to introduce her just yet.

Hammerson's small earpiece blipped softly, and he touched the stud to open the comms – *Let's roll*, he thought.

"Send him straight in," he said.

Everyone knew who he meant, so the room fell silent as they waited.

Hammerson folded his arms, watching his team. His soldiers were the most highly trained on the planet. They were the sharpest thinkers, the toughest, and by far the deadliest. And right now, he watched them all staring at the door like schoolkids waiting for the principal.

It might have been Casey Franks who started pounding on the wooden armrest of her chair with her metallic fist, but soon all the HAWCs took up the beat until it was near deafening in the room.

A couple of moments later the handle turned, and the door opened. Alex Hunter, the Arcadian, stood in the doorway. He was now shaven, still hugely fit and robust-looking. His blue-gray eyes moved from Hammerson to the group.

The pounding immediately stopped, and the entire room of HAWCs just stared, wide-eyed. Bernadette Cooper looked confused.

Sam Reid got to his feet. "*Arcadian,*" he yelled, as the other HAWCs shot upright.

* * *

Alex could hear the thumping, like a giant heartbeat, long before he got to the briefing room.

He grabbed the doorhandle and paused to take a breath. It wasn't nerves – he wasn't sure he even had the ability to get nervous anymore. It was more a building eagerness to be on-mission again.

He pushed the door open. The thumping stopped instantly, and he saw the huge form of Sam Reid on his feet, yelling the name he hadn't heard in years.

Colonel Jack Hammerson stood at the front of the room, his face as stern as ever.

"Captain Hunter," he said with a slight nod, which was about as close as you got to a warm greeting from the man.

Alex looked over the room, taking in his fellow HAWCs. Some, like Casey and Sam, he'd been on countless missions with, and some he only knew by reputation. When he saw them all together for the first time since – he struggled with the thought for a moment – since he had lost his family, he felt a small bloom of joy.

"Take a seat, Captain. Everyone else at ease, and do the same." Hammerson waited as Alex walked among the group.

Alex shook hands as he went, embracing Sam like a long-lost brother. In fact, that was what Sam seemed like: a big brother. And he knew the big guy would die for him if need be.

The huge man reached out with both hands to grab Alex's shoulders and look deep into his eyes. "Good to have you back, Alex." He half-smiled. "I missed you, man. And if you tell anyone I said that, I'll have to kill you."

Alex laughed softly.

"See, the big lug's gone soft without you here, boss." Casey Franks held out her new hand to fist-bump him.

"Casey." He bumped her metal fist and then grabbed her arm and held it up. He turned the artificial limb, looking at it for a moment.

"I remember," he said softly, his vision clouding as he was cast back to the Well of Hell mission when Casey had held the bomb on the other side of an interplanetary portal when it closed – taking the bomb, and Casey's hand and part of her arm, with it.

He remembered her on the ground, her teeth gritted and eyes furious as she held the stump, refusing to cry out in pain.

Casey opened and closed the fist. "Good as ever," she said.

He then gripped her hand. "Press."

She did, and then gripped hard as her sneer pulled her lip up.

After another moment he nodded. "Yeah, about ten times the power of a normal human fist. Not as good as ever; better than ever." He looked into her eyes. "That'll work just fine."

"Damn right," she replied.

Alex then looked around at the other HAWCs, nodding to each, until there was a single hand clap like a rifle shot.

"Okay, listen up, people." Hammerson's voice was raised. "You know when they call us in, the shit has already gone south. And this is as bad as it gets."

The HAWCs sat, silenced and waiting.

"We are facing a terrorist-generated scenario that could be described as a potential extinction event for our great country." Hammerson looked along their faces. "Let me cut to the chase. Hang on to your asses, because time travel is real."

He waved down the questions and continued. "A US company called Janus has developed a device that harnesses tachyons, subatomic particles that can travel faster than the speed of light – and, it seems, time itself. They use these particles to create a bridge that can be traveled across, through time. Right now it has destination limitations."

He gestured toward the woman standing a few feet away. "I'm going to hand over to Bernadette Cooper, chief science officer attached to the CIA, who has expertize in physics, chemistry, and biology, and has been involved in debriefing the Janus team and working with the project for a while now. She will take you through more of the details." He turned. "Agent Cooper."

Alex looked at the woman; he'd never met or heard of her. She was maybe mid-thirties, athletic, and he could tell by her intelligent eyes that she would be competent. But she was nervous as hell in front of the huge Special Forces soldiers.

"Thank you, Colonel." She walked a few paces forward and cleared her throat. Then cleared her throat again.

"Waiting." Casey grinned up at the woman.

"*Franks*," Hammerson warned, and then nodded to Cooper.

"Soldiers," she began. "Until recently everyone thought time travel and time machines were science fiction or all theoretical.

They're not. They exist. They work. And we can send objects and people back in time and then return them to our present day."

"Back to the future," Casey sneer-grinned.

"Yes, but without a DeLorean," Cooper replied, deadpan. "We are out of the realm of the theoretical, and therefore as well as being cognizant of the effects of traveling through time, we also need to be aware of the paradoxes."

"I know these," Sam said. "A temporal paradox, or time travel paradox, is a logical contradiction associated with the idea of time and time travel itself." Sam's brows were slightly furrowed. "But they're supposed to be logical impossibilities."

"Yes, but now everything has changed. We need a new approach, new rules, new thinking, and even new ways to deal with the paradoxes," Agent Cooper replied.

"The genie is out of the bottle," Alex said.

Cooper nodded. "Unfortunately, yes. And it's not going back in."

Casey raised a hand momentarily. "I read that a paradox is where you create a time machine to go back in time and kill Hitler. But if you do, and are successful, and Hitler doesn't exist anymore, then there was no reason to create the time machine in the first place."

"That's right." Cooper looked from Casey to the group. "Similar to the grandfather paradox – you can't kill your own grandfather as then you wouldn't exist to go back and kill your own grandfather." She folded her arms. "There are a lot of examples, and we've always believed, as Lieutenant Reid said, that they were nothing more than logical impossibilities."

"But not all of them," Alex said. "There are some instances where the past might be able to be altered. And mistakes, errors, or crimes, erased completely."

"Yes. That's what we believe. Or at least that's what we

now believe." She nodded. "And then, we might have no knowledge of them, because they never happened."

"Except for the person who went back – they might still remember. Right?" Alex pressed.

Alex glanced at Hammerson, who was watching him closely. The man's expression never changed but he gave Alex an almost imperceptible nod.

Cooper shrugged. "We don't know if that is true or not yet. But that's what we may find out, to our benefit or detriment, very soon."

Hammerson folded his arms. "This is where it gets messy." He gave the team a detailed overview of the Janus Institute and the machine itself, and explained how the plans for the device had been leaked to the North Koreans.

"HAWCs," he said finally, "we proceed on the basis that the mission is green-lit, and happening any time from now. The bell-ring moment will be when the North Koreans initiate their jump – it will give off a tachyon signature we can home in on. We plan on arriving at the place where they launch from just hours after they leave." He looked along their ranks. "And we will be following them back in time, and then tracking them down."

"So . . ." Sam sat forward, and his six-foot-five frame made the chair beneath him squeal in protest. "We're time traveling. Exactly how far back?"

"You'll love this." Hammerson allowed himself a smile. "Agent Cooper." He nodded to the CIA woman.

She faced the group, her expression closed.

"Four hundred and twenty million years. To primordial Earth, the Silurian period." She looked at each of the HAWCs' faces.

"That far back? Will we be able to breathe?" Sam asked.

"Yes, the oxygen levels are higher than now, in fact, but there had been an atmosphere for a hundred million years by then," Cooper replied. "That we know. But I won't lie to anyone; it's a period we know little about. The fossil remains are scant at best."

"So, we could be walking into unknown situations, with unknown non-human adversaries, while tracking armed human adversaries," Alex said. "We need more intel."

"I agree, and I'm it," Cooper replied. She picked up a remote from the desk beside her, pressed a button, and the back wall illuminated. She then called up a representation of the entire world, flattened, showing the oceans, continents, and islands.

"Our world, today."

She pressed another button on the remote.

"Taking us back in time now – fifty million years, one hundred million ..." She continued to press the buttons. "Two hundred million years ago, three hundred . . ."

The continents had broken up, some had sunk, some had merged with other landmasses to create entire new islands and continents. All were totally unrecognizable.

"And at just over four hundred million years ago we arrive at the Silurian period." She lowered the arm holding the remote but continued to look at the map. "The world's glaciers had melted so it was mainly a water world. After another few million years, those major landmasses – we call them super islands – will collide to create the continent Laurussia, through the merging of Laurentia and Baltica."

She pointed with the remote. "Between them is a vast sea some 600 miles long by 100 miles wide. The majority of our petroleum beds came from the marine fossil deposits in the shallow seas that formed after that point."

"So, here's what we believe they're planning based on intel from our deep cover intelligences sources." She put the remote down and turned back to the group. "We expect the NKs will be trying to detonate several small but powerful – and very dirty – nuclear devices. We computer-simulated how they could cause the maximum long-term damage and we found that timing the devices to go off decades or centuries apart would maintain a high level of contamination for many millennia." She folded her arms. "If the North Koreans can corrupt that shallow sea and stop life for an extended period, then no sea life, no fossil sedimentation, no oil. You know what that means: no genesis of wealth for our growing nation, so potentially, no nation."

"So many changes," Sam said.

Cooper nodded. "And that's why there are so many missing pieces in the fossil record for that era. We may encounter things that are . . . unexpected."

"We?" Alex's eyes slid to Hammerson. "The risk factors are off the charts. We'll be in absolute hostile territory, moving fast. There will be no time for babysitting civilians."

Cooper walked forward and stood in front of the seated Alex Hunter. She looked down at him. "I can run a marathon in two hours twenty. I have hand-to-hand combat skills, and I'm weapons trained with target proficiency to 300 feet. With over eighty percent pure shots."

Casey scoffed. "That wouldn't get you past first culling for HAWC tryout."

Cooper ignored Casey and continued to focus on Alex. "I'll be the closest thing you have to an expert on that period of time. I won't slow you down, and I might just save your lives."

Alex saw the strength in her conviction. Without specialist briefing notes, and the terrain and situations they might face being such a gray area, having the specialist made sense. He continued to stare, and she didn't wilt.

She smiled. "And it's Agent Bernadette Cooper. But people call me Bern."

"Fine." He smiled back grimly. "Just keep up, or you'll be left behind, *Agent Cooper*."

"Bern, baby, Bern." Casey grinned.

"Okay, people." Hammerson's voice was loud in the room. "Meet and greet is now over. I want everyone down to WRD for kit out. I'm thinking our human adversaries won't be the only things back there that will try and kill you, so full combat equipment and armor." He saluted. "Dismissed."

CHAPTER 13

USSTRATCOM, Nebraska, Sub Basement 4 –
Weapons Research and Development

Alex Hunter and the HAWC mission team traveled down in
the secure elevator to the second-deepest level beneath the
USSTRATCOM building. None of them spoke, their heads
full of what they'd just heard.

The entire subterranean complex was encased in sealed
titanium and lead shielding that made the basement levels
impregnable to a nuclear blast and impervious to electromag-
netic pulse attack.

The design was like an upside-down wedding cake, with the
larger test facilities at the top, then the smaller R&D laboratories, and then the lower-level containment cells for biological
specimen testing and hazardous materials work. That level
also contained the heavily fortified room, called 'the box', that
was used for Alex to restabilize himself following a mission or
those times when the inner demon howled too loudly in the
core of his mind.

The research floor they headed to was where Sam Reid's
internal MECH endoskeleton had been developed, and Casey

had had her robotic prosthetic attached. It was also where the android, Sophia, had been created.

The android was developed to be a combat unit with reinforced chassis, fusion reactor power source, and AI programming. It was expected to fight alongside soldiers in hot conflict zones. And even bond with a soldier to act as their guardian – as Sophia had been bonded to him. That's what it was designed to do. But nothing ever goes to plan.

Alex drew in a deep breath and let it out slow. It was weird; now and then he still felt her in his head. He blinked several times and focused on nothing but the heavy steel elevator door in front of him.

He had mixed feelings about the place. For the most part he appreciated it as the source of the defensive and offensive weapons tech that enabled him to get his job done. But it was also where the former head of R&D, Walter Grey, had worked. The bespectacled, diminutive scientist had lived in his laboratory like a turtle within its shell, only emerging to try and help rescue Alex. And for that, he had been brutally killed by Sophia. Like in an old horror story cliché, the scientist had been killed by his own creation.

And that was another death, Alex mused glumly, that had happened because of him.

Alex stared straight ahead at the heavy elevator door, his own thoughts tormenting him.

Everyone dies, he thought. *Except me.*

* * *

Sam Reid stood just behind Alex as the door slid open to reveal Dr. Andrew Quartermain waiting for them. The scientist stepped back as Alex Hunter walked out.

"Sir, I . . ." He saluted. Sort of.

"Don't do that," Alex said.

He dropped his hand. "Captain Hunter, sir, it's good to see you back, and, ah, I just wanted to say . . ."

Alex went past the scientist, leaving him staring. Casey Franks laid her bionic arm on the young man's shoulder. "Keep it up, Doc. I think you can get him to sign your t-shirt on the way out."

Sam chuckled as Quartermain turned to Casey.

"I just wanted . . ." He sighed, refocused, and walked fast to keep up with the female HAWC. "How's the hand and arm?"

"Excellent," she replied. "Did you know I even have a sensation of touch?" She lifted her hand and rubbed the thumb and forefinger together.

"I do – that's why there were so many sensors embedded into the nerve beds." He grabbed her skeletal-looking hand and turned it over. "Plus, see here, the tiny arrays of sensors on the fingertips."

"*Ahh*, yeah, I thought they were just for grip." She nodded.

"They're for both." He grinned. "No extra charge."

"Nice." She laughed. "Hey, feel free to cut my other arm off; I want two."

"Knowing you, it'll probably be bitten or blown off next mission." He checked where the flesh of her arm fitted into the prosthetic socket. "Excellent seal, and nice bonding." He grinned at her. "I do good work."

"I second that," Sam jumped in, nodding.

Quartermain beamed. "Thank you, Lieutenant Reid. Your MECH internal infrastructure still satisfactory?"

"No complaints," Sam replied.

"Upgrades coming soon." Quartermain nodded. "We've been finalizing many more advancements." He looked up at Sam. "We can replace anything these days. Except the brain."

"That's fine. Still using mine," Sam replied.

"Really?" Casey grinned over her shoulder at the pair.

Sam snorted and glanced at the scientist. "When it comes time to replacing Casey's brain, all you'll need to do is insert a piece of paper with the words: *kill everything* written on it."

She nodded. "Simplifies things."

Quartermain turned to take in the rest of the team. The HAWCs, numbering six, comprised Alex Hunter as team leader, Sam Reid, second-in-charge, Casey Franks, Bill Brandt, Eric Gonzalez, and Ito Yamada. He greeted each by name, but then he came to a woman he didn't recognize.

He stopped in front of her. "I don't know you."

"She's with us," Alex said. "Consultant."

"Bernadette Cooper," the woman said. "Chief science officer attached to the CIA. Advanced degrees in physics, chemistry, and summa cum laude in biology."

"Good, good." Quartermain lifted his chin, refusing to be overshadowed in his own laboratory. "You'll come in very handy." He walked around her. "Five-nine and a bit, athletic figure, maybe 160, 163 pounds."

"Do you mind?" she said in an offended tone.

"The armored suits need to be lived in for however many days you will be on-mission. A good fit is critical. Data matters. So I do mind." He smiled thinly. "It may be the difference between life and death. Yours, of course."

"Got it," she said. "Sorry, my first time."

"No problem." He brightened. "You'll be fine. But I'll run a bio-scan on you so the suit will be printed and tailored. I already have all the HAWCs' physicals." He rubbed his hands together. "Now. Follow me to the armory and let's talk about the mission kit out."

After passing through several security checkpoints they entered the armory and Quartermain stepped back as the HAWCs and Cooper formed a half-ring in front of him. Sam folded massive log-like arms and stood behind Casey.

"The colonel has briefed me about your mission parameters, terrain, environment, and risk factors." He half-smiled. "I'm sort of envious. I want to go. And I don't want to go. What you will encounter will be unbelievable, and could also be unbelievably dangerous."

"Environmentally, what can we expect?" Sam asked.

"From the Silurian period? It's 420 million years ago, so there's not much in the fossil record. However, we know the oxygen levels will be slightly higher than now, and there might be a pervading smell of sulfur and methane due to active volcanism. Oh, and it should be a lot warmer and more humid than it is today – probably high eighties to mid-nineties, and humidity constantly at eighty percent at least."

The HAWCs groaned.

Quartermain nodded and continued. "Plus, there was little or no ice at the North or South Pole, so sea levels were higher at that time – up to five hundred feet higher than today. In fact, the planet is mostly ocean."

"Will we need to take that into consideration?" Alex asked.

Quartermain nodded. "I think—"

"Yes," Bernadette Cooper finished. "As the majority of our petroleum beds came from the marine fossil deposits in the shallow sea, then it makes sense for the North Koreans to target that sea."

"So, they'll be taking to the water," Alex said.

"Bastards," Casey said softly.

"But taking out our oil doesn't only affect our economics," Sam said. "Sure, we'd be a poorer, less powerful nation without it – if we existed at all. We probably would never have the might to engage meaningfully in the Second World War. But there's also the after-effects of the radioactive contamination – who knows what sort of mutations would appear?"

"New lifeforms. Or distorted old ones," Alex said. "Right in our own backyard."

"Not just our own backyard," Quartermain said. "Millions of years later, during the early Triassic, the continents merged again: Asia, Africa, America. That means anything here would be able to just walk or fly over there." He shook his head. "If this is their plan, these guys might be signing their own death warrants as well. Because some of those distorted lifeforms might well be us human beings."

"The end of us all," Sam said.

Quartermain rubbed his chin. "But Agent Cooper is right. We need to take the water into consideration. I think you may need the ability to dive in it as well."

"More gear?" Sam asked.

Quartermain nodded. "But minimal. Just means the suits I provide will need an airtight visor and oxygen supply. But that's not where the weight is going to come in." He looked up with a grim smile. "The weaponry required against potential formidable predators will need to be significant."

"What sort of predators?" Ito asked. "I wish to take my sword."

Quartermain held up a finger. "What sort of predators? Good question, and no easy answer, as, again, very little data on contemporary Paleozoic fossils has survived. However, I have done a little research and looked at the footage from one of the Janus group's filmed jumps, which captured footage of an animal. It was a herbivorous creature called a *Lystrosaurus*. It has a beak, is about the size of a pig and is from a very ancient order of creatures called therapsids, which are a cross between reptiles and mammals."

"The size of a pig . . . with a beak?" Brandt said scornfully. "Forget the weapons, we should take a grill."

"Sure, if you want to risk dying," Cooper said. "Be aware one of their other scientists, James Chen, did a solo jump and was torn apart by something a lot more formidable than the *Lystrosaurus*."

She pinned Brandt with her gaze for a moment before continuing. "The Silurian is a geological period spanning from the end of the Ordovician to the beginning of the Devonian period. Due to scant fossil evidence of anything dinosaur-like, many scientists assumed it was a fairly benign era. But new fossil fragments are surfacing every day. You've just got to know where to look."

She pulled out her phone and called up an image – it was of a bony fish that looked a little like an armor-plated steelhead trout.

"*Megamastax amblyodus*," she said. "Newly discovered and the largest aquatic vertebrate known in the Silurian fossil record – we thought they didn't grow larger than a few inches in the oceans, then we discovered this three-foot-long specimen."

"*Ooh*, three foot." Brandt raised his eyebrows. "Is that what killed Chen? This is getting serious." He winked at Casey.

"You don't understand. This creature represents a hundred times increase in size on what we thought was possible." Cooper frowned back at the big HAWC. "Then we found this . . ." She called up another image.

It was from a dark, broken-open piece of shale, alongside which a soda can had been placed for size comparison. The thing embedded in the matrix was a tusk-like tooth, backward curving, with barbs along its conical length. It was broken off, but the fragment was bigger than the can.

Sam whistled. "What's it from?" he asked.

"It's called the Great Basin tooth." She shook her head. "And that's just it; we don't know what it's from. This is the only fragment we found. We're not even sure if it's aquatic or terrestrial." Cooper lowered her phone and looked at each of them. "Think of it in this context: say we dig down to this place right here in a few hundred million years, and we come across the city and its outskirts. We might find out that the dominant species was humans, and they grew to an average height of around five-nine. We also find the remains of a few dogs, cats, pigeons, and, further out, moose, and a few eagles, and from that data surmise that this was also a fairly benign area."

She stared at the group. "But we never find our basketballers who are seven feet plus. And out in the forests we have Kodiak bears that stand nine feet tall and can weigh 2300 pounds. And don't forget down south we have alligators that grow to twenty feet."

"But at least those are not as bad as dinosaurs," said Casey.

"We don't really know. They could be as bad or worse. Or at least there could be things that filled the same predatorial niche." Cooper chuckled mirthlessly. "Bottom line, we should hope for the best but plan for the worst."

"Always count on nature to let loose its war machines," Alex said softly.

"No running away from those suckers," Casey said. "Give us the firepower and we stand and fight."

Cooper turned to Ito. "And maybe take a little more than a sword."

The group was quiet for a moment or two, until she stepped back and nodded to Quartermain. "Over to you, again."

"Thank you, Agent Cooper, a good summary. And yes, we have to assume there might be mega predators on land and sea to deal with so we will be taking a range of weaponry, grenades, and equipment that can operate in a range of environments." He paused and seemed to collect his thoughts. "But remember, we need to balance weight with portability. I also want the mission members to retain their personal defensive punch in an aquatic environment."

He turned to Bernadette Cooper. "You've interviewed the Janus team?"

She nodded. "I have."

"I'd like an opportunity to do that. They're quite brilliant. I'm in awe of their work on the tachyon pathways that they've harnessed, or as they call them, *time bridges*. They've made some intuitive scientific leaps that are technological magic." He shook his head in wonder. "I have a thousand questions." He turned back. "And almost as many concerns."

"Like what?" Cooper asked.

He shrugged. "Tachyons are one of the most chaotic particles in existence. Sure, they can break the rules of light, speed, time, and perhaps even dimensional travel. But as I mentioned, they're chaotic, and I can't imagine how you keep them under enough control to be able to hitch a ride on their stream, or bridge – without getting . . . tipped off."

Casey Franks guffawed. "Now they tell us." She folded her arms and looked at the scientist from under lowered brows. "Doc, just exactly what could happen if some poor sap like me managed to get *tipped off* one of those bridges?"

Quartermain lifted a hand, palm up, and his mouth turned down momentarily. "Perhaps the Janus team would be best to answer that one, or best placed to explain how, or if, they have solved the issue. It's all theoretical, and at this stage it's all guesswork."

"Stop wriggling and tell us what *you* think," Casey demanded.

"Well, um . . ." He pursed his lips for a moment. "Perhaps, one might find themselves tipped off somewhere unexpected, into a time zone not their own. Or a place not their own. Or a dimension . . ."

"We get it. There'll be risks," Alex said. "Doesn't matter. We're committed to the mission." He looked at each of the HAWCs, who all nodded without hesitation.

Alex turned back to Quartermain. "Suits first. Mission expectation is for only a few days. But as we'll be searching extremely hostile terrain, we may find ourselves living in them longer."

"I understand," the scientist replied. "I'll be generating maximum camouflage, extreme defensive armor shielding, on top of high durability."

"Good. I want as many advantages over our adversaries – human or otherwise – as we can load up on," Alex said.

"We will have other advantages as well," Bernadette Cooper added. "The Janus team has been continually working on improving their technology. Our temporal bridge generator will be safer and more accurate than the NKs' model. Also, the model the NKs stole needs a destination platform to arrive on and return from. Ours doesn't. We just have to have a tachyon identification pellet with us, or even better, inserted under our skin, so the device can find us anywhere."

"The pellet will be inserted," Quartermain confirmed.

"Good. I'd hate to lose my return ticket during the mission – be a long walk home," Sam said.

Quartermain led the team further into the armory, where they saw that already there were several body-shaped suits lining a wall. Quartermain indicated the ones at the rear first.

"All are ballistic-proof and have biological armor plates with high mobility areas. Some have significantly more plating depending on the, ah, resistance the wearer is expecting in a combat scenario."

He stopped between two of the suits. "I'll be generating suits that will be a combination of these two."

The suits he motioned toward were black with streaks of green through them like a tiger stripe. "Adaptive camouflage skin that will change hue depending on the time of day or night, and also type of cover. They're also cooled internally for comfort in high heat and/or humidity environments, but that cooling will also bring down the external heat signature."

He turned and smiled. "So night hunters who rely on thermal vision won't find you so easily."

The team nodded their understanding.

"They look heavy," Cooper observed.

"Fairly heavy, but they're MECH assisted, so you'll basically be driving them." Quartermain tapped on one of the chest plates with a knuckle. "Biological plating, and stronger than titanium." He turned. "Can stop rounds of most calibers; although a .50-cal will crack them, it still won't penetrate." He grinned. "Though you may end up with a decent set of bruised ribs."

"Small price to pay if I took a direct hit from a .50-cal," Casey added.

"I think so too." The scientist nodded.

Quartermain then moved to the next suit. "The suits will be multi-layered. Standard mission, and also combat mode with heavier shielding. Helmet can be removed as a single piece or can be auto engaged and then retracted into the suit neck when not in use." He pressed a tiny stud on the neck and a visor slid up and over the head and face.

He pointed to the now solid-looking facial plates with four eye lenses. "As you can see, the first level is full armor with quad optical multiple vision spectrums of thermal vision, light amplification, motion sensitivity, and varying levels of magnification. And for going aquatic . . ." he pressed another stud and the heavier shielding pulled pack to reveal a clear plate, "full shatterproof nano-glass mask. There'll be a recessed pack on the back that stores a half-hour's oxygen. It's a small amount of below-water time, but the upside of the miniaturized units is they can refill themselves and then compress within twenty minutes above water."

He kneeled to highlight the devices on the aquatic suit's calves. "See these?" He didn't wait for a response. "They're the jets. Inflow at the top, high-pressure water expelled at speed at the rear. I actually tried them out in the base pool and they work extremely effectively. Maneuvering is done by the hands and feet." He looked up and smiled. "You literally fly under the water."

"What's the top speed?" Bill Brandt asked.

"Two speeds: there's cruising at around three knots, and bursts of top speed at around ten knots." He stood and then walked back to the group. "And of course, various slots and pouches for armaments."

"For my sword?" Ito asked.

"I'll make you up a back scabbard," Quartermain replied, and then turned. "Any more questions?" he asked.

"How long until we get them?" Bernadette Cooper asked.

"I can generate all the composite suits by end of day. Yours included." He smiled.

"Wow," she replied. "How do you . . .?"

He shrugged. "Like I said, it's biological armor; we grow them. Ensures there's a perfect fit to form." He looked at their faces. "Anything else?" He waited another moment, and then walked to the wall and pressed a small button. "In here." The blank wall slid back, and lights came on inside. "I've suggested some defensive kit. See what you think."

"Sam, take them in," Alex said.

Sam turned and saw Alex's slightly haunted expression. Colonel Hammerson had asked Sam to keep an eye on him, because even though Alex was in top physical shape, his mental state was still an open question.

"You got it," Sam said, and led the HAWCs into the next room.

CHAPTER 14

Alex stayed put and Quartermain walked over.

"Something else, Captain Hunter?" he asked. The scientist noticed that Alex Hunter looked as big and dangerous as ever, and those eyes of his, which sometimes shone silver, were burning into him intensely. He stopped a few paces from the big HAWC.

"Yes, there is," Alex said. "On this mission, I need a DOG. I've heard you've made some refinements." He stared down at the smaller man.

"Is that all? I mean, yes, good thinking. A Defensive Operational Ground unit would work on this assignment." He nodded, and then looked up. "I heard your android performed superbly on your Well of Hell operation."

"It, *he*, saved us all," Alex replied.

"That's excellent." Quartermain waited. "Something else?"

"Yes. I need it linked," Alex pressed.

"Linked?' Quartermain's brows came together. "It will have a neural mission-link to you. Just like last time."

Alex shook his head. "Linked to me, yes. But I also mean that its underlying psychological patterning needs to be imprinted with some*thing* else."

Quartermain stared for a moment. "Overwrite its AI logic? Hmm, I guess it's possible, but it's never been done. But why? And linked with what?"

"With . . . Torben," Alex replied. "I would take the real animal, but the danger is too great. Plus, I want the real dog waiting at home for when Joshua comes back."

"Comes . . . back?" Quartermain gulped and stared for a moment. *This doesn't sound good*, he thought. *Not good at all.* He shrugged. "Um, okay. I think the neurological patterning can be transferred."

"Good," Alex replied.

"And yes, you're right, we have made some improvements to the DOG androids. Certainly there are some things that might be beneficial for where you're going. Luckily, I do have a MK-III model right here and ready to go." He crossed to a slot in the wall that had a touch pad and typed in a code.

From a dark portal a box slid out on a moving ramp, and Quartermain took something that looked like a small remote from its top, lifted his hand to his mouth and spoke into it.

"Authorization Quartermain RX471382. Initiate." The scientist lowered his arm.

The suitcase-sized box had no obvious seams, but it broke apart, unfolded, elongated, and its corners smoothed out.

Quartermain smiled as he watched Alex run his eyes over the android. He knew that Alex had been one of the first HAWCs to work with versions of a DOG many years before. From that boxy prototype, which had been little more than a mobile gun, they had become intelligent offensive and defensive weapons with highly complex software that made them "bond" with their mission companion. Like the one Alex had used on his Well of Hell sortie.

But the new version was a whole new ball game. "I present Defensive Operational Ground vehicle, DOG, MK-III." He folded his arms.

The metallic creature looked like a large smooth canine. When sitting, its head came to about waist height.

Quartermain spoke into the handheld device again. "Audio input." He lowered the device and then spoke directly to the DOG. "Jungle camouflage."

The skin of the creature immediately turned a dappled green and black stripe like the HAWC suits.

"Desert camouflage." The android took on a patchy sandy and brown skin. "Night camouflage." It then changed to a non-reflective black.

"It'll assess its environment and do that automatically," Quartermain said.

"Very good," Alex replied. "Aquatic?"

"Yep. Becomes surround-reflective. Means it will simply look like the water source it is in. There are more terrain variations, but you get the idea."

"I like it." Alex nodded.

"Also equipped with now-standard combat lasers, incendiary output, and multiple-caliber armaments. Limited of course as there won't be anywhere to restock the ammunition. But the lasers will be inexhaustible, and the underlying power source is a fusion generator that could potentially run for a thousand years."

Alex frowned as he looked at its very dog-like face. "Hey, are they what I think they are?"

Quartermain chuckled. "A couple of small personal changes I made." He walked to the front and laid a hand on the android's head. "I did this for fun. And aesthetics. But it kinda works." He turned to the metallic creature. "Open mouth."

The mouth opened, displaying rows of razor-sharp teeth. "Bite power like a great white shark, can be used for everything from cutting a hole through thick jungle foliage like a high-speed machete, or for silent guardian work." He shrugged. "I like them because they make this bad boy look more *real.*"

Alex laid a hand on its head. "And you think we can link it?"

"Yes, I think so . . ." Quartermain looked up. "But will Torben let us?"

"He will," Alex replied confidently.

"Okay, then bring him in." Quartermain stood but paused, tilting his head to look up at Alex. "Just remember, it won't really be Torben. And Torben will not actually be linked through the android – I think. What it will be instead is a facsimile, an inserted copy of the real being. The AI's algorithms will create an approximation of Torben from his brain patterns. RX471382 will think it's Torben, and it will act like Torben, but—"

"I get it, it won't actually be Torben. I know that," Alex said. "But that will be enough."

"Why?" Quartermain asked. "Why do you want that?"

Alex drew in a breath and then let it out slowly. "Torben now has a strong bond with me. But he had an even stronger link with Joshua, and I know there are some residual fragments of my son held in Torben's mind." He looked across to the scientist, his eyes glistening. "I want that with me."

After a moment, Quartermain nodded. "I think I understand. Like I said, bring him in, and I'll make it happen."

"One more thing." Alex stepped in close to the smaller man.

"Yes?" Quartermain resisted the urge to step away from the big HAWC.

"I want you to stay on top of the Janus team. Keep pushing them to solve the near-term tachyon bridge limitations." He seemed to think about it for a moment. "When I get back, I want those bridges formed so we can select a time and destination. I have somewhere important I need to be. No one and nothing else matters. Can you do that?" he asked softly.

"Oh." Quartermain suddenly began to understand why Alex had come back for duty. "I understand. You have my word. I won't let them sleep until they've solved it. I promise."

Alex lowered his head, and he exhaled as if a great weight had been lifted from his shoulders. "Thank you."

Quartermain brightened. "Now let's join the team in the armaments room. I have some neat new kit to show you."

* * *

Alex followed the scientist into the armaments room and saw his team either trying out different weapons or talking softly. Casey Franks was at the knife table, and Eric Gonzalez looked to be trying to impress Bernadette Cooper with his knowledge of firearms and explosives. He was bouncing up on his toes, perhaps in an attempt to be taller than the CIA woman. For her part, Cooper seemed amused, but interested in what he was telling her.

Quartermain had already laid out some weapon suggestions on a long table and Alex looked them over as the young scientist described them. Alex already knew what most of them were as he had been keeping abreast of the USSTRATCOM Research and Development Weapons progress. Sam joined him and listened in.

"Rifles and hand weapons, with various pistols. You get to choose." Quartermain indicated a range of guns. The HAWCs usually had a preference for larger pistols with high-end stopping power, with smaller-caliber handguns for portability or as a backup weapon.

Quartermain walked to the next table which displayed two rifles. Alex moved closer as these seemed different, or at least new variants of weapons he had used before.

The scientist picked up the smaller one, which was the size of an M16 but had a smoother profile. The weapon was matte-black, but when he flicked a small switch a row of lights came on along the barrel.

"Laser rifle, Rev-6. Alterations include greater powerpack life with eight megawatts of energy from a miniaturized, self-contained fusion engine. Discharges beam size in multiple variations and also has rapid recharge capability," he said.

"How many shots until recharge required?" Sam asked.

"Two hundred pulses or twenty seconds of continual beam. Anything still standing after that, I suggest you simply run." Quartermain laughed but stopped when he saw the stony expressions on the pair of HAWCs. "Okay, like I said, it can be set to single pulse, or rapid-fire use that generates a stream of condensed light – it'll cut through anything. Plus, computer-assisted sighting means you can't miss."

"Ten bucks says the Beast can." Casey thumbed at Bill Brandt and grinned broadly.

Brandt gave Casey the finger.

"Recharge in under two minutes," Quartermain continued.

Sam picked up the larger model. "I'm assuming this is its big brother?"

"Correct. The laser cannon." Quartermain proudly took the larger weapon from him and held it under his arm. He strained to hold it up. "Presenting the Model T40 laser cannon. Forty megawatts of power from a larger fusion engine. Thicker beam size that'll punch a dinner plate–sized hole through anything. Thought it might come in handy where you're going." He bobbed his head. "But bigger energy pulse means faster energy drain, and slower recharge. Consider it personal heavy artillery. For emergencies."

Quartermain looked across to the HAWCs. "I have two ready for field-of-fire testing. There's a bit of weight with these guys as they need more shielding due to the bigger reactor."

Sam held the cannon under his arm. The longer dark weapon with bulbous tip on the end of the barrel looked like something from a sci-fi movie. Sam was a big man at six-five, and the internal MECH structure in his body meant the weight was nothing to him.

"Yeah, this'll do just fine," he said.

Brandt held up a hand. "Calling it. Bigger hits means I'm betting I ain't missing nothing. This time." He grinned and winked at Casey.

"I'll still take that bet," she shot back.

Quartermain stopped before another bench. On it were several objects, including some small silver balls roughly the size of a half-dollar.

"Standard pop grenades. High-impact percussive force. They can be used as a throwing projectile to detonate on impact or can be stuck to an object and timed to go off up to ten minutes later. Throw a handful of these at multiple converging adversaries, and it'll ruin their whole day." Quartermain lifted one and pressed a small stud on its surface. Red lights came on and spikes appeared all over it. "Each of you will get a dozen of these, carried in one of your hip pouches."

The next item looked like a dark, metallic tube with tapered ends and a rail slot. One end had an inch-wide hole inside. Quartermain looked at it lovingly.

"Grenade launcher." He turned the ten-inch device in the air. "Or my version of it. Will attach to the laser rifles and cannon via the slide rail on the undercarriage of the barrel. Discharge is a pulse of pure, sticky plasma that is around 54,000 degrees Fahrenheit, about five times hotter than the surface of our sun."

He looked at each of the HAWCs and nodded. "I know, cool, huh? And it's my personal invention – pure plasma harnessed as a weapon – awesome. Works on the same principle as ball lightning. The light is compressed via optical electrostrictive pressure. Meaning a shell of compressed air is a self-confined energy source constrained in a nonlinear optical medium."

Casey nudged Brandt in the ribs and shrugged. The big HAWC just rolled his eyes.

Quartermain pointed. "Will fire a pulse up to 300 feet and vaporize anything it touches on contact. You could vaporize an elephant." He held up a finger. "One important thing; these are your break-glass weapons. You get three high-energy pulses, and then you are out for good. No recharge, as plasma is understandably energy-hungry."

"Oh boy, can't wait." Casey's eyes blazed.

He looked into each of their faces. "Questions?"

"Can we try 'em?" Casey asked.

"Sure can. The range is set up and ready." He turned. "Ms. Cooper, have you fired a weapon before?"

"Of course," she replied. "I have both handgun and rifle training."

"Excellent. I still suggest you get some practice on these as well, as there are a few differences to get used to – the weight, zero recoil, precision – you understand."

"I do." She nodded. "Looking forward to it."

"You're with me, Bern babe." Casey grinned.

"One more thing," the scientist said, and pulled out a flat-looking suitcase. "I've got an above and below raft . . ."

"Above and below? What's that?" Sam asked.

"It can dive. The canopy shell is open ribbing, but if you need to take it under water, you can. It's lightweight and uses a similar propulsion to the calf-jets in your suits. Top speed is only five knots. It'll take all of you and save you having to swim if you need to cross a large waterway." He shrugged. "We know very little about many of the inhabitants of the inland seas at that time. The Kevlar ribbing will give you some protection, and the size of the craft might just make it harder for a Silurian sea denizen to swallow you."

"I heard that," Sam replied.

Alex hefted the raft pack. "Around ten pounds; we'll take two in case one gets damaged. I'll carry one . . ."

"I've got the other," Brandt said.

Quartermain got to the end of his weapons bench. "And finally, I have two turbine propulsion camera drones. Link right into your gauntlet comms systems." He opened a case and lifted the foot-long black oval object with four small pipes attached to each end. He placed it on the countertop and fiddled with some controls, and the almost soundless small device lifted from the ground. The jets swiveled backwards and propelled the drone forward, and it circled the small room at speed and then landed at their feet. "Max speed is twenty miles per hour and it returns high-resolution images. Works exactly the same under water. Nice piece of kit, if I do say so myself."

"Yep, pack 'em." Alex turned. "Gonzalez, they're your babies."

"On it," Gonzalez replied.

The HAWCs tried out various weapons in the subterranean firing range, made their final selections, and Quartermain locked in their individual kits for delivery.

Then Alex looked at his watch and turned to his team. "HAWCs, we stay on base tonight. As soon as the NKs jump, we follow. Expect that to happen any moment. A helo is on stand-by to drop us right on their jump point. But we can't let them get too far ahead of us. If they detonate even a single device in a strategic position, it might change – or destroy – everything."

"Confrontation designation?" Bill Brandt asked.

Alex looked at each of his soldiers. "We are the sword and the shield, the last line of defense, and the one that never breaks." His expression was as stone. "No negotiation. They want us to cease to exist. So I want them to cease to exist. Confrontation designation is kill on sight."

"*HUA*," the HAWCs responded as one.

Even Bernadette Cooper nodded.

Alex turned to Quartermain. "As always, a pleasure."

Quartermain grinned and gave a half-salute. "Any time, Captain Hunter. Your kits will be with you in an hour." He nodded toward the android DOG. "I'm hoping we will have established the link with Torben and your DOG by then as well. Happy hunting."

Alex nodded, and then led the team out.

CHAPTER 15

Gila National Forest, New Mexico, USA

Soong-Li watched as her team assembled. Counting herself and Shuchang, there were ten of them. She scanned their faces, and then their physiques. Some she trusted to do their job. Some she'd watch. And others she did not.

She looked down at the packs they'd be taking with them – the fissionable material had been engineered into powerful and highly polluting nuclear devices. The lead shielding was kept to a minimum to keep their weight down, but each package still weighed around sixty pounds. Some of the bigger men would be carrying several apiece.

Her team had brought all their weaponry, equipment for living rough, and a large raft that was in an enormous crate that took two of the soldiers to carry. It contained a small outboard motor that would move the burdened raft laboriously slowly.

The raft was required, as most of their trip would be conducted over water. Right now they had all been dropped in Gila National Forest, at a spot that they had assessed as being the coast of the interior seaway separating the mega islands that would one day become the heartland of the United States.

Their mission was simple – they would be traveling by water to deliver their bombs to the area where the oil-bearing petroleum beds of Texas and New Mexico would be one day. There were ten of them, each one timed to go off 100 years after the last. They would create a gigantic ulcer in the inland sea that would fester and corrupt all life for countless eons, thus disrupting the collective base of nearly a quarter of a trillion barrels of oil and approximately twelve trillion cubic feet of natural gas. These riches were the foundation of the United States' empire, and once removed would prevent the nation from ever rising to the level of great wealth, technical superiority, and military power it possessed in the current world.

After all, it was American interference in their civil war in support of the South Koreans that had split their country in two – if that had never happened, then Korea would be unified under their first great leader and their power would be unbounded.

Soong-Li walked a dozen feet away and inhaled the dry air slowly as she briefly admired the scenery. Above them was a large bird being carried on the thermal updrafts. Perhaps it was an eagle. But she had seen very little other wildlife.

She had been told to expect that the time and place they were going would look nothing like this. And the denizens of that place might be strange and dangerous. She still found it hard to believe – time travel in general – that they could actually go somewhere so long ago, when the Earth and its lifeforms were still in their infancy.

Without even thinking about it, she reached up to touch the small jade amulet around her neck, and rubbed its carved surface with her thumb.

Shuchang called her name and she turned to him.

"We're ready," he said.

She nodded and walked toward the team. One looked sullen, insolent, others impatient, and the rest simply nervous – good, she hoped they were all on edge. She'd not met many of them, but she was in charge due to her technical expertize, assertive personality, and links to senior party officials.

She would chat to each of them in a short bonding session, check their equipment, and then they could begin.

The team had arrived at their meeting point via several helicopters, coming in low and fast and from different directions. Only one chopper remained, and that contained the temporal gateway device that would establish their bridge to send them back. It would then depart, but return in five days, and initiate the link again – they would either return or they would not.

She looked slowly across her assembled team and wasn't unhappy with what she saw. All of the team were soldiers to some degree, because in North Korea, everyone did service. The only outlier standing before her was a party official, their watchdog, who would be useless to her, and the mission.

If he suffered a tragic accident, she would not care. And if he hindered her command, then he would definitely suffer a tragic accident. She didn't need him.

The others she did need, and those were the ones she greeted. The first was Captain Junfeng Yang. He was a man who looked competent, confident, and had obvious self-control. He would command the military team and had been ordered to respond to any of her directives. But she was under no illusion that if she seemed to be faltering, he would assume control to ensure the mission was completed successfully.

Next was Lingyun Zhang, their marksman. She shook his hand and welcomed him. Zhang carried a high-powered hunting rifle, and though all the soldiers were armed with grenades, rifles, sidearms, and knives, he was charged with ensuring that threats were taken down long before they reached them.

She went and stood in front of the next man, who was a head taller than her. Quinfan Chen looked as brutal as his reputation suggested. He was a battering ram of a human being, and though she didn't like the way he looked at her – she saw disrespect in his dull eyes, and perhaps lust – if he did his job well then she would not complain.

When she'd read Chen's background papers, she'd noted with mild amusement that he had been a high school javelin champion. He had even brought along three six-foot spiked poles as spears. She scoffed softly. If that made him a better defender of their team, she would not question them.

There were also two soldiers who looked to be barely out of their teens, but the fervor of duty burned in their eyes, and they were physically fit, so would hopefully do their jobs as beasts of burden, defenders, and warriors. The first was Jin Baek, short but muscular and with a protruding, toothy smile, who bowed when she addressed him. The next was Kwan Myung, taller, but just as young, and still with a rash of pimples on his cheeks. They would do, she thought.

The last man in the group was the party official, Yan Guo. He had a receding chin and looked weak and fearful. He was already sweating profusely. He was the assembly's watchdog, snake, and informer all in one stooped-shouldered, thinning-haired package. Every foreign mission had to have one of those toads attached. She resented it, but even with her good contacts she could not dislodge this political tick.

Soong-Li crossed to greet the female team members. Tian Wu, their science officer and paleontologist, would hopefully help them avoid trouble with the local wildlife. The woman was young but confident, friendly and good-natured. However, she was physically tiny at around five-foot-two, and Soong-Li hoped she'd be able to cope with the physical challenges that lay ahead. Regardless, Soong-Li liked her.

And lastly there was Jia Sun, an engineering physicist, who was tasked with arming their bombs. She would also be advising on the best place to drop them. Her role was critical, but the bespectacled woman was like a nervous mouse, not knowing where to put herself.

Soong-Li turned away from the group, shielding her eyes from the sun, and faced the massive helicopter waiting on a patch of flat land like a giant black dragonfly. She nodded, and the team of men rushed out to place the forty-foot locator pad on the ground.

It was covered in sensors, and its position would be marked by their satellite down to a fraction of an inch – it needed to be placed in the same position for their return in one week. If they returned.

The raft was inflated, and all their equipment loaded into it. She then called for the team to board the boat. Before they did, she quickly walked a few paces, turned over a stone and hid a small device under it. It was a disrupter, and would initiate after they had left. The device would create a small EMP pulse that would scramble the Americans' technology just as they were initiating the tachyon bridge. She doubted it would stop them, but it might at least throw them off. Every advantage counted now.

She then went and sat in the raft. It seemed incongruous that a team of North Korean people were sitting in a raft, on a grassy plain in the middle of the day. But she could not be sure if they would arrive on dry land 100 feet from a coastline, or in the sea 100 feet from the shore. After the gruesome results of their test run, it was best that they were able to float if it was the latter.

She twirled her finger in the air, and from within the helicopter a blue glow began. She was certain that the Americans would be looking out for their tachyon radiation signature and would immediately converge on the site when they detected it. But there would be no clues left for them here. Once they had departed, the helicopter crew would dismantle the mat and vacate the area at top speed.

Soong-Li knew that the one course of action the Americans had was to use the Janus Institute's device to try to follow them back. But if that device was suddenly destroyed, then they would be left with nothing other than the knowledge that they had failed. By the time they had constructed another one, their lives would be altered forever. If they were even born. She smiled; that plan was already in motion.

The tachyon beam's glow intensified, and Soong-Li felt her skin tingle and an odd itch spread out from deep inside her head. In another moment, the stream picked her up and she felt a stomach-flipping sensation of speed and swirling colors, as if she were in the barrel of a gun that was all light and motion.

Soong-Li didn't know if she blacked out or not, or if she was out for a second or an hour. But when she blinked open sticky eyes the once-dry air of the American midlands and the bright sunshine were gone, and she was sitting right on the edge of a brackish coast that smelled like a mangrove swamp at low tide. Around her the air was oppressively hot and humid, and alive with the sounds of insects. *Big* insects.

They'd arrived. They were still sitting in their raft, but on muddy ground, not water.

Soong-Li stood. "And so, we begin."

The group gathered around her, waiting. She liked that even Captain Junfeng Yang was subservient to her. She looked at each of their already sweat-streaked faces.

"They will come for us. And they will probably arrive around here." Her eyes stopped on Lingyun Zhang, their marksman. "You will wait here, climb a tree, and slow them down. We will return for you when our mission is complete. Understand?"

Zhang blinked a few times and swallowed. But he then nodded and turned away, perhaps to find a tree to climb.

The sky was a murky twilight, but they still had many hours of daylight yet. She clicked her fingers. "We take to the water." She pointed east. "That way. Silence is best."

She looked to the hulking form of Quinfan Chen. "Bring the raft."

He looked from Soong-Li to Captain Yang.

"*Hey,*" she said forcibly up into his face. "Look at me, *only me*, and do your job."

But the big man continued to look at Yang, who nodded. And only then did he set about dragging the raft eastward.

CHAPTER 16

Alex read the information on his wrist comms unit, and immediately the familiar thrill shot through him. "Heads up, people, tachyon signature has been confirmed – Gila National Forest, New Mexico. Mission is *go*." He looked up. "*Move it.*"

The team scrambled. Alex yelled more orders, but everyone knew what was expected of them. First they climbed into their body armor and habitat suits, which they'd be living in for the week. Their armaments were already laid out, and they did a brief weapons and ammunition check before slotting them in, fitting them on, and sliding them into special pouches.

Ito was delighted with the special sheath across his back that would lock his sword in place. Before stowing it there he half-drew it from the hard scabbard he would leave behind. The gleaming blade was a katana and been in his family for over 250 years. He looked lovingly at it – it was a slightly curved, single-edged blade with a small, squared guard to accommodate two hands, and had been crafted during the *shinshintō* period by master sword maker Minamoto Kiyomaro. His were said to be the finest battlefield swords in existence.

Ito smiled; this sword had tasted blood in battle many times, and he had no doubt it would do so again. His lips moved in a silent prayer or chant and then he slid the blade slowly over his back and into its sheath.

All the team had their plasma grenade launchers slotted onto the rifles. Alex watched as over to one side, Casey helped Bernadette Cooper kit out and load up. He was pleased that the non-HAWC woman was a fast learner, and looked to be fitting right in.

On the pad two high-speed helicopters were powering up, and in ten minutes the HAWCs came up out of their bunker-style accommodation on the USSTRATCOM base and headed over to them.

The regulars on the base stood back, no matter what their duties were, and just stared. Most knew of the HAWCs but they were still in awe of them.

They'd also heard of the secretive Special Forces squad's team leader, the one known as the Arcadian, who had the near-mythical legendary status of being *the man who couldn't be killed*. Because he'd already been dead – they'd heard the whispers – and he'd come back.

The HAWCs, huge, and in their black battle armor with their visors over their faces, further contributing to their robot-like appearances, looked other-worldly. However, lowering their visors was also an orientation field test, as they'd be wearing them over the next few days, so it was better to become familiar with the different spectrums and fields of vison now rather than when they hit the ancient terrain.

Alex and Brandt hefted the raft packs. Sam, and the equally mountainous Beast Brandt, carried the larger laser cannons. Alex also carried the DOG. He and the team quickly loaded everything onto the choppers.

Alex looked back at one of the buildings. Standing in the large window of his office was Colonel Jack "the Hammer" Hammerson. Alex nodded to him, and the man returned the gesture.

Alex then jumped inside and banged an armored fist on the chopper's steel door. "*Go.*"

Immediately the two helicopters lifted off at speed and veered sharply toward New Mexico. The several hundred-mile trip would take nearly two hours in the high-speed craft, which were loaded with extra fuel. But then, the next trip, the one where they travelled 420 million years, should theoretically occur in the blink of an eye.

As Alex leaned back in his seat, he said a silent prayer that Quartermain would push the Janus team to solve and perfect the shorter jump software. Not just his sanity, but everything he was and had, and would become, depended on it.

He rested his head back against the cabin wall and closed his eyes. To anyone else in the craft he looked like he was catching a few z's, but in reality he was reliving a moment from not too long ago where he'd caught a football thrown by his son and kissed Aimee goodbye.

As planned, and almost exactly to the minute, the pilot informed them they were coming up on the NK jump site. Alex returned to the here and now and looked out through the small window at the terrain below. It flew past as they came in low, but they were still doing close to 200 miles per hour. They had just come out of a lush, green river valley, the water invitingly mountain-stream clear but probably bone-chillingly cold. They then began to cross a dryer plain of low-lying bushes and open patches of prairie grass.

"There," Bernadette Cooper said, pointing at an innocuous, flattened area of grass.

She used her comms system to connect to the pilots. "Slow and hover."

She held in her hands an object that looked like a pocket calculator but which Alex knew was a device for measuring residual tachyon particle discharge.

She continued pointing. "That patch of open ground was where they jumped from."

"Take us down," Alex said into his mic.

Both choppers began to ease closer to the ground and softly touched down. Once settled, the HAWCs leaped out, dragging their weapons and equipment with them.

"What have you got?" Alex asked Cooper, who was still reading data from the device.

She walked a few dozen paces, turned a little and then looked down at the dirt. She nodded. "Yeah, they were here, and then they initiated a stream bridge and went back." She looked up. "It's been just over two hours since we got the tachyon signature, so that's their head start. We need to run 'em down."

Alex twirled a finger in the air. "HAWCs, get ready to jump." He turned. "Hey, we're not going to land on top of them and be ambushed are we?"

"Unlikely." Cooper replied. "Micro changes to the environment, weather, and chronology, mean we should land close, but not on them." She grinned. "I hope."

Alex chuckled. "That'll have to do."

The six HAWCs, including Alex, formed into two lines, with Cooper at their center. Alex and Brandt were at the front carrying the extra weight of the portable rafts, and Alex also held the DOG case.

Ito Yamada half-drew his sword and checked the blade's already razor-sharp edge. "Be ready, *Kazeshini*," he whispered. The name meant *Wind of Death*. Ito, like many former samurai warriors before him, had named his blade, even calling to it in the heat of battle as they fought together as a single unit. He grunted his satisfaction and slid the sword back over his shoulder.

Casey looked up at the blazing sun. "Next time we see you, you'll be 420 million years younger." She guffawed and looked ahead to Bill Brandt. "This is gonna be a hoot."

"*Oh, yeah.*" Brandt grinned. "Look out, dino-freaks, some real super predators are on their way."

"Team formed up and ready," Alex said. "Visors," he yelled.

The HAWCs and Bernadette Cooper initiated the visors that covered their faces. But for now they would just use the clear armored screen and not the heavier combat version with the range of viewing spectrums.

"Torben . . ." Alex began to initiate the android, but then stopped. He'd wait for now. Instead, he reached down and placed his hand on the box, smiling at it. For some reason he felt comforted by it. After another moment he faced front and steeled himself.

The team had their transponders implanted in their necks, meaning that the stream should find them, wherever they were, and drag them onto the bridge when the return was initiated. At least, that was the plan.

Bernadette Cooper spoke into her mic to the helicopter. "*Launch.*"

They glowed blue.

Then came a flash.

And they were gone.

* * *

Hidden under a rock, the small disrupter had sent out its pulse just as the tachyon bridge was initiated. The HAWCs' time stream was unbroken, but like a still pond's surface when a breeze blows up, it became choppy and disorganized. Things were changed.

* * *

In Landsdowne Street, outside the Janus Institute, Joon Feng and Hyuan Wan, two agents from the North Korean assassination squad, quickly prepared in the back of the unmarked white van, while their driver, an administrative agent, kept watch.

It was still early as they donned Kevlar vests and then replaced their dark suit jackets over the top. They also loaded up with sidearms, grenades, extra speed-load clips, and various knives. Joon Feng would also wear a vest that contained around ten pounds of C4 plus a detonator strapped to his wrist.

Both men smoothed down their jackets. Though the bulky armaments would not pass close scrutiny, they only needed to get inside the building. Coming out was a secondary problem, and the van would not wait if they stayed inside longer than their mission called for.

Their orders were simple – destroy the tachyon bridge device. Kill all personnel. And if time permitted, copy all the latest advancements and transmit them over Wi-Fi to a local signal station which would transmit them to Pyongyang.

Doreen Peng had reported that there was minimal security and the offices should be filled only with scientists and technicians, so they didn't expect a high level of resistance. Both men expected the surprise nature of their attack would mean they would have several minutes to kill and destroy the Janus infrastructure and its people. The explosions would start a fire, and as the first responders on the scene would be the fire brigade, there should be enough confusion and evacuations from the other floors that there was a good chance they could both escape. When they got home, they would be heroes.

The three men synchronized watches, nodded to each other, and then without another word slid back the van's side door.

The two assassins crossed the street, dark suits, dark glasses, and heads down. Then they walked in through the front doors, entered an elevator, and pressed the button for the laboratory offices on the fifth floor. Both men faced forward – so far, so good.

In the elevator they were alone and as they were slowly ascended to their destination they opened their jackets and pulled their sidearms.

Joon Feng rolled his shoulders – the bomb vest was uncomfortable, and he needed to ensure he had good fighting mobility. His plan was to plant the bombs and initiate the timer before leaving. But if there was trouble, he was prepared to blow himself, and his attackers, up.

The elevator pinged, and the door slid back. They knew where they needed to go – Doreen Peng had given them a map of the office layout.

Both men exited fast, guns up.

They burst through the Janus Institute lab doors, screaming to generate maximum confusion among the technicians they expected to see going about their business in the large open-plan tech company. But all they encountered was a single being, big and hulking, planted in the center of the empty floor. And facing them. Seemingly, waiting for them.

It was not what they were expecting. But as they were professionals they had orders and mission plans, so they stuck to them – they started firing.

* * *

Colonel Jack Hammerson only had confirmation the agents were coming when they had entered the elevator.

As the doors burst open, Hammerson held his position in the center of the room. To his left were the laboratories and data center, and to the right were meeting rooms, and some auxiliary spaces. Behind him was a large conference room and then nothing but huge windows overlooking the streets below.

The two men in dark suits came through the double doors fast. They had guns up and when sighting Hammerson, were confused for only a moment before they began firing.

The HAWC commander could tell they were professionals from the way all their shots struck on head and heart targets, and their centering was good.

But he had already deployed combat shielding, and the full armored suit he wore also had the visor down over his face. The bullets were not of a high enough caliber to worry him, smacking into the suit's plating with little or no effect. After a dozen rounds they stopped.

"My turn," Hammerson said. The men now decided to rush him.

Hammerson knew he had much heavier guns built into his suit gauntlet, but using them would have more than likely obliterated the laboratory.

Perhaps the two NK attackers thought the size of the suit would make it cumbersome, and it *was* big and heavy, but it was also MECH assisted, and that meant Hammerson could move far faster than normal human capabilities allowed.

The major mistake the first of the North Korean men made was coming in too close. Maybe they expected to be able to identify a seam or opening in the armor plating and fire a round or two into it. But Hammerson just took two lightning-quick steps, shot an arm out, and grabbed the guy's jacket. With his other arm, he backhanded the man's face so hard, the impact caused his head to bounce all the way over onto his shoulder with an audible snap of bone.

Hammerson flung the man's body aside and turned to the final intruder.

The second NK agent had undoubtedly witnessed enough of the suit's capabilities, and paused in his attack.

"Surrender or die," Hammerson said, and took a step forward.

The man ignored him and swerved around him, picking up speed.

"Your choice." Hammerson turned to track him.

The North Korean tore his jacket open and sighted on the door leading into the main laboratory where the tachyon drive was kept. The man had obviously decided that fighting to the death with this hulking thing was not his mission priority, and was doomed to failure anyway, so he headed for the Janus nerve center, fast.

Hammerson caught only a glimpse of the mass taped to his torso – the wires, the timer, the sealed packages – but he knew exactly what was about to happen.

"*Like hell*," he yelled as the guy went through the door.

Hammerson was on him in a few steps, but the North Korean had already hit the ignition switch and the small clock ticked down its few seconds to detonation.

For the first time in Hammerson's life he felt a degree of panic – everything rested on the Janus team being able to bring his HAWCs back using the primary device in this laboratory, and, just as importantly, complete their work on the shorter-term jumps for Alex Hunter.

That meant everything else was secondary. Nothing else mattered. Not even him.

Hammerson lunged at the man, grabbed him and pulled him in close. He then picked him up, spun, and headed back out, fast.

Hammerson held the screaming man in tight to his armored chest and went through the wooden partition closing off the conference room. Then he headed for the bank of windows.

Colonel Jack Hammerson didn't even blink as he accelerated, and he and the now furiously screaming agent went through the large windows and out into thin air, five stories up from the street below.

For Hammerson everything now seemed to move in slow motion. And just as he moved past the shattered glass, he heard the timer *ping* and then his world turned blinding red and volcanically hot.

The detonation was bigger and more powerful than he expected. And he knew he wasn't far enough from the labs. The amount of C4 turned the man in his arms into little more than gobbets of flesh and shards of bone.

The explosion crystalized the glass in the windows for around four stories of the building, but being closest to the Janus lab level it sent a shockwave inside that caused a high level of destruction to the labs and equipment.

Hammerson himself was propelled backwards by the blast, to collide with the building façade and then bounce back to plummet the last fifty or so feet to the unforgiving road.

He hit. Hard. Bounced and then skidded to a stop. His armor was dented and smoking, and he lay still.

* * *

Hanley and Rashid, plus the technologists, were let out of their secured rooms to stream back into the decimated lab.

Hanley ran straight to the tachyon chamber and breathed a sigh of relief when he saw it still intact.

"The machine is okay," he gasped.

Rashid's hands moved over one of the still-working consoles and his jaws clenched. "Wait." He spoke through gritted teeth. "*Oh no, oh no, oh no*. There was a disruption to the stream."

"What?" Hanley spun to his colleague. "Did the explosion . . .?"

"No, not us. But something out in the field." Rashid frowned. "Something screwed with the tachyon bridge and frayed the time stream."

"Oh, God no." Hanley grimaced. "Did they make it?"

Rashid stopped typing and sat with his eyes wide. "Not all of them."

CHAPTER 17

Alex and the team stared straight ahead as a blue ball of light appeared in between them and then grew to envelop the entire group. It grew brighter and brighter, and in the next second, Alex felt his stomach flip and a sense of weightlessness.

He fought to try and take it all in, but his senses were scrambled as he seemed to fall into a tunnel of light. He couldn't see his HAWCs, Bernadette Cooper, or even his own body. But just as he began to wonder how long he had been sliding along a bridge created by a stream of faster-than-light particles, he was out of it, and gravity, and reality, kicked in again.

But he wasn't on firm ground anymore. He wasn't on *any* ground anymore. Instead he was falling.

He hit the boggy earth hard, probably from about fifty feet up, and being in his heavy armored suit he created a four-foot-deep impact crater in the wet soil. Right beside him, Tor hit the soft earth as well, still in case form.

Around him he heard the impacts of his team, and as his momentarily addled brain counted them off, he knew he'd come up way short of the expected number.

He shook off the effects of the fall and rose to one knee to find he was in calf-deep, bath-warm, brackish water. He immediately pulled his gun in tight to his shoulder to scan the terrain.

The sounds of a jungle began to start up again after the team's splashdown had probably startled them to silence. But he saw immediately that this place was different from the dozens of other jungles he had been in before.

He turned slowly; there were a few trees, but mostly things that looked like fifty-foot-tall stalks of asparagus. Some of the growths had more tangle than branches and they were draped with soft vines or hanging curtains of a substance that might be lichen but looked like a sort of moldy gossamer.

There were also no frog croaks or animal sounds. But the buzz, chirrup, and squeak of insects was extremely loud. And they sounded like they came from creatures a lot bigger than those back home.

As Alex continued to scan his surroundings, he saw something climb a rotted log – it was about a foot long, flattened, and armored like a giant wood louse, but out front it had a pair of vicious pincers. He couldn't see its legs, but had the impression there were dozens of them working underneath its shell.

He retracted his visor and inhaled the air, smelling rotted plants and methane, and a hint of sulfur. But the heat and humidity felt the same as every tropical jungle everywhere.

Alex got to his feet, and saw that several of his team were doing the same.

"HAWCs, *sound off*," he yelled.

One after another the HAWCs began to identify themselves – he heard Gonzalez come back, then Ito, and then Bernadette Cooper. He waited a few seconds more – he was still three short.

"Sam, Franks, Brandt, sound off, *now*." He went to the longer-range mic. "HAWCs Reid, Franks, Brandt, come back." He tried again, and again, but there was nothing.

"What just happened?" Gonzalez asked. "Where are they?"

"Something went wrong," Alex said.

"Are we even in the right place?" Gonzalez asked. "And the right time?"

"Cooper?" Alex turned.

Bernadette Cooper looked at a small device she held. "Star mapping now." After another moment she began to nod. "Yep, good, Silurian period star charts say we're in the right place, right time, but off target." She looked up. "Somehow it looks like we miscalculated the geography, and it placed us about three stories up. Thank God for these suits, or I'd be pretty busted up now."

"Just as well we weren't over rock," Gonzalez remarked. "Suits or no suits, we'd be seeing double for a week." He looked around. "Where's the rest of our team?"

"Hold on, hold on. I can track them via their implanted chips." She turned slowly. "Okay good, they're here. Wait, two of them are. But at least those two are together." She turned and pointed. "But they're about sixty miles west-north-west. Might be why you're not getting them over your comms system."

"Who are they, and who's missing?" Alex demanded.

"The retrieval pellets embedded in their necks all have an ID number. Identifying now." She said. "Okay, the two HAWCs northwest are Brandt and Franks." She frowned as she turned one way then the other. "But Sam Reid is not here."

"Out of range?" Alex suggested.

Bernadette Cooper slowly shook her head as she checked the data again. "It's telling me he never completed the jump." She looked up at him. "He fell out of the tachyon stream."

The team went silent, and just stared at her.

"What does that mean?" Alex asked evenly. "Is he still back home? Is he alive?"

"He traveled. But to where, I don't know," she replied. "It all depends on when and where he landed." She tapped her lips, thinking it through. "If he retains his pellet, he may be brought back with the rest of us. But . . ."

Alex glared. "But, what?"

"I just don't have the answers." She sighed. "But one of the things the Janus team theorized was that they believed time moves differently on other time streams. What might be a week for us might be a day, or a week, or fifty years for Reid. Or a thousand," she finished softly.

Alex nodded. That was their lot as a HAWC. He couldn't do anything about it now, and he absolutely could not let himself be thrown by the news. They lost HAWCs on missions all the time.

He tried hard to suck it up but knew that Sam was like his big brother and best friend all in one huge package. He forced himself to refocus on the here and now.

"Okay. Sam Reid is over 250 pounds, has internal MECH architecture, a laser cannon, and is in a HAWC enviro-suit. As long as those Janus assholes didn't drop him into a volcano, he'll survive, and we'll link up back home." He glanced at Cooper and then turned away.

He hoped his friend would be okay, but they had their own challenges right now – they had no satellite, so the comms they used were more short range with a weaker signal. Plus, the Silurian period still had significant active volcanism, and that threw out a lot of extra magnetism.

Alex slowly turned about, looking for a route through the miasmic, slimy gray-green mush surrounding them. To his right there were weird mangrove-like tree things lifting from the bog, and other fern frond plants clinging to their trunks and the crooks of their branches. To his left there were stands of things like bushes, but they had glossy bulbs rather than feathery leaves or palm fronds.

He knew from his mission briefing notes that many plants in the Silurian period weren't real plants at all, but instead giant fungi, liverworts, mosses and lichens, and other softer variants of growth that grew far larger than in their own time.

The rest was a guess, as these plants didn't fossilize well, and so more than likely they'd be encountering things their experts didn't expect or couldn't even imagine.

There was also a heavy mist, and there was so much vegetation around them, under them, and above them, it made the air itself seem green. He inhaled again, this time ignoring the stink of rotting vegetation and swampy water, instead detecting brine, which told him they were close to a seashore. It was mind-bending to realize that only a few minutes ago they'd been standing on a dry plain, and then in a heartbeat were in a thick jungle swamp on the edge of a sea.

All around him there was sound and movement. He checked his wrist sensors to get a bearing on the North Koreans. Just like his own team, the NKs would give off a tachyon radiation signature for several days after traveling along the time stream. It would allow him to follow them, but they needed to close the gap within forty-eight hours or they'd have to hunt them by tracking – near impossible to do if they took to the water.

He quickly found the NKs – they were heading northwest, tracking along what he expected was a potential shoreline.

Alex turned, holding up his sensor – the NKs were about five miles north, but his missing team members were sixty miles northwest – a lot further away, but at least in the same general direction.

"Casey and Brandt, boss?" Gonzalez asked.

Alex pointed with a flat hand. "NKs went that way. Priority mission objective is to track them down and eliminate their threat. Casey and Brandt are up there too, but a lot further out. I'm hoping they will also follow the NK signature and come down at them from another angle. If not, I guess we'll see them on the ride home."

"Sam Reid?" Ito asked.

Alex glanced at Cooper, then back to Ito. "I'm sure we'll see him back home."

Ito grunted, nodding once, but his eyes were unreadable.

"This way," Alex said, and pushed through the calf-deep mud and water, followed by Bernadette Cooper, then Gonzalez, and Ito, who was tasked with covering their rear.

After five minutes they came up on a dry bank a little higher than the surrounding swamp. Alex tested the comms again, then half-turned to his team. "Gonzalez, anything on the scanners?"

The man lifted his gauntlet scanner and turned slowly. "Lots of movement. In close this place is teeming with life, though nothing over fifty pounds." He nodded toward the gauntlet. "But further out, I've got bigger impressions."

"How big?" Cooper asked.

"Varying," Gonzalez replied. "Length around thirty feet, one on the edge of the scanner range is close to fifty. Not coming at us right now."

"Some of your unexpected fauna?" Alex raised his eyebrows at Cooper.

She nodded. "I can't imagine what they are. But I'd love to see them." She grinned. "From a distance."

"If it stays at a distance, it stays alive. And maybe so do we," Alex said. "We'll be long gone by the time whatever they are decide to lumber on over." His team assembled around him.

"What're our first steps?" Cooper asked.

Alex just let his eyes move over the landscape. Surrounded by veils of gauze-like mist, and under a heavy canopy of barely recognizable jungle growth, it was hard to know.

"We need to get our bearings." He half turned. "Gonzalez, send up a drone. These guys have at least two hours on us. Let's see if we can spot them. And find me a launch waterline that's not a tangled swamp."

Gonzalez pulled out one of the tube-shaped devices strapped to his belt and set it down. He worked his gauntlet to bring it online and then the four small jets whined to life and the small dark metallic avian lifted off.

While the drone soared higher, Alex placed the case he had been carrying on the ground. He straightened to stare down at it for a moment.

Quartermain had said he had completed a transference link with Torben, his – or rather, Joshua's – dog. He was about to find out if the transference had been successful. If it was, the android would believe it was the animal. And if not, well, it'd still be useful as a battle droid in this potentially hostile terrain.

"DOG, ah, Torben, initiate."

The case-like box broke open, lengthened out, and the flat panels seemed to fold in on themselves. The body shape morphed into the outline of a large canine.

To begin with, its exterior, which was composed of a super-hardened tungsten shell that covered advanced electronics, armaments, a fusion core, and a processor running sophisticated AI software, seemed a mottled, moving color, but then it orien-tated itself to its surroundings and changed to matte-black with ragged green stripes.

"*Ho-l-y* shit," Gonzalez breathed. "It's a giant fucking dog, man."

The android stood and turned slowly, taking in the human beings staring back at it. But then it saw Alex, and it rushed forward, jamming its hard, muzzled head into his stomach. Alex smiled and couldn't help but lay both hands on either side of its head. Before he even thought about what he was doing, he was rubbing the hard surface.

"Hi there, Tor," he said softly. "Good boy."

He guessed this answered the question about the transfer bonding being successful.

"It knows you." Cooper sounded impressed.

"That it does," Alex replied. "Because . . . we were mission-linked back at home base." He didn't have time to explain the longer story of what, how, and why. He looked at the metallic animal. "Tor, we've got work to do."

The android looked up, and even though Alex saw that the eyes were black on black, and he knew there were camera lenses inside, he felt Tor was looking up at him with his remembered familiarity, loyalty, and love.

"One hundred feet. Patrol. Go."

In a blur, the dog immediately vanished into the fungus jungle.

"Armed to the teeth, and near indestructible." Gonzalez grinned. "That is some cool piece of tech, boss."

Alex nodded and turned to the east where the smell of the sea was strongest.

Bernadette Cooper stood next to him. "They'll take to the water, if they haven't already," she said. "They have to detonate their nuclear packages in the inland sea to destroy the future petroleum beds. If we're lucky we'll hear their boat motors. And if not, we can still track their radiation signature. For now."

"Well, ain't that romantic?" Gonzalez nodded to the sky.

Rising in the east was the moon. But this was no normal moon; instead it looked smoother and was a massive yellow disk almost the size of a cantaloupe in the sky.

"It's huge," Alex said.

"Yep," Cooper replied. "Did you know that the moon is moving away from us at just over an inch a year? 420 million years ago it was about 8000 miles closer."

"I know now." Alex smiled. "And I'm betting with a moon that close its magnetism will have a significant effect on the tides."

"You got it," Cooper replied. "They may rise and fall fifty to a hundred feet."

Alex looked around. "No wonder it's so boggy here. Probably gets inundated."

"No sign of the NKs. But here's a potential launch site," Gonzalez said, and leaned over to show Alex the small screen on his gauntlet. The drone had found a small bay with a rocky shore about one klick north.

"Good. That's where we're going." He started to head off. "*Torben*," Alex called, and the android animal fell in beside him.

* * *

420 million years in the future, and nearly 700 miles away on Jack Hammerson's ranch, the huge form of Torben, the genetically engineered German shepherd, had been dozing in the morning sun on the front porch.

Until he heard the familiar voice of Alex Hunter saying his name. Then he snapped up to a sitting position and his eyes turned a ghostly white.

He saw everything.

CHAPTER 18

"Nothing," Casey said as she tried her comms system for the fourth time.

"Well, ain't that just fucking peachy. That busted-ass time machine dropped us somewhere on Earth, maybe, hundreds of millions of years ago, and lost us. We're fucked." Bill Brandt threw his hands up.

"Shut up, Beast. You're alive, ain't you?" Casey replied.

"For how long?" He turned to her. "Take a look around; we're not in Kansas anymore."

"*Meh.*" She shrugged. "Just another wet-assed jungle."

He groaned. "So, whatta we do now?"

Casey tried to think. Right now, she didn't know if her fellow HAWCs were even alive. And if they were, whether they were one mile or a hundred from them. All she knew was that they had been sent here on a mission. And were still on it.

"We need to find 'em, and link up. We must be outside comms range and our mission briefing notes told us there might be some interference for long-range messaging." She sneer-grinned. "Remember, no satellites."

"Yeah, no satellites, no electricity, no lights, no bars or burgers," Brandt huffed. "Maybe we'll smell their cooking."

Casey stared for a moment, her mind working. "Brilliant," she said, and worked her gauntlet computer for a moment. "But it won't be their cooking we'll smell. Remember what the CIA chick said? Once we ride the tachyon stream, we'll stink of its radiation for a few days."

"So?" he asked.

"So, the NKs will also stink of it." She half-smiled as she looked at her small gauntlet screen. "So will our brothers. *Annnd,* here we go . . . got 'em." She nodded. "Or got someone."

"Hey, no shit." Brandt came and looked over her shoulder.

Casey orientated her gauntlet and then pointed southeast. "That way. Fifty-two miles."

"Fifty-two fucking miles. Ah, fuck," Brandt complained.

"What else you gonna do?" Casey scowled. "We suck it up and get moving. If we maintain speed, we can link up in a day and a half."

Brandt looked around at the dark, boggy landscape. "Yeah, a walk in the park." He stopped to switch his vision spectrum from dark-adapted to thermal. "Can't see shit in thermal," he growled. "Every-fucking-thing here is hot and wet as a whore's bathhouse."

Casey chuckled softly. "Just be thankful the suits are water-proof. I don't think I'd like to meet a prehistoric leech as it's sliding up my ass right now." She turned on the spot. "You know what? I don't think I want to meet a prehistoric anything in this swamp."

"I do," Brandt said. "I want to shoot a dino." He laughed. "And I want to bring back its head for my wall."

"Then this might be your lucky day, Beast," Casey replied. "I got several big signatures a few miles out. And they're between us and where we need to go."

"Cool." Brandt lifted his laser cannon. "I wonder if Reid has used his yet."

"I bet he has. Can't wait to see him." She chuckled. "I bet he's pissed as all hell at us." She nodded ahead. "Let's get moving."

* * *

There was a blue flash and Sam Reid landed, hitting the ground at an angle. He skidded thirty feet, rolled for a while, and then was still. He groaned, feeling like he had been shot out of a cannon. Everything hurt. He stayed on his back, breathing hard.

He was a big man at six-five. But the addition of the HAWC armor over his MECH-assisted body with the surgically grafted MECH endoskeleton meant he probably weighed close to 800 pounds.

He sat up and tested his limbs right down to fingers and toes – everything still worked. But there was something wrong with the suit visor as it seemed cloudy, and he tried to retract the lens shield, but it wouldn't comply. And the helmet wouldn't retract back into the suit. In the end he manually dragged it off his head and looked at it – the armor was scarred and even looked aged.

"What?" He turned it in his hands, examining it.

Just minutes ago, it had been brand new. Then he noticed he had a beard, long, and there was something else – when he had left, he'd had a crew cut, and now his hair fell beyond his shoulders.

"What the hell is going on?" he asked no one but himself as he got to his feet.

Sam turned slowly, and then exhaled long and loud. "Well, shit."

He spoke into his wrist comms. "Boss, come back."

There was just the crackle of static.

"HAWCs, anyone, come back," he tried again, and again, but there was nothing. He lowered his arm. "This ain't good."

Sam then tried everything he could think of to identify his position. Find his team. Or even the North Koreans. But after a while he knew he was alone.

"Something went bad," he muttered.

He looked out over a dry and arid landscape with a few piles of boulders, some rising twenty feet. It was hot at around eighty-five degrees, but a dry desert heat.

There were also a few stunted bushes dotted about and he squinted at them and saw they were an arid-adapted tussock-like grass, and there were also a few stands of olive trees. He'd done his homework before coming and one thing he knew for sure was that these were not something that had even existed in the Silurian period.

"Where the fuck did I end up?" He turned and felt the hair against his neck and also the beard now hanging down over his chest. He reached up. "How long was I traveling?"

Sam quickly pulled his knife and cut off a good foot of chin hair, examining it. He knew how fast his whiskers grew, so somehow his trip had taken months or even years. He had either slept – no that probably wasn't right – or remained in suspended animation during the trip. And he'd been told the actual tachyon bridge traveling should have been over in the blink of an eye.

He felt down his suit and found scrapes and holes in the damaged surface. He'd lost the laser cannon, and, pulling a handgun, he saw it was corroded. The only thing he had left that worked was the knife, as it had no moving parts.

His mouth was dry, and he pulled the small emergency canteen and shook it. It had fluid in it, but it tasted murky and he spat it out. Quickly checking his rations, he found them rotted as well.

He let the beard hair fall to the ground and sheathed his knife. So now he had another problem – in this heat, he'd need to find water, food, and shelter, and a place to think.

He squinted into the distance, where he thought he could see dust rising, as if something was approaching. If he had a working visor, he could have amplified it.

"Friend or foe?" he asked in a whisper.

The hair on the back of his neck prickled and just as he turned, the roar from the boulders behind him startled the hell out of him.

Lion's roar, his brain screamed. And he knew that the reason an attacking lion would roar was to freeze its prey to the spot.

Sam's training and lightning-fast reflexes meant he didn't have to play by those rules, and he quickly spun just as the twelve-foot-long, 700-pound desert lion leaped at him.

He caught it and used its momentum to fling it to the side, but the huge claws still raked against his armor, gouging the aging biological plating deeply.

But the beast hadn't given up and came back at him. This time he took it head-on and the massive lion reared up, mouth open a foot wide, showing huge upper and lower dagger-like canines that could crack a man's skull like an eggshell if caught between them.

Sam's boots skidded along the dry, hard-packed surface as he took the weight of the great beast's charge. He now wished he had left the helmet on, as one of the animal's paws, as wide as a dinner plate and showing hooked claws, managed to catch his cheek, opening a deep cut.

"*Arrgh.*" He punched at the head, hard, and knocked it to the side. "Fuck off, kitty," he yelled, and braced as the animal immediately rounded on him again, its eyes wide with fury – and hunger.

Out in the desert, he bet prey was scarce, so the big cat wasn't going to give up on a large hunk of meat like him so easily. Sam knew then, it was either kill or be killed.

"So be it."

The lion leaped again, and Sam caught it and lifted it, holding the struggling beast above his head only for a second, before using its momentum to slam it down on the hard-as-stone ground with all the force he could muster from his own strength combined with his MECH hydraulics.

There was a crunch as the neck bones were crushed by the impact.

The beast lay still.

"I warned you." Sam stood over it, sucking in breath and waiting for his jittery nerves to release some of the adrenaline from his system. He closed his eyes and worked to slow his heartbeat.

After another few moments, he opened them and saw that he wasn't alone.

"What now?" he asked.

* * *

The Saran of Gaza was in the lead chariot. Just behind him on either side were two other chariots carrying the Saran's favored warriors and generals.

In the twelfth century BC, he was the leader of the Philistines across the entire Levant, an area that included the lands of modern-day Israel, Gaza, Lebanon, and Syria.

They were hunting lions for a trophy so the Saran could impress the court with his skill and virility. Scouts had reported there was a particularly massive specimen of Gazan lion in this area.

He had brought with him two of his most accurate spearmen, plus two generals, his son, Prince Artur, and further behind them a retinue of bodyguards, and even some court women.

The Saran was under no illusions about the danger of his quest as the animals were huge and fearsome, and even speared could still kill half a dozen men before they succumbed to their injuries.

His warriors were ordered to protect him even at the loss of their own lives. If anything happened to the Saran, they would meet a grisly and slow death.

As they approached a stand of boulders one of the men pointed. "There, sire."

On the top of the rocks one of the biggest male lions the Saran had ever seen was stalking something just out of sight.

"Faster," the Saran ordered, and the charioteer flicked the reins. The horse broke into a gallop, bouncing over the scrabbly hard-packed earth and sending a dust cloud into the air behind him.

In the scabbard just to the Saran's side were three needle-sharp spears, and he held the railing with one hand and drew forth one of the spears with the other.

The plan was for him to skewer or at least strike the beast first. It didn't matter if the other warriors finished it off, as long as it ended up dead, and the first prick was his.

They gave the pile of boulders a few hundred yards' berth as they knew the lions liked to perch on high ground and launch themselves at their prey.

But just as they came around the rocks, there was an almighty roar, an attacking roar, and the charioteer pulled up the horses while the other two chariots did the same.

"By Dagon, what am I seeing?" The Saran stared.

A giant man with flowing, straw-colored hair, and wearing strange armor the Saran had never seen before, was fighting the biggest lion he had ever laid eyes on. The giant had only his bare hands for weapons, and incredibly, he seemed to be winning.

One moment the lion reared up, standing on its hind legs, at which height it was even taller than the huge man, but it was thrown to the side. Then it spun to come back, its eyes wide with fury and bloodlust, and it leaped, all bristling mane and jaws open.

But with a speed that was well beyond anything the Saran had ever witnessed, the giant caught the charging beast and lifted it high above his head. He then slammed it down so hard and fast that the thump raised a dust cloud.

The animal lay still, defeated.

"By all the gods." The Saran's mouth hung open. "Who is this man?"

The giant turned to them and stared back unflinchingly.

The Saran nodded. "Proceed," he said. "I wish to see this man up close."

When they were just fifty feet from the giant, they stopped, watching him breathe heavily.

"A mighty deed, giant. Who are you?" the Saran asked.

The man looked up and his brows came together for a moment before he spoke to them, but it was in a language none of them could understand. He saw their confusion and seemed to try several more languages, but still only a word or two sounded familiar.

One of the Saran's generals spoke up. "I think it is like the language of the Nazarites."

"He does not look like a Nazarite. His hair is the color of the sun." The Saran tilted his head. "Then ask my question again," he commanded. "In the tongue of the Nazarites."

The general did as asked, and the man responded. In turn the general translated what he understood.

"I think he said he is stranger to these lands. His name is Samson."

CHAPTER 19

Sniper Lingyun Zhang was about fifty feet up in the crown of one of the soft and spongy tree-like growths. He had dragged branches down and around himself, and also smeared himself with mud and moss to further create a living ghillie suit. His training in the North Korean Special Forces had prepared him for enduring absolute hardships, as well as expert concealment, and how to take an adversary's life in just seconds.

Even the barrel of his sniper rifle was wrapped in threads of a mossy growth, concealing its long, straight shape, which rarely existed in nature and therefore made it stand out. He brought it up to his face and looked down the scope.

The Americans would be coming soon. Or they were already here. They would be experts, like him, but he had something few had – a level of patience that was beyond normal human endurance. He could wait in place without moving a muscle for not just hours but days, if need be.

He used his scope to scan the weird jungle. When they came, he only needed them to show a fraction of their body or head and he could hit it. With the claymores he had secreted down below and a few other surprises, he thought he could hold them in place for hours. And every minute he kept them anchored here was another minute his team got closer to fulfilling their objectives.

From time to time he saw movements, but they were just the tiny denizens of this hellish jungle. Everything here smelled of rotten cabbage, or was sticky, or soft, or warm and wet like overcooked noodles.

From behind him he heard something softly squelch in the darkness. *The Americans*, he thought; *they have somehow got around me.* Zhang carefully turned to look over his shoulder where he guessed the sound came from, but even though the huge, yellow moon lit the night sky, it was a weak light that left far too many shadows.

The massive tree-like things rising from the sodden ground and other smaller clumps closer to the jungle floor all offered too many places for concealment. All he saw were more shadows within shadows that remained impenetrable even with his night scope.

He sniffed. He was sure he could smell something like bad meat, mixed with a rotten almond odor. He frowned into the darkness; had that shadow been there before? Was it a bush, or rock? He tried to remember seeing it when he was on the ground, but he had been too focused on finding and scaling a good tree at the time.

He squinted into the gloom for several moments and then carefully lifted his rifle so he could view the area through the light-amplification lens again. But what he thought had been a bush or rock wasn't there anymore.

The plants moved and then fell still as if there had been a slight breeze. Which there hadn't. This was something alive – or maybe someone, an American, was in there. And who or whatever it was, it was drawing closer.

He moved his rifle scope over the terrain, and thought he saw the tail end of something entering a line of ragged plants that looked like the sagging wings of dying birds. The thing had been big and bulky. Not a human, then.

He turned his scope back around in the direction he expected the Americans to appear from. He was hopeful they would arrive and that maybe the thing with the vile odor would find them first.

More stealthy movement. Whatever was in there was breaking his concentration. He had to see what he was up against.

He pulled out a powerful flashlight. He knew he was contravening protocol, but assured himself he would only blink it on for a second or two so he wouldn't lose his night vision.

He aimed the small but powerful light and switched it on. The intense light temporarily lit the dismal jungle, and in that split second of illumination Zhang saw the shape of the thing just before it pulled back into the shadows again.

Zhang's breath caught in his throat at what he thought he'd seen, and he quickly swung the scope back around. He squeezed his eyes shut for a second to try and readjust to the darkness.

Impossible, he thought. *How had it got through the claymore lines?*

He looked through the scope and quickly found the creature again. It was still on the move, and coming toward him now. A few seconds later it was at the base of his tree.

He edged forward to frown down at the abomination. It reminded him of something he had seen when his father had taken him to the seaside wet markets when he was a boy. There had been a giant deep-sea crab, all covered in spines, waving feelers, with claws that were as long as he was. It had scared away his sleep for many nights. And right now he felt that same sense of dread, because the thing right below him looked the same, except this hulking nightmare was easily twelve feet long.

He continued to stare at it, his eyes almost bulging now, because the worst thing was, the monstrosity was feeling around the trunk of his tree. Looking for a way up.

Zhang brought the scope to his eye again and watched as the animal's long and segmented feelers tapped at the trunk. And below those long whip-like feelers there were two black bulb eyes on stalks as big as fists that seemed to move independently.

Both of the black bulbs aligned to stare up at him, and with the head raised Zhang saw the mouthparts – they were overlapping serrated plates with buzzsaw-like blades inside. When he was a child he had seen a praying mantis capture a beetle and begin to eat it alive, its powerful and sharp mouth machinery chewing right through the beetle's exoskeletal armor plating. And his gut told him that's what would happen to him if that thing made it up to his perch.

But luck was with him, as he then spotted the shape of the American soldiers coming through the foliage toward him. Four of them. He ignored the beast below and focused on his mission orders.

He had good, clear shots, and at this range, he knew he might hit several before they could react.

Zhang exhaled, focusing, and then squeezed the trigger.

A center chest shot, and the soldier was blown backwards into the murky jungle.

He quickly jacked in another round and fired. But to his surprise, the group had already vanished into the dark jungle faster than he expected any human could.

He cursed but knew he had at least hit one of them. It hadn't been a headshot, but he bet the man must be injured. No one could take a high-velocity 7.62 millimeter round and not have a hole in them, even if they wore a bulletproof vest.

He looked back down at the monstrosity below him. *Come on, smell them. There's more of them and they're bigger*, he mentally urged the thing. *And now one of them is wounded.*

Then, to Zhang's horror, the creature raised one front leg and placed it against the tree trunk. Long pincer-like claws were on the end of the barbed legs and they gripped the soft bark. It was going to climb.

* * *

Alex led the remaining HAWCs through the boggy swamp. They didn't need light sensors as the yellowish twilight glow given off by the huge golden moon above them was more than enough to see by.

He also didn't need his suit's other electronic sensors to warn him as his own physical senses screamed to him about the danger all around them. There was life here in myriad forms, and it made his scalp tingle.

Many times creatures scuttled or slithered from their path. Some looked like three-foot-long, soft-bodied salamanders with frog eyes, paddle tails, and needle teeth. Others had a hard carapace and might have been a form of crustacean or insect. Cooper might know the difference. But right now, as long as the animals remained this small and didn't attack, they had no chance to penetrate their HAWC suits, so he'd just kick them aside and not worry about them.

And then the real threat manifested – from a different and potentially more dangerous predator. The shot came out of nowhere, blowing Gonzalez off his feet and back into the mud behind them. The second shot came a split second after, but the HAWCs' reflexes were honed by years of hard-core training, and they had already taken cover and were searching for the shooter.

"Gonzalez, you okay?" Alex called.

The man groaned. "Yeah, suit plating defrayed the impact, but it hurts like a bitch. That was a sniper rifle with a high-speed round." He moved behind a slime-covered bunch of tree roots.

Ito covered Bernadette Cooper and the pair edged up beside Alex.

"Yes, a high-end sniper rifle. Heavy-caliber," Ito said. "He will be somewhere up high."

Alex nodded. "Seems the NKs left us a welcome party." He leaned around the tree trunk. "I want to speak to this guy." He turned. "I want him alive."

Gonzalez got up, leaned carefully around the tree and aimed his rifle out into the darkness. "Anyone got eyes on the bastard?" he said as another bullet smashed into the tree trunk he was hiding behind.

"*Dammit.*" Gonzalez pulled back.

Using the second rifle rapport, Alex moved the scope on his own weapon, trying to see where the shot had come from. Though he doubted the bullets could penetrate their suit armor, the impacts would still be painful and could crack ribs. Not so much a problem for him, but a cracked rib was painful as hell and reduced fluid movement and mobility.

He needed his small team to be in good physical condition for what lay ahead. And there was also the possibility a direct shot to their glass visor might splinter it – which would be a serious issue if they needed to go aquatic. And they couldn't rule out the possibility the sniper had heavier armaments, like a grenade launcher – combat suit or no combat suit, a direct hit from a grenade might blow them to pieces.

Alex looked along the tree line – or what passed for a tree line in this ancient time. There were several large tree-like plants which Cooper had explained were more like light-pole-tall fungi stalks with bulbous fronds of things like clusters of grapes at the top. The sniper had to be up in one of those, bedded in among the foliage. But he must have been keeping his head down, as even with Alex's enhanced vision he couldn't spot him.

There weren't that many other places of concealment, so it was almost like the marksman was daring them to come look for him – and that raised a question. Alex quickly looked out at the ground-level terrain ahead of them. And then he saw the first claymore, with a line running just a few inches up from the ground. And then a little further to the right, he saw the almost invisible line of another whose fragmentation plate was hidden. He bet there'd be more, creating a fence around the sniper.

"*Claymores,*" he said into his mic to his team.

He didn't need to say any more – they all knew that the NKs used a range of anti-personnel mines, favoring the Chinese-built Type-66 frag devices. They were deadly, and literally took a soldier apart with a high-velocity spray of ball bearings and fragmentation casing.

"Initiate war mode," Alex said.

He brought the combat visor with the heavy armored plating down over his face. He now operated with vision from the synthetic feed from the hardware and software as the quad vision lenses took over.

Thermal didn't give him the flaring outline he hoped for and he switched back to night vision, which delivered a phosphorescent glow over the reeking shoreline. But even with the advanced equipment he still couldn't find their adversary. And the sniper was doing exactly what was expected of him – keeping the HAWCs bogged down.

Every minute he and his team squatted in the mud, the sniper's team drew further away. Soon they'd drop their first nuclear package. Time was against them. Alex knew he needed to act.

He turned to the group. "Keep looking for our friend in the trees. But I want him alive." He turned away. "Time for a circuit breaker."

Alex whistled the same tune he used to call Tor, and sure enough, in seconds the metallic dog appeared by his side.

Alex stared into the android canine's dark eyes for a moment and felt the prickle of the familiarity in his mind as the DOG in turn reached out to this new-found consciousness. The connection to Tor was strong and comforting. "Find him. Incapacitate, no kill. Note claymore explosive positions. Go."

The android bounded off and Alex turned. "Get ready for him to be flushed out." He nodded to Ito. "Stay on Cooper."

The Japanese man nodded and then grabbed Cooper's arm and tried to pull her lower. In turn she elbowed him away and drew her gun.

* * *

Zhang saw the thing place another leg against the tree trunk. And then another. He knew he had no choice now, so he carefully reached down along his body to a thigh pocket for a grenade. He understood that if he detonated it, he might dissuade the beast, but he would definitely give away his position.

To hell with it, he thought, and flipped the pin.

If it came down to dying in gunfire exchange with the Americans or being eaten alive by a giant land lobster thing, he knew which option he'd take. He dropped the grenade straight down at the multiple feet of the huge crustacean.

* * *

The blast forced the HAWCs to hunker down.

Alex already had the heavier combat shielding in place, so he continued to watch even though he felt the fragmentation spray pepper his suit. It left indent pit marks but they were not enough to penetrate the tough armor.

Alex called Tor back in while they assessed the situation. Already the flash of light had dissipated and the miasmic-yellow gloom quickly returned.

"Did our sniper just blow himself up trying to get away?" Gonzalez asked.

"Unlikely," Alex said. Anyone got eyes on what?"

"Movement," Ito said. "Base of that tree, about two o'clock."

All eyes moved to where he indicated. But for now all they could make out was some gentle movement among the soft-looking bushes, as if something was creeping through them.

"Looks like the blast didn't stop whatever it is," Gonzalez said. "Means it's got one tough-ass skin or armor covering it."

"I see it," Alex said.

As they watched, the creature emerged.

"Holy fuck. What the hell is that thing?" Gonzalez said incredulously. "Anyone order the lobster?"

Alex turned. "Cooper."

Bernadette Cooper snuck forward with Ito at her side.

"Go to night vision." Alex turned back to the jungle. "Base of that limbless tree about two o'clock. Tell me what that thing is."

Cooper stared. And then amplified and enhanced her vision spectrum. "Oh, wow." She breathed. "It looks a bit like a *Pterygotus*. That's a genus of giant predatory eurypterid."

"Once again in English?" Alex requested.

"They were a Silurian period arthropod, um, a giant sea scorpion. But they were aquatic, and only sometimes came into the shallows to hunt or lay eggs." She shook her head. "That creature has got to be twelve to fifteen feet – we don't think they ever got that big or that formidable-looking."

"I'm guessing it's another surprise that never made it into the fossil record, then," Alex observed.

"Yeah." She switched between night vision and magnification on her quad lenses. "It looks different, so maybe a variation. Hmm, perhaps even a different species altogether." She turned. "Like I said, we really have very little idea what to expect of the species we may encounter here."

Alex turned. "Wasn't this supposed to be the age of amphibians and arthropods? Is everything going to look like that?"

"Maybe, but it was also a time of variations, combinations, and even creatures that looked like mergers between mammals and reptiles, or had the characteristics of both amphibians and arthropods."

"That's seriously weird," Gonzalez said.

She shrugged. "Nature was rolling the dice, trying things out."

"It's going after the sniper – looks like it found him before we did." Alex turned. "Were they – *are they* – carnivorous?"

"If it's anything like the *Pterygotus*, you bet they were," she replied. "They were one of the alpha predators during the Silurian period. Ate anything smaller or slower than they were."

Alex turned back just in time to see the massive arthropod grip the tree trunk and begin to lift its bulk upward. In the flaring green of their night vision they had a better view of the thing. It looked like a giant, spiny, heavily armor-plated cockroach, with two formidable-looking pincers out front like a true scorpion. It also had sharp legs that dug into the fleshy tree trunk as it climbed.

The thing must have weighed around 1200 pounds, easy, but with the sound of ripping bark the horrifying creature gradually lifted itself away from the ground.

"It's going after him." Alex watched it climb. "Looks like the guy is definitely on the menu."

CHAPTER 20

Zhang looked down at the monstrosity again and cursed – it was still coming up. From where he was he knew it was too high to jump, however, the boggy ground might somewhat cushion his fall.

But even if through blind luck he jumped and didn't break anything, his short legs would make slow progress over the marshy landscape, and he had no idea how fast the thing could move if it pursued him – and he bet it would. It would likely run him down in seconds.

And then there were the Americans. Would they shoot him on sight? Why not? After all, he had administered what he thought were kill shots on them. Why would they show him mercy in return? Zhang was fully prepared to die. But not to throw his life away.

He quickly turned one way then the other – if he couldn't go down, then he'd go somewhere else. He used the sniper rifle to survey the other treetops. The tree he was in was around sixty feet tall and had a thick fleshy canopy. There were small fig-like berries on some of the branches that gave off a cloying sugary scent, and small insects hovered around them. In the darkness he couldn't tell if they were flies, bees, or something else entirely.

But just about twenty feet to his right, there was a similar tree slightly lower down, and if its canopy was as soft and spongy as this one, it would make for a soft landing. If he made it.

He quickly glanced down again.

The massive creature was motionless, watching him now, its head tilted upward and its two bulb-like eyes twitching. They only stopped moving when they caught sight of him looking back.

He knew that with the size of its boxy head and its proximity, he could not fail to miss it if he shot it. But he had no idea if its brain was inside that horrifying head or somewhere else in its weird alien body, because he was sure he'd read somewhere that insects had a long brain running all the way down their backs and not just packed into their armor-plated heads. Plus, the thing had just walked through a grenade detonation and was unharmed.

He felt his stomach roil with indecision as time ticked by. Was it not better to hand himself over to the Americans than be eaten alive? In return they would want information, and perhaps he could gain their support, and give them false data – how would they know what was true and what was a lie?

He eased back and looked again at his target tree – it was so far, and he had no run-up other than just springing out and hoping he was propelled far enough to latch on to it.

The sound from the tree trunk told him the creature was nearly up to him. *No choice*, he thought, so he pushed his rifle up over his shoulder and started to ease his way out.

The tree shook a little, not from his movements, but from the much heavier thing scaling it. He heard the raking of its sharp dagger-like claws on the moss-covered bark, and the cloying almondy odor was becoming overpowering.

Zhang looked at his target tree – if he made it he was sure he could vanish into its foliage without ever touching the ground.

He got up on his feet with legs bent and mentally prepared himself, judging where he'd hit and what his first move would be: to scramble into the thick foliage and hopefully disappear. Even if the thing saw him, and scaled down to try for the next tree, it would pass closer to the Americans than to him – let them deal with it, he thought.

Zhang tensed his thigh muscles and then sprang forward – just as the nightmarish creature made it to the canopy top, shaking the tree as it went. The movement wasn't much, but it caused Zhang's feet to slip a little and lose some of their traction. He sailed into space, but from the moment he left he knew he was off by about two feet. He sailed into open air knowing he was going to fall short.

Zhang just caught the tips of the branches with his fingers and prayed they were strong enough – if not to support him, then at last to allow him to swing in closer to the trunk.

But luck was against him, as the few hanging branches he grabbed were soft, and the bulb-ends squashed in his hands like grapes and their juice made his hands slippery. He slid down the branch strands and then plummeted to the ground to land with a muddy splash.

Everything hurt, but he turned over – just in time to see the massive creature scuttling down the trunk of the first tree and leaping the last few feet in its urgency to get to him.

Zhang pulled the rifle from over his shoulder. But the barrel had been forced into the soft, greasy earth and was clogged with mud. He changed his grip and held it like a club as the thing advanced on him, now barreling through the soft undergrowth in its haste or hunger.

The sniper backed up, deciding that to surrender to the Americans was the lesser of the two evils facing him right now – a bullet, or being eaten? It was an easy choice. But he had left it too late.

The thing was burrowing through the soft, fern-like ground cover like a bulldozer, making soft clicking noises he imagined came from its chitinous mouthparts, as if it was licking its lips.

Zhang scooted backwards, but not fast enough, crying out and lifting an arm as the thing overtook him. It used its pincers to grip and hold him in place. Filling Zhang's vision were the thing's bulbous eyes on stalks as they stared down dispassionately at him. He punched up with all his strength into its hard-shelled face as the buzzsaw mouth opened like a lot of razor-edged sliding doors. His hand went in.

* * *

"It's got him." Gonzalez shouldered his weapon and sighted along the barrel. After a moment he lifted his head. "No shot. Orders, boss?"

Alex stood. "I want him alive."

As they watched, they saw the man lift his arm to fend off the massive arthropod creature. His hand went straight into the mouth, and with a blur of blade-like teeth, the man screamed as blood spurted, and he tugged his arm back, but now without his hand.

"We better hurry, or there's not gonna be much left of him," said Gonzalez.

Alex knew that without a clear shot, they needed to physically intervene. He turned.

"Tor." The metallic animal was at his side in a blink. "Protect, retrieve."

The metallic animal knew immediately what Alex wanted and leaped into action.

It crossed the hundred feet of ground between the HAWCs and the attack, and as it sprinted, its armor dappled and changed color as its adaptive camouflage helped it meld into the jungle surroundings.

Gonzalez stood. "Oh boy, I'm dying to see what dog-bot can do."

The group watched as Tor picked up so much speed in the last ten feet it became airborne and struck the arthropod mid-section. Though the creature was more than three times Tor's size, and heavily armor-plated, the android's titanium teeth crunched into the carapace and ripped away a dinner plate–sized chunk of shell.

The arthropod turned away from the North Korean soldier to engage the more formidable adversary. Huge pincers nearly as long as the dog opened and gripped the metallic animal. They held Tor in place and then slowly dragged the bot toward the creature's mouthparts, which were still covered in dark blood.

Mandibles opened wide to expose the powerful, and already moving, serrated plates. But the android was no normal creature of this time or place, and Tor turned front on, opening its own jaws – hardened carapace versus titanium as they came together – and after an audible crunching, when they pulled apart, a portion of the arthropod's face was missing.

At that point the crustacean decided to disengage with its attack and released the dog. Or tried to. Tor held on for a fraction longer and then let go, but rather than move away it planted itself in front of its larger attacker. Tor's mouth hung open, and a red beam shot out. It swiped from the top to the bottom of the creature's front, between the moving eyestalks, and a second later the huge crustacean creature simply fell in half.

"Yeah, I'd count that as a definite kill." Gonzalez chuckled. "Glad he's on our team."

Alex nodded and whistled.

Tor turned.

"Bring the man," Alex said, and then looked about. "Everyone keep your eyes open. There may be more of those things out there."

Tor grabbed the soldier by the collar of his jungle fatigues and dragged him backwards through the mud and undergrowth. He finished by releasing the man on the ground between the HAWCs, and then stared down, perhaps on guard against him making a move for a weapon.

The North Korean grimaced as he held his wrist, which still pulsed hot blood around a stump with an inch of sharp bone sticking out the end.

"Seal that," Alex said.

Gonzalez stepped forward. "Hold him down."

Alex put a boot on the man's chest, and Ito held his legs. Gonzalez then opened a side pouch and drew out a pencil-like apparatus. He slid a thumb down its side and switched it on, eliciting a small light at the tip.

"I could give you something to knock the pain back a few notches, but you tried to kill me, so fuck you, buddy." He grabbed the stump. "This is gonna hurt like a bitch."

He brought the small laser cutter close to the bleeding stump, and then slowly took the beam from one side of the ragged wound to the other. There was the sound of sizzling flesh, and the smell of cooking meat filled the air.

The North Korean screamed, and Cooper looked away as a slice of his arm-flesh dropped off, leaving a cleaned and cauterized stump, with the hard bone still protruding slightly.

"I should take that bone back a bit as the flesh will shrink around it. But that'll hold until he gets medical care. Or he decides to . . ." he laughed grimly, ". . . leave us for the NK version of heaven." Gonzalez then clicked his fingers in front of the man's face to get his attention. "One more thing." He tapped his own chest where there was a sniper bullet scar on the armored plating. "I hold a grudge, asshole."

Alex took his boot off the North Korean's chest and stared down at the man, who groaned and grimaced as he held his still-smoking stump.

"*Hey.*" The man's eyes slid to Alex. "English?"

The man looked up at the black-clad giant whose eyes shone a little silver in the darkness. After a few seconds he shrugged. "No very good."

"That'll do." Alex crouched. "You tried to kill us, so we owe you nothing. From now on you're just excess baggage. We just saved your life, but you've got to give us a reason to keep you alive." He pointed at the stump. "Or we'll peg you out here so the big bugs will eat you alive. Got it?"

The man stared for a moment more, then nodded. But Alex could see by the hardness in his eyes that he was unlikely to give them much.

"How many of you are there?" He waited.

The man slowly raised two fingers.

"Bullshit," Cooper said. "They'd need more than that just to carry their multiple packages."

"Strike one," Alex said. "If you get to strike three, we won't kill you. We won't have to. This place will eat you." He still saw the dead-eyed resolve in the sniper's eyes.

"How many bombs do you plan to leave here? And have you deployed any yet?" Alex waited again.

"Bombs?" The man frowned. "No, we just, ah, explore."

"We already detected your radiation trace. So that's strike two." Alex leaned forward and grabbed the man's stump and squeezed it a little. A few drops of blood oozed from the blackened end. "This is so the predators can smell you. And find you quicker." He turned. "Tor."

The android canine loomed over the soldier. It bared its razor-sharp teeth and stared down with its black, gun-barrel eyes.

The man tried to cringe away, but Alex held his arm.

"Last question. What is your mission route and destination?" Alex smiled grimly.

The man shook his head. "I am just soldier. I not told plan."

"Strike three." Alex stood. "You are no use to us. Strip him down and tie him to a tree."

"Hey, you can't do that," Cooper complained.

"He tried to kill us. He will again." Alex stared and his eyes were smoldering mercury in the strange yellow gloom. "Our mission is to save the United States. This guy will slow us down, and given the chance, try and sabotage us."

"You can't know that." She looked deeply uncomfortable. "I won't be party to this."

"You're not." Alex clicked his fingers and Ito and Gonzalez began to pull the man's shirt off and undo his belt.

The man frowned, but he pressed his lips together in a straight line of determination.

From behind them came a rumbling through the undergrowth and Alex spun, gun up. Another of the hulking arthropod creatures was charging down on them, and Alex initiated the plasma grenade launcher and fired a single pulse at it.

The super-hot foot-wide discharge of plasma was like ball lightning and around 50,000 degrees. It hit the thing front on, and continued through its body. When it finished there was a glowing hole that kept burning and widening, from front to end.

In seconds all that remained of the creature were the six spiked legs, which fell outward to the soft earth where their still orange-glowing ends sizzled as the muddy water covered them.

Alex turned back to the North Korean. "See? They can already smell you and are coming in for a free meal." Alex's eyes were dead as he leaned forward. "I've found that carnivores like to eat the soft parts of their prey animals first."

The HAWCs lashed the now naked NK's outstretched arms to a few small cork-like trees, and then Alex had them spread his legs and lash them as well.

"Let's move out," Alex said.

The team gathered their materials, and Alex glanced back. The sniper's eyes went wide as he realized they were serious, and he began to panic.

"North," he said.

"We already know that." Alex kept walking.

"*Texas*," the man shouted now.

Alex held up a hand and the HAWCs stopped and waited.

"Speak. And live. At least a little while longer," Alex warned.

"My name Lingyun Zhang. I soldier." He breathed heavily. "My fight over. I fail."

Alex was unfazed by the admission. "I repeat, what is your mission destination, and number of team members? Number of bombs?"

Zhang held up five fingers. Then another four from his only hand.

"Nine," Alex said.

The man nodded. "We travel water. Drop bomb. Ten of them. No drop yet." He seemed to struggle with the words and spoke some Korean for a moment. "Bombs, ah, go big . . ." He flicked his fingers open.

"Explode," Gonzalez offered.

"Yes. Explode. Ten bomb. Every one hundred." He shut his eyes.

"Over a thousand years. Just as we suspected," Cooper said.

Alex walked closer to the man and pulled one of his knives. "You bought yourself a little more time." He brought his face in real close to Zhang's. "But one mistake, and you are dead. Got it?"

Zhang stared blankly.

Alex straightened. "Let's get after them. We've wasted enough time here." He turned to Gonzalez. "He's in front of you. Watch him. If he screws up, shoot him and leave him."

They waited while the North Korean scrambled back into his clothes, then Alex checked his wrist gauntlet one last time, and they headed north.

CHAPTER 21

"Where the fuck is my man?" Hammerson demanded of the scientists.

The HAWC commander had a black eye and a split across the top of his nose from the explosion and fall from the Janus lab. Quartermain had checked him over, and he bet the tough HAWC commander's body ached in a hundred different places – not that the Hammer would ever admit it.

All they could focus on was what the Janus guys had just told them – some HAWC mission team members hadn't made it to the Silurian destination. They were there, but miles away. But that wasn't the worst of it – Sam Reid hadn't made it at all. Hammerson's face was furious. He didn't like the answers he was getting.

Hanley raised his hands. "We don't know. *Yet*. But he still has his tracker installed."

"Then initiate the recall; bring him back," Hammerson growled. "Or send him to the original mission site."

Hanley and Rashid glanced at each other.

"They can't," Dr. Andrew Quartermain observed, and turned to the two scientists. "Can you?" The room hung in silence for a few long seconds.

Hanley was first to shake his head. "No." He exhaled, and then looked nervously at Hammerson. "We can't find him to lock in on him. Like I said, *yet.*"

"How long?" Hammerson demanded.

"We're working on it," Rashid offered. "Something went wrong at the initiation point. Somehow the bridge and its stream got distorted. We think—" Hammerson glared and Rashid held up his hands, palms outward. "Okay, look, we told you there were risks. We're working on this right now. Give us a few days."

Hammerson exhaled through his nose; his lips were pressed together furiously tight as he growled deep in his chest. He turned to Quartermain. "Stay on top of these guys." He turned on his heel.

At the door he paused in front of the female HAWC stationed there. "Keep me informed."

"Sir," she said, saluting.

Marion 'Pinch' Pinchella was five-nine, late twenties, with dark hair pulled back so tight it revealed a scar in the center of her forehead that could be seen running up into her scalp. She was dressed all in black, and had a black bomber-style jacket, so she could secrete numerous weapons and armor about her body.

Quartermain watched Hammerson exit through the now repaired lab doors. He turned back to the two scientists.

"He can get very impatient when he doesn't see results. And then he gets angry. And then he acts. You won't like that." He smiled. "Shall we get back to work, gentlemen?"

* * *

Sam wandered in the land of the Philistines. He had refused to become a soldier for the Saran and had escaped them. Perhaps that was his first mistake.

It was soon after that he had come to the village of the Nazarites. He understood the roots of their language, and unlike the Philistines, who treated him with distrust and hostility, the people here greeted him with open arms and hearts. They took him in, fed him, and housed him.

Many of the women admired the blond giant with his ferocious beard and hair halfway down his back, and in turn Sam came to love the people here and have affection for all of them. But this was not where his heart was. As the months passed, he continued to hope he would be transported home one day.

Sam often reached up to feel the small pellet still embedded in the skin of his neck. While that was there, he believed he would see his beloved Alyssa and be home with her again one day. He had to believe that, because anything else just led him toward a depressive madness.

Over time he found peace among the Nazarites. He devoted himself to them, and his great strength and size, and his willingness to defend them and any other oppressed peoples, made him their champion.

The stories of Sam grew, and no matter what he told people, they called him Samson, which meant *child of the sun* – probably because of his hair color. Sam had heard the Nazarites whispering about him having divine power gifted to him so he could be their protector.

He knew of the stories of the great warrior of biblical mythology, and wondered if he was being mistaken for him. Or, if through some mad twist of time travelling fate, he was actually . . .

No, he pushed that thought from his head. He was 1st Lieutenant Samuel Reid, of the HAWC US Special Forces. That was all.

He would help the Nazarites, but there was a poisonous side effect of him aligning himself with them. It made a mortal enemy of the Philistine soldiers, who Sam dealt with swiftly and brutally. He needed no weapons other than his bare hands, and he had the strength of ten of them, or more.

But Sam knew he couldn't stay with the Nazarites. He must leave, or eventually, the army would come and obliterate them all. And a spear through the chest, if it got through his internal MECH shielding, would kill him the same as it would any man.

One of the young women, Dalila, who had a schoolgirl crush on him like no other, followed him around, giving him the ripest dates and cups of cool well-water on the hottest days. She would often smile and wave at him, and he would return the gesture. Sam knew there was peace and life here. But not for the Nazarites if he stayed.

He knew Dalila would be devastated with his leaving. But he would rather have her upset than dead. Than all of them, dead.

CHAPTER 22

Soong-Li sat in the middle of the inflatable boat next to Shuchang. She tried to make sense of her compass, which kept changing as if the magnetism of the poles was shifting or somehow being interrupted by stronger forces.

"*Ach*, must be the volcanoes," she muttered. "Too much magnetic interference."

She checked her wristwatch – it was still a few hours until sun-up. For now, they moved close to the shoreline. Every now and then the keel of their boat bumped over submerged logs. Or something else.

She had posted the huge form of Quinfan Chen to the front of the boat. There had been early disagreement over him holding his spears too close to the inflatable's edge, but eventually he had agreed to wrap them as long as he was able to keep them within reach.

Next were the two young soldiers, Jin and Kwan, who cradled their rifles, always at the ready. Just behind them was Yan Guo, the party official. The man sat hunched over, looking ill and worn down already, and jumping at every shadow and sound. She still bet he would be the first of them to crack and fall away. Soong-Li doubted he would sleep a wink, compounding his physical and mental decline.

Soong-Li then turned to her two scientists, Tian Wu and Jia Sun, and was happy to see both of the young women still looking more excited than fearful. They chatted and compared notes on things they had seen so far.

Beside her, Shuchang's eyes were half-closed, as if he was fighting off sleep. She examined his features, and even with a layer of perspiration and grime, she found them pleasing to the eye. She liked him, always had. And she knew he liked her, as many times she had caught him casting sideways glances at her. But he had to know that the party and their mission came first. If they made it back, then perhaps they might have time to celebrate together. Just the two of them.

Soong-Li then looked over her shoulder to Captain Junfeng Yang at the helm, guiding them. The man nodded once to her. Calm and confident as ever, she thought gratefully.

He, like the rest of them, had been relieved to be able to remove the huge and heavy packs from their shoulders, and the packages now sat together in a big radioactive pile at the front of the boat, under Quinfan Chen's rump. That made her smile; *no offspring for you, big lump.*

She turned away and inhaled, smelling the swampy brine, and looked out to the horizon where the enormous yellow moon was just setting.

It would be going down in the west, so at least that gave her some primary bearings. Also, their time-to-speed rate was noted by Captain Yang, and that gave her a distance bearing. She felt they were still on track.

She reached down into one of her large pouch pockets for her night vision goggles and pulled them over her head. She turned to the shoreline, and saw the tangle of dark roots, some hanging fronds like ragged curtains in a haunted house, and also now and then the luminous glow of the eyes of beasts hidden in the darkest of shadows – even her night vision optometrics couldn't penetrate that gloom. But from the height of some of those sets of eyes, she estimated they belonged to large creatures.

She turned back to scan the water. For the most part there was no breeze, and the surface was oily smooth, the water so warm there were small heat vapors rising from its languid surface. From time to time, she heard the splash and movement of water as something came up, either to take a breath or just to get a glimpse of them as they motored by. She didn't mind – as long as they left her alone, she would be happy. *Tread softly and leave no footprints* was her mission motto.

They had arrived in the northeastern part of New Mexico and still needed to travel many hours and miles to the first of America's future petroleum beds. They'd set the timer on one of their packages for one week. By then they would be long gone. They'd lower the bomb and then turn east, to the next drop-off points – placement was critical for maximum coverage. The latter drops would be timed for 100-year intervals.

They'd then continue on into Texas for three more package drops. She estimated it'd take them several days if they weren't interrupted by hostile local creatures or the Americans. However, she was confident that their marksman, Zhang, would have slowed them down and put her mission team far enough ahead that they'd never be run down.

They traveled slowly as their boat was overloaded. She didn't mind that Yang was using low revolutions as it also kept the noise down. They all needed rest, but not yet. So that meant the hardest part was staying awake, as it was easy to slip into a trance-like state with the monotonous noise and the continual bath-like warmth. But Soong-Li knew there were things below the water that would be trouble if she drifted off to sleep and then fell over the side. As if to underscore this point, there was another splash out in the darkness and a small wave buffeted the side of their boat.

"Quinfan," she said softly.

The huge man in the bow of the boat turned.

"Stay alert." She nodded out at the water. "Sea creatures."

He nodded and turned back to face front, with one hand on the raft wall and the other pulling free one of his javelin spears. Jin and Kwan also turned to keep watch ahead on either side of the bow.

The soft orange glow from the coming dawn in the east gave Soong-Li a sense of relief. She regarded herself as a strong character, but the shadows hid things that no human had ever encountered before. She preferred to see what was coming at her so she could fight it or evade it.

She glanced at the dark shoreline in the distance. They were only around 500 feet from land, but soon they would need to turn away from it and head directly out into the sea. She didn't like the idea of losing sight of the shoreline.

Right now she heard the strange calls from throats large and small. She hated this place. Maybe saying goodbye to the land was the safest option. She hoped so.

She inhaled and let out the breath slowly. A week – just a few days, she thought. We can make it. Then when she got home she would be a hero. *I will only think of this*, she demanded of herself.

They continued for another fifteen minutes, and she calculated that it would still be some hours before they reached their first drop point. But then she noticed something odd; their boat seemed to slow.

Soong-Li turned to Captain Yang at the rear, and he frowned and then looked down at the motor to see if it had slipped into a lower gear or had some other mechanical issue. He then looked up at her and shrugged, his frown further creasing his brow.

The boat slowed a little more and in the next minute stopped in the water altogether, even though the engine was still going, churning water. Confused now, everyone inside the craft looked one way then the other, and then back to Yang.

The captain shut off the engine, then peered over the side into the inky water for a few moments before reaching back for his flashlight.

"What is it?" Soong-Li asked, but he just put a finger to his lips.

The silence hung heavily around them as the man leaned out, closer to the surface of the water.

"What do you see?" Soong-Li pressed. "Have we run aground?"

Yang held the raft edge with one hand and his flashlight in the other. He flicked it on and suddenly Soong-Li saw the man's eyes go wide. He had time to make a single exclamation before something whipped up out of the water.

Soong-Li yelled a curse, Shuchang woke in panic, and the rest of the boat's passengers screamed and tried to edge away from the rear of the craft as they watched the captain struggle with what looked like a rope-thick, mottled green tentacle, which had wrapped itself around his head and face.

As they looked on, another tentacle slapped the side of the boat and slithered up and over the edge. Inside the boat the humans reacted with panic, becoming a mass of tangled limbs as they tried to get away, all toward the front, and of course, the craft rocked ominously.

If that wasn't bad enough, the huge form of Quinfan Chen stood up. He had one of his spears in his hand, but then thankfully dropped it and instead lifted his rifle, pulled it in tight to his shoulder and began to fire into the water, only narrowly missing the tops of his comrades' heads.

Jin and Kwan also began to shoot, and the gunfire, plus the screaming, added to the sense of mass chaos and fear in the small boat. It started to tilt to one side.

Soong-Li turned quickly. "*Sit down,*" she screamed, while everyone was still trying to scramble even further into the bow.

Quinfan sat heavily but continued to fire – badly. Bullets whizzed past them, went overheard, and one smacked into Captain Yang's kit pack.

"*Stop, you imbecile,*" Soong-Li screamed. "Just stop."

She then pulled her own pistol and moved to the stern. One of the slimy tentacles touched her ankle but she ignored it as she went for the entangled man. The captain was fighting against the beast as more and more long, ropy tentacles came over the side. He had pulled out his knife to blindly stab at the rubbery, muscular mass. But it did little damage, and if the thing felt pain, it showed no sign.

Soong-Li took aim, but it was impossible to hit the whipping tentacles, and also the captain's body was in the way.

It was then that the sea creature began to pull itself up beside the craft, and one huge, plate-sized white eye rose from the water to get a better look at the prey it had gotten hold of.

The thing was like nothing they had ever experienced, with far too many tentacles for a normal octopus, and just visible at the water line was a huge, ribbed shell.

The scientist behind Soong-Li, Tian Wu, yelled a single word: *nautiloid,* in a high-pitched scream, and then the rear of the craft began to go under as the weight and bulk of the creature dragged it down while it lifted itself higher.

It was a terrifying sight, but it finally gave Soong-Li a larger, steadier target other than the creature's fast-moving limbs. She calmed herself, aimed, exhaled, and then fired.

The bullet was loud over the water, but at this range it was impossible to miss the huge, bulbous head. Immediately the water exploded all around them as the thing fell away, and the tentacles were quickly dragged back over the side – including the ones still holding the captain, and, horrifyingly, taking him with them.

As he was hauled over the side, Soong-Li dived and grabbed at his quickly vanishing legs. But the thing attached to him was a lot bigger and more powerful than she was, and she began to slide over the edge herself.

"*Help*," she screamed, and Shuchang leaped into action. He landed beside her, firstly holding on to her back to stop her slide.

"Grab him," she ordered.

He did as asked, and together they pulled Yang back up.

Junfeng Yang flopped into the boat, his eyes wide. He sucked in almighty breaths. Covering his face and neck were painful-looking, golf ball–sized red welts.

"Giant octopus," he blurted out.

Soong-Li helped him up but turned to her science officer. "It looked different; what was it?"

Tian Wu sputtered.

"Well?" Soong-Li demanded.

The woman swallowed. "He's sort of right. I think it was a *Sphooceras*, a very primitive cephalopod from the Silurian period. But it had ten arms instead of eight. Like a cuttlefish." She grimaced. "But they don't get that big, or we didn't think they did. No bigger than . . ." she held her hands about a foot apart, ". . . this."

Captain Yang wiped his wet hair back off his face and scoffed. "That thing was 500 pounds. Maybe more." He coughed up some water. "So strong." He looked at his hands, which were covered in an eye-stinging black mucus, but then looked up at Soong-Li. "Thank you."

"Of course." She half-smiled. "I need you."

Soong-Li then turned to the glowing horizon. "Let's get moving. Daylight is approaching. And I want to finish our job before any other creatures decide to try and make a meal of us."

CHAPTER 23

Alex was first into the small open area in the jungle. He held up a hand. "Take five."

He retracted his visor, and the team did the same. They'd been trekking for an hour, and the going had been hard. And so far they still hadn't reached a clear or safe place to take to the water, and the ground alternated between knee-deep brackish swamp, and sticky sludge.

They had stopped on a small mound that was like an island of liverwort among the stinking coastal miasma. It gave Alex a few minutes to grab some water, get his bearings, and collect his thoughts.

He sat down and picked up a smooth egg-sized stone, turning it in his hand as his mind worked. He couldn't help wondering if the Janus team had solved the short-term jump problem – he prayed with everything he had that they would. There was only one reason he was here – and when he got back he was going to make things right.

As if summoned, images suddenly rushed his mind of the day Aimee and Joshua were killed, and it filled him with a grief so deep he felt cramps in his belly. But then it bloomed into something hotter and more deadly. A chained beast rattled in his mind.

When we get back, we'll find them, it whispered. *And when we do we will make them pay a price that'll make them wish they had never been born.*

Without even thinking about it, Alex's hand tightened on the rock he held, and it popped and squealed as if in agony before it exploded in his fist. He lowered his head, crushed his eyes shut and breathed in and out for a few moments. Then he shook his head to cast out the demon. He couldn't afford to allow it to take over now while there was work to be done.

Alex wiped the rock dust from his hand and pulled out his canteen. While he sipped, he watched his team. Gonzalez and Ito crouched beneath a shrub-like plant, and Cooper gave the North Korean captive a sip of water. The man still seemed furtive and held his stump by the wrist. Alex didn't trust him one bit.

Both camps were here to complete a mission. The North Koreans had come to destroy the United States. The HAWCs were here to stop them. He bet in both their minds, nothing had changed.

Alex cursed and looked away, tamping down his murderous thoughts. Glancing at his arm of his suit, he saw that a green, glistening growth had begun to creep across the armor plates – mold and fungi were on and in everything.

He turned to face the walls of strange plant life around them. Without seeing them, he knew eyes were on them. There were beasts in there. He could smell them, smell their exhalations, smell their droppings.

In front of him a tiny creature just a few inches long snuck out on a green limb that was like a smooth piece of garden hose. Its destination was a small round bug that had its head burrowed into the stem. As Alex watched it approach, he saw it slow down, and then from an inch out, a tongue like a hard spear shot out to skewer the small beetle, and then reel it in.

The crunch and pop of the prey bug's carapace was loud for the size of the tiny predator, and it reminded him that here it was kill or be killed – and that went for the confrontation with the North Koreans that was coming, too, Alex thought.

* * *

Gonzalez closed his eyes and tilted his head back. He exhaled, loudly. "You know what? We've been here less than a day, and I already hate it."

Ito grunted. "You get soft."

Gonzalez scoffed, keeping his eyes closed as he gave an upside-down smile. "Oh, you like it here?"

"No," Ito replied. "I ignore it."

"Yeah, right." Gonzalez chuckled. "Nobody can ignore this shithole's heat and stink."

"You just like complaining." Ito half-smiled.

"Yep." Gonzalez clasped his hands on his stomach and relaxed.

* * *

Above them a golf ball–sized thing that looked like a knot of bristling hairs moved out onto a limb as it was being pursued by one of the spear-tongued creatures in pursuit of a quick meal.

But when the spear-tongued bug got within range, the black bristling ball exploded into hundreds of separate tiny creatures, with long legs, waving antennae, and a tail with a red tip.

Spear-tongue shot its bolt anyway, and hundreds of the bristling bugs leaped for freedom – showering down on the HAWCs below.

* * *

"Fuck.' Gonzalez sat forward and brushed his check.

Ito, just to his left, turned and saw about two dozen tiny crawling things on his arm. He brushed at them as they made their way upward, perhaps thinking he was another tree. He engaged his visor to seal them out.

Gonzalez, who was directly under the shower, managed to get several dozen on his face. And then down his neck. He suddenly found out what that red-tipped barb on the insects' tail could do.

"*Argh*. They're in my suit." He jumped up. "*Shit*, the fuckers are stinging me."

He danced for a while, uselessly slapping at his armor as Alex walked over and grabbed the front breastplate of his suit to lift him to his feet.

"Stay still," he ordered. "Freeze flush."

Gonzalez looked up, his face red. "Yeah, yeah, right, boss." He quickly closed his visor and discharged the suit's coolant to flush the inside of his suit. Momentarily his visor misted with freezing vapor, and he felt the sudden relieving but painful chill of the icy mist that filled the suit with dry, cold air that was about twenty degrees. This was an emergency feature – if the suit's pilot encountered flames or other extreme heat environments it was a way to immediately reduce burning.

The human body could tolerate it for several seconds without getting hypothermia or freeze burn. But the tiny bugs couldn't. In seconds they were all dead.

Gonzalez retracted his visor, sighed, and nodded. "Yeah, that worked." He grimaced. "Covered in bug bites, though."

"Be more careful," Alex said. "And monitor yourself, in case those things were venomous."

"Sir." Gonzalez nodded.

Ito slapped him on the shoulder. "Do you still hate it here?"

"No way, I feel much better about it now . . . *smartass*."
He grinned through his discomfort. "But I gotta tell you;
I really feel like I want to shoot something."

"Break time's over," Alex said. "Gonzalez, you finished
feeding the bugs?"

"Yes sir, donated my pint today." He grinned and saluted.

The group filed out, heading north, and following the coast,
and soon the jungle opened, the ground hardened, and they
came to the small bay.

At the water's edge Ito crouched and touched some faint
indentations in the mud. "The North Koreans took to the sea
here." He pointed over the ground. "Here and here, and here,
I think maybe nine or ten people. All in combat boots – some
men, some women."

Alex nodded. "Then we take to the water here as well."

Bernadette Cooper stood beside him and watched the
murky water for a while. It was mostly oil-smooth, but now
and then it swirled and bubbled.

"I don't think we're going to be alone out there." She
turned. "Over surface or below?"

Alex also watched the water and saw the telltale signs of
life. "I'd prefer to navigate below the water as it'll create less
turbulence and attract less attention." He thumbed over his
shoulder at their prisoner. "But that guy doesn't have the gear,
so . . ."

"Oh yeah," Cooper replied. "We'll need eyes in the back
of our heads. Think of it as crossing an alligator-infested
swamp."

Alex half-smiled. "Except we don't know what the alligators look like, how big they can get, or how many there are."

"That about sums it up." She grinned back.

"Just another day in the office." He turned back to the
water. "Okay, everyone, we're going aquatic."

"Nice day for a swim," Gonzalez replied.

Alex took the raft pack from his shoulders and handed it to Gonzalez, who set about constructing the craft. It was torpedo-shaped and the framework ribbing was filled with a liquid silicone mixture which, when solidified, gave flexibility and strength, and also neutral buoyancy. The panels were made of Kevlar – thin, but high strength and tougher than steel.

The group set about doing their jobs, and the only one who stood back was Lingyun Zhang, who pretended not to understand, but watched everything like a hawk.

* * *

The North Korean sniper saw the craft being constructed, and carefully looked it over for any weak points and places he could sabotage. Though his days as a marksman were over, the mission wasn't. He decided that he would slow the Americans down or sabotage them completely.

The American soldiers had stripped him of all his weapons. They seemed extremely formidable and he knew a direct assault would lead to his death. But the female with them, though dressed as a soldier, didn't move like them. He saw she had a full complement of weapons. So she would be his target and eventual armory.

The former sniper grimaced as his stump ached again. The missing hand meant he would be an idle veteran if he made it back home. He would be nothing. Better to die here a hero than return a broken man.

He knew what he had planned would probably mean his death. However maybe it would lead to the deaths of the Americans, too. Whatever occurred, he must not let them catch up to Soong-Li and his comrades.

He was ready to act, and to die. His time of glory was near.

CHAPTER 24

Around fifty miles further north of Alex's group, Casey suddenly went into a crouch and waved Brandt down.

He dropped and crawled up beside her. "What've you got?"

"A herd of things that look like buffalo," she replied.

"I see 'em." He blew air between his lips. "Except they ain't buffalo. What they is, is ugly as fuck."

"They're eating the moss, so probably no threat." She lifted her head. "We go around."

Casey sighted a path, but it was around a stand of growths like twisted mangroves that rose fifty feet. Shawls of glistening, rag-like mosses hung from their slimy branches. As she looked for the best path through, there was a commotion among the herd.

She turned back and saw that just behind the herd the plants were moving gently, as if being pushed in a wave. Or pushed aside. Then the plants to the left of them began to slowly bend forward.

"Something's coming. Predator," she whispered.

The herd had stopped eating and raised their heads. They froze, as if listening, or smelling.

Everything seemed to stop. Even the wind.

And then the attack came in an explosion of noise, muscle, and teeth.

"Ambush attack." Brandt hunkered down.

Casey stared as from the side of the herd a creature about fifteen feet long, powerful, and easily weighing 2000 pounds, exploded from the wet foliage to crush one of the plant-eating beasts to the ground.

"Holy shit," Brandt breathed. "A fucking monster."

The creature had an enormous, oversized head that split open to reveal forearm-sized tusks either side of its upper and lower jaws. Casey thought it looked like a giant wolf with no ears, but instead of fur it had leathery plates, and at the end of its four powerful but squat legs were long talon-like claws. It set about raking the skin of the beast it had just caught, eliciting squeals of pain as strips of flesh were peeled from its body.

By now the herd had panicked. And they ran. Right toward the two HAWCs.

"*Run*," Casey yelled.

"Fuck that. I ain't running from mutant cows." Brandt widened his stance and pulled the laser cannon from over his shoulder to hold it under his arm. "Go time."

As the first of the plant-eating beasts bore down on him, he pulled the trigger. He hadn't calibrated the beam size, so a two-inch thick burst of super condensed light was spat from the bulb end of the barrel to cross the hundred feet between him and the first of the charging animals.

The beast exploded in a shower of charred flesh that rained down around them.

"*Hoowee.*" Brandt couldn't contain his grin.

He moved the barrel and inciner-blasted another of them. "Hell, yeah," he yelled. "That's what I'm talkin' about. Back the fuck up, ladies." He fired a few more times, missing twice.

"Get your ass to cover," Casey yelled.

The herd stalled, and there was mass confusion among them as they sensed the danger to their front but had no experience with how to deal with this new threat.

But from behind the mass of bovine-like creatures, more of the carnivores appeared out of the darkness. A lot more. In addition to their huge size and brute strength, they were fast, agile, and very efficient hunters – and obviously intelligent enough to know to creep up on the herd by staying downwind of them.

The herd had never before encountered Brandt's laser cannon. But they had obviously run into the carnivores before, because they immediately decided those horrors were their biggest threat. So they charged again, en masse, right toward Casey and Brandt.

Brandt lifted his cannon again, but noticed the charge was running low. And there were at least twenty animals running at him now in a wall of fear and muscle, and the ground beneath his feet was shaking.

"Okay. Nope." He turned and ran, following Casey.

The pair of HAWCs headed to a massive knot-like growth of roots. There was no path through, but it was the largest thing close by that might give them shelter from the stampeding beasts.

The running herd enticed the carnivores. Also, hardwired into a predator's DNA was the inclination to choose their prey based on size or weakness, and one of the wolf-beasts spied the small and slow-moving pair of bipedal creatures out in front and went for them instead.

The bear trap–toothed mountain of fury charged at Casey, who spotted it when she glanced over her shoulder.

"Incoming," she yelled, and then realized she wasn't going to be able to outpace the horror. So she turned to face it.

It was on her in the blink of an eye, but she raised her newly acquired MECH arm and with lightning speed brought it down on the center of the animal's skull just as the huge jaws opened to take her in.

There was a crunch like the breaking of a giant eggshell as her fist sank into the bone to crush the brain matter. The huge creature dropped dead at her feet.

Casey yanked her gore-covered arm out and looked down at the thing as it juddered in its final death throes. "That's right; fuck you." She grinned, but then saw more of the beasts charging her position. She turned and ran.

From behind them the sound of the massacre was near ear-splitting as screams mixed with roars and tearing flesh filled the air, along with the salty scent of fresh blood as a cloud of pink mist rose over the kill site.

Casey and Brandt made it to the twisted, slimy roots just as some of the huge bovine-like creatures rumbled past them.

As they scaled higher, Casey saw the gleam of water through the foliage around them. That probably meant the seashore or a lake was beyond – it was what they were looking for.

Many of the lumbering beasts charged onward, around the root structure they were in, and hit the water, barreling in before beginning to swim.

The HAWCs grabbed the root-like growths and swung up quickly as the sound of the slaughtering got closer below them. About twenty feet up, Casey turned and saw there were about six of the huge predators, and no matter which way she looked at them she couldn't determine if they were mammal, reptile, or something else altogether. But they were huge, powerful, and had leather-like, folded skin all over their bodies that looked like large armor plating. As she stared she thought they reminded her of a cross between a wolf and a Komodo dragon, but stubby and more powerful, and with the backward-curving teeth or tusks. They were bigger than those of any land predator she had ever seen.

"What the hell are they?" Brandt spat.

"Something straight from Hell," Casey replied. "Or from a Silurian Hell."

Brandt turned to peer through the root tangle. "Through there must be the sea that we were supposed to make it to. Perhaps we can use the raft and go around all these monsters."

Casey nodded. "Not a bad idea. It's where our team expected to catch up to the NKs."

There was a scream from the direction of the sea, and the pair swung around to see that about a dozen of the plant eaters had found themselves out in deeper water.

"Something's going on out there." Casey squinted through her night vision lenses. "The water; there's something else in there with them."

The water began to thrash and churn, and the animals started swimming back toward the shore. Then the pair saw what was instigating the second panic – around the bison-reptiles who were furthest out, huge jaws erupted, crushed several together and dragging them down in seconds.

"Well, that's just fucking great. Monsters on shore, monsters in the water." Casey bared her teeth. "Welcome to paradise."

"I'm guessing that the idea of taking to the water right now just got nixed," Brandt said dryly.

"Nope. The NKs will take to the water, and I know the boss will too." Casey shrugged. "It's our only chance to find 'em." She watched the massacre out in the water for a while longer. "But maybe we don't launch from here."

"Yeah, that works for me." Brandt chuckled. "So what now?" He looked up over the sights of his huge laser cannon, noticing it had nearly restored to full charge. "We could just sit here for a week until they initiate the bridge home; that'll still work, right?"

"We're on a mission, and the Arcadian brought us here for a reason. We use our brains to find a way to join the party." Casey retracted her visor. "Remember what Bern said? If you wanted to fuck up Uncle Sam's oil supply by nuking the places where it formed, where would you go?" she asked.

Brandt bobbed his head as he thought about it. "Where the biggest deposits are, or are going to be, and, uh, that would be ..." He shrugged. "Maybe New Mexico, and around there, I think."

Casey nodded. "It's where I'd target. And I bet that's why the NKs started from here – they're thinking the same." She nodded south. "And that's that way." She turned back to her partner. "Maybe we can pick up their trail."

"Unless they take to the water," Brandt replied.

"That's right," she said. "But we keep going and see if our comms can pick our team up as we get closer." She grinned. "And on the way, you might just get a chance to use that big-ass blaster again."

"You see what this bad boy did back there? That cow fucking exploded like a balloon full of hot jello." Brandt grinned, lifting the weapon. "And I didn't bring it just because it looks good on me." His expression became serious. "Let's do this, Franks."

Casey nodded. The water behind them had settled to stillness again. But when she turned back the other way, she saw that the carnage on the killing field continued. "Okay, then. Make a hole."

Brandt lifted the cannon, reset the pulse size, targeted the biggest predator, and fired. The massive toothed beast was hunched over a dead animal one minute, and the next there was a hole a foot wide in the side of its body.

Its eyes went wide before it simply fell over on its side, its heart not only having stopped beating, but completely gone. There was no blood as all the tendons, veins, and arteries had been seared closed.

"You like that, hell pig?" Brandt guffawed. "You want some more?" He put a hole in another one.

"Make room, the real killers are in town," Casey said as the other animals scattered. She slid down to the ground. "Okay, Beast, let's double-time it."

***

Alex was in the front of the torpedo-shaped boat. Cooper was next in line. Gonzalez was at the rear, with Ito close to their prisoner on the port side.

The North Korean, Zhang, groaned and held his wrist. Ito ignored him.

"Is the pain bad?" Cooper asked.

Zhang stared for a moment. "I no understand."

Cooper pointed at his stump. "Pain." She grimaced and held her own hand. "Bad hurt?"

Zhang nodded. Cooper turned to Alex who had his back turned. "Can I give him some morphine? Might keep him quiet."

Alex half-turned and shook his head. "No. That's our stock." He looked down at the man. "He's Special Forces; he can deal with the pain."

Cooper frowned and shook her head. "His groaning is not great for stealth traveling."

Alex turned. "If it was one of us who'd been captured, we'd be silent. Because we'd already be dead." Alex glanced at the North Korean. "Right?"

Alex saw Zhang's eyes quickly shift away. In that split second, Alex knew the man understood every word they were saying.

Alex stared for a moment longer, but the NK kept his eyes on the bottom of the boat. Alex faced front again, but his senses were now split between potential dangers ahead, and those within their own boat.

The craft moved at around five knots, and even though the propulsion was a near-soundless jet, the push of water around the bullet-shaped bow still created tiny waves and made a small noise.

From time to time, Alex saw swells and eddies out on the oil-slick calm water, and he knew from their appearance that there were creatures below that were of considerable size. He and his HAWCs were ready, but even though the framework of the boat had exceptional strength, he knew a serious attack would destroy it.

Behind them, the shoreline was shrinking to little more than a line on the horizon, and their direction would lead them even further out into the wider sea and deeper water – and deeper water meant even bigger predators.

It was just a few moments later that Alex's senses prickled, warning him of an impending attack. But it was from close by.

Alex spun, his body able to react far faster than any normal human, and was in time to see the North Korean lunge at Bernadette Cooper and punch her with his stump. The protruding bone spiked her exposed cheek and would have been extremely painful – for both of them. But in the few seconds of her shock, Zhang grabbed her blade from its sheath.

The man yanked it free but didn't try to thrust it into Cooper or one of the HAWCs, instead going for the boat's ribbing, obviously hoping to penetrate it or at least severely damage it.

Cooper yelled, and the other HAWCs lunged, and before the man could stab the blade in, Alex moved almost in a blur and grabbed the North Korean's wrist.

Alex held it with one hand, his own expression deadpan, and the man stared back, his eyes momentarily blazing in surprise and anger. Then he grimaced as Alex exerted more pressure and the man's remaining hand bent back until there was an audible snap of bone. The blade dropped and Cooper snatched it up.

Alex stared into the man's face. "Remember when I said if you behaved we'd keep you alive?"

The man just stared, pain, fury, and defiance still in his eyes.

"You failed." In a single motion Alex yanked the man from his seat and threw him over the side and a good twenty feet out from the boat.

As the man spluttered to the surface, Gonzalez waved. "That's for the bullet, asshole."

Alex faced front as Cooper protested.

"He was an enemy prisoner," she said as she held a hand to her bleeding face. "He was an asshole, but there are laws, rules, about that."

Alex turned slowly. "Agent Cooper, you're lucky to not be sitting here with only one eye right now. Or be dead." Alex stared. "We're 420 million years before those laws and rules you mention even exist." He smiled, but there was zero humor in his expression. "Besides, he might make it to shore."

Ito grunted. "And now, I think, that solves a problem for us." The Japanese HAWC turned back to the front. "Because now we can dive."

Alex nodded. "That it does, Mr. Ito. Everyone, prepare to go deep."

He watched Cooper for a moment as she quickly placed a med-pad on her painful but thankfully superficial wound. Cooper winced. 'That little bastard,' she muttered.

She refused to turn to where they could still hear the man floundering in the water, and her expression was untroubled as she engaged her clear visor.

Alex turned back to the front and in the next few seconds, their visors all engaged, the craft sank below the dark water.

* * *

Lingyun Zhang came to the surface and tried to suck in a ragged breath, but instead drew in a lungful of the bath-warm salty water. He coughed, gagged, and then vomited.

He found it extremely hard trying to stay on the surface with only one hand – and a broken one at that – and the salty water made the seared skin on the end of his stump sting like fire.

He watched the American craft head away. And then it submerged. He stared in disbelief – not one of them had even looked back. He had been schooled all his life into believing Americans were weak and stupid, and he had expected them to give him a warning, and maybe tie him up. But not throw him over the side.

He turned about and saw the faintest line of land to the west. It must have been nearly a mile away, but there was no fear of hypothermia in the warm water. It would be hard, though, and his missing hand was an enormous liability that would tax his energy and speed. And that meant fatigue might catch him before he finally got there.

He began to swim in breaststroke style, and immediately had to adjust to the missing limb as he couldn't scoop water and made little forward progress.

It took ten minutes before he managed to craft a stroke that achieved maximum speed, and just as he was making good progress, he felt something surge past beneath him. He smiled; the Americans had come back. What he had learned about them had been correct after all, and they would pick him up.

Zhang would be happy to be tied up, and he would act defeated and groggy, and if it took an hour, or a day, or several, he knew another opportunity for sabotage would present itself. And next time, he would act faster.

The surge came again, closer this time; close enough to push him slightly off course. Lingyun Zhang ducked his head below the surface and looked down, hoping to catch a glimpse of the submarine boat.

The water was clear, and the sun was high enough in the sky now to create shawls of sunlight that hung down for at least fifty feet. But beyond that it became darker and then became a pitiless black.

Something passed underneath him just on the edge of the blackness, and a second or two later he felt the surge wave again. The thing had been moving fast, very fast, and he suddenly doubted the American craft had that capability.

Lingyun lifted his head, sucked in a deep breath, and then looked back down into the depths. As he watched, this time he saw something rising from the dark-blue gloom, something that grew in size. He only needed a few seconds more to know it wasn't the submarine boat. And it was coming up. Straight up.

He jerked his head up to scream uselessly for help.

The monstrous sea creature breached the surface and its gigantic jaws displaying huge, dagger-like teeth that reminded him of prison bars opened wide to take him in.

The colossal prehistoric eel was ribbed with cartilage rather than bone, which was one of the reasons it never fossilized. But it was a 100-foot-long pipe of solid muscle.

It hunted in the upper layers of the primitive sea, and a morsel like Zhang was a welcome gift.

The last thing Lingyun Zhang saw were those long, dagger-teeth prison bars closing around him, shutting out the light forever.

CHAPTER 25

Something must have gone wrong, Sam thought, for perhaps the hundredth time. How long had he been stranded here now, a year, ten? He had long ago lost track of time.

His huge body was shackled, and he was being dragged up toward the mountain pass by the Philistines.

His blond hair had been tied back, but it still hung almost to his waist, and his beard touched his chest. At six-foot-five he was tall back home, but here he was a giant among men, and his huge shoulders exploded outwards, carrying massive log-like arms that were currently tied at the wrists with two-inch-thick course rope.

He muttered to himself, lost in his own thoughts. Everything he had had been taken from him and destroyed, and he was dressed in only a loin cloth. Even the precious, tattered picture of his beloved Alyssa was gone, and he wondered if she even remembered him. Of course, in the here and now, she wouldn't exist for several thousand years.

How long, how long, how long?

He had stayed in this land because where else could he go? At this time, America was populated by many small native American nations. And England was still in its Bronze Age.

So, he had embedded himself with the Nazarites, and it had been peaceful. But only for a while. Because he quickly learned that the Philistines subjugated them and were a cruel and tormenting race. Many times he had defended the Nazarite shepherd folk from them.

For this, his reputation as their defender had grown. That had earned him the ire of the Saran, who had originally wanted him to join their army. When he had refused, forcibly, the Philistines had branded him an enemy and an outlaw.

His great size and strength made him outlier and outlaw both, and there was a bounty on his head. In the end the Saran had ordered that a dozen Nazarites would be killed per day unless Samson was handed over to them.

Sam knew that the Nazarites wanted to protect him, but he also knew they really had no choice. And so, he had finally allowed himself to be captured to avoid the Nazarites being massacred and having their villages burned to the ground.

They were brave, and shouted courageous words of support as he was led away, but they all knew that without him as their protector and their champion, they would soon be put under the whip and the sword.

The Philistines led Sam up through the steep and winding mountain pass of Ramath Lehi, miles away, at least, from the Nazarites.

Sam was lost in his thoughts, in his depression, and in his growing anger. How much longer must he endure this? Forever? Or until he was put to death?

He wondered how they would do it and what they would make of him – trying to behead him would not be easy as their blades would not be able to cut through the MECH endoskeleton that ran right throughout his internal muscular and skeletal system. And if they burned him alive, what would they think of the metallic skeleton left behind? They would think he was a demon.

Beside him, the closest soldiers jeered and tormented him every mile, and every step. He was more than a head taller than their biggest man, and they reveled in the fact that he was bound. They thought they had brought him low and rendered him harmless, but Sam had let them do this. He could break free when he wished, but he needed to be seen to be captured. Only then did the Philistines say they would leave the Nazarites in peace.

Their weapons were crude – spears, swords, maces, and other instruments that looked like clubs with bronze clenched fists or animal heads at their top.

And then from the scraps of their language he had learned, he overheard their leaders saying they planned to drop him off at the next garrison, and then turn back to punish the Nazarites for sheltering him, even though with him captured the Philistines had promised to leave them in peace. That was supposed to be their bargain.

Sam's body ran with blood from the pricks of their spears, and he wished he had Alex Hunter's rapidly healing metabolism. But as he didn't, he felt every blow, stab, and cut.

Thinking about Alex made him wonder if his friend was trying to find him. Or had he, too, been flung off into some alternate timeline and was also lost?

Lost, yes, I'm lost and maybe we all are. We fucked with time itself, and it turned around and bit our asses.

He shook his head at their folly as another stab hit him in the back of his shoulder. He didn't even bother turning. He knew his well-trained mind was finally fragmenting, and a part of him wanted it to give out, so he could just lapse into somnambulance, be a walking zombie. But that was a small part. Because there was another part of his mind that began to coil and burn and thrash. And that part demanded he stop them. Here. Now.

They were just moving through the Michmash pass, a narrowing in the mountainside rocks, when above them a storm that had been gathering for hours grew more ominous. As they reached the narrowing of the mountain pass, the sky boiled with clouds roiling in bilious shades of purple and black. Lightning surged, and so too did Sam's determination to end this. One way or another.

The next stab into his back grated against one of his ribs and was red-hot agony.

Then came a blow to the side of his brow with a metal club, making him see stars, and in his dizziness he went down on his knees. His brain seemed to short-circuit for a moment. Lighting and thunder exploded across the sky as the first of the raindrops began to fall – big, heavy, and blood-warm.

Perhaps it was bad luck or his MECH armor attracting the lightning, but the next jagged bolt came down to touch on him, jarring him, and blowing him along the ground.

Maybe the Philistines thought he was trying to escape, as they begin to use their clubs to beat him manically, and their spears to pin him down, piercing his flesh.

Then, as one large, skull-headed club came down toward his temple, Sam's reflexes took over, and his hand shot out, grabbing it in a grip the Philistine soldier could never break.

The bronze-headed mace had part of an animal's head on the end that looked like a jawbone, and just as Sam held it, another bolt of lightning forked down to touch it, and the discharge raced right throughout his entire metal alloy MECH skeleton, agonizing him from the inside.

Like an infuriated beast, Sam's rage exploded, and he rose up, using his enormous strength to break the ropes binding him. All reason, planning, and mercy had left him. All that remained was animal rage, and pain, and fury – and the desire for bloody revenge.

Sam turned to face the army, his eyes blood-red from the lightning strike, and he roared so loud and long he tasted blood in the back of his throat. Then he charged.

It was like a dream, or a nightmare. He didn't know how long he fought, but he swung the animal head club up down, left and right, smashing skulls and splintering bones.

His titanic strength overwhelmed the Philistine soldiers, and in the narrow pass they had nowhere to go. The massed troops surged forward from the rear, but the ones in front couldn't flee or even get out of the way of the giant berserker, who obliterated them, their smashed bodies piling up around him.

The rain fell heavily now, and beneath Sam's feet in that dark mountain pass, the ground was becoming a bloody mud, gritty with bone fragments and slippery with gore and viscera.

Grown men panicked, screamed and died, and some threw themselves off the cliff to die on rocks 500 feet below rather than face the monstrous wrath of Samson.

Eventually, the remnants of the army fled, leaving him alone. Breathing hard, Sam looked down at his hands and arms, coated in red, which the rain washed quickly away.

The storm broke as he walked out on a flat rock looking down over the valley and saw the retreating army.

The sky broke open, letting through a few sunbeams, and one of them touched the rock Sam stood upon. From far below he heard the Philistine shouts, and a few pointed at the huge warrior with the long beard and hair down his back staring out upon them.

A small part of him wanted to pursue them, but that quickly turned to revulsion at what he had done. He dropped the club and turned to the mountaintop.

Where to now?

He couldn't go back to the village, but he couldn't be so far from the Nazarites that he couldn't protect them.

Because he knew now that if the Saran couldn't punish him, he would punish the Nazarites instead.

He sucked in a deep breath and let it out. His body ached and he needed food and water. And somewhere to recover.

I'm an outcast, he thought miserably. *A man without a country, a home, or family. This is my life now.*

The giant HAWC turned to leave the path and make his way across the mountainside to where he knew the deep caves were.

CHAPTER 26

Soong-Li used her sleeve to mop her brow. The day had been long, hot, and energy sapping. Waves of humidity rolled over the glass-smooth water and made their bodies slick with perspiration.

She turned to look over her team. Most just dozed or stared at nothing. Even the indomitable Captain Junfeng Yang looked exhausted, and although he kept up a strong, set jaw and calm expression, his complexion was pale, and his eyes were rimmed with dark circles. The fight with the creature from the waters had drained him.

Many more times throughout the day, they had been buffeted by unseen things from below the water. And the times they had lost sight of land had made it even more unsettling – because the thought of going over the side would mean they were lost at sea with no shoreline to swim to.

Soong-Li knew the team needed to rest, stretch their legs, and even cook some warm food, and when she saw a spit of land coming up that didn't seem overgrown with jungle like everywhere else, plus had a small beach to pull in at, she made up her mind.

She had originally been determined to keep pushing ahead, and keep the Americans far behind them, but fatigue would cause mistakes, irritability, and maybe discord within the group. She felt she had no choice.

"Captain." She pointed. "Pull in at the beach. We take a rest for ninety minutes."

He nodded and turned the boat toward the small beach. From the team there were audible sighs and murmurs of relief. It was the right decision.

As they neared the spit of land they saw that it had many small shrubs like rotting broccoli, and the ground was marshy, covered in a kidney-shaped plant or lichen. Every now and then there was a tall trunk of something that resembled a lamppost, which was devoid of branches or leaves but instead had lumps of some sort of glistening, bumpy growth at its crown.

There would be little shade, but each of them had brought bright personal shelter cloths that doubled as blankets.

As they came in on the soft sand, Soong-Li issued orders, and the giant Quinfan Chen, plus Jin and Kwan, were tasked with scouting for safety. Tian Wu, their science officer, and Captain Yang would start a small fire and cook some of their rations. Jia Sun, the engineering physicist engineer, and Shuchang would desalinate and clean some water, and the useless bureaucrat Yan Guo could just stay out of their way and observe.

It didn't take them long to complete their tasks, and with one hour of their rest time remaining, the team spread their shelter cloths between the weird trees to create small tents they could rest under. Even Yan Guo managed to erect his own, and in seconds his snoring rang out over the small spit of land.

Soong-Li would take first watch, then hand it over to the captain for the final thirty minutes so she could get some rest. Already her eyes drooped and she felt the effects of the food, warmth, and bone tiredness making her feel sleepier than she ever had in her life.

The group settled down in only a few minutes, and Soong-Li squatted under her own shade cloth. She drew in a deep breath, smelling the stink of low tide, farty sulfur, and rotting plants. There was the constant background sound of insects singing as a droning *zumm*, which calmed and relaxed her. And, thankfully, it appeared mosquitoes and sandflies hadn't evolved to bother them. The water at the beachline was so calm there was only the lap of the tiniest waves. She struggled to stay awake.

Checking her watch, she saw she still had fifteen more minutes until she handed over the watch to Captain Yang. She sipped brackish water and blinked her eyes several times. She tried to focus on what their next steps were to be, and how much longer it would take them to reach their first package drop point. Provided they weren't capsized by the weird things below the surface, she felt that they were still on track to complete the task in a few days or at least in under a week.

She looked forward to being home, and as she thought this her mind fogged. One minute she was under her shade tent, and the next she was walking through a field of apple blossom trees in the park near her house. She smelled their scent on the cool crisp air and their bouquet was so heady she could almost taste it.

Soong-Li smiled in her sleep, not even realizing she had stepped out of reality, and into a pleasant dream.

* * *

The ancient slime mold in the top of the tree-like growth sensed the exhalations of the bipedal creature below it. For most of its life it spent its time sprouting buds that were tipped with a sticky and heavily scented nectar to attract the large insects to feast on them. Then when the insects sampled it, they became stuck, and the buds would lean in on themselves to enmesh the animal. Once done, the slime mold would fold them into its body, and slowly digest them using a highly corrosive acid.

However, if it detected a particularly large or injured animal close by, the massive blob-like entity, which was a cross between a plant, animal, and fungus, would go hunting.

Primitive dot eyes were arranged on the lower half of its form. It left the canopy of the tree and slid down the fibrous trunk. Though it couldn't yet *see* the animal underneath the barrier, it knew it was there, and knew it was large enough to sustain it for days.

It sped up, allowing its weight to pull it down quickly as the salty scent of its prey's perspiration stimulated its hunger.

* * *

The scream wrenched Soong-Li from her sleep so violently she felt her heart thump brutally in her chest, and the remnants of her beautiful dream of home exploded like a shattering window pane.

She quickly checked her watch and saw that she was late to rouse the captain. She jumped to her feet. There were people screaming, running, shouting, and she pulled her gun and began looking for the attacker, man or beast.

The screams came from Jia Sun, their mouse-like physics engineer, who hopped from foot to foot, her mouth wide and still emitting the siren-like din as she pointed at the shade canopy where Yan Guo was sheltering.

"*It killed him.*" She shrieked.

Soong-Li raced over and skidded to a stop before it, pulling his shade cloth away. Beside her now was Captain Yang and then Quinfan Chen and the two young soldiers. They all pointed their guns at what they beheld. But no one pulled the trigger as confusion reigned as to what exactly they were seeing, and what they could do about it.

Yan Guo still sat with his back against the strange tree trunk. But sliding down and now covering one side of his body and half his head was some sort of gigantic blob of jelly. To add to the nightmare, several stalks seemed to be growing from it, and the black dots in each stalk probably meant they were a simple form of eye.

"What is this . . . abomination?" Soong-Li yelled. She was aware her voice sounded like a tremulous quaver. "You, biologist, tell me," she demanded.

Tian Wu, her hands up over her mouth, spoke between her fingers. "I think . . . I think it's some sort of slime mold."

Yan Guo's legs moved languidly, and they saw the jelly slide lower over him, covering his left side completely and inching over his face and head down to nose level. It also covered the tree trunk, locking him in place.

Then the man's mouth inched open, and he let out a low animal moan.

"*Ach*, he's still alive." Captain Yang grimaced.

Behind the layer of jelly, they could see that Guo's eyes were open, but the organs weren't there anymore; the eye sockets were just dark holes surrounded by red.

"I think it is . . . digesting him," Tian squeaked.

"While he's still alive," Captain Yang whispered, not able to hide his horror.

They all looked back at the man and saw that Yan Guo's clothing on his right side was also gone and the now-exposed skin was beginning to redden as it, too, was dissolved. The blob slid down over his mouth and chin and his moan was shut off.

"Digesting him," Soong-Li repeated, feeling the burn of stomach bile rise to bite the back of her throat. "Get him out." She turned away.

Yang issued orders and pointed for Quinfan Chen to grab the man's legs, being careful not to touch the advancing blob of mucus dripping down over his body, as it was obviously living, and very acidic.

The huge man tugged on Yan Guo, and then tugged again, but the glutinous mass proved far stronger and more solid than he expected – it held firm to the tree trunk, and also to its prize.

As the huge man dragged some of the body out, Yan Guo's legs wriggled, and the fingers on his only exposed hand clenched and unclenched.

"Oh no, he's still in there." Jia Sun blanched and spun away, holding a hand over her mouth, but it did no good as a stream of vomit sprayed from between her fingers.

Tian shook her head. "No, I think it is just involuntary muscle spasms." She stared. "The slime mold must have liquified the contents of his skull by now."

"He will not come out." Quinfan Chen let go of the legs.

"The man is dead," Yang said softly.

Quinfan Chen turned. "But can we be sure, if he still moves . . .?"

Soong-Li lifted her sidearm and fired into Guo – once into the head, and once into the heart. It was like striking a side of beef at an abattoir, as the body took the bullets with only a slight jerk as the rounds impacted the flesh.

She turned to the big soldier. "*Now*, the man is dead."

Quinfan Chen blinked a few times and stood upright. Soong-Li holstered her gun and turned to Captain Yang, who nodded to her.

Soong-Li turned back to the thing engulfing the body of Yan Guo. Her mouth turned down. "If we had spare fuel and the time, I would burn this revolting mess to ashes." She turned about, spotting more of the blobs in the branches of the other tree-like growths. It seemed they were lucky Yan Guo was the only one of them caught.

"*Yech*; I think there will be no more rest time. We're leaving."

The group backed away from the revolting sight and began to gather their equipment, readying themselves for departure. Soong-Li turned back and saw the young soldier, Kwan Myung, staring, watching the living blob of jelly, which seemed untroubled by the bullets and simply continued inching lower over Guo's body. The young man's face was pale and that made his pimples stand out. Already they were worse than ever, probably due to the grimy humidity coating his skin.

"Hurry," she said, and the man snapped out of his fugue and headed to their boat.

I hate this place, Soong-Li thought again as she gripped her jade amulet briefly and then stepped back and checked her wristwatch.

"*Madam*," Captain Yang barked.

She turned.

"On the sensors," he said and pointed into the distance. "They're coming."

"Of course they are." Soong-Li sighed, knowing the American craft might be faster than theirs. She turned about and saw the stand of plant growth a little further up the headland. She spun back to the body of Yan Guo, still being engulfed.

She couldn't outrun them, and a firefight would suit the Americans more than her team. Instead, perhaps she could slow or surprise them in some other way.

Her eyes narrowed as a plan formed. The useless official might be of use after all. She could set up a dummy camp and create a focal point for the approaching Americans. They would head in to investigate while her group waited in the tree line ready to spring an ambush.

It would work, and at a minimum, kill some of the Americans, dent their capabilities, and allow her team to get far ahead of them again. At best, they might be able to kill them all. Anything was possible now.

"Captain," she said. "Light a small cooking fire next to Yan Guo. Place an empty rifle next to him." She pointed along the coast. "Then, we move to the trees there and wait for our pursuers to arrive. When they investigate, we shoot to kill."

Captain Yang looked from Yan Guo to the trees along the spit of sand. "Yes, that might work."

"Good." Quinfan lifted a spear in each of his large hands. "I did not bring these just for fishing."

Soong-Li paused. "One more thing. Rig grenades to go off. Many of them together." She lifted her head. "Can we remote-detonate?"

"Yes, of course," Yang replied.

"Do it," Soong-Li said, and turned back to keep watch over the water. "Now, hurry."

Yang and his soldiers quickly constructed what looked from a distance like a campsite around the rapidly dissolving carcass of their former party official. She was sure that from out on the water it would look like the man was resting, while waiting for his tea to boil or food to cook.

They also set up some of the other shelters close by to make it look like he wasn't alone. Then Soong-Li had them quickly move their boat across to the stand of bushes on a narrow peninsula just around a small bay. They dragged the raft up and over the mud to the other side to wait on the water for their escape.

The scientists waited by the boat and the fighting group returned and concealed themselves in the slimy plant growth, waiting to spring their trap.

Soong-Li gritted her teeth and said a small prayer that her soldiers could identify the American team leader and perhaps take him and a few others out. The Americans would undoubtedly be professionals, but the surprise attack should cause enough confusion in their ranks to make them all vulnerable for a few seconds.

She didn't know why, but she enjoyed this part of the mission – a hunt was always entertaining, and after watching that sniveling Yan Guo be eaten, she felt she and the team needed some uplifting entertainment.

Soong-Li turned to look back at the opposite bay through the trees and saw her two science officers hunkering down already. She made a guttural sound in her throat – at least some of them needed entertainment.

"They come," Yang said.

She lifted her field glasses and narrowed her eyes as she stared out into the distance. Through the heat vapor rising from the sea she could just make out a growing dot rising on the horizon as if surfacing.

She lowered her glasses. "Quickly now."

The four soldiers moved into position. Quinfan was a dozen paces closer than the rest of them, and even though he had his rifle, he kept it over his shoulder and instead carried three spears in his hand. His mighty arm could throw them a great distance and he boasted he could hit a sparrow's eye from a hundred paces. But even he knew that for him, closer was better, so that his spears retained their full impact and penetrative power.

"Wait until they are ashore," Soong-Li said. "I want accurate kill shots."

Yang nodded and spoke some soft commands to his team.

"Should we not just shoot to injure them?" Shuchang asked. "Maybe it will slow them down even more if they have to tend to their wounded," he added.

"It will slow them down even more if they are dead." Soong-Li snorted softly. "The Americans know why we are here, and they will shoot to kill." She turned way. "So will we."

In the distance the torpedo-shaped craft slowed.

"They've spotted Yan Guo's body." Soong-Li smiled. "Here they come."

CHAPTER 27

"It's a camp," Gonzalez said as he magnified the scene with his visor lenses and peered through the rising heat mist. "We got 'em."

Their submersible had come to the surface when they detected the radiation and just glided slowly on the silky, warm water. Alex looked along the shoreline, already spotting the camp, but seeing no movement.

Bernadette Cooper checked the radiation readout again. "It's weird. I'm getting a high readout, but not from that area."

"Are the bombs there or not?" Alex asked. "They're our priority."

"Yes, somewhere," she replied.

"I think it is probably a trap," Ito said.

"Undoubtedly a trap," Alex replied. "But we need those bombs, at all costs. So we've got to gamble." He turned. "Stop the boat."

Ito did as asked, and the boat glided to a standstill on the glass-smooth sea.

"Going in is high-risk if it's an ambush," Cooper remarked. "Sensor says the devices are in there somewhere, but I can't pinpoint them."

"They expect us to bring the boat in so they can spring

their trap." Alex said. "That's why you and I are going for a little swim." Alex turned. "Ito, Gonzalez, cover us. We'll swim in and come up next to the camp. Eyes out for snipers."

"Shit." Cooper sucked in a breath and engaged her visor, and then blinked a few times, either from nerves or to clear her vision. "Here goes my field-of-fire test swimming in the aquatic suit." She chuckled nervously.

"Just stay close to me," Alex said. He engaged his own visor. "Voice check."

Cooper nodded. "Loud and clear."

Alex took one last look at the shoreline, and then slipped over the side. Cooper did the same.

Below the surface the water was clear, and if they weren't in their suits they would have felt the tropical warmth. Alex allowed himself to sink down about ten feet, and noticed that already small ammonoids were bobbing toward him like floating, striped lanterns in a hazy blue sky.

Below them the water was probably only about fifty feet deep, with a sandy bottom, all crisscrossed by creatures that had been sifting the sea floor for a meal or sliding past on a large gastropod foot.

Alex pointed toward the shore and Cooper gave him a thumbs-up. The pair then engaged their propulsion units and traveled like a pair of torpedoes to the beach. As they closed in on the shore the water got muddier, reducing their vision to about a foot, and then Alex felt the bottom under his hand. He reached out to grab Cooper and stop her.

"We've lost vision, and we don't want to swim into a snag. It's shallow enough to walk. Give me a minute." Alex carefully raised his head above the surface and slowly surveyed the shoreline.

All was clear, and he stood. The water came up to his waist. He tapped Cooper and she also stood, and then the pair waded up onto the muddy shoreline.

"No movement," Alex said into his mic. "Any unfriendlies?"

"Nothing. All quiet on the scopes. But too warm in there to detect anything on the thermal," Gonzalez replied. "Sleeping Beauty is still out cold."

"Why is he alone?" Alex asked. "Heading up the beach now."

"Roger that. We got your back," Gonzalez said.

Alex retracted his visor and headed up toward the North Korean camp. Normally he would have liked his partner to spread a little wider, but not being a HAWC, Cooper needed cover, so he kept her in close. She retracted her visor as well and sniffed the air.

"Swamp," she said simply. "And something else."

As they approached the campsite, he could see it was empty, plus the guy they had assumed was sleeping wasn't a guy anymore – he was covered in a massive blob of jelly that had oozed down over his body. Alex stopped.

Beneath the jelly they could just make out a red, and rapidly degrading, skeleton.

"*Holy shit*," he whispered.

Up closer now he saw that someone had placed a hat on top of the mess, and from all over the glutinous blob multiple eyestalks like those on a snail slowly lifted and bent toward them.

"What the hell is that thing?" Alex asked.

Cooper cursed softly. "If I had to take a guess, I'd say it's probably some sort of primitive slime mold. Or an advanced one that somehow got cancelled out by evolution."

"Thank God for that," Alex said.

He turned slowly. "Gonzalez, nothing but bodies and ghosts here, do you have eyes on—"

The two bullets smashed into Alex – both were direct hits on his chest armor, pushing him back a step.

Cooper crouched and Alex spun.

"Deploy shielding," he barked.

His suit had reacted automatically after the attack and deployed the combat shielding, and would also throw armor plating over his face so his vision would come from the quad lenses.

But as Cooper wasn't attacked, her own reaction times were a second or two slower and in the split second before her shields were fully deployed Alex sensed the incoming projectiles – right toward her.

The first spear or lance was headed directly for Cooper's face, and Alex's body took over. His heart sped up to nearly 200 beats per minute and the world slowed around him.

His movements were so fast, to everyone else he would have moved in a blur as he lunged, shooting out an arm and knocking aside the first six-foot-long, needle-tipped spear.

The second was coming right behind it, but this one he caught from the air, and in one fluid motion, he spun and threw it back at the deliverer with every ounce of titanic strength he could muster.

By now Cooper's armor and face shielding had deployed. But just as Alex released the projectile, he sensed rather than heard the electronic *ping* of a remote device, and their world turned red hot and blinding as they were both lifted and blown backwards through the air.

* * *

Captain Yang counted down the seconds, giving the pair of American soldiers another few feet until they topped the small rise and entered the dummy campsite. The larger of the Americans kept himself between the North Koreans and the smaller figure, but Yang had a clear shot at him and focused his scope on the center of the man's chest. He knew his men would be doing the same, except for Quinfan who would be readying himself for a spear throw. Yang bet his giant was itching to take them on hand-to-hand. He half-smiled. "Fire," he said softly.

The North Koreans opened fire, and Yang managed a direct hit while someone else scored a partial strike.

Out in front, Quinfan stepped away from his hiding spot, a spear in each hand, and drew his huge arm back. He threw the spear, immediately changing hands with the spare and throwing that as well. The first traveled in a direct line toward the smaller soldier's pale face.

Yang smiled as he watched it all unfold as if in slow motion. His first bullet strike was better than the second and the high-velocity impact with the tungsten carbide penetration tip should have cut through any armor the man wore. Yang expected the American to have been killed or at least knocked down. But instead, he only took a single backward step.

Then, just as Quinfan's first spear arrived, the bigger man moved impossibly fast and knocked the projectile aside as if it were nothing, and then, still at a lightning speed, he darted in front of the smaller soldier.

Incredibly, he reached out to grab the second spear from the air before it struck home. Yang's smile vanished as he saw that the American wasn't finished. Instead, he pirouetted, and then launched the spear back at Quinfan, and much harder and faster than their own giant had thrown it.

The spear caught Quinfan along the top of his shoulder, leaving him with a painful gouge in his flesh. Then, like a giant, tantruming child, Quinfan stamped his foot to roar his surprise and anger.

Yang stared as he heard Soong-Li curse. The two younger soldiers were dumbstruck, and for the first time Yang felt that engaging these American soldiers head-on might not have been such a good battle tactic after all.

He turned to Soong-Li. "We should leave, now."

She gritted her teeth in anger, and her words came hissing out. "Detonate, now. Everyone else, fall back."

Yang lifted the remote and pressed the tiny button. The entire camp exploded in a huge orange cloud of heat and debris. He didn't wait to see the results but was confident the pair would now either be in pieces or severely injured.

The group pulled back, all except Quinfan, who lifted his remaining spear and started to make his way along the stinking beach to where the Americans had been blown out into the water.

Just then, he dropped to his belly and began to crawl along the brush line. Yang suspected he had caught sight of one of their adversaries. Was it possible?

"Soldier Quinfan," Yang hissed. "*Fall in.*"

The giant soldier ignored him and continued to snake closer to the Americans' position.

"*Captain,*" Soong-Li ordered.

Yang looked from her to Quinfan, and then made a guttural sound in his throat and followed her. But he moved slowly, still watching the burning camp with interest. He guessed Quinfan was aggrieved at taking the hit and wanted some payback.

The Americans had to be injured, perhaps mortally, after being within the grenades' blast radius. Maybe letting Quinfan have some fun might be worthwhile. And his success would motivate their team to greater efforts.

Yang got to the line of mushy plant growth that his group had passed through and turned to squat and watch.

* * *

Alex spun to grab Cooper, getting in front of her as the blast spread over the camp and shore area. In the blink of an eye they were lifted by the percussion wave to be thrown twenty feet out into the sea.

Their red-hot armor sizzled as it made contact with the water, and debris rained down over them.

Alex immediately got to his feet and dragged Cooper up with him. "You okay?"

She placed a hand on his shoulder to steady herself, but nodded. "Head's ringing like a bell. But I'm okay." She shook her head to clear it. "Guess that answers the question of whether it was a trap or not."

"Anyone got eyes on them?" Alex asked as he retracted his face shielding.

"Shots came out of the jungle about a quarter click north-ward along the coast. No attackers have reappeared, so they must still be in there," Ito said.

Alex turned. "Or they're behind that line of shrubs." He looked out along the shoreline that stretched away into the humid mist. "Must be water on the other side."

"They wanted to slow us down. Maybe take us out," Cooper said. "We need to get after them." She began to wade up out of the water, but Alex grabbed her.

"Hold on. There might be more surprises waiting for us up there." Alex checked the shoreline again. "Not sure we can go around. We might have to follow them overland." He turned to her. "Wait here." He strode out of the water and spoke over his shoulder. "Ito, I'll scout what's over the rise. If it's clear, be ready to bring the boat in. We might have to drag it up and over. Give me three minutes."

Alex left the water. He knew he was taking a chance but banked on the North Koreans already having departed. If they were still there hiding, he knew he'd run into a hail of bullets, but he needed to clear the field for his HAWCs.

Alex began to run along the beach.

* * *

Yang pulled out his field glasses and focused in closer on the large, body-armored American coming over the rise. Around him he saw that the once-slimy sand was now crisp on the surface from the heat of the blast, and the flying shrapnel had given it a pocked, moon-like appearance.

The man's armor also looked singed, but undamaged. The American headed straight to where Quinfan was hiding, and just as he came abreast of him, Quinfan rose up.

The American was a tall man at maybe six-two, but Quinfan was easily close to seven feet. And for someone so big, he was incredibly fast – the spear was already in his hands and coming forward to jam into the only exposed area on the American – his face. Before the American could react, the lance had already found its target, and all the man was able to do was move enough so the needle-sharp tip didn't enter his eye.

However, Yang was not surprised to see the weapon still went in hard, dragging a deep line of fire across the flesh of his cheek. It wasn't the desired kill strike, but enough to make any warrior flinch.

"Good," Yang grunted. "Now finish him."

But even as Quinfan went to pull the spear back and take another thrust, surprisingly, the American's hand flashed up to grab the spear.

The huge and powerful Quinfan tried to press it further, but his adversary held it in an unbreakable grip, and then brought his other forearm down on it like a club, unbelievably, breaking it in two.

Yang was surprised but satisfied that Quinfan was already bringing up his other hand, which was holding his revolver. He fired repeatedly into the American's torso, until his magazine was empty. But the soldier's armor was superior to anything the North Korean had ever seen, and if the shots even bothered him, he didn't show it.

Instead, the American used his other hand to grab the huge Quinfan by the neck. And lift him.

Yang knew from his medical sheet that Quinfan weighed in at around 300 pounds, but the American extended his arm and raised him half a foot above the sand.

"*Impossible*," Yang breathed. As he watched, the American then carried Quinfan backwards – with one hand. Quinfan continued to batter at his adversary's head with the empty gun, making a clanging noise on the helmet that echoed across the empty beach.

Yang blinked. He thought he could see the man's furious eyes shining silver, and even from his place of concealment he heard the American's animal growl as he picked up speed and then rammed the giant Quinfan into one of the large hairy tree trunks.

In a flash, the American brought the broken end of spear he was still carrying up and jammed it into Quinfan's shoulder, pushing it in hard – piercing him, and nailing him to the tree.

Rather than pain, a shocked expression filled Quinfan's face. He roared and cursed and tried to free himself, but the American just stepped back, his eyes calm. And then he looked up.

Yang followed his gaze and noticed a slight movement from above. He lifted his eyes further to the tree's top, where a three-foot-wide blob of mucus had dislodged itself from the sticky canopy and begun to gently ooze down the trunk toward the North Korean's pumpkin-sized head.

Quinfan stopped his struggling to look up, saw the approaching abomination, and must have remembered what happened to Yan Guo. He then began to curse and wriggle furiously on the spike.

The American reached up to touch the end of the spear, checking it was stuck in firmly. He smiled grimly into Quinfan's face and said something.

Yang lifted his rifle with thoughts of either saving his man, or of avenging his death, flooding his mind. Captain Yang watched for a second or two more, his mouth hanging open in disbelief. The American had lifted his man as if he weighed nothing. And then pinned him to a tree like a collector would a butterfly on a corkboard.

Logic took over – if the man could survive a bomb blast, multiple point-blank bullets and take down Quinfan so easily, Yang knew that taking him on would be folly.

He lowered his rifle. Besides, taking a shot would reveal his position. And then be suicide. And if there were more soldiers like this American on their boat, then his entire team would be at risk of total mission failure.

The American glanced up at the lowering blob and then down to Quinfan's face. Then he smirked, and turned away.

"Thank you for your service, Quinfan." Yang carefully withdrew to the other side of the spit and to their waiting boat.

CHAPTER 28

Fifty miles north of the HAWCs' position

Casey Franks stood with her hands on her hips and stared out over the water. Brandt came and stood beside her.

"Well, we either double back, or we keep going," Brandt said.

"Go back? To what?" Casey briefly turned to him, and then shook her head. "Ain't no going back now, big guy."

She crouched, picked up a short stick, and smoothed out an area of mud. "This is what I think." She began to draw. "We've turned up here, probably a good way north of our team. We know, or we strongly believe, the NKs are coming at us, as they head toward what'll one day be Texas and New Mexico."

Brandt crouched on his haunches, his forearms resting on huge thighs. "And our guys are right behind them."

"Maybe." Casey drew more small circles in the mud. "You and I still have comms, which tells me that over short range we're good. So, we head south. Either we'll pick up the comms of our team as we get closer . . ." she looked up, ". . . or we run into the NKs, who will be sandwiched between us."

"And we slow 'em down or kill 'em all." Brandt smiled grimly. "Now that's a plan I like."

Brandt stood and dropped the raft from his shoulders. "Time to get wet." He immediately set about constructing the craft. "Stick close to shore, or head out?"

"Head out about half a mile. We'll stay in sight of the shore, but we'll have a greater comms range if we're on open water." Casey looked out over the sea. "We'll head in if we encounter shit weather, or run into a giant, pissed-off local."

It only took the huge HAWC fifteen minutes to set up their boat, and together they pushed it into the murky, knee-deep water. As they did so, Brandt bent and shot out a hand, then lifted something that looked like a weird crab-insect. Its many legs crawled in the air and a tail with a crescent-shaped pincer on the end flicked beneath it, splashing him.

He held it up. "I'm eating this guy later." He tossed it into the boat.

Casey grinned, looked down, and then jammed her foot down on something. She reached into the water and lifted a strange creature that looked like a hard-shelled, shovel-headed animal, with a fish tail. It flipped madly in her hand.

"Make that two. Not sure what this sucker is, but you can't live on rations alone, right?" Her MECH hand compressed, crushing the thing's head. It immediately stopped moving and she tossed it into the boat next to Brandt's scorpion-lobster.

Together the pair climbed in and Brandt started up the propulsion system. Then they quickly maneuvered away from the shoreline. It was after around thirty minutes of constant traveling that Casey looked back to see that the land was just a line in the distance.

"This will be far enough for now," she said.

Brandt nodded and adjusted their course, moving them south and parallel to the shore. The smell of brine from the warm water, and the sun now high in the sky, could have made them think they were on some sort of fishing holiday instead of in an ancient period on Earth, long before even dinosaurs ruled.

Casey worked hard to stop from dozing, but then eased up straighter and frowned. She turned her head, listening.

"Hey, you hear that?" she asked.

Brandt cut the drives and they glided in a drift for a moment. The sound came again.

"*Jezuz*. Yeah, I do," he replied.

It came again. Louder and closer this time – it was a low moan, and so deep and pervasive, it seemed to go right through their bodies to vibrate their bones.

"What. The Fuck. Was that?" Brandt asked.

Casey slowly shook her head. "No idea, man."

The sound came again, and she looked over the side.

"But I think it came from down there."

* * *

Alex finally reached the top of the spit and saw the tracks where the NK boat had been dragged up and over to another small beach on the other side. They were already gone, but he doubted they were far away, and he walked back out through the heavy growth and waved at Cooper.

He touched his mic. "Bring the boat in, we need to go overland."

Cooper joined him, walking past the huge NK impaled by the spear. The slime mold was nearly on him, and the once aggressive giant implored her to help him, perhaps knowing that the male soldier would give him nothing.

Before she could even speak, Alex shook his head. He then turned about and then whistled. In seconds DOG had unfolded, gone over the side of the boat and came up on shore.

Alex looked down at the metallic face. "Scan for traps."

DOG shot off into the jungle.

"Your face," she said. "That needs treatment."

Alex reached up and touched the deep rip that ran from the corner of his mouth to just under his ear.

He felt the pain, but not from the wound, as it had already stopped bleeding. But as his fingers alighted on it, the wound sizzled, and small puffs of steam rose from it. He clenched his jaws to ride out the pain.

"What's happening?" Bernadette Cooper frowned and stepped forward. "Your wound. It's, it's, *healing.*"

In seconds his flesh had smoothed, leaving just a purple scar. But even that was beginning to lighten out.

He lowered his hand. "I'm a fast healer," Alex replied.

"That's not possible," she said, staring.

"And neither is time travel." He turned away as DOG came out of the line of jungle and then back along the length of slimy sand.

The android stopped and sat in front of Alex, and he looked into its eyes. Tor sent him images and impressions, straight into his mind.

He half smiled. "I know, I know, I should have sent you first." After another moment Alex nodded, and then turned to Cooper. "They've gone. No more traps. But we need to pick up speed – we're running out of time."

CHAPTER 29

Soong-Li had directed her boat out into the open sea toward what she had calculated was the first of the future petroleum beds. Each bomb had to be dropped in the right place at the right depth for maximum long-term corruption of the environment.

In another hour they were coming up on the first drop point when Jin Baek called out that he saw land in the distance.

She turned to glance at the young soldier, and then with her brow creased faced where he pointed – there should have been nothing but a 200-foot-deep warm and shallow sea in front of them for hundreds of miles. In her pre-mission research she had read about the collision of the super islands to form Laurussia, and another island called Baltica bearing down on the landmass. It would smash into it eventually, and then in another 100 million years be torn apart again to one day become northern and eastern Europe. But those mini continents should be hundreds of miles out in the center of the sea.

She put a hand over her eyes and squinted, and then she saw that Jin was right. On the horizon was a dark line that could only be land.

Soong-Li was confused as to what she should do next. There should be nothing there. Not a continent. Not a super island. Not even a small island. And not in a place where the first of the nuclear packages was to be lowered.

Have we got it wrong? she wondered.

She couldn't think for a moment – should she just set the first bomb on that land instead, given it was in her target location? Would that have the same effect as dropping the bomb in the sea?

Captain Yang had slowed their boat, awaiting her directions. She leaned toward Shuchang.

"That land shouldn't be here," she whispered.

He nodded and turned to her. "Neither should we. But we are." He tilted his head. "It is on our path. And the detonations would be easier to organize and accomplish if we only had to deposit the devices on land."

"Agreed." Soong-Li sat back and then faced Yang. "It is on our route. We will investigate."

Yang opened up the throttle and the small boat kicked forward again.

It was around fifteen minutes before they could make out the geography of the unexpected shoreline a little more clearly. There were lumped rocks, some with jagged edges, and in most areas strange jungle came down to touch the water. Other places consisted of just barren, volcanic-looking stone.

But what caught their attention and made them all stare was what sat just to one side of a massive up-thrusting of rock.

"Is that a building?" Shuchang scoffed in disbelief. "That can't be a building."

Soong-Li held a pair of field binoculars to her eyes and just stared. "And yet, I think it is. And not just some sort of mud hut. But large architecture." She continued to look at the structure as they approached, noting its size and strange form until it vanished behind a hill.

They maneuvered their boat in toward one side of a swampy beach, which featured black mud with twisted roots, and rotting plant, fungus, or other material hanging limply from skeletal-looking branches.

The miasmic smell was of sulfur and decomposition. Soong-Li stayed in the boat as Jin Baek and Kwan Myung leaped out to try and haul the vessel up onto firmer ground. It was no easy task, and even a dozen feet from the water they sank in up to their knees and the sucking mud fought them every step of the way. If not for the pair's youthful energy they might have all needed to get out into the mud. Or leave the boat for the tide.

Ten minutes later, the men had tugged the boat high enough for them to disembark. The mud here had dried and compacted and was obviously above the tide line. Tracks showed that various creatures had been crisscrossing the shore, but thankfully, they all seemed to be small.

Soong-Li put a hand over her eyes. Just up from the beach there was a rising slope and beyond that she expected there was around a mile of terrain to cover before they came to the structure they'd seen. She had no idea what it could be, but this island or mini continent was either in their way, or *was* their way, and the first of the nuclear devices could be planted here.

"I feel . . ." Shuchang turned slowly, ". . . that we're being watched."

"Or perhaps it's just your nerves," said Soong-Li scornfully, but felt the same prickle on the back of her neck. She briefly turned about. "And if we are, and whatever it is leaves us alone to do our work, we could not care."

"Will they leave us alone, though?" Shuchang replied, and turned to her. "Think about it; if there are sentient beings living here and they are curious about us, or what we're doing, they may investigate what we leave behind. And then . . ."

Soong-Li froze. She hadn't thought of that.

Her mind conjured another race, perhaps some sort of human being that had evolved here. Or maybe they were giants like those in ancient Korean legends. But Shuchang was right; with intelligence comes curiosity. Maybe there were creatures here curious enough to find, dismantle, or destroy the devices.

She made up her mind. "Then we have no choice but to protect our interests. If there are beings here, we need to find them, and perhaps conquer them."

"What?" Captain Yang looked confused. "This is not our mission."

She rounded on him. "Our mission is the successful planting and detonation of the devices. That cannot be achieved if there are potential saboteurs close by." She lifted her chin. "Besides, whoever they were, they might have technology or weapons that would benefit our Great Leader," she rationalized. "Whatever desirable technological assets they have must be obtained." She was about to turn away when she looked back. "Before they are all incinerated in the blast, that is."

Yang exhaled loudly and turned away from her.

Soong-Li then faced her team. She needed someone to watch their boat. They could have deflated it and packed it down to bring with them, but as it was now mud-caked and damp, and they didn't have the hulking Quinfan to rely on, it would require at least two of them to carry – a burden she didn't want when they might need all the hands they could get.

She looked at each of them – she needed her soldiers and her science officer. The only people she could dispense with were her friend Shuchang, and Jia Sun, their engineering physicist. That made sense as they would be leaving the bombs in the boat for now.

Regardless, she felt she had no choice. She ordered both of them to stay behind. The advantage was that the team was now small enough to move quickly in and out of the jungle.

Shuchang looked at her forlornly, obviously not happy about being left behind. Soong-Li saw his expression, sighed, and then walked a few paces from the group and called him over.

"I have a bad feeling about this," he said softly.

"You have a bad feeling about everything." She smiled. "You'll be safe here."

"No, no, I'm not worried for myself." He tilted his head. "I'm worried about you."

"Foolish man," she said, but she liked that he worried about her. "I'll come back. I'll always come back." She glanced over her shoulder at the group and then back to Shuchang. "I want you here where I know you'll be safe."

"Really?" He gave her a crooked smile. "That makes me feel a little better."

She reached out to grab the front of his shirt, wanting to pull him closer, but knew the others would perhaps see it as weakness and mock her.

After a moment, she just released him. "Be here when I return."

"I'll wait forever," he whispered.

Soong-Li turned away and rejoined the group. She then directed them forward, ordering Kwan to cover their rear and putting Jin out at point. Though he used his long blade to hack a path, the plant life was soft, in some places having the consistency of overcooked asparagus rather than hard bark.

Going uphill, it didn't take long for the ground to dry beneath their feet. Living things scurried in the weird pulpy foliage around them, rarely revealing themselves, and the few times they did, the creatures looked like slimy, shovel-headed alligators, or long-legged cockroaches.

One larger creature, which must have been twenty feet long with six legs, an arrow head, and shark-like teeth, needed more forceful encouragement to move on, but finally left with a few bullet holes in it.

Tian Wu tried her best to identify many of the species, but some were too strange, or too different from anything she knew, and she mostly just shook her head and gave up. Perhaps seeing them with flesh on their bones instead of just their fossilized fragments crushed between layers of shale had confused her.

It was when they were only a few hundred feet from the top of the hill that they came across a path, wending upward but at an angle. They agreed it must have been an animal track, but what was more interesting were the prints in the drying soil.

"What made these?" Soong-Li sked.

Tian examined them. "So many. But from a single creature with many legs, I think," she said. "Look, there are more."

The scientist followed the tracks for a dozen paces as the group watched. She pointed at one spot on the ground and then another. "A six-foot gait. Three-inch-deep indentations in hard-packed earth. Possibly means an animal close to nine feet tall and weighing around 500 pounds." She looked up. "And there were several of them."

"They're footprints?" Jin said incredulously. "They just look like holes."

Tian looked up. "Ever seen the marks a crab leaves on the sand?" She stood. "Like that."

"So it's a giant crab?" Soong-Li couldn't believe it, and frowned, trying to imagine a giant shelled creature standing upright and walking up the path.

"Might make for a fine dinner." Captain Yang followed them for a few paces. "Unless there are so many, we end up being their dinner."

"That's why we brought the army." Soong-Li turned. "So we don't end up anything's dinner, yes?"

Yang's face was deadpan. "Tell that to Yan Guo."

Soong-Li narrowed her eyes. "Yan Guo was lazy, unobservant of his surroundings, and a dead weight. He got what he deserved." She turned away.

The group followed the path for several more minutes, and none could shake the feeling of being watched. But when they moved into a slight clearing on the hill, they stopped and stared in confusion at what lay before them. And their confusion turned to disgust.

Soong-Li balled her fists. "What is this abomination I am seeing here?"

"It is, uh, I have no idea." Yang turned to the other soldiers. "Cover me." He walked carefully forward, gun up, and eventually stopped before the first of the strange things.

The captain stood there for several seconds just staring up. In front of him, and all across the slope, were things that looked like scarecrows. But they weren't just old clothing or animal hides stuffed with straw; instead they were the desiccating bodies of animals, with either their bones pushing through the skin, or their internal meat drying out completely inside their exoskeletons. And they were all spread-eagled on wooden crosses.

Yang prodded the one before him with the barrel of his rifle. He half-turned. "It's dead. They're all dead."

"I hope so." Soong-Li approached, the rest of the team behind her.

She looked around at the line of jungle surrounding the clearing and then back up at the animal directly in front of them.

It looked like some sort of lizard with tufted hair on its back and limbs. The face had a short snout with powerful jaws, plus conical teeth indicating it must have been some sort of carnivore.

"It's big," she said. "It must have weighed close to 500 pounds when it was alive. Plenty of meat. Why leave it here?"

"Maybe they are air-drying the meat," Jin Baek said. "My uncle does this with duck meat."

"These are no ducks." She turned briefly to him, and then pointed to another of the scarecrow-like effigies. "And does he leave the meat out to rot down to the bone like this?" she sneered.

Jin shook his head.

"This is proof of intelligent life; brutal, but intelligent." Soong-Li exhaled slowly. "And I care less about why it was done, and more about who it was done by."

"Something we haven't seen yet," Yang replied.

"Obviously." Soong-Li stepped back. "Captain, be on alert."

"I am, always." He gazed steadily at her.

Soong-Li paused for a moment as the group headed off. She turned slowly, scanning the stinking, fungus-like jungle. Her neck prickled again, and she narrowed her eyes.

"I know you're in there," she whispered.

After a few more seconds, she hurried after her team.

* * *

The hill got steeper. They continued to follow the track, which now took them back into thicker jungle.

Soong-Li stopped several times, listening. She couldn't shake the feeling they were now being followed, and the sensation of being watched never left her.

Stopping before a wall of vines and fungus and examining it for several moments, she turned to Captain Yang, her head tilted inquisitively. Yang nodded to her, then let his eyes move over the slimy undergrowth. He held up a hand and the group waited to see what he was doing.

Soong-Li watched intently as the man put his rifle under his arm and walked carefully toward the near-impenetrable tangle.

He stopped a few feet from it and turned one way then the other, and then looked skyward at its upper limbs. After a moment, he moved his gun under one arm and reached out with his other hand to grab the hanging vines and part them, creating a hole.

Suspended in the gap like a ghastly Halloween mask was a face, or what might have been a face. There were hard plates, quivering mouthparts and black bulb eyes on stalks. It was there, just for a second or two, and then it was gone.

Yang made a strangled noise in his throat and leaped back, letting the vines drop. His heel caught a rock and he fell onto his ass, but still lifted his gun.

Soong-Li saw that even the battle-hardened captain's hands were shaking.

"What was that?" Kwan asked in a small voice.

To Yang's credit, he jumped to his feet and crept forward again, and this time used the barrel of his gun to part the vines.

Of course, there was nothing there. He peered in further and after a second or two stepped back.

"I think it was . . . our observers," he said.

"It looked like an arthropod," Tian whispered. "Maybe the makers of the footprints."

"Be alert," Soong-Li said again redundantly, not knowing what else to tell them. But this time a small voice in her head whispered to her that it was a bad idea to go there.

She shut out the thought and nodded to Jin Baek. "Proceed."

They continued until suddenly a long mournful sound filled the air around them and deep vibrations tickled their bones and made their teeth hurt. Soong-Li couldn't determine if it was from some sort of animal or instrument like an ancient Korean *nagak* horn, but it was bass-deep, low, and unsettling.

Many in the group cringed, and Captain Yang, Jin and Kwan held up their rifles and turned slowly, but it was impossible to track exactly where the noise was coming from.

"It sounded like a whale," Jin whispered. "But from where?"

"I think . . ." Yang shook his head, "it's coming from all around us."

After a moment, Soong-Li crouched and placed a hand flat against a rock protruding from the ground. "It's vibrating. Maybe it is coming from below us. Inside the island."

"What could cause it? An earth tremor?" Tian asked in a small voice.

The group stood in silence for a moment longer, just listening, but still not able to pinpoint the source of the strange emanation.

And then it stopped.

Soong-Li blinked, feeling the silence weigh heavily on them now.

"And that is that," Captain Yang said softly.

"It seems so." Soong-Li still felt unsettled. She wanted this investigation over. "And now ... we continue with our mission."

The group started up the hill again but continued to follow the track to make faster headway. It was after another fifteen minutes that Soong-Li began to think there was something different about the land, a different feeling, and it was Captain Yang who pointed it out.

"No animals," he said as he looked around. "No animals, no insects, no movement, not even a sound. Nothing is living here."

"Or everything has left," Tian added. "The land is not barren, as there is plant life. And with plant life comes plant eaters. But sometimes land can be vacated if there is a large enough predator around."

"Large predator," Soong-Li scoffed, swallowing down her nerves. "Let's hope no larger than my predators and their guns." She nodded to Jin and Kwan, who grinned in return. But Captain Yang remained impassive.

After ten more minutes they reached the crest of the steep hill, and the group spread out. They stood catching their breath and stared at the object they had come looking for.

"I don't believe this," Tian said.

"We are in the wrong place. Or maybe the wrong time," Yang whispered.

"No, this is the right time and place," Soong-Li replied. "But that thing is not." She raised her binoculars to her eyes. "It's definitely the building we saw from the water."

It was a structure. Or maybe more like the remains of a city. And it was mind-blowing in its size and design.

They were 420 million years in Earth's primordial past, eons before humanity's ancestors even existed. But what they beheld was already ancient.

Vines entwined colossal columns that rose like titanic fingers from the surrounding plant life. It was astounding to see them in this time and place, but what was truly alarming was the sheer size of them: each of the columns had to be 200 feet high and at least fifty feet around.

Between them there was a raised dais supporting a collection of stones, each the size of a school bus and in strange geometric shapes of some sort of Euclidean design, fitting together with absolute precision.

Soong-Li thought what was in between those massive stones might have been a huge tabletop, fifty feet in length, toppled beside a rounded stone plinth, obviously its base, and on its surface was etched other-worldly designs in whorls, lines, and mad scribblings.

Soong-Li felt a creeping sickness like a cold bile settling low in her gut as she looked over the structure. It wasn't just its sheer size that was alarming and intimidating, it was also the absolute stillness surrounding the buildings. The whole place was eerie.

"They are old. And yet this time period is so long ago." Yang turned. "How?"

"They look old. But I'm not sure they are in decay." Soong-Li turned. "The size. Who could possibly have built them?"

"They must be giants," Jin muttered. "Maybe there were giants living at this time? There were said to be *Dokkaebi* . . ."

"Be quiet, young fool," Soong-Li growled.

She knew the *Dokkaebi* were giant goblin-like creatures from myth, and stories of them were used to scare children. Not soldiers.

"That looks like a ceremonial altar." She turned to Tian. "The question I have is, are they terrestrial, or are they visitors?"

Tian's eyes widened. "Visitors?"

"Yes."

"You mean like from somewhere else . . . other than Earth?" Tian frowned.

Soong-Li scoffed. "Well, I don't mean from Australia. Or anywhere else, because humans don't exist yet. Someone or something built those. And it was something that was here hundreds of millions of years before humans." She handed Tian her field glasses.

The young scientist held them to her eyes. "The altar is covered in symbols, writing, I think."

"Can you read it?" Yang asked from behind.

"It's picture glyphs, like a mix of Egyptian and Mayan. But not the same. I can see there are symbols that could be mathematical. Each image could be a word, an entire sentence, perhaps an expression, or maybe even an equation." She half-turned. "And no, I cannot decipher them. Languages are not my specialty."

"And so big," Yang observed. "If we were closer, we might not be able to take it all in. I don't think they were made by something the size of human beings."

"Or maybe they were," Tian replied. "Maybe they were designed in deference to their gods and with those gods in mind. After all, look at the size of the pyramids."

Soong-Li took the glasses back and scanned the area around the ruins. "There's no movement. No anything." She lowered them. "We must take a closer look."

The group moved a little further along and found a towering flat wall. Its size was awe-inspiring. But the grotesque thing carved upon its façade froze them to silence for many minutes.

They stared up at the carved image that had also been painted in now fading colors to give it depth, and an almost lifelike perspective. If an artist could take every nightmarish creature imaginable and meld them all together, they might come close to the depiction on the cliff-sized wall.

Spanning what must have been land and water was a monstrous, hulking beast with blazing red eyes, a face hanging with tendrils or tentacles cascading down over lumpy shoulders, and with muscular, scaled arms ending in clawed hands.

"Was this their god?" Tian asked breathlessly.

Captain Yang grunted. "I think, maybe, we should go around. I have a bad feeling about this place."

"Do not be fearful," Soong-Li scoffed. "Just as we paint dragons, or Europeans place gargoyles on their cathedrals, this thing is most likely an imaginary beast." She turned back, glancing from Yang to the group. "We have come this far and are not leaving until we have investigated. This race is obviously intelligent, and maybe they have something we can use."

"We should at least try to communicate with them," Tian agreed.

"I don't like it," Yang pressed. "It is my military judgment that we avoid this area and return to our primary mission."

"Your advice is noted. And now, follow orders," Soong-Li insisted.

Yang glared at her for a moment, but then turned away. "Then we proceed?"

"Yes," Soong-Li replied curtly. "We will travel beyond this, uh, temple. We will see if anyone is home." She turned away.

"I wonder what they could be like?" Tian mused. "Who or what can they possibly be to exist 420 million years before us? Who are they, and how did they get here?" She turned. "And what happened to them?"

"All good questions. Let us find out." Soong-Li nodded to Captain Yang.

Yang hesitated for a moment and then instructed Jin Baek and Kwan Myung to move out at the front of their group. The young men glanced at each other and then did as ordered.

It took them twenty minutes to skirt around the enormous structure, such was its size. The columns seemed to touch the sky, and up close the group saw that the alien geometry of the design was like nothing ever created by humans, nor ever likely to be.

The huge edifices seemed hewn from single pieces of stone, but up close they could see that the blocks were in pieces so well cut that they fitted together almost seamlessly.

Beyond the gargantuan stone structure, something else came into view.

"A village," Soong-Li whispered, feeling the urge to be quiet now.

They approached what looked like a settlement with domed hut-type structures, and wide laneways between them. The group stopped about 100 feet from the first of them.

"Strange," Tian observed. "The huts are far more primitive than the design and construction of the columns and altar. And look at the doorframes." She turned to Soong-Li. "Our doorframes are taller than they are wide to accommodate the human shape. They reflect our form. But look at these."

Soong-Li saw what she meant. The doorways were broader than they were high. "They don't look as ancient as the ruins. So where is everyone?" she asked.

"Maybe they are also gone," Tian replied.

"Captain, send in your man," Soong-Li ordered.

Both the young soldiers looked to Yang, and they met each other's eyes before Yang turned back, his expression stony. "No."

"What?" Soong-Li frowned in disbelief.

"No," Yang repeated. "It is my job to assess the risks, and I believe this is not a risk we should be undertaking. It is wasting time, and has no bearing on our mission outcome and may even jeopardize it."

Soong-Li looked at the man from under her brows, assessing him for several long seconds. Jin, Kwan, and Tian were like children watching their parents fight, glancing anxiously from one to the other.

Perhaps they knew that Soong-Li was like a force of nature, but Yang had more weapons and the loyalty of the young soldiers. This interaction would determine what happened with the leadership structure and perhaps the mission.

Soong-Li knew she could not afford to back down as that would allow Yang to assume control, meaning that at best, she would have to become a submissive member of the team. And at worst, she might be killed or forced from the group.

Her expression was implacable. "Listen, Captain. This is important for you to understand." She walked closer to him, never relinquishing eye contact. "I was selected to lead this mission by the Committee of Generals, who are so far above your head you cannot even see them."

Soong-Li's expression hardened even further. "Be careful that your risk-avoidance speech doesn't begin to sound like a call for insurrection. That would not end well for you."

Yang just stared back.

She knew she was taking a chance, as the senior military man could simply shoot her dead, right here, right now – and then claim she had been a victim of the creatures on the land or sea.

Behind him, the two younger soldiers visibly paled and shifted from foot to foot.

"I speak for the Party." Soong-Li took a step forward. "You are loyal to the Party, Captain, yes?"

The man blinked.

And on seeing that single blink, she knew she would prevail. But she didn't want to just prevail, she wanted to dominate – and for everyone to see her dominate.

"Say it," she demanded. "Pledge your loyalty to the Party."

Yang's eyes burned, but after a moment, he straightened. "I am a loyal member of the Democratic People's Republic of Korea and pledge my undying loyalty to the Great Leader."

She glared. "And . . . to me." Soong-Li folded her arms, waiting, and turning the heat of her glare up several degrees.

"And to you," he said, and gave her a small nod-bow.

Soong-Li grunted her acceptance and turned away. "Captain, send in your man."

Yang nodded, still at attention. "Jin Baek."

The young man snapped to attention. "Yes, sir."

"Reconnoiter," he said curtly.

Jin nodded and turned to face the first hut.

Kwan whispered, "Good luck." And then the young man set off.

CHAPTER 30

Standing at the controls, Ito took the torpedo-shaped submarine into a dive. The HAWCs, along with Agent Cooper, had engaged their clear visors, and with the sun directly overhead, plus being away from the coast, the brackish water quickly cleared.

The raft was ribbed, strong, but largely open around them. And it had no real defenses other than those that the soldiers carried with them. So the HAWCs needed to adapt their attack or defensive strategy, as in the water most of their armaments were limited in range or power. Their laser weapons were green-light, free beam, and still retained their cutting power, but only over short distances. For now they would cruise below the surface, but their oxygen supply needed to be replenished every 30 minutes.

Alex sat in the front, facing forward, cocooned in the warmth of his suit, and felt the movement of the water around him. As all the helmets had linked communications, he could hear the even breathing of his team and was satisfied that all sounded calm and in control. He could even monitor their heartbeats from his master unit.

Beside him was Tor. The DOG was folded back into its case-like shape again. Though the android could operate within an aquatic environment, he wasn't equipped with jet propulsion like the HAWC suits, so for now, he was a passenger.

Alex reached down to place a hand upon it. With the real animal's consciousness and brain patterns mapped into its synthetic synapses, he wondered whether it dreamed. And if it did, of what. Leaving his hand on Tor's case, he probed the synthetic mind, and found images there, images of Joshua, of himself, and of Aimee.

A lump formed in his throat, and he swallowed it down. The grief made him feel weak and unfocused. He wanted to stay with the memories, but knew that the reason he was here was to make sure they would "be" again. Nothing else mattered.

At that moment their craft slowed as its tapered nose ran into a huge, near-transparent mass that began to enfold them.

"What the hell?" Alex turned, confused – and annoyed that he had not been doing his job.

It appeared they had plowed into a large blob of jelly that might have been a prototype of a jellyfish. Its gossamer filaments were stretched and broken, but a few stuck to Alex's suit and he wondered whether they had evolved stings yet.

"Sorry, team." He wiped them off and let them drift away. "Didn't see that coming."

"Neither did the sensors," Gonzalez said. "Five hundred pounds of snot."

"Nice." Cooper chuckled.

Around them, the warm sea was becoming clogged with smaller varieties of the same jelly-like things. "Take us down to the bottom, Mr. Yamada. See if we can get under them," Alex said.

The nose angled downward and soon they left the layer of jellyfish behind and were nearing a sea bottom that was only about 100 feet below the surface. The sunlight just faintly striped the bottom, which was marked with tracks criss-crossing the sand.

"Trilobites," Cooper said.

Next, they overtook a rug-sized shelled creature that moved across the sea floor, legs tucked up underneath it, its oval segmented body gouging the sand in its path as it searched for a meal in the top layer.

Things like sea fans waved in the current, grabbing and siphoning food, or they rapidly snapped backed into their soft tube shells when something startled them. At these depths only a few nautilus shells scooted by, trailing striped tentacles, their large, round eyes turning to observe the submersible with interest.

After a few more moments, they saw another of the trilobites, but something else had also found it.

"Hey, check out that weird-ass thing," Gonzalez said.

The creature hovering over the trilobite was about three feet long, roughly oval-shaped and on both sides of its flattened body were undulating flaps or groups of paddles. From its head two flat, hammer-like eyes protruded on stalks, and both were pointed down at its prey.

It slowed down a little as they came abreast of the thing, and just one of its hammer eyes swiveled toward them.

"Oh my God; I think it's an *Anomalocaris*," Cooper said. "They predated even the Silurian period. They should have been extinct for millions of years by now."

The creature's eye turned away from them, and as they watched, two trunk-like appendages unfurled from its front. They looked like twin elephant trunks but with a row of spikes on their underside.

The creature then shot in fast and scooped up the trilobite. The twin trunks compressed, and they could hear the cracking of the trilobite's carapace through the seawater.

"Holy shit, see that?" Gonzalez exclaimed. "Double jumbo attack."

"And that's why they were one of the first apex predators of the Cambrian period," Cooper said. "Their very name means 'anomaly', because they seem to be made up of many different creatures all glued together."

"Glad they were small then," Alex replied.

"Who's to know?" Cooper said. "They shouldn't be here. We know next to nothing about them, and fossil evidence is fragmentary. For all we know they got a bit bigger, or a lot bigger."

Alex grunted. "Let's hope we don't run into its big brother then."

"And let's hope we don't run into another of the primordial super predators." She started. "It's called an Orthocone s—"

"Orthocone squid; a cephalopod." Alex turned. "With a shell, right?"

Cooper nodded. "Well, yeah, that's right."

"We've met before." He turned away. "I don't care how big these things get. They take a run at us, we'll cut them in half." Alex pointed forward, and Ito responded by accelerating.

In a few more minutes Alex's suit warned him that his oxygen was running low, so had Ito take them to the surface.

When they breached, the team set to replenishing their supply and retracted their visors. They inhaled the salty, humid air, and most just rested.

Alex turned slowly – they were in an endless sea and above them a magnificent, cloudless, azure sky. Both the sea and sky were unchanged from horizon to horizon and Alex closed his eyes and let the sunshine warm his face.

It seemed this part of the world was empty; flying animals hadn't evolved yet, and the air would belong to no one or nothing for another seventy million years when insects would be the first to evolve wings.

He opened his eyes and looked over the side into the water's steel blue depths. Above them there might be nothing, but below, that was where the giants already lived.

His suit told him it was at capacity oxygen, and he closed his visor. "Mr. Yamada."

Ito nodded, he and the team closed their visors, and then he started the craft, taking it down in seconds more.

The seabed started to angle gently downward, and the depth increased. When the water was about 120 feet deep, Alex had Ito take them back up to the mid water level. His senses prickled at the sensation of life around them. In the craft there were multiple units for monitoring movement, and proximity alerts. Many times the small screens had warned them of things out in the blue depths, ranging from a few feet in length to silent behemoths gliding past just out of sight.

Alex remembered Agent Cooper's briefing on the life-forms they might encounter. Though most creatures big or small wouldn't worry them, there was the massive tooth she'd displayed that was the size of a soda can. It looked like something that might sit easily in the mouth of an alligator – if one grew to around 100 feet long – and something that big *would* be a problem.

He'd take no chances. All the big guys swimming around down here would be *encouraged* to stay well back from them. If their craft got attacked and damaged, they could leave it behind and still operate in their suits. But their job would be much harder.

Alex looked down at the small panel before him, noting that they were traveling at a depth of around fifty feet in 160 feet of water. They were still within the sunlight layer, but below them the water began to darken, creating shadows.

After another fifteen minutes the sonar pinged again, and he saw a shape on the screen out at starboard. Five minutes later it was still there, keeping pace and staying parallel to them. Then it turned and came at them, staying out in front and just out of sight. But Alex felt it go past, and Ito confirmed that he had needed to compensate for its wake to keep them on course.

Whatever it was, it was big at around fifty to seventy-five feet, or maybe even bigger, because it had a fluctuating form, as though it was compressing and then releasing its musculature. And now it was swinging back to take another look at them.

Alex guessed it liked what it saw, because it fell into a parallel swim again just out of sight on the port side. He tried once again to get his technical sensors to reconstruct its signature, but they were all over the place and the thing refused to be identified. It wasn't streamlined as he would have expected from a large sea-going predator like a shark, raptorial whale, or sea reptile. Instead, it was still repeatedly contracting and then spreading into a more amorphous shape.

He had no idea what it could be, but then again, no one really knew what things inhabited this ancient sea world. For that matter, Cooper had told them that there were periods in Earth's distant past that were just paleontological blanks – no one had any idea what happened and what lived there for tens of millions of years. The Silurian period wasn't entirely like one of those, but they sure had plenty of knowledge gaps.

Alex turned. "Cooper, you seeing this?" he asked.

Bernadette Cooper looked up from the tiny screen on her wrist gauntlet and nodded. "Yeah, I see it, but I have no idea what it could be. Its shape, even its size, seems to change. My database is refusing to even speculate."

"Whatever it is, it's big and keeping abreast of us, checking us out," Alex said.

"Might be a territorial display," Cooper replied. "Or it's deciding if it can eat us or not."

"Yep, that's what I'm thinking." Alex stared out into the blue depths. His vision was far sharper that any normal person's, and he could just make out the smudge of something there, effortlessly keeping pace with them. "I don't want to blast it if I don't have to, but if it comes closer, I'm going warn it off."

"Send out a drone, boss?" Gonzalez asked.

Alex nodded. "Good idea. Let's see exactly what our big friend is. Might be something benign we can ignore. And if not . . ."

"And if not, we cook it." Gonzalez laughed and set to preparing one of the underwater drones for launch.

"And away." He released the black, two-foot-long cylinder, and like a fish the small unit shot out into the gloom toward the bogey, with the HAWC operating it via his gauntlet.

"Could be a cephalopod. There were several ancient species inhabiting the Silurian oceans," Cooper said. "And in myriad different forms. That might also explain the weird shape-shifting we're getting."

"And the interest in us," Ito added. "They are a very intelligent animal." He continued to speed the craft forward. "There is a story in Japan about an old man who lived in a cottage on the water with his dog. An octopus started to come in at night and steal the leftover dog food. The man kept moving the dog's bowl, but the octopus would always find it. Finally, the man stopped leaving the food out in the bowl for the dog."

"What happened then?" Cooper asked.

Ito turned to her. "It took the dog."

"Got it." She exhaled through pressed lips.

Alex's eyes went from the smudge in the distance back to the feed from the tiny screen that relayed images from the drone. As yet, they hadn't turned on any lighting, but with the drone's small, streamlined size, and the near-silent water jet propulsion, it would be able to get in close without being detected.

At around fifty feet out, they began to make out the shape of the thing. But still nothing made sense, as it seemed to be just a huge mass of muscle, scales, and either spines or bristled hairs.

Gonzalez took the drone in another ten feet, and then the thing expanded in the water, going from approximately fifty feet across to about a hundred as something like a canopy unfolded. A pair of large red eyes opened. Then more. Lots of large red eyes.

"A cephalopod," Cooper breathed.

"I don't think so," Alex replied.

The thing had tentacles, but they seemed to hang from a monstrous face, and from its rear a pair of membranous wings opened. Colossal limbs that emanated enormous power also spread wide.

"What the hell is that?" Gonzalez whispered.

Alex felt a small niggling pain begin in the center of his head, as if he was being probed. So he probed back.

And then the images came.

He saw a planet devoid of life. Somehow he knew it was Earth. Its oceans were acid baths, its air a toxic mix of sulfur and other caustic chemicals, and the moon, nearly smooth, and so close it felt like you could reach out and touch it.

Something crashed into that primordial Earth – a ship, or pod, or egg, and stayed dormant for countless millions of years. Perhaps waiting. Waiting for a suitable environment to develop, or life to evolve with enough mass to sustain the new arrival.

Time meant nothing to it, as it measured its lifespan in the age of stars, not in the passing of tiny, captured planets around a yellow dwarf sun. But Alex saw that it had come for domination, and already it was the master of its domain.

The images came quickly, and Alex didn't know if they were being fed to him because the creature wanted him to know, or if Alex himself was teasing them out.

One thing he knew was that this entity was no cephalopod, but something vastly older, and more intelligent, and it had been here since the beginning – and expected to be here at the end.

Then Alex realized it was also interrogating his own mind and memories. It was fascinated by his intelligence, and intrigued, because humans were a lifeform it did not know. But it wanted to.

Then, horrifyingly, Alex knew why – it wanted to know them because it wanted to control them. And taste them.

He then felt the thing in his mind try and draw him to it. And not just him – he felt Ito accelerating the craft toward it.

He tried to pull his consciousness back and shut down the thing's probe into his own mind. But it wouldn't let go. "*Back up, back up*," he ordered.

The submersible stayed on track. Alex turned and saw that Ito was staring straight ahead, ignoring him.

"*Lieutenant Ito Yamada*," Alex yelled into his mic.

The man blinked, and then his eyes focused on Alex.

"Back up, *now*," Alex demanded.

This time Ito did as commanded, and their craft veered away in an arc and then accelerated.

Gonzalez was still watching the feed from the drone, and his brows came together. "Hey, boss, it whited out." He looked up. "We lost it."

But Alex hadn't lost it. He pulled his pulse rifle and trained it on the thing that was keeping pace with them. He fired a continual plasma blast into the blue gloom, and the beam struck one edge of the creature.

In an explosion of turbulence and bubbles the monstrous thing vanished, and with it went the images from Alex's head.

"What was that?" Gonzalez asked. "That was no squid."

"It wasn't," Alex said. "I saw inside its mind. There was intelligence there. But no pity, or what we know of as humanity." Alex was still watching over his shoulder. His wrist gauntlet told him the surrounding water was now clear, but his gut told him they were still somehow being observed.

He turned. "It didn't evolve here. It came here," Alex said. "It's been here since the dawn of our world. Waiting. Perhaps it can't die. Or die as we know it."

"That's insane," Gonzalez said. "It's some sort of space traveler? Then where is it now, uh, I mean, in our time?"

"I don't know," Alex said. "Maybe gone."

"The old gods," Bernadette Cooper muttered.

"What?" Alex turned back to her.

She was examining the images Gonzalez's drone had captured and was enlarging one of them.

"Stick with me here as I might sound a little crazy." Cooper sighed and looked up from the tiny screen. "I think I know what it looks like. There are stories of some smaller seaside villages in old England and other places in Europe, that worship an ancient deity called Dagon. It looked something like this."

"Lovecraftian," Alex said. "Fiction."

"We thought so," Cooper said. "Until we found the ancient caves in Innsmouth, in England. They were thousands of years old and had depictions of some sort of great creature, which looked like that. It used to come ashore, it and its minions, and the villagers used to sacrifice people to it."

"Can't beat the old English hospitality," Gonzalez said dryly.

"This thing is intelligent. And it wants us." Alex turned. "It wants to control us. And consume us."

"Consume us?" Cooper asked.

"It's powerful. Tried to draw us in," Alex said.

"I felt it. It was like being trapped and I couldn't break free. By myself, that is," Ito said. "Without you, I would have been gone."

"It's still out there. Just on the periphery of our sensors. I can still feel it." Alex turned back around. "We need to capture those NKs' bombs and finish our mission. Then find our people and get the hell back home." He exhaled. "One problem at a time."

CHAPTER 31

Jin had no choice. But he wanted to appear stoic, brave, and in control – even though he didn't feel it. He hated the way his legs trembled a little and his heart beat like a hammer in his chest as he approached the nearest of the large domed huts.

He saw up close that it seemed to be made of some sort of sand composition mixed with a shiny resin that had been smoothed over or piled upon itself when wet and then dried. And it smelled odd – a little like fish heads left to dry in the sun.

Jin moved closer to the edge of the doorway and stopped just outside with his back to the wall. He glanced at his team and saw Soong-Li nod to him, her brows knitted as if impatient. He turned away and tried hard to slow his breathing so he could listen. After a moment he was satisfied there was no sound from within, and he darted his head out for a quick glance and then quickly pulled it back.

He had seen no movement, but it was dark inside, and there were too many shadows to be sure.

Here goes, he thought. He stuck his head around the doorframe again, and this time stayed there so he could take his time examining the inside. But again he saw nothing menacing.

So he stepped out.

Framed in the doorway and with the sunlight behind him he knew he was exposed – the interior was dark, so if there was something or someone in there, they could see him without him seeing them.

"Hello," he said a little above a whisper as he strained to see. "*Hello.*" A little louder.

No response, no movement, so he stepped in and just to the side, and he paused, just turning his head slowly. The ceiling was high at about twelve feet, and he wished he had asked for a flashlight as there were still too many shadows and no windows. But he thought he could make out some decorations hanging on the wall. As he got closer he swallowed noisily when he saw they were some type of crudely nailed animal skins, and jawbones, and some of the strangest skulls he had ever seen. It all reminded him of hunters' trophies.

One of the largest things in the sparse room was an odd-shaped table, with nothing on it. But leaning against a wall were several long and stout poles that were sharpened at one end – spears, he guessed. And why not? After all, the huts looked primitive.

He glanced back at the strange table that was jammed at the rear of the hut and hidden in the shadows. Then Jin tilted his head – he thought he could hear a soft crackling sound. No; not crackling – it was wetter, more like tiny bubbles popping, softly, a little like sticky froth.

He followed the sound toward its origin – which seemed to be the strange table – and reached out to run his fingers lightly along its top.

It was about five feet high and seemed made of some sort of stone or maybe a rough form of ceramic. There were no joins, but there were a few spikes and protuberances along the edges.

He paused, listening; the sound seemed to be coming from underneath the table, and he slowly crouched.

He saw now that the sides of this piece of furniture were a mass of flat, interlocking plates, many covered in course bristles like spines, and all resting on poles or pipes that ended in cruel-looking spikes.

As it was now right in front of him, the smell of rotting fish was more powerful, but nonetheless he leaned in closer, frowning. There seemed to be a bunch of smaller plates that were between two fist-sized, bulging stones that shone like dark oil. Were they decorative gems? he wondered.

Jin slowly reached a hand toward a small mound of froth emanating or leaking from between some of the bristled plating. He scooped a finger through it, then rubbed his thumb and finger together – it was slimy, and bringing it closer to his nose, he was immediately repelled by the rank odor.

"*Foof.*" He grimaced and wiped the mess on his shirt.

The young soldier then looked down at one of the dark glass-like bulbs or gems, and decided that if he could work one free he'd keep it as a souvenir. He pulled out his blade and reached for the gem with his other hand.

But as soon as his fingers alighted on it, it popped out, on a stalk. Then came the other one beside it. And at their tips were tiny white dots, three of them, and they all aligned.

Eyes! Jin's mind screamed, and he sprang backwards, landing on his rump as his breath caught in his chest.

His mouth dropped open. He could only stare as the thing that he had thought was a table lengthened and rose higher and higher, to about nine feet, nearly scraping the ceiling.

He realized then that this wasn't a piece of furniture, but instead was the hut's occupant – a giant, long, crustacean thing that now stood on six legs, with two more branching from its sides, and two more again that it held out before it and which ended in strong-looking pincers.

Its head was cone-shaped and sat on the huge shell body. But worst of all was its face, which was a vision from his worst nightmares – tooth-edged mandibles worked feverishly and parted to reveal things inside that looked like tiny buzzsaws, and multiple spines and feelers protruded that never stopped their quivering motion.

Jin was still on his ass, frozen to the spot, as the thing loomed over him. He realized that this was the creature that had been taking the grisly trophies, and he suddenly felt the warm spread of his own urine inside his pant legs.

Perhaps the disgust he felt in himself unlocked his muscles, because he scrambled to his feet and turned to run. There was no way he was going to end up another skin hanging on the wall.

He made it to the doorway and saw his team standing there, maybe a little closer, and just as he felt the kiss of sunlight on his face, there came a vice-like agony across his shoulder.

The thing had him and had stopped him dead.

"*Help*," Jin screamed, as the pain in his shoulder intensified.

* * *

"What's keeping him?" Soong-Li sighed.

She looked about, conscious of the stillness of the place. "It's empty," she said. "Let's move closer."

"You have sent in a scout," Captain Yang warned. "Let him do his job."

Soong-Li slowly faced the captain. "And if he's in trouble, we're too far away to help, yes? We advance another dozen feet." She turned and walked forward, satisfied when she heard the team follow her.

But she stopped when she heard muffled sounds and scrabbling from within the hut. What could he be doing? she wondered.

Even though she was only around seventy feet from the hut Jin had entered, she lifted the binoculars to her eyes again.

She adjusted the light setting on the small dial, but inside the hut it was still too dark to discern anything.

Just as she lowered the binoculars, Jin burst from the doorway – but he didn't get more than five feet, as from behind him emerged an enormous creature that took her breath away.

"*Demon,*" she whispered.

The powerful-looking, multi-legged thing's shape was like an opium-fueled nightmare where a man had somehow been fused with a giant crustacean. The back end was all lumped armor plate with sharp legs, and the front torso rose with a huge shell on the back, two sets of arms, one with claw-pincers, and smaller plating over its belly.

The small head had two twitching bulb eyes that remained on Jin, and it reached out with one of its segmented arms to grip his shoulder in its toothed claw and stop him in his tracks.

Jin wailed, and even from their distance they could hear the crunching of bone and tearing of tendons and flesh.

The fear-shocked Soong-Li surprised herself by pulling her weapon, and Captain Yang and Kwan Myung also had their rifles in tight to their shoulders. Without thinking about it, Soong-Li advanced toward the thing, but her hand shook and she had no clear shot because the young man was being held in front of the massive creature. From behind her, Tian's scream was like a continual ear-piercing siren.

As the group watched, the other pincer grabbed Jin's other arm between the elbow and wrist, and with a swift compression accompanied by the sound of a cooked chicken being pulled apart, the severed hand fell to the ground in a spurt of blood and with Jin's bone-chilling scream.

"Shoot it, shoot it," Soong-Li yelled.

As they watched, the pincer-claw holding Jin's shoulder also came together with a sickening crunch, and the bones and meat easily separated. The young man's head flopped to the side as blood jetted out. But Jin's eyes were still wide, and his mouth opened and closed as if he was gulping for air or trying to form words.

A perfect shot didn't matter anymore, so Yang and Kwan began to fire, and their high-powered rounds smashed into the thing's carapace. Bits of shell flicked away, and the massive crustacean backed into its dark doorway, dragging Jin's body with it.

"Cease fire," Yang said.

Silence ruled again but only for a few moments, as from all around the camp came the slight sounds of scraping and scratching, and what sounded like heavy plates rubbing over one another.

"What is . . ." Soong-Li began.

"The huts," Yang answered.

Soong-Li's mouth snapped shut as the noise rose, and she saw that the captain was right; from within the dozens of other huts, things were beginning to stir.

Yang trained his gun on one hut then another before he spoke without turning. "I think we should leave now."

"Jin," Kwan said forlornly.

"Is dead," Yang answered. "And so will we be if a lot of these things attack us."

From somewhere that was hard to pinpoint came the deep moaning sound of the horn, or bellow, which moved through the air and right through their bodies.

"That sound again," Soong-Li whispered.

"Maybe . . ." Yang began, ". . . it's a call to arms."

He backed up as from inside the dark mouths of the huts bulb eyes emerged first, then the nightmarish heads, followed by the clay-colored bulk of the of the gruesome creatures.

"I think we should go back to the boat now," Tian whispered.

The being that had attacked Jin re-emerged to fill the doorway of its hut, and this time it held the bottom half of the man. It lifted the legs dangling from a viscera-trailing groin to its mouth, and the buzzsaw plates worked feverishly to feed on the ropy, glistening intestines and bloody flesh.

Yang pulled a grenade from his belt and popped the pin. "Run," he yelled, and tossed it, and it bounced and then rolled to the thing's feet.

The group sprinted off in several directions as the grenade exploded. As they went, Soong-Li looked over her shoulder to see the orange ball of an explosion tear most of the hut and the shelled creature to pieces.

Good, she thought. *Rot in hell, monster.*

The group ran back toward the monolithic altar and columns, and just as they neared the base, a line of the creatures scuttled out to block their path. Yang, who had been leading, changed course, but once again, they were anticipated, and another group appeared to block their new path.

From behind them, beside them, and in front, more of the creatures filled the area, now totally closing them in. Their plates jostled against each other, making a heavy bumping, grinding sound, but once assembled, they all stood just watching the people, with the only movement being the twitching of their strange bulb eyes on their quivering stalks.

"What now?" Soong-Li asked.

Yang snorted derisively. "Perhaps this is where you get your chance to communicate with them." He turned to Tian and raised his eyebrows.

"I don't know . . . how?" Tian squeaked.

"Try." Soong-Li also faced the small scientist. "We are surrounded. No choice. Do it."

The young woman blanched, and her chin trembled. "I can hear them. But it's just buzzing, pops, and squeaks. All I can do is try and mimic it."

"Then try. They may like it," Soong-Li ordered. "Or we are all dead anyway."

Tian took a hesitant step forward. She swallowed, noisily. And began.

* * *

Back at the boat, Jia Sun shot to her feet. "Did you hear that? It sounded like gunfire." She clutched her hands. "What should we do?"

"I . . . I'm not sure. Maybe it was, maybe it wasn't. We should wait." Shuchang hated his indecisiveness. But the last thing he wanted to do was go running into the strange jungle, when Soong-Li had asked him to guard the packages and their boat. If anything happened to them, he feared she would hate him. And with good reason, he decided.

There came another faint noise, and this one caused Jia Sun to grimace in fear. "That was a scream."

"It sounded like a bird call," Shuchang offered.

"There are *no* birds yet," Jia hissed through her teeth at him. "We need to do something."

Shuchang got to his feet. "Our orders are to remain here."

"They're in trouble," Jia implored him.

"And if they're not, and we leave the bombs, she'll be mad at us," Shuchang replied.

"Soong-Li could be hurt," Jia Sun said calmly now. "You could save her. That would make her happy, yes?"

Shuchang looked to the jungle in the direction the noise had come from. It had sounded far away. He looked across at the concealed boat. There was no way they could take all the bombs. But he also had a bad feeling in his stomach about Soong-Li.

If he did nothing, and she was hurt, he'd be a coward, and worse, he might lose her. He decided. "I'll go. You stay."

"By myself?" Jia Sun's eyes widened. "No, I can't."

"Hold it." Shuchang held up a hand, tilting his head to listen. "I think . . . I think they're coming back."

Jia turned to the sounds of movement from the jungle.

Shuchang was relieved. Suddenly a complicated situation had been resolved. He walked toward where the jungle was moving. But when he got to its edge he froze.

Words wouldn't even form in his mouth, and behind him he heard Jia make a small sound like a squeak. The creatures that muscled out into the open were almost twice as tall as he was and looked like constantly twitching insects or crabs.

Shuchang felt light-headed from fear.

He pointed at them. "*Gaa . . .*" was all he could summon.

The closest creature reached toward him with a huge arm or leg that ended in a claw.

Shuchang fainted.

* * *

Soong-Li had a rope tied around her neck, along with Captain Yang and Kwan. She tried not to think of the gruesome fate of Tian or blame herself for asking her to try and communicate. But the monsters' response had sickened her to the pit of her stomach.

They had stripped them all and the revolting creatures now tugged them along like naked puppies. Or maybe ducks to the slaughter.

The only hope she had was that Shuchang had escaped. Maybe he would still plant the bombs, maybe he would make it back home. And maybe he would bring back a rescue team, she hoped ridiculously.

There was a hissing and popping from the buzzsaw-like mouths of the creatures and then they stopped, waiting for something.

They all turned, and Soong-Li and the other humans did too. And then from out of the rancid jungle, another group of the crab-people appeared. And one of them dragged a rope, and what was attached to it made her heart sink.

She smiled forlornly as the naked Shuchang and Jia were dragged closer, and their rope was attached to Soong-Li's own. But then Kwan, Jia, and Captain Yang were separated from them onto a different rope.

The arthropods prodded at them and pinched at their flesh. In seconds more the trio were tugged away in the direction of the village.

"Stay strong, we will come for you." Soong-Li said forlornly.

Yang looked over his shoulder, his face was devoid of expression. He shook his head. "Save yourselves." He said and then vanished with the rest into the jungle.

Soong-Li sagged as she continued to stare at where her three compatriots had been taken. After a moment, she became aware that Shuchang was talking.

"The bombs . . ." Shuchang began.

"Do not matter anymore." She smiled sadly. "I'm sorry."

"Sorry?" he asked.

The huge arthropod people set off toward the mouth of a huge and ominous-looking cave that loomed before them.

"I'm sorry we did not have time for each other." She reached out to take his hand.

She felt it trembling, and she squeezed it, trying to radiate confidence and comfort to him.

The pair walked side by side as they entered the gloom of the cave.

CHAPTER 32

"Land ho," Casey said.

"This is bullshit. Shouldn't be there." Brandt's thick, black brows came together as he turned to her. "Did we fuck up somewhere?"

"I dunno, we're kinda flying blind here, big guy." Casey adjusted the lenses on her visor to amplify the approaching landmass. "But unless we got turned around and are heading back to where we came from, or somehow traveled a few hundred miles further out than we expected – both unlikely – then we just found something that wasn't on any of the extrapolation maps."

"Never trust experts," Brandt growled, and then looked up. "Hey, if the NKs saw it, would they land?"

"We would. They would," she replied. "If it's on their detonation route, it'd be easier to plant their bombs on land."

"Then full speed ahead, coz I suddenly feel like kicking some NK ass." Brandt pulled his cannon from over his shoulder and checked the charge. "Lock and load."

Casey took them into a rocky cove, unbeknownst to them only a few miles around the coast from where the North Koreans had landed.

The pair leaped out and pulled their craft up the beach a little. Both then crouched behind a pile of rotting fibrous-looking tree stumps and scanned the muddy beach and the tangle of growth just up from them.

"What a surprise, more shitty, hot, and wet fungus-jungle," Brandt complained.

Casey snorted. "What, you were expecting? Florida?"

"Look." He held out an armored hand. On the back there was the beginning of green slime growing.

Casey looked from the slime to his face. "Can't imagine what's going on in your tighty whities then." She guffawed and nudged his hand away. "Quit bellyaching, let's go to work."

The pair headed in, from time to time following what might have been animal tracks, but mostly they had to cut, rip, or just push through growths that were like bags of mush or giant mushroom stalks.

"My sensors are picking up sound from up ahead," Casey said.

"Our guys, or theirs?" Brandt asked.

"Soon find out." She sped up.

They threaded their way along a hillside and then down into a rugged valley that was devoid of plants and becoming more volcanic-looking. There were pools at the bottom crusted with different-colored salt minerals, and areas of broken pumice, and craggy cliffs.

"Whoa." Casey slowed. "Coming from in there."

It was a cave in the cliffside, but of enormous proportions. Steam leaked out from its top to drift away in the humid air.

"Fly a damn plane in there," Brandt said, and looked around. "No tracks."

Casey glanced down. "Ground is too hard-packed to carry a print. Still picking up movement from down deep." She stared into the enormous dark cave. "I'm going to amplify the sound."

She worked her suit controls so as to isolate the noises from the inside of the cave and restrict all others.

After a moment she turned. "Water, or the sea. Maybe the cave drops below sea level and there's a tidal surge going on in there." She looked up at the steam drifting out from the top of the cave mouth. "That looks like water vapor, so maybe there are some volcanic pools bubbling away down there."

"Check it out?" Brandt asked.

Casey looked around the entrance and was about to turn away when she spied something out of place. She crossed to it and lifted the object.

It was a jade amulet no bigger than a bottle cap. But it was smoothed, and on one side was a swirling sun. She crossed back to Brandt.

"This looks like something one of the NKs would wear." She turned back to the cave. "Did they go in there, maybe seeking shelter?"

Brandt walked a few paces closer to the entrance and adjusted the setting on his optics. "Can't see shit – too hot for thermal imagery. Might even be too dark for light enhance." He turned to her. "Go, no go?"

Casey thought the amulet was an indicator that the NKs were in there – or at least one of them was. Just as she was about to enter, the situational dynamics changed.

The scream came from back the way they had come – and it was human.

"Shit." Brandt spun to Casey. "I know goddamn pain and fear, and that was it."

"Yep, double time." Casey began to sprint back in the direction of the cry.

* * *

Brandt eased through the soft branches, and then stopped dead. "What the . . . *hey*, what the fuck am I looking at here, Franks?"

Casey joined him and squinted at the strange scene. "Holy shit. If I didn't know better, I'd say we just found the lost tribe."

"This crap is insane; shouldn't be here." Brandt spat.

"Let's keep it together. Gather intel." Casey replied. "NKs might be in there."

The pair of HAWCs stared out at the chaotic spread of village huts. There didn't seem to be any design or rationale for things like streets or paths; there were just clumps of the dwellings, some merging into others, almost like they were organic. They looked like things you would see inhabited by wasps or stuck to rocks at low tide.

The pair slowed. Normally they would use simple hand signals, but both now had their combat visors engaged and had internal mic access.

"Big," Brandt said. "But they look primitive, don't they?"

"Cover my ass while I have a look-see." Casey eased her back up next to the open doorway of the nearest hut, while Brandt covered the rest of the village.

She allowed the visor to switch from normal ambiance to dark adapt, and quickly peered around the corner then pulled back. When nothing jumped out, and nothing was moving, she took a longer look.

The hut was empty save for a large table-looking thing at the rear.

"Clear," she said, and pulled back again.

"Further down,' Brandt said. "That faint heat source again."

The pair eased through the tomb-silent village, moving from one hut to the next, and finally came to a larger shelter from which the faint heat source was emanating.

Casey retracted her face shield and sniffed deeply. "Blood."

"The scream," Brandt replied.

The huge man had his back to the hut beside the wide doorway. Ready?" he asked. "On three, and two, and . . ."

He and Casey went in fast and took up positions inside and just on either side of the doorway. Casey immediately covered her face with the visor to block out the stench.

"Looks like this is as far as the NKs got. Or at least some of them," Brandt said.

"Fucking abattoir," Casey seethed.

The hut was littered with the remains of bodies – or rather skeletons, which still glistened with strands of meat and gristle. Even the skulls had been broken open like fruit to get at the soft pulp inside.

"Cannibals," Brandt spat.

"Cannibals? Nah, that's people eating people. Unlikely that humans did this." Casey crouched and used her scanners on the remains. "The bones are still warm. This just happened." She sighed. "I'm betting this was who screamed; and if it was, it was their last. Just hope it was quick."

Brandt walked around the hut, kicking a few of the bones aside. "Were they ripped apart in here, or were they dumped here like trash after the feast?"

Casey looked over the mound. "I count the remains of two, maybe three bodies. Probably not the entire team." She looked across at the huge HAWC. "Maybe some got away and got to the cave. Or were herded in there."

Brandt snorted softly. "I wanted them dead. But not like this." He turned to her. "I think our mission just ended."

"I think you're . . ." Casey held up a hand and tilted her head. Brandt stopped talking and listened as well.

From outside there was a soft noise, a little like bubbles popping. Then there came a soft clicking noise like hundreds of knitting needles all working furiously.

Casey turned slowly toward the open doorway. "And here we go."

"I am not fucking ending up like these assholes," Brandt said, and hefted the huge laser cannon.

The pair of HAWCs edged toward the doorway, and Casey stole a glance outside.

She pulled back. "Fu-*uuck*."

"How bad is it?" Brandt asked.

She turned to him. "On my in-the-shit scale of one to ten, it's a fifty."

"Fine with me." Brandt laughed as he looked at Casey. "Party time."

Both of the HAWCs engaged the heavier combat armor which also came up over their visors.

Casey turned back to grin at him, and even though she knew he couldn't see it, she bet he was grinning too.

"We fight our way back to the beach. And get the fuck out of here," she said. "Hundred bucks says I take more down than you do."

Brandt guffawed and opened the cannon's pulse size to maximum. "With that extra hundred I'm winning, first round is on me."

The big man turned to bump armored knuckles with Casey.

They counted down.

And then the pair burst out of the hut, firing as they went.

* * *

Casey Franks and Bill 'Beast' Brandt fought back to back. But the shelled monstrosities kept coming. And coming.

They put holes in them, but the creatures didn't go down from a body shot. Only Brandt's laser cannon obliterated them, a single sun-hot pulse from it slicing through a dozen at a time. But after a few pulses it needed to recharge, and there were more of the creatures joining the attack every second.

Casey threw grenades and fired head shots into the horde. But it was as if the very ground or sea was vomiting more of them up.

The smell of burned shellfish filled the air, and that damn clicking of their arms, or legs, or whatever they were, never stopped.

The creatures stood about nine feet tall, and looked like upright crabs, but they weren't dumb animals because they communicated with each other, coordinated their attacks, and obviously lived in these damn huts.

An organized attack came from their left flank, and as both HAWCs turned to concentrate their firepower there, the right flank surged, catching Casey. Her remaining good arm was grabbed by one of the pincers, and if not for the heavy armored suit, her hand would have been separated from her arm.

She reached across with her other MECH-powered hand and grabbed the huge claw, squeezing and crushing the carapace with the sound of breaking pottery, and leaking white fluid.

"Hurts, doesn't it?" She laughed out loud.

She and Brandt formed up again, but the great strength of the HAWCs and their training wasn't enough as they gradually tired and were pushed further and further back.

"You're not fucking eating me," Brandt screamed as he fired his sidearm or lashed out with his armored fist, while he waited for the laser cannon to recharge.

"We need a circuit breaker," Casey yelled back, and threw one of her remaining grenades. It was effective in that it blew apart three of the things, but ten more took the places of their obliterated compatriots.

Casey knew what was happening. They were being pushed all the way back to the huge cave. In another fifteen minutes, they were at its mouth, and Brandt's cannon had recharged enough for him to fire a wide reaper-style beam across the front ranks, cutting in half at least twenty of the powerful crustaceans.

Brandt bumped up against Casey. "They want us to go in, don't they?" he yelled.

"That's my reading. But we got no choice," she said. "We're dead meat out in the open. At least we got rock at our backs in there."

"I hope that's all we got at our backs," Brandt replied.

The pair retreated a little more, and this time, the shelled creatures didn't advance. The more the HAWCs approached the cave, the more the weird crab people paused their attack.

"They won't go in," Brandt said. "Maybe there's something in there even they are afraid of."

"Well ..." Casey said, and delivered a few more head shots. "If there's something in there that's their enemy, then it gets to be on my team."

"Works for me," Brandt replied.

"Goin' in." Casey backed into the cave, followed by the big HAWC.

CHAPTER 33

Present day – The Janus Institute, Landsdowne Street, Cambridge, Massachusetts

Quartermain nodded as he watched the Janus scientist work. "Brilliant, brilliant," he said.

Rashid Jamal continued to type long strings of code into his computer. He spoke without turning. "If the tachyons are too fast for us to harness and control the stream jump-off points on a bridge, then we simply have to bend to their will."

"Work with them, rather than against them," Quartermain offered.

"Exactly." Phillip Hanley watched with folded arms. "If they won't slow down, then we'll speed up."

After another moment Rashid stopped typing and held his hands over the keys as his eyes moved rapidly through the code. He began to nod. "Yes, yes, that might work."

Quartermain clapped, knowing he was under instruction to force the scientists forward. It had taken them many decades to create, cross, and return on a tachyon stream bridge successfully. But he would push them to go to the next steps in a matter of days. To hell with sleep.

"Then let's test it right now," he said.

"Is that safe?" Pinchella, the female HAWC sent as his bodyguard, asked. She wandered closer.

Quartermain turned to her and raised his eyebrows. "Is anything right now?"

"No." Pinchella half-smiled back. "That would make life boring, right?"

He smiled at her. "And who wants that?"

Though no one had seriously thought Quartermain needed backup against the Janus scientists, he was more concerned that the NK agents might try to infiltrate again to either obtain any new refinements to the technology or mount another attack to slow them down. Hammerson's orders to Pinchella were direct and simple: *Don't even let them get close. Take them down, hard.*

Rashid turned to Hanley; his lips turned up at one corner.

The man stared back. "Confidence level?" he asked.

"High," Rashid replied.

"Then let's do it," Hanley replied. He turned to face the technology team. "Okay, people, prepare for a stream jump. I want a camera pod readied and on the plinth in five minutes." He clapped his hands. "Come on, let's hustle."

"How far back?" Rashid asked. "Still not sure I've conquered all the bugs and I'm not able to timeframe it down to the . . ." he snorted softly, "day, or week, or year, or . . ."

"We get it," Quartermain replied.

Rashid's smile was almost apologetic. "Well, it's more like biting off my stream-jump epochs in millions of years at the moment."

"Then just go back one million years," Quartermain suggested. "This was prairie land here. Wide open plains. Nice and dry, and we should see the difference from a Silurian landscape immediately."

"I can do that," Rashid said, and started to prepare the jump instructions for the tachyon drive.

In five more minutes the camera was readied and running. Quartermain, Pinch, Rashid, and Hanley were all masked-up and in standby mode. Behind them were the six technicians who were completing their pre-jump duties and standing back with goggles on, also watching.

The equipment was given a final check and then the chamber was sealed.

Rashid looked around, smiling. "Ready, everyone?" he asked.

"Let's see what we got." Hanley folded his arms. "Mr. Jamal, let's proceed."

"Hey." Pinch motioned for Quartermain to come and stand by her.

He did, and she nudged his arm and winked.

He liked the tall and super-fit woman. He liked that she was looking out for him. And though his rational mind knew that was part of her designated role, in his heart he still fantasized that she did it because she fancied him. Just a little.

As he stared at the HAWC from the corner of his eye, her dark eyes slid to him. Although he would bet that she saw little more than a pencil-necked geek, he didn't care.

As he watched, the corner of her mouth twitched up a fraction. He blushed and turned away, but felt her eyes still on him.

"You okay?" She asked.

"Yeah, sure, don't worry about me." He grinned.

"But I do worry about you." Her dark eyes bored into him. "And not just because it's my job."

That small smile again, and Quartermain nearly swooned.

"Ready," Rashid said, waiting.

Hanley took one last look around the sealed and recently rebuilt laboratory. "Okay." He sucked in a deep, lung-filling breath, let it out, and then said: "*Initiate.*"

Rashid started the process over again and the tachyon drive commenced its familiar soft blue glow. The beam shot forward to envelop the plinth that held the camera box. It flared until it was too bright to look at directly and then vanished.

"Delivered." Rashid read data from the screen and focused as intently as if he were performing open heart surgery. "Okay, okay, according to the software it's arrived at its destination, the Pleistocene period, one million years ago. Hopefully the tech is working, it has an unimpeded vista, and it's capturing good film for us."

"Just some images of a prairie will be all we need for confirmation." Hanley checked his wristwatch. "Okay, that's long enough. Bring it back."

Rashid nodded once, never taking his eyes off his console. Again his fingers flew over the keyboard.

"Got it," he said softly. "Locking on. Generating bridge."

Quartermain watched, his heart pounding. He knew if this was successful, then they were only weeks, if not days, away from being able to perform near-term jumps. Then they could work on honing it down to the minute and second they wanted to return to.

The tachyon device glowed once again, and Quartermain felt the familiar tingle in the center of his head, like an itch that could never be scratched. The plinth glowed as the camera was returning.

The smudge of blue light formed, no bigger than a basketball. Then oddly it began to expand – getting bigger and bigger, far bigger than the camera ever was.

"Something's wrong," Rashid said.

"What is it?" Hanley glanced at his colleague and then back to the plinth.

There was a bright flash, and everyone waited a second or two for their eyes to readjust. But before that could even happen, there was a brutal animal roar so loud it felt like it went right through them to chill the marrow in their bones.

Quartermain's eyes flicked wide, and the breath caught in his throat.

"Get behind me," Pinchella yelled, and grabbed the scientist. She dragged him back behind her, then reached inside her jacket and pulled two guns, aimed them, and planted her legs in a wide stance.

Quartermain could only stare at what was standing inside the sealed tachyon chamber on top of the plinth, which had been crushed under its weight. The hulking beast must have weighed 1000 pounds and stood six feet tall at its shoulders, which were massively lumped with tawny-colored muscle. Curving down either side of its jaws were two long tusk-like teeth, and it was breathing hard and fast from fear and confusion. It turned luminous yellow eyes on them.

"*Oh, God,*" Quartermain whispered.

The beast fixed its eyes on the four closest people and began to coil its huge limbs.

Here it comes, Quartermain thought, and felt a prickle of fear run through his body.

The scientists backed up, but Pinchella punched a place on her chest, and armored plating telescoped up and over her head.

Quartermain recognized it as the more discreet body armor he had developed for urban operations. The female HAWC stepped forward, holding both her guns up, ready to meet the monster head on.

Quartermain wished she had chosen something a little heavier caliber against the beast, as he doubted her twin nine-millimeters were going to do anything other than irritate it. Unless she got it in the eye or the roof of the mouth, that was – something he wouldn't put past the ability of a well-trained HAWC.

Quartermain turned to see that Rashid was totally ignoring the beast and keeping his cool as he typed furiously. He stopped and looked up.

"Initiating," he said.

Just as the animal leaped, he hit a key, the blue glow enveloped the animal, and then came the usual blue, eye-blinding flash.

The glare died away and the muted darkness returned. The creature had vanished, and everyone exhaled, slumped, or closed their eyes, shoulders sagging.

Pinchella allowed her armor to retract and slowly lowered her guns. "What. The fuck. Was that?"

"*Smilodon*, I'd say," Quartermain said softly, and swallowed in a dry mouth. "One of the megafauna alpha predators of the Pleistocene epoch. They were alive around a million years ago. And lived right around here." He began to grin. "As far as the timing was concerned, I'd say that was a success."

Hanley smiled wearily, but then turned to Rashid. "How did we get that monster instead of our camera? Have we got a bug in the code?"

Rashid shook his head. He had already been quickly scanning the lines of instructions. "Nope." He turned. "You know what I think? I think we got the camera as expected. But it was inside that thing."

"Of course." Quartermain began to laugh softly. "You brought the camera back successfully. But the camera just happened to be inside a giant saber-toothed tiger."

Hanley nodded, his smile widening. "We went fishing . . . and caught a whopper."

Rashid shrugged. "But the bottom line is, we're still on track." He looked across to Quartermain. "I think we can solve the near-term destination mapping within the next few weeks."

"Make it happen. But make it in the next few days," said Quartermain. "I'll let Colonel Hammerson know. He'll be pleased." He then turned to Pinchella and put a hand on her arm. "Thank you."

"Just another day at the office." She grinned and placed her hand over his, giving it a squeeze.

CHAPTER 34

A recognizable blip appeared on Alex's sensor. Then another.

"Got 'em. Casey and Brandt." He waited another moment for the third. "Come on, big guy, where are you?"

Alex kept staring, hoping to see Sam Reid's signature. But after another few minutes there was still nothing.

"Dammit, Reid." He exhaled and stared at the only two HAWC signatures on his tracker. He couldn't wait for him – but if he couldn't get to Sam, then he'd just get what he could. He'd prioritize getting his HAWCs. Maybe they had intel on Sam, or maybe not. But regardless, the extra firepower would be welcome. Alex read the coordinates of his other two missing HAWCs again.

He pointed. "Eleven clicks, north-northeast." He turned to Ito. "Give it all we got."

Ito nodded and the craft surged forward.

"Are they moving?" Cooper asked.

Alex shook his head. "Stationary."

"What about the big guy?" Gonzalez asked.

Alex shook his head. "Nothing – yet. Either he's out of reach, or already back home."

He turned away, knowing in his gut that Sam wasn't home. He looked again out at the endless blue walls of the warm sea surrounding them and felt a sensation of disquiet in his belly.

"Why are they stationary?" Cooper asked. "There's nothing out here."

"Maybe they lost power. Becalmed," Ito replied.

"Knowing the Beast, he's probably fishing." Gonzalez grinned. "Gonna be good to see Franks and that big lug again."

"Something's not right. I got that feeling," Alex said.

"That ain't good," Gonzalez replied.

Alex turned to his remaining team. "Be ready."

* * *

It was just twenty minutes later that Alex had Ito surface, and he squinted into the distance. "Land," he said.

He had his visor retracted and he closed his eyes and inhaled. "I can smell it."

Cooper used her lenses on maximum amplification and confirmed it. "Yes, yes, just on the horizon, a landmass. But it's not just an island; the sensors say it's huge." She looked up. "There should be nothing ahead of us but sea for hundreds of miles."

Gonzalez laughed out loud. "Gee, seems our maps from 420 million years ago were out just a tad. Who'd have guessed?"

Cooper turned. "This isn't a tad; this is a significant landmass."

"And that must be where Casey and Brandt are," Alex replied. "They must have found it and gone ashore."

"Maybe they made camp. That's why they're stationary," Ito said. "This would make sense."

Alex nodded, but he was doubtful.

"Something else," Cooper said, and looked up with a

crooked smile. "The radiation readings are lifting off the charts. I think our bombs are there too."

"Then that's why our HAWCs are there," Alex replied. "Means the NKs are there. And if they're caught in a firefight, that might make our guys dig in." Alex turned. "Take her down again, Mr. Yamada. If someone's watching the water, it might be best to give them a little surprise."

They all deployed the clear aquatic visor down over their faces as the craft submerged. It would take them another fifteen minutes to arrive, and he just hoped Franks and Brandt could hold out that long.

He stared straight ahead as the craft powered through the clear water. Schools of weird, bony-headed fish were persuaded out of the way by the nose of their submersible, and just on the periphery of his vision, he saw shadows lurking in the blue gloom the size of great white sharks, but in shapes that were more like armor-plated tanks with fins.

Alex ignored them and focused – he remembered Jack Hammerson's words from what seemed a long-ago mission: *When your team is in trouble, there are only two paths to take – rescue or revenge.* Time would dictate which it would be.

"Shallowing out," Ito said as the bottom came up fast underneath them.

They slowed as they began to pass through long strands of kelp infused with all manner of life.

Alex squinted at some larger formations on the sea floor, hidden among the kelp forests, that he could have sworn looked like huts. *Impossible*, he thought, and refocused on the planned profile of the mission ahead.

"Twenty feet," Ito intoned.

Alex looked up to watch the mirroring effect of the water surface above them – their craft was a long dark fish and rising rapidly toward them.

"Ten feet." Ito began to count down, but Alex stopped him.

"Park it. We walk from here," he said.

Ito shut down the engines and they glided gently to the sea floor, where he secured the vessel. The crew eased out and Alex also initiated DOG. Together the four humans and the android canine walked along the sand toward land.

Alex was first to raise his head and scan the shore. He could see a beach, and shifting through his different vision spectrums he saw a boat that must be the NKs' craft hidden among some bushes.

"They're here," he said, and carefully scanned the undergrowth for any snipers. But other than the normal background warmth on his heat sensors, there was nothing.

The others came to the surface.

"Gonzalez, check for the HAWC boat. Ito and Cooper, with me as we examine the NK vessel." He looked down at the DOG standing beside him. "Tor, security circuit. Scan for threats. Go."

The android version of Tor exploded from the water like a missile and sped into the undergrowth. The four humans followed to complete their allotted tasks. Alex moved Ito out to the right flank, and he took the left, with Cooper following close behind him. She held her sidearm in a two-handed grip and moved it over the line of thick jungle.

The four had engaged their combat visors, and Cooper read the readout displayed on her facial screen indicating the radiation signature.

"Rad count rising – we're very close," she said.

"Got it," Alex said.

Alex and Ito stopped to scan the heavy growth just before the mound of branches and debris covering the NK boat. Alex saw DOG return and stand motionless. It sent the message directly to him – *no perceivable threats*.

"Let's see what we got," Alex said, and he and Ito pulled the covering from the boat and pointed their guns inside, looking for hidden traps or anything else that had been secreted in the North Korean craft.

Cooper jumped straight in and began ferreting among the supplies and other boxes. She quickly found the nuclear packages and counted them off.

"There are ten here. Either they've only just begun to deploy them, or they haven't started yet."

Alex retracted his visor, and the others did the same. "My guess is that they were as surprised as we were by this landmass."

Cooper nodded. "They expected to be dropping these things in open water. They might be scouting for a suitable drop point on land." She looked back down at them. "For now, they're all inert. Should we dismantle them?"

"How long?" Alex asked.

"She shrugged. "Three to five minutes per package."

"No, we need that time." He looked out at the jungle. "Something happened here. They wouldn't leave the packages unguarded. Something must have forced them to abandon them."

"That something might have been our HAWCs," Ito said. "They took off and our guys went after them."

Alex nodded. "Maybe. Whatever happened, we need to find our people." Alex turned. "Gonzalez, what've you got?"

Gonzalez joined them. "Nothing. If our guys are here, they came ashore somewhere else." He looked back over his shoulder momentarily. "Something else; looks like a skirmish. A couple of NKs and the tracks of something else I can't identify bumped up against each other. Looks to me like the NKs lost and were herded out."

"Carried out?" Alex frowned.

Gonzalez shook his head. "Nope, there are footprints in the center of the weird tracks. They were shuffling, but they were on their feet."

Alex grunted, and then opened his mic and tried to contact the two missing HAWCs again. This time he boosted the signal. "Franks, Brandt, come back." He walked a few paces out into the open. "Franks, Brandt, what is your operational status?"

He waited a few more moments. "Dammit." He opened the mic again. "HAWCs, we are initiating tracking and coming to you. Out." He turned. "Team, we're moving."

Alex checked his scanner and programmed it to search for the transponders implanted in all the HAWCs' necks. The tracker first found him and his team, and then after a few minutes it found Casey and Brandt several miles inland.

"Okay, I've got 'em. Still stationary," Alex said. "Let's go get 'em."

"What about the boats, and the bombs?" Cooper said. "This is our primary objective."

"I know." Alex doubted the NKs could get past them, but on the off chance they did, he'd hate to have them sail away with the bombs and leave his team chasing them again. But he needed his HAWCs and didn't want to leave Cooper behind.

"DOG," he said.

Tor sped to sit in front of him.

Alex put his hand on the android's head and crouched in front of it. The thing's black lens eyes stared back into his own, and for a brief moment, he felt Tor's consciousness, and its desire to please him. He bet if it had a tail, it would be wagging.

"Guardian mode." He pointed at the NKs' boat. "No one is to touch this vessel."

DOG's eyes flashed red for a moment, and it trotted to the boat to sit with its back to it, facing Alex.

Alex led his team out and looked over his shoulder to see the android animal watching him leave. He could have sworn he heard a small electronic whine of dismay.

* * *

The team moved quickly along the tracks, but after just ten minutes Gonzalez stopped. "Hey, what's wrong with this picture?"

"Everything," Alex said, and edged forward toward a lumpy object lying on the ground.

"It's clothing." Gonzalez used the muzzle of his gun to lift some of the material. "Not HAWC. But no blood. So they stripped down." He went to one knee. "Yep, it's the North Korean army camo-uniform, with weapons still in holsters and packs." He quickly went through a few of the pockets and pouches, drawing out a few grenades, sidearms, knives, and a picture of a young woman and child.

"Why'd they strip off?" Cooper asked.

"Maybe they had no choice." Alex lifted a shirt that was ripped. "They didn't strip, they were stripped. Humiliated. This is degradation stuff, to dehumanize them. The Viet Cong used to do this to prisoners. It lowered resistance, made the soldiers feel more vulnerable."

He walked a few paces forward. "Here, bare footprints in among those spiked prints." He lifted his head to look along the track. "They were herded in here, stripped down, and then moved on, one behind the other."

They continued on up the slope for another twenty minutes, following the pathway and keeping an eye on the tracks. They passed through a thicker part of the jungle but were still able to move easily as the branches, vines, and hanging shawls of growth were soft like overcooked vegetables. The path soon narrowed, and up ahead they saw another clearing, but it was the smell that got their attention first.

"Death," Ito said.

"It's not . . .?" Cooper began.

Alex looked at his tracker. "No, not the HAWCs. They're further in." He slowly looked around at the miasmic jungle. "We need to check it out. See who or what it is."

He led them on. And he prayed he wouldn't finally find Sam Reid.

CHAPTER 35

Sam returned from the hunt with the huge deer over his shoulder, but as soon as he neared the village he knew something was wrong. There was no sound of children laughing, no smoke from cooking pits, and no Dalila sitting on the stone wall watching out for him.

At the arched entrance to the village, he shucked the deer carcass from his shoulders and walked forward, hunting spear in one hand, the other resting lightly on the scabbard containing the long skinning knife in his belt.

It was then that the Philistine garrison commander, Gargus, stepped out, a cruel smirk twisting his lips.

Sam stopped and stared. He knew enough of the Philistine language now to speak and understand it. "Where is everyone?" His grip tightened on the spear, and he was confident he could skewer the man before he could even blink. "They better not be harmed, or there will be blood."

"There will only be blood . . ." the man's smirk remained, ". . . if you do not do as I tell you." He folded his arms. "Drop your weapons and kneel."

Sam didn't move, just letting his eyes slide across the empty village. He saw then the brown stains on the ground and had a sinking feeling he was already too late.

Sam spoke through gritted teeth. "If they are dead, I will tear you—"

Gargus snapped his fingers and several Philistine soldiers appeared. Each had a villager in their arms, with a blade to their throats – there was the village elder, Marcus, his wife, Arina, and then there was Dalila.

"*Run, Samson,*" Dalila had time to shout before the hand went across her mouth to squeeze off her words.

Sam's shoulders dropped in defeat. He knew he couldn't get to them all. And the blood already spilled told him the Philistines were hungry for more death. He knew he was defeated without feeling a single blow.

"I cannot." He dropped his spear. Then the knife.

Gargus grinned. "I am to deliver you to the Saran, alive. But first I have been ordered to declaw you." His smile widened. "Hold out your arms."

Sam sucked in a huge breath and did as asked. The entire time he kept his eyes on Dalila, knowing what was coming.

Their biggest soldier came forward with an axe, and in a huge chop brought it down across both of Sam's forearms.

The villagers screamed and Arina fainted.

Sam just glared, sucking up the excruciating pain. Blood ran freely, but his hands remained on his arms. The flesh was cut, deep, but there was no chance the axe could cut through the internal MECH infrastructure running throughout his body.

"What dark magic is this?" Gargus growled.

"*The hand of God,*" Dalila yelled, before she was shaken roughly back to silence.

Gargus stepped forward and ran his hand over Sam's arms, shoulders, and chest. Then he looked up into Sam's face and his expression became crafty.

"Samson, the slayer of lions . . ." he smiled cruelly, ". . . should know there are many ways to declaw a big cat."

He snapped his fingers and ordered a blade be heated.

Five minutes later, with Sam's wounds bound and his hands tied behind his back, and several warriors holding him, Gargus stepped in front of him.

"She says you are the hand of God. Or have the hands of a god." He tilted his head. "The rumors say your strength is in your strange white hair." He smiled. "Or maybe it is in those pale eyes."

Sam remained like a block of stone.

"Look at my face," Gargus hissed.

Sam remained mute and stared only at Dalila.

"*Look at my face!*" Gargus shouted.

Sam remained motionless.

Gargus held out a hand behind him. "Without those eyes we will make you a stumbling beast of burden for the Saran until you rot." He lifted the white-hot blade.

Sam stared straight ahead as the searing blade approached his eyes. As a HAWC he had been trained to ignore pain and torment that would send a normal human being insane.

He breathed calmly, and in his mind he transported himself away, taking himself back to a time when he sat in a park with Alyssa, and she handed him a tiny wildflower, which he'd held in one of his huge, rough hands – a small and delicate piece of love, in the hands of a brutal warrior.

The blade touched his first eye – the pain was excruciating.

But the darkness that came was worse.

CHAPTER 36

Two hours prior to Alex's landfall

Casey and Brandt sprinted down into the depths of the stygian cave. It was narrowing but was still the size of a railway tunnel. They had left the crab creatures long behind, but had discovered a new torment, that seemed even worse.

They could hear the scuttling sounds of the swarm of acid-spitting freaks that were right behind them. And not just on their heels, but also on the walls and covering the cave ceiling overhead.

Already their pitted armor was beginning to degrade and fatigue, and the acidic shit was still raining down on them. They both knew they didn't have long in the safety of their suits. Brandt had already discarded a shoulder brace, and they could only hope they would win the race before the acid made it through to their skin.

But it was a race to the unknown, and Casey worried they may end up somewhere even worse. Those big-shelled freaks had herded them in here for a reason, and she bet it wasn't just to feed themselves.

There was a side tunnel coming up, smaller, perhaps only

about ten feet around, but maybe it would provide a better place to defend themselves against the coming horde.

"In here," Casey yelled, and as she headed for the opening she pointed back at the scuttling masses coming after them. "Clear the deck."

Brandt lifted the laser cannon and sent a wide-beam pulse of pure plasma, like a rolling ball of lightning, back at the monstrosities. It flew back, bounced, and everywhere it touched, it vaporized hundreds of the things. But for every one that was fried or disintegrated, ten more took their place.

Both HAWCs charged into the smaller tunnel, ducking underneath a line of wickedly sharp and weird-looking stalactites. They immediately felt the change in the floor as it became spongy, and their suit sensors told them the heat and humidity had gone off the charts.

After running in about a hundred feet, Brandt turned back, and his brows came together. "Hey, Franks," he said as he slowed.

Casey looked over her shoulder and saw that the big man had stopped. She did too.

"What?" She frowned, knowing they had no time.

He pointed. "The acid critters; I think they stopped following us."

"Huh?" Casey turned back and switched her vision spectrum to night vision, and then amplification. Beast was right; there was nothing following them into the smaller cave.

"Good," she said, and sucked in a few deep breaths.

The pair stood in silence for a moment before Casey tilted her head. "Hey, something . . ." The floor seemed to quiver beneath her boots. She took a few more steps as her suit joins on her limbs were starting to seize up.

She retracted her visor. "This don't feel right."

A gentle breeze blew past her, and it stank like bad meat. She allowed her suit to test it, and her inbuilt analyzer judged it as methane, nitrogen, oxygen, and high levels of carbon dioxide.

The breeze died away. But in the next instant it came again, although it had changed direction. This time the gas mix was like the surrounding atmosphere.

But then a few moments later it changed again. It was almost like . . .

"Oh, fuck no," she said.

"What now, dead end?" Brandt turned. "We turn back or go on and find another way out."

Casey looked around. "Oh, there ain't another way out of here. Unless you want to be shitted out some big fucking thing's asshole."

Brandt scoffed. "What does that—?"

"Run," Casey yelled.

She began to run back toward the entrance, and Brandt didn't hesitate to follow. As they did, the ground shivered under their feet, and then the walls rippled.

The pair of HAWCs tried to run faster, but their failing suits were working against them now. And then from up ahead, they saw the wave coming at them – the entire tunnel was closing, in a giant peristaltic wave.

"I was right, we're inside something's fucking mouth," Casey yelled, engaged her visor again, and then dived at Brandt, linking arms with him. "Dig in." She pulled her blade and swung her arm back, sinking it to the hilt into the leathery wall.

Brandt did the same, and then the crushing wave hit them. Unfortunately, the HAWC armor was already weakened, and the thousands of pounds of peristaltic pressure came down, tearing at their limbs and compressing hardest on the largest parts of them – their torsos. But the blades and their strength held out, and they weren't swallowed down a monstrous gullet to some sort of giant acid bath in a lake-sized belly somewhere.

After the wave passed over them the tunnel opened up again, and Casey and Brandt wiped slime from their visors.

"We gotta get the fuck out of this thing." Brandt staggered to his feet, but the ground shifted constantly now, and it was hard to maintain his balance.

Casey knew that they'd never make it back to the mouth. And even if they did, it might be closed tight, and those weird-looking stalactites weren't just three-foot-long teeth but prison bars.

"We'll never get there before the next wave hits us," she yelled, as a deep moan permeated the atmosphere. They felt the thing begin to shift again, and Casey imagined it was sliding deeper back into its hidey hole.

Now it was obvious why the little acid-spitters hadn't followed them – they knew exactly what this cave of horrors was.

Casey grabbed at Brandt's shoulder as they heard the next peristaltic wave coming down the tunnel – or as they now knew, down the throat – toward them.

"We'll never make it to the exit. So let's generate our own." She pushed him. "Make a fucking hole, soldier."

"Oh, yeah." Brandt pulled the huge cannon up tight under his arm. It was pitted from the acid-spitters, but he widened the pulse, and fired it directly into the wall beside him.

There was a flash of light and heat, and the end of the cannon melted. But there was also a bloody explosion, immediately followed by a storm of movement, and in the chaos they saw the three-foot-wide ragged hole they'd made in the wall.

The creature was thick, three feet of flesh, but the hole had been seared and cauterized by the plasma burst.

Casey was first through, diving headfirst and rolling to her feet. She turned, willing her partner on, and a second later the huge man followed, worming and wriggling, but because of his size he got wedged.

Casey grabbed Brandt's shoulders. "You big-assed Beast." She tugged as Brandt fought to escape, just as the monstrous creature began to retract furiously down the tunnel. Casey used her robotic arm to hold on, and, screaming her fury, finally dragged Brandt out.

As the thing went past they saw the huge head, like a massive sightless worm, and at the tip, meshed teeth like a Venus flytrap.

"Fuck you too," Casey yelled, and fired a few pulses of her own laser rifle after it.

The sound of it withdrawing began to fade, and she sucked in a deep breath, her shoulders sagging as the adrenaline began to leak from her system.

Brandt scoffed. "Did we just get eaten by a fucking worm?"

She looked up at him and grinned. "Man, this place is fucked up."

The pair laughed and then she straightened. Her armor grated, and one of the arms refused to bend at the elbow.

"Well, this is shit," she said. "Suits are compromised. Might have to ditch or they'll end up our coffins."

"Do we want speed or security?" Brandt asked.

"I want to get the hell out of here, fast," she replied. "And if I wanted security, I would have stayed home."

Brandt took off his helmet, breathed in deeply through his nose, and then coughed. "Stinks in here."

Casey did the same and lifted her chin. "I also smell seawater, coming from deep down somewhere. Maybe this cave leads to the sea." She turned. "Acid-spitters, monster worm, or the sea?"

Brandt grinned. "I could do with a bath."

She grinned back. "I coulda told you that on the chopper in." She turned to bang the back of her fist against his chest. "The sea it is."

The pair spent a few minutes shucking off their HAWC armor but removing and keeping any tech and weaponry that still worked – which wasn't much, but included their gauntlet monitors. Brandt shook his head as he stared down at the melted cannon.

"Thanks for everything, buddy." He dropped it.

They then headed down into the dark depths, just in their Kevlar skinsuits.

CHAPTER 37

Alex, Cooper, and the HAWCs followed the stench of death, which was like a highway through the jungle. As it became more powerful, Alex slowed his team and together they crept forward toward a small clearing. They stopped behind the last line of jungle growth and stared up at what was pegged out on the hillside.

"For fuck's sake; crucifixions now?" Gonzalez spat. "Who would do this? Our guys wouldn't." He turned. "Fucking animals."

"Could there be another team?" Ito asked.

"Unlikely," Alex replied. "But I think the threat level just went up a few degrees, and we might have more problems than just a team of NKs right now." He let his eyes travel over the surrounding jungle and then back to the track they were on.

"Move out." He looked along the line of the macabre displays – there were things lashed to x-shaped crosses. Some were just skeletons, or the empty shells of human-sized insects. But others still had meat on their bones. And then he stopped at the last one. The newest addition.

"Oh, shit," Cooper said. "That's a person."

As one, the group shut their helmet visors.

"I think we just found one of the NKs," Gonzalez growled through gritted teeth. "This is medieval-level shit."

"We're going in. We need to check that human body," Alex said. "Everyone, eyes out." He briefly scanned his surroundings to ensure the torturers weren't waiting in ambush or taking delight in their response. When satisfied they were alone, he took the team in, moving at a low crouch toward the body.

The group stopped to stare up at it.

"Looks Asian, North Korean, female," Cooper said. "Or what's left of one."

"This is bad shit," Gonzalez seethed.

Alex nodded. "There is a culture here – primitive and barbaric, but still a culture." He looked up. "I can't tell if this is a warning, or some sort of offering to their gods."

"Could they be human?" Ito asked. "The beings who did this?'

"Impossible," Cooper said. "Humans don't even begin to evolve for another 420 million years. I can't imagine what did this."

Alex had seen torture before. But its purpose was usually to get the victim to talk. Here, the young woman's jaw was missing from the nose down. From her ripped-open neck her esophagus protruded like a piece of broken pipe, and her eyes had rolled back and were now sunken and milky. Blood had run down and dried on her bare chest.

Gonzalez was still muttering curses. "Jesus, man, you don't torture people by tearing their mouths off. They can't answer questions like that."

"Her tongue is missing. They took it. I don't think they wanted to talk to her. They wanted to hurt her. Or make an example of her so the others would talk." Ito made a small grunt and half-turned. "Or maybe to stop her talking."

"Could it have been her buddies?" Gonzalez asked. "Maybe she had turned traitor or something."

Alex shook his head. "No, they wouldn't burn time doing this." He looked along the rows of other scarecrows. "Besides, some of these things have been here months, years maybe." He walked across and stood in front of one of the things that bore a rough resemblance to a long frog, with extended arms. "And I have no idea what some of them even are."

"Some sort of convergent species?" Cooper offered.

Alex looked back at the human figure. "We're done here. But we are now moving on high alert." He turned. "Our guys are out there, so we find them, ASAP." He waved them on. "Double time."

They moved at a trot now, and soon breached the hilltop and saw the massive structure of columns and stones. They went to ground and scanned the area.

"What the hell is this?" Alex asked. "This shouldn't exist. Why is it here?"

Cooper shook her head. "Your guess is as good as mine. Its size and workmanship . . ." She exhaled. "It exceeds the scale of the pyramids or Cambodia's Angkor Wat." She pursed her lips. "We need to take a closer look."

"We're on the clock; we pass through it, but that's all. No time for sightseeing until we've recovered our people," Alex said.

He waved them on.

The team climbed steps of colossal proportions and walked in through the columns that towered above them like mighty redwoods. A few minutes later they stood looking up at the carving on the wall.

"That is badass," Gonzalez breathed.

The group scrutinized the carved rendition of the hellish beast.

"I think this is a demon. Known as *Akkorokamui*," Ito said.

"No, not a demon. I think it's the thing we saw in the water," Cooper said softly, and turned to Alex. "The old god."

"Looks like a demon to me." Gonzalez turned. "Hey, maybe they sent us back to Hell by mistake."

"Shut that down, soldier," Alex said, and faced Cooper. "Continue."

Cooper nodded and walked a few paces closer. "I think . . . I think this is what they referred to as an elder god. One of the great old ones."

"That's no god I would pray to." Gonzalez turned away.

"But others did," Cooper replied to him. "There are many involved in dark magic and other underground religions who believe that there was a race of super beings that existed long before all other creation. Whether they formed here or came from somewhere else in the cosmos is unknown. But they were thought to have vanished long before humanity even evolved. Some say they still exist deep in the bowels of the Earth . . . and are simply sleeping." She turned to Alex. "That's why they're referred to as the slumbering gods, who intrude into our dreams."

"Or nightmares." Alex looked up at the horror. "We thought Lovecraft made it up."

"He might have dreamed it. Like many have," she replied.

"It lived in his dreams," Ito said hopefully. "Maybe in his imagination."

"Lovecraft wrote about it." Cooper frowned, seeming to be searching her memory. "It went something like this: '. . . *the Great Old Ones who lived ages before there were any men, and who came to the young world out of the sky. Those Old Ones are gone now, inside the Earth and under the sea; but their dead bodies had told their secrets in dreams to the first men, who formed a cult which had never died.*'" When she finished, her face was pale.

"It lives underground. So, it *is* a demon. Or maybe a devil." Gonzalez tilted his head. "Hey, you know want? Maybe it is *the* devil." His lips pulled back from his teeth in a grimace and he crossed himself. He made a guttural sound in his throat. "Dream or no dream, this thing is freaking me out."

Alex stared up at it. "I saw that in my mind." He remembered the thing he'd seen hovering in the water on the drone's camera. He remembered how it had the intellect to probe his mind. To *intrude* into his mind. Was this the same thing? he wondered.

In his gut he knew it was.

"Let's get moving. We've got work to do." He led them off.

The HAWCs crouched just outside the clusters of huts and slowly looked over the village. There was no movement or sound they could detect. Alex also saw from his tracker that his missing team members had been there but had moved off to a place just on half a mile away.

"Tracking says they went in. Same as the North Koreans – but the NKs seem to have been marched in under guard," Gonzalez said.

"Those huts," Cooper said. "I've seen something like that building material before. Usually on tidal flats. They're not built but excreted."

"Excuse me?" Gonzalez turned. "It sounded like you just said they were *excreted*."

"Whatever they are, our people are not in there now. We go around," Alex said.

The HAWCs pulled back and they slid around the village, hive, nest, or whatever it was. As they moved through the growth, they came across burns and breaks in the foliage.

"Laser burns. Lots of them," Ito said. "Our guys were fighting against something every step of the way."

"Whatever was living in that village, I bet," Gonzalez said. "Looks like they were fighting all the way from here to wherever they ended up."

The HAWCs and Cooper sped up, and soon came closer to the cliffs. Then, breaking from their cover, they stopped before the huge cave. Though the ground outside was rocky, it was still torn up, and some of the soft plants had been obliterated.

Alex stared at the huge dark cave mouth. "Did they seek shelter, or were they pushed in?"

"They were still fighting here," Ito observed.

Alex looked around. "We both know Franks and Brandt; those guys don't give up, and they don't miss." He turned slowly. "Just like in the village and the jungle; so where are all the bodies?"

"They must have taken them away. Many cultures did that," Cooper replied. "Or . . ."

Alex turned to her. "Or?"

"Or they weren't affected by the HAWCs' weapons." She exhaled as she shook her head. "We have no idea what we're dealing with, so we have to take into consideration an opponent that is vastly different from us. Maybe vastly more formidable."

"Well, that's a great thought." Gonzalez shook his head in frustration. "Shoulda brought my slingshot."

"Doesn't matter." Alex sucked in a deep breath. "Armor up, we're going in."

The HAWCs and Cooper initiated the heavier combat form of their suits, checked their weapons, and then Alex led them in.

Almost immediately they saw that the cave angled downward, and the sound of water emanated from deep inside.

"Franks, Brandt, come back." Alex tried to reach out and connect to their comms again. But this time instead of no response, he got static. It was as if their receivers were close, but were either using a different frequency, or being blocked.

Alex retracted his helmet visor and inhaled deeply. "Seawater," he said, ignoring the suit tech and reaching out with his own physical sensors. He was immediately flooded with impressions of life.

This time he picked up Casey and Brandt, but they were very far below them. And alive – for now. And then came the crawling intrusion into his mind again, just like when he'd seen the monstrous thing beneath the sea. It was also here.

They continued heading down, and a stagnant wind wafted up at them that seemed like it was breathing pure evil.

The group began to pass by side tunnels and some shallow caves that branched off the main one. They slowed as they saw that some of the alcoves had what looked like the remains of fences, high, some with gates on them.

"Prisons," Ito said. "Or holding pens."

"For who?" Cooper asked. "Why would they imprison people, or other creatures, down here?"

"There's something else in these caves. Lower down," Alex said. "I can feel it."

"Is it our team?" Cooper began.

"No." Alex turned. "Non-human. But there's intelligence there."

"The old gods," Ito repeated Cooper's words.

"You know what I think?" Gonzalez said. "They were caging things in those pens to be sacrifices to that weird-ass old god of theirs." He groaned. "I am not liking this one bit."

Ito turned away from the pens. "Do you think they imprisoned our people?"

"No." But Alex had the same thought. "We find our people. Kill anything that gets in our way. Then we bug out," he said.

CHAPTER 38

Twelfth century BC, the Levant – beneath the
Philistine grain houses

Sam Reid was shackled to a huge grinding wheel. A rough
cloth had been bound around his eyes, which had finally
stopped leaking fluid from the destroyed orbs.

The turning pole he was chained to was too thick even for
him to break, so his life now was to push the pole, hour after
hour, day after day, as endless wheat grain was thrown under
the huge stone wheel for him to crush down to powder.

The air was thick with dust and rasped at his throat.
With that and the grit he breathed in, his thirst was a never-
ending agony. But there was no one to quench it, no one
would dare, as he was an outcast, a criminal, and one day set
to be executed by order of the Saran himself, when the amusement of having captured the mighty Samson, the giant of the
Nazarites, wore off.

At night Sam resorted to catching the rats that crawled
on his body and drinking their blood and devouring
their flesh. He was becoming an animal and was stripped
down to little more than rags around his waist. His ruined
eye sockets still burned with pain, and his body was scarred

and marked with bruises and cuts from the regular beatings he received.

Without his sight, the attacks came without warning, and once a blow had landed on his neck that was so hard and heavy, he was nearly knocked unconscious. He recovered quickly, but the tachyon bridge transponder inserted under the skin crunched when he moved, and he knew it had been damaged. He also knew that with the transponder gone, he was trapped here, and crushingly, knew he would not be going home now.

Thankfully they hadn't yet detected his internal MECH armor. He knew it would be a miserable and agonizing way to die, being bound while they flayed him alive and then separated his muscles so they could pull free all his metallic skeletal infrastructure.

He had been here years now. Did time pass the same back home? Or was he in some sort of separate dimension where this time was nothing more than the blink of an eye?

He tried not to think about it, and instead focused on his beautiful Alyssa, waiting for him back there. Her face comforted him. He imagined her drinking wine on the front porch. Laughing in the sunshine as she gathered flowers. Or helping deliver a new foal. If he couldn't be with her, he could at least dream of being with her. Because the one thing they could never cut free were his memories.

He ground his teeth, hard, and tried not to sob. But try as he might to master his emotions, anger still swelled, as he knew he had now been robbed of touching her again. But also of ever speaking to her, feeling her, loving her again. He saw her beautiful brown face, large, liquid dark eyes, and full soft lips.

He couldn't help the wail that escaped his lips then turned into a roar of fury. Immediately he felt the lash across his back. It just made his anger swell to even greater heights, and he pushed the wheel faster, the many-ton grinding stone picking up speed.

"*Alyssa,*" he screamed. "*Alyssaaaaa!*"

The walls shook as faster and faster he went, until he heard the splintering of wood and crack of stone. He'd bring this entire place down on them, he thought. Kill them all. Kill himself. Free himself. If he couldn't free his flesh, he'd free his spirit.

He was running now, but just as the ground was beginning to vibrate and rock dust poured down on him, a loop went around one of his ankles, bringing him to his knees. And he stayed there, weeping, as the lashes rained down on him.

But his anger remained. One day they would make a mistake. And on that day, he would bury them all.

Lieutenant Sam Reid, Samson, now back on his feet, pushed the wheel, his enormous body scarred and filthy, as he waited for his opportunity. Until then, he would shut himself off from the pain and degradation being inflicted on him.

His one hope was that his brothers and sisters in arms, the other HAWCs, had been successful and made it home. After so many years he had given up hope of them ever finding him and rescuing him. It didn't matter now.

* * *

That night Sam heard the guard's soft whispers. The Saran had chosen a date for a festival to their decrepit god, Dagon. They thrilled at the rumors about the entertainment – there would be feasting, wine by the jug, and in the main temple arena, there would be animals, slaves, and prisoners, all tormented and slaughtered for the enjoyment of the bloodthirsty crowd of Philistine elite.

All of it would be working up toward the evening's major and final event. And that was to be Sam's ending.

Sam had no idea how that would occur, but he could imagine the Saran choosing something that would inflict the most humiliation and pain on his body. He knew the man didn't want to just kill him; he wanted to send a message to his own people and the Nazarites, that none should stand against him. And if they did, then they should be prepared to suffer the same fate as Samson.

Sam knelt. He couldn't even tell the difference between light and dark, but he knew there was a high barred window up on the wall, and a cooling breeze wafted in through it.

As he knelt there with his face turned to it, he imagined a bright moon throwing a soft glow in on him, and he held up his shackled hands in its direction.

Sam prayed. But not for freedom, or a quick death, or even a painless death. He prayed for something far darker.

He prayed for vengeance.

CHAPTER 39

The Janus Institute, Landsdowne Street, Cambridge, Massachusetts

Rashid sat back from the screen in time to see his friend and colleague, Phillip Hanley, rub his face, hard, with both hands. They were both running on very little sleep, but he thought his partner looked ten years older than only a few months ago.

He knew stress would do that.

"Phillip," No reaction. "*Phillip.*"

"Huh?" Hanley looked up. "What is it?"

"That should do it." Rashid smiled. "I can pinpoint date, time, and geography." He pointed at the screen. "I can also now see where all our team members are."

"Good; now we can tell that asshole, Hamm—" He stopped himself and his eyes slid to the ever-present female HAWC and watchdog, Pinchella, who glared at him.

Quartermain stepped forward. "Don't worry, we'll tell the colonel. He will be delighted with the news." He walked closer to Rashid. "You said we can pinpoint our team? Show me."

Rashid nodded as he worked the screen, but then his eyebrows came together. "Yes, but—"

"But what?" Hanley asked.

"I can see that the majority of the HAWCs are all together in the Silurian period right now. But the big HAWC, Sam Reid." He shook his head. "He's close, I mean timewise, he's far closer to us in the present. He's only around three thousand years ago. But something's wrong."

"For fuck's sake, be clear; what do you mean something's wrong?" Pinchella growled.

"He was thrown off the tachyon bridge, and into another time stream. This says he's been there . . ." He made an incredulous noise. "Ten years."

"*Ten years.*" Hanley exhaled. "But they've only been gone a few days."

"Time distortion." Rashid nodded sagely. "I hypothesized this could happen."

"Shit." Hanley ran his hands through his thinning hair, and then looked up. "Is he, ah, alive, do we know?"

"Unknown, but his transponder is not working properly – weak signal – I can't grab it to get a good link." Rashid sighed. "There's just enough residual imprint to tell me where it is – where he is – but not enough to collect him and bring him back."

Hanley folded his arms tight across his body. "Can we boost the—"

"No," Rashid cut in.

Pinchella's eyes burned into the men. "Well, you two better work on a plan to get him back, or by God . . ."

Quartermain put a hand on her arm. "If he can't come back, then someone needs to go get him."

"That's not all." Rashid grimaced. "His brainwaves are a little, ah, disjointed."

"Great, so we can send someone back, and they find the big guy is insane, and he doesn't recognize whoever drops in to get him. Or fights them," said Hanley.

"Unless it is someone he trusts." Quartermain lifted his chin. "Or loves."

Hanley slowly turned to him. "Go on."

"That might work." Rashid liked the idea. "We send someone back who can identify him. All they need to do is grab him and hold on. As long as he recognizes them and doesn't fight them, then we enlarge the tachyon print to create a double envelope to bring them both back." Rashid rubbed his chin. "But it'll have to be someone he'll let get close. Real close, and immediately. Because if they can't, or he won't let them hold on to him, we'll drop him. And this time maybe lose him for good."

Quartermain looked at Pinchella. "I know someone."

* * *

Jack Hammerson stepped out onto his front porch to smoke a cigar. He saw that Alex's mountainous dog, Torben, was still sitting by the broad opening at the top of the steps. Had been for most of the day.

Hammerson was still wary of the beast, and they were pleasant to each other, but neither fully trusted the other.

"You need a drink there, big guy?" he asked.

The dog didn't move at all, but continued to stare out over the wide, open landscape to a stand of eastern red cedars a quarter-mile in the distance.

Hammerson went and leaned on the railing, drew in a mouthful of smoke, and let it out in a long satisfying stream. He couldn't see anything out there that might have kept the dog in such rapt attention, so he turned.

"What's on your min—?"

He stopped mid-sentence, and his brows came together. The dog's lips were pulled back, exposed the huge canine fangs, and its eyes were completely white.

"What the hell?"

Hammerson slowly approached the huge animal and bent to look into those bone-white orbs – there was something there, an image. Just for the briefest of moments, he thought he saw Alex's face.

"*Jezuz*, you're linking. Seeing it all." He straightened. "This must be agony for you, seeing it, but not being able to help."

The dog continued to sit with its frozen snarl.

He snorted softly. "Or maybe you *are* helping."

Hammerson's phone rang, and he looked at the ID, and then answered it. "Quartermain?"

"We think we can get him; Sam, I mean. We can bring him back," the scientist said.

Hammerson closed his eyes for a moment. "Make it happen. I'm on my way."

CHAPTER 40

As Alex led them deeper, the cave became narrower, and the ruggedness of the upper caves gave way to a smoother rock that looked like cooled lava but was pocked with holes. They followed the downward-sloping path, and with every step it became more humid, the walls now slick with running moisture and slime. They also had to be careful where they walked, as there were now different sorts of pools containing not water but puddles of slime that stank of ammonia.

"Looks biological. Excreted," Cooper observed. "Whatever is down below comes up from time to time." She turned to glance over her shoulder. "Maybe to the pens."

"To feed," Alex said. "Or be fed."

He immediately wished he hadn't voiced those thoughts as it shut down conversation and made the group even edgier. But he hoped it was also making them hypersensitive and alert, as he had a feeling they'd be encountering something that already knew they were coming and perhaps was waiting for them.

Liquid dripped down on them like rain and plinked into the slime pools and large pools of water that gave off steam vapors into the already humid air. Some of the larger ponds swirled with life, but the brackish murkiness of the water prevented them from seeing what moved beneath the surface.

Alex led them, Cooper came next, followed by Gonzalez, and then Ito. After a moment Alex stopped the team and stared down at the edge of one of the larger pools.

"HAWC boot mark," he said.

Sure enough, there was a boot print sunk into the soft mud.

"But they're facing the other way," Cooper said. "Were they heading out? How did we miss them?"

"We didn't," Alex replied. "Print impressions go from toe to heel – they were backing up. They were still being forced deeper into the cave by something following them." Alex nodded down at the prints. "Boot size is about a fifteen, so must be Brandt." He looked up. "Let's move it."

They continued, passing by stains on the ground, and some degraded dead creatures. Alex noticed that the carcasses were from various species, some with exoskeletons, and some that might have been reptile-like animals. But they didn't seem old; it was more like they had been somehow . . . softened.

Then he found something that stopped him fast. He bent to pick the object up.

"What've you got, boss?" Gonzalez asked.

Alex turned the thing over in his hands, and then brought it close to his shoulder – it matched. It was a piece of HAWC armor, the shoulder section that created a cover for the joint.

"Is that one of ours?" Ito asked.

"Yeah." Alex rubbed at the edge. It wasn't complete, but it wasn't broken off either, it was more rounded somehow, like the thing had lost its structural integrity and become malleable. Like the bodies he had just seen.

"Big plate, must also be Brandt's." Alex continued to stare at it, wondering what it could mean.

"Why did he take it off?" Cooper asked.

Alex looked up. "I don't think he did. Voluntarily."

He turned slowly – there was nothing now, and no sign of any more discarded HAWC armor plating. Alex knew the armored suits well and bits didn't just fall off them. This piece must have been purposely removed, or . . . or he had no idea. He threw the piece to the ground and waved his team on.

As they continued down, Alex's mind began to be overwhelmed by the impression of life all around him. He looked from one side of the passageway to the other, but failed to see anything obvious, and that worried him more than a herd of great beasts coming at them – he knew something was there, somewhere, but they were keeping themselves hidden.

If he had more time he could find them . . . Then, just as the group walked past one of the larger pools, something emerged and lashed out at Gonzalez's leg.

The HAWC's reflexes were like lightning, and no sooner had it lunged at the man than he brought his gun around to fire a small pulse at the thing, putting a hole right through it.

"*Fuck off,*" he yelled at it the now-dead thing.

The group crowded round, staring at the creature. It looked like a hand with several digits attached to its front, and a single long finger at the center. On the end of the longest finger were two fangs or talons, for gripping, they guessed.

"No discernible eyes. Hunts by vibration." Cooper frowned down at it. "Can't really tell if those are scales covering it or an exoskeleton."

"Weirdest damn thing I've ever seen," Gonzalez said. "Tried to make a meal out of me. But found the HAWC armor a little too tough."

Cooper retracted her face shield and crouched. She drew out her knife and pressed on the thing's longest center limb near the fangs.

"I see," she said as a drop of milky fluid was expressed. "This is why it attacked something dozens of times its size – venom. Might be enough to stun or even kill you." She turned it over and they saw that under the fangs was a round mouth like a lamprey's.

Cooper snorted softly and looked up. "Then, when you're down and out, it crawls up out of the pool to latch onto its prey and maybe start to digest it."

"Fucking gross," Gonzalez said, and lifted his gun, pointing it at the thing. "I think I'll shoot it again."

"Look at your knife," Alex said to Cooper.

Cooper turned the blade over. The side where she had pressed the long digit that excreted the venom was all pitted.

"That's HAWC steel, Vanadium carbide, and near unbreakable," Alex said. "That venom must be powerfully acidic."

"And that little fucker must be one pretty tough hombre to keep that shit in its belly," Gonzalez added.

Behind them, the pool water swirled.

"Danger." Ito turned to point his gun at the pool.

"On your feet," Alex said to Cooper. "Time to go. Seems there are more of them and they're still hungry."

Around the group more of the pools started to shimmer and ripple with life. As Alex watched he saw something drip down onto Gonzalez's shoulder. Immediately the armor plating started to sizzle.

Alex looked up, and at first saw nothing but darkness. But then he concentrated and saw movement on the cave ceiling.

"Face shields back up," he yelled, and hit the illumination bar on the forehead of his suit, which immediately cast a strong beam a hundred feet up to the cavern ceiling.

Above them the ceiling squirmed, jostled, and wriggled with life. It seemed the puddles weren't the only place these creatures lived, as out of every moisture-laden crack, crevice, and recess, they emerged – dozens at first, then hundreds, and then they just kept on coming.

As more and more of the creatures crowded the cavern roof above them, their acid venom dripped down like a steady rain.

It was as if they were salivating at the meal to come. Suddenly Alex realized what those degraded-looking carcasses were that they'd passed – animals that had been caught out in the acid rain. If he and the HAWCs hadn't been wearing the hardened armor, they would have suffered the same fate.

Alex turned to the cave depths. "Move it," he yelled, and began to run.

The team followed, firing bullets and beams at the creatures in their path, but from behind them they heard a growing wave of scuttling and popping sounds as a torrent in the tens of thousands pursued them.

The creatures' long digits created a leaping-hopping movement that propelled them forward and also allowed them to move extremely fast for an animal their size. Alex didn't need to turn to know that the ceiling, floor, and even the walls were coated with the things, and they couldn't afford to fall, or even slow down, or they'd be overwhelmed.

Alex drew his gun, turned, and used the wide laser to create a scythe effect over an area around them. He must have slayed hundreds. But it only bought them a second or two, and as the acidic saliva rained down, he saw that his armor was beginning to pit. Now he understood why and how Brandt's shoulder section had come away – either the acid had corroded the internal seal, or he had pulled it away himself as he and Casey had also fled deeper into the cavern – just like they were doing now.

Suddenly Alex's suit's warning system started intoning that it was suffering a loss of integrity. He knew the others would be experiencing the same. Time was nearly up.

He looked over his shoulder and saw a biological wave coming at them – it looked like there were millions of the jumping, scuttling, and sliding things, and the noise of their approach in the echoing cave was overwhelming everything else.

Alex yelled as he ran, "Grenades."

He and the HAWCs pulled grenades, one in each hand, and threw them into different areas of the cave, and in among the heaviest concentrations of the acid scorpions, as he now thought of them.

The explosions came one after the other and shook the ground beneath their feet. The blast echoes belted away into the darkness. And then a different kind of rain began to fall – as well as acid rain, mud, and sand, fragments of the obliterated creatures and rocks showered down around them.

But the wave continued, and for the first time, Alex suspected they would be overrun. They were like a plague of locusts, and soon the HAWCs would be in among them, fighting. Alex didn't want to think about what that acid could do to flesh if it was able to degrade the HAWCs' super-hardened biological suits in a matter of minutes.

One of the acid scorpions leaped from the roof to land on Alex's helmet and squirt the acidic bile over one of his visor's quad lenses. Immediately, the lens failed, and Alex cursed, reached up and crushed the monstrosity in his hand. Another landed on his neck, and this time Ito shot it with a precisely aimed beam of condensed light.

"Thanks," Alex said over his shoulder.

Alex ran on, but then strangely he picked up the mind of the android canine back at the boat, which was watching them and what was occurring, perhaps seeing it through Alex's eyes. For the first time, he felt the impression of fear from the android.

Not for itself, but for Alex.

CHAPTER 41

Brandt led Casey as they ran down a narrowing cave. Ahead there was nothing but darkness on darkness . . . until the last dozen feet, when there came a soft glow.

"Something coming up," Brandt yelled over his shoulder, and started to run harder.

And then, there was nothing.

"*Shit!*" Brandt went over the edge.

Casey, about half a dozen paces behind him, dived, shot out her hand and grabbed his nearest flailing arm by the wrist. Her other hand, the robotic one, she speared into the rocks to anchor herself.

The huge HAWC was suspended in the air as Casey held on.

"*You. Fucking. Heavy bastard,*" she groaned as she slowly began to drag him back in.

The pair then fell back, breathing heavily.

"Thanks." Brandt sat up and laughed. "What a day, huh?"

"Yeah. And it ain't over yet." Casey got to her feet and walked to the precipice.

The cave had ended at a cliff edge that dropped several hundred feet down to a huge underground body of water that looked like a large black lake. Luminescent fungus or lichen ran in veins around the wall casting a ghostly glow over the scene. Around the dark lake there were many small impenetrably black tunnels.

Casey stared down at it for a moment before pulling a glow stick, igniting it, and dropping it. It hit the water, and then it kept falling below the surface until it vanished.

"How deep do you figure that was?" Brandt asked.

"That stick dropped for at least sixty feet before vanishing. So deeper than that. Not great for us. Any deeper and we might not be able to use it to swim to the outside sea. We gotta find out if that's our exit or not." She turned to Brandt. "Did you keep a drone?"

"Yeah, just one left." He reached into a slot on his thigh and pulled out the small torpedo-shaped tech.

"Good man." Casey took it and readied the device. "Time for a deeper dive." She initiated it. "Here goes." She tossed it out, and the pair watched it fall toward the black lake.

The small drone splashed down, a light came on at its front, and then it immediately took off in a corkscrew dive, winding lower as it went.

Casey lifted her arm and watched the data feed and images on her gauntlet screen. "Fifty feet – big cavity down there. A hundred feet – still nothing but black and rock." She shook her head. "And that's our dive limit."

"We could free dive that," Brandt said. "But if there was no exit, we'd black out trying to get back to the surface."

As Casey watched, the small drone began to accelerate.

"Whoa, what's going on here?" She frowned. "Slow down, little buddy."

"What the hell's it doing?" Brandt looked over her shoulder at her screen.

Casey's frown deepened. "Must be caught in a current or something. Maybe a tidal flow."

"Could we ride that out?" Brandt asked hopefully.

"No, it's already down 200 feet – huh, now 500. Something's wrong. Now 1000, 2000, 5000 . . . it's still accelerating." She shook her head. "This is nuts."

And then the screen whited out.

"How fucking deep is that hole?" Brandt asked incredulously.

"In this primordial world? For all we know it goes all the way to the center of the Earth." She lowered her arm. "One thing we know now; we sure as shit ain't gonna be able to swim out that way." Casey lifted her strong flashlight and panned it around. "He-*eey*, hold the phone . . ." She stared across the water to another huge opening she had spotted on the other side.

But there was something weird about it.

"I see it, but that doesn't look naturally formed to me." Brandt frowned. "They look like steps. Big-assed steps."

Casey nodded. "That's what I think. Jesus, they've got to be ten feet tall."

"Steps of a giant," Brandt said. "Who could build that down here? And who the hell could use them?"

Casey stepped forward and peered down to the black water. "They've got to lead somewhere. Just over the lake."

"Might be our best bet. How do we get there? Swim it?" Brandt asked.

"Only if we have to. Because I'm not doing laps in that ink without a damn good reason." Casey got right down on the edge. "Something else down there. See there? Could be a platform, or dock."

Brandt got down with her. "Yeah, yeah, but too small for sailing on that pond. But I also see something like chain rings set in the rock. Maybe for tying boats off."

"It's ancient. Who knows what it was for?" Casey pulled back. She leaned out and shone her flashlight up to the left. There were just sheer walls. Then she moved it to the right, and began to nod. "Yeah, I think I found a way."

She followed a narrow ledge weathered into the rock face with her beam that wound around its craggy surface until it came to another broader area of tumbled rock. And something else. She stopped moving her light.

"*Ho-lee-y* shit." Her brow was furrowed. "You seeing this? Tell me that ain't what I think it is."

"Yeah. Yeah. I see it." Brandt straightened. "If I had to guess, I'd say it's a fucking spaceship."

"I'm looking right at it, and I still don't believe it." Casey shook her head. "It's enormous."

Jutting from high up in the ancient rock wall, and looking like it had been there forever, was the gigantic nose of a craft emerging from the titanic tumbled stone blocks as though it had crashed and burrowed into the earth, thousands, or maybe millions, of years ago.

The craft was covered in a skin of moss and hanging with fronds of lichen. There was also a huge hole in its side. From the hole there was a pathway that had later been carved into the rock.

"Whatever was in there survived, and is now out," Brandt said.

"Out here," Casey added, and followed a smoothed path from the craft to the edge of the lake of water at the bottom of the shaft. "And I'm betting in there." She looked down into the pitch-black water.

"I don't get it," Brandt said. "Is this our planet or not? Who, or what, came out of that? What the fuck is going on here?"

Casey pulled back. "This is 420 million years before we even evolved. Maybe whatever came out of there died long before we even shaved our asses and stood on two legs."

"I hope so, because by the look of those steps, whatever came out is a lot bigger than we are. And I mean hundreds of times bigger," Brandt said.

"It's not just its size," said Casey. "This thing, or these things, had space travel nearly half a billion years before we did."

"This is above our paygrade." Brandt turned to her. "I say we keep going. Get the fuck out of here and just report it to the boss."

There was a sound from below, and both HAWCs immediately fell silent.

"Something's happening down there," Casey whispered as she hunkered down to watch. "Here we go."

As they watched, a line of the nine-foot-tall crustacean beings appeared from one of the smaller tunnels at the lake's edge. Just a few, but they were dragging a rope and attached to it were all manner of creatures, some crawling on multiple legs, some slithering on their bellies, and then at the end, two naked human beings tied around the neck.

"Holy fuck. Tell me I'm not seeing this," Brandt said.

The two humans were a young man and woman, slightly built, naked, and Asian.

"Can't, because I'm seeing it too," Casey whispered. "North Koreans."

As they watched, the two people looked around, and by chance, the male spotted the HAWCs up on the ledge. He immediately began calling, beseeching, begging for help. The young woman turned and then joined in, creating an echoing din in the cave.

Casey and Brandt hunkered down lower.

Brandt scoffed. "Yeah, right, you motherfuckers. You were gonna destroy the US from the past. And now you want us to save your asses? Fuck you."

As they watched, the tethered line of animals and people was anchored to one of the round metal rings on the end of the wharf platform. The shell people seemed to freeze in place for a moment, and above the screaming of the people,

Casey could just make out a small grating noise in among the popping sounds coming from the crab-creatures' mouths.

"They're talking to each other," Brandt said.

"Or to something else," Casey replied.

Then came the bellowing horn-like sound, which seemed to reverberate up from somewhere deep below the surface of the lake. Its cadence jarred their senses.

Casey stared down into the dark water, and her brows slowly came together. "Hey, remember that glow stick that vanished?"

"Yeah," Brandt said.

Casey felt for her sidearm, the only weapon she had left after the acid-spitters. "I think it's coming back up."

CHAPTER 42

Alex dodged around steaming pools, and more of the monstrous creatures lifted themselves from their murky depths to spit at them as they passed by. As he ran he spotted one of the laser cannons – Brandt's, he realized – and saw that its long barrel was now melted-looking and covered in holes. It looked something like taffy.

Just like Brandt's armor, Alex's shoulder plates, which were bearing the brunt of the dripping acid, were the first part of his suit to fail.

An idea formed in his mind. The things were not invulnerable, but there were too many to fight. They needed something to take them out en masse.

Quartermain had told him that the lasers were powered by small fusion energy cells. As Alex ran, he pulled his rifle up and broke open the power cell carriage, exposing its tiny, glowing heart. He reached for the charge inhibiter that kept the size of the energy pulses in check and crushed it with his thumb. He then bent the barrel, meaning the pulse was trapped. Finally, he pressed the discharge switch, and the charge began to build – but with the barrel broken, and the inhibiter damaged, the energy build-up had nowhere to go.

"Fire in the hole," he yelled, and turned to toss the laser rifle over the heads of his team at the oncoming horde.

He and the HAWCs accelerated. He had no idea just how big the blast was going to be, or even if it would bring the entire cave down around them all. But they had run out of options. Without the mad gamble, they would slowly be worn down, caught, melted, and then probably eaten. He just hoped that Casey and Brandt hadn't already suffered that fate.

Two hundred feet further on, the gun screamed an overload warning and then the detonation came – it was less an explosion than a balloon-like flash of super-heated plasma.

"*Hit the deck,*" Alex yelled as he threw himself to the ground. Cooper, Ito, and Gonzalez dived forward to lie flat, hoping their disintegrating suits would hold together well enough to shield them.

The gun's power cell created a small nuclear-fission detonation like a tiny sun that lifted the temperature to over a thousand degrees in a second. The massive light and heat wave went past them, and then shut off as completely as if someone had flicked a switch.

Alex lifted his head and looked back over his shoulder. Of the perhaps tens of thousands of tiny acid-spitting creatures that had been pursuing them, only a few stragglers remained, most of them wounded and disorientated and now staggering off into the darkness.

Alex got carefully to his feet and turned slowly, examining the cave. Then, satisfied, he sucked in a deep breath, and let it out. "I think it's over," he said.

Ito and Gonzalez jumped to their feet, and Cooper slowly rose and then bent, holding her knees and heaving in air. She looked up. "That was . . . intense."

Gonzalez took a few steps and there came a grinding sound from his suit's joints. "Hydraulics are damaged," he said, and raised an arm. "Not working. Getting heavy."

"Yes, mine too." Ito twisted at the waist and then turned. "It will now require work to move the suit, draining our energy and reducing our speed and mobility. Or we remove them and hope we don't run into any more of the acid-spitters."

"Cooper?" Alex asked. "How you doing?"

Cooper shook her head. "No choice; I'm going to have to ditch it. The suit must weigh 200 pounds and I can't move in this thing without it working smoothly." She retracted her helmet visor, which slid slowly back with an audible grating sound. "Anyone got an umbrella?"

Alex laughed softly and walked a few paces away. The cavern was still angling downward and remained enormous.

With his visor retracted he could smell the ocean, and he closed his eyes and reached out with his mind, trying to find his missing team members. But instead he was immediately flooded with impressions of somewhere else – somewhere far away – it was the monster, the old god again.

His mind glimpsed moonless shorelines of black beaches, and seaborne growths that had washed up and rotted on their dark sands. Corpses littered the waters, and at the center of a lake was a darker area that seemed to have no bottom and perhaps reached all the way to the center of the world itself.

He jolted back from the horrible impressions and knew they were being inserted into his mind. Alex blinked a few times as he stared into the dark depths of the cave.

"We were being chased, herded, down that way." He turned to his team.

"I think that's a good reason to go another way," Cooper replied.

Alex nodded. "It is. And if I didn't think our HAWCs were down there I'd back out."

"You think they could have survived, boss?" Gonzalez asked. "Casey and Beast, I mean."

Alex chuckled. "You couldn't kill that pair with a nuke."
He hoped that was true as he turned away again. "We go on.
Ditch any parts of the suits that are weighing you down. Try
and keep your gauntlet sensors and any working weapons. The
inner suit has a tough Kevlar weave – they're not bulletproof,
but right now, we need to balance physical protection with
speed and mobility." He laughed darkly. "And I'm guessing
bullets are not going to be what we encounter from now on."

They jettisoned most of their heavy armor and continued
on for another half-hour.

Alex was concerned that he still couldn't contact Casey or
Brandt and bet that the acid-scorpions had also damaged their
suits and that was why they were offline. But he also couldn't
pick up their life emanations. Usually with people he knew
well, like Casey, if they were close, he'd feel it. But for some
reason, she was just gone.

* * *

Alex came to a large cavern with multiple exits, and he walked
a few paces toward one of them. It seemed empty and devoid
of life. He went to the next, and then turned slowly, taking
them all in. The place looked like some sort of terminus where
trains shot off into their own tunnels heading to unknown
destinations.

"Which one, boss?" Gonzalez asked.

With the majority of their suit tech having failed or been
discarded, Alex relied on his own exceptional senses, which
could even detect different light spectrums and gave him
better illumination than the others obtained from their gun
barrel lights.

The group spread out, and Alex walked across the mouth
of a few more of the tunnels, feeling nothing but dead air,
which undoubtedly meant there would be no way through.

But a few of the entrances had a line of large and wickedly sharp-looking stalactites hanging down, as well as dagger-like growths on the floor that were nearly as large. He stared in at one, and his senses started to prickle.

Just across from him there was another similar cave, and Ito was about to step inside. As Alex watched his HAWC, he detected the faint odor of an exhalation from deep within the cave, and he suddenly knew what it meant.

Almost faster than the eye could track, Alex shot across to grab the man back out.

"What is it?" Ito asked.

Alex held up a hand. "Watch." He then fired a single round into the smaller cave, just beyond the row of sharp growths.

Immediately the front of the cave revealed itself as a mouth as it snapped shut, and then the monstrous thing withdrew back into the impenetrable darkness.

"*Hoy*, that cave was alive." Ito staggered backwards. "I was going to step inside."

Gonzalez was beside them in an instant with his gun up. "What the hell was that?"

Alex turned to Cooper, and she shrugged.

"Maybe some sort of nematode. They've been around for hundreds of millions of years, and actually grow big in caves. They get bigger the deeper you go."

"*Jezuz*, man, I'm just glad we have nothing like that back home," Gonzalez added.

"Maybe not for long," Cooper replied. "In 2023, an ancient form of giant nematode called *Panagrolaimus kolymaensis* was found frozen in the Siberian permafrost. It had laid there undisturbed for nearly 50,000 years." She laughed dryly. "And here's the kicker. They were able to revive it."

"Why would they want to bring that shit back?" Gonzalez complained. "That's asking for trouble."

"That it is." Alex turned away. "Everyone watch your step. Nothing in here is what it seems."

He looked across the mouths of several tunnels, and from the largest he sensed the presence of his missing HAWCs.

"This way." He led them on, and they continued down into the Tartarean darkness.

* * *

Alex tried to balance speed with caution. He finally had an impression of Franks and Brandt – both alive.

"Got 'em," he said. "We're not far behind."

"How?" Cooper asked. "Our trackers are destroyed."

Gonzalez laughed. "The Arcadian don't need all that fancy tech. He can see round corners."

The tunnel they were in was constricting, and Alex slowed, and then stopped.

The HAWCs waited behind him.

"It's in there. The other intelligence. It knows us." He closed his eyes. "And it can see us."

CHAPTER 43

As Casey and Brandt watched, a shape began to appear in the dark water. It seemed to fill the lake, and as they stared, a pair of large red eyes opened in its center. Then more eyes opened around those, dozens of them, hellishly red, and they seemed to burn with an evil intelligence.

"*Ho-l-y* shit," Casey breathed.

The thing broke the surface. Its twenty-foot-wide head was a mass of bristles and scales. Dangling from under the clusters of eyes were tentacles, not eight or ten but dozens of them that curled and writhed, with oily convolutions, never remaining still.

It kept coming, and they saw that folded down hard on its back were wings, and it had hugely muscled shoulders and tree-trunk arms ending in three-taloned hands ten feet across.

The crustacean people pulled back in awe, reverence, or perhaps fear.

"They were calling to it. That's what they were doing." Casey stared.

"And it came," Brandt whispered.

The tethered animals, numbering about a dozen, were going mad with fear, and the two humans scrabbled at the rope around their necks and screeched even louder to Casey and Brandt. The naked woman held up her hands to them, pressed together, beseeching.

The massive beast towered over them, showering them with water and looking like it was reveling in their fear. Almost at once, the entire group of roped beasts silenced. Even the two people dropped their arms and stood calmly as if in a trance.

"What just happened?" Brandt asked. "Why did they . . .?"

And that was when it took them – the huge tentacled face leaned forward, and the ropy coils opened to display a massive, toothed mouth that enveloped the entire group, pulled them from the ropes, and with an audible crunching of meat, bone, and shell, devoured them all, including the people.

"It ate them. All of them," Brandt said blankly, his eyes wide. "And they just fucking let it."

"It somehow shut them up. They had no choice." Casey Franks frowned at the thought. "It somehow got in their heads. And then, the danger dawned on her. "Oh, fuck no. We gotta get the hell out of here."

Before they could move, the beast lifted its multiple red eyes toward where the two HAWCs hid, and Casey felt the screech in her brain. It locked her muscles, froze her, and like a mental ice pick, dug into her mind, peeled back her resistance, and then took control.

Both of the HAWCs got to their feet and slowly made their way along the narrow path in the cave wall toward the water.

And the waiting ropes.

* * *

Alex stopped and placed his hand against the wall – something had changed. Where before he had felt the impressions of his missing HAWCs in his mind, plus another more alien presence, now he only felt the alien. It was if somehow his missing team members had been eclipsed or absorbed by the thing.

He had an agonizing thought: absorbed . . . or *consumed* by the thing.

Alex began to run, quickly outpacing his team. That macabre thought alone made him accelerate, moving along the narrowing cave at an impossible velocity. He dimly heard Gonzalez, Cooper, and Ito, a way back now, calling after him and sprinting hard to try and keep up.

His team only had their flashlights, some pistols, and a range of knives, and he knew that those weren't going to be nearly enough to win a battle with what he imagined they would encounter.

He was close now, he could feel it. The tunnel he was in became filled with the smell of brackish seawater, and in his mind's eye Alex saw the desolate dark shorelines, and the hide of a leviathan that dwelled in the sunless depths.

He was just about to give another burst of acceleration when he came out into nothingness as the tunnel ended.

He spun in the air and shot out an arm to catch the lip of the cliff edge and hang on. He swung toward the rock wall and quickly pulled himself back up, then stood in the center of the tunnel, blocking his team members from going over like he had.

As his team arrived, even the toughened HAWCs were struck dumb by the jarring scene before them. Brandt and Casey were tethered by the neck with a thick rope to an iron ring set into the ground. The pair stood motionless. But the worst of it was the monstrous being that towered over them.

"Oh God, the monster carving from the temple," Cooper whispered.

"Dagon," Alex said. "It's real."

He looked quickly about, taking in the steps, the spacecraft, the deep pool – and spotted a narrow path in the cliff leading down, but knew they wouldn't have time to rescue the pair of lost HAWCs. The colossal horror was already reaching over them, its bloom of tentacles opening like the petals of a ghastly flower, ready to take them in.

"Fire at will," Alex yelled, and together the four of them hailed bullets down at the thing.

Alex knew the rounds would be as effective as throwing peas at that monstrous hide, but all he hoped to do was distract it long enough to buy his colleagues some time. He wasn't even sure the monstrosity would react.

But it did. And not in a way Alex expected.

A searing bolt of pain blasted through his head. Gonzalez, Cooper, and Ito collapsed to the ground, holding their heads and moaning in agony.

The pain felt like someone had set his brain on fire. But buried within the attack was a command – *stop* – and a demand: *join with me.*

Alex's unique physical makeup allowed him to weather the agony of the intrusion, and instead of buckling, he not only fought back, he also reached out to probe the mind of the colossal being that had risen from the bottomless pool in the buried grotto.

Alex saw into the thing's head, and visions of its home world crowded in. It was a water planet where the seas were black and corrupted. Rotting bodies floated on the surface as their flesh turned to sludge and their skeletons sank to the bottom, where they would disintegrate into the fetid ooze.

Its kind had consumed their world entirely, and it was now a celestial wanderer seeking a new home. It had arrived here a billion years ago. With its fuel exhausted, it had been unable to land and had crashed here.

It had found a primitive world, the Hadean period on Earth, devoid of life, but it knew that when living creatures evolved and rose from the primordial ooze, it would rule them for an eternity. It wasn't immortal but lived at a different rate from anything on the planet. It could live for another million years, or a billion.

And then Alex saw its plans for his species. When evolution lifted human beings to domination, it would be there, waiting for them. And it would harvest them as both food and slaves.

Eventually our world would become like its world: corrupted and lifeless. But before then, the human slaves would build it another ship, and when the Earth became that toxic swamp, it would leave and continue its search for another world to dominate, consume, and destroy. It would take the remaining humans with it to serve as food on its voyage.

He also saw that the creature wasn't fully grown and would eventually be the size of a mountain. Now he understood why there had been five mass extinctions on Earth. This creature had gorged itself, and then had needed to hibernate for millions of years so its feeding ground could restock.

Behind Alex his team had risen, zombie-like, to their feet, and were making their way down the steep path in the cliff wall to join Franks and Brandt, who stood with slumped shoulders awaiting their fate.

Alex knew what was going to happen – the thing was a consumer – it was going to eat them, and in doing so it would not only absorb their flesh, but also their minds and memories. That's what it meant by *join with me*.

With every fibre of his being he knew this creature needed to be destroyed. And if it couldn't be destroyed, it needed to somehow be restrained or imprisoned. Forever.

Alex saw the crab-creatures waiting for his HAWCs. Perhaps the arthropod race were slaves the monster had brought with it on the craft that had crashed. Maybe they had been the custodians of the previous planet this thing had subjugated before traveling to Earth.

It didn't matter now; they too needed to be destroyed or entombed.

As his last three team members joined Casey and Brandt on the platform, Alex managed to keep resisting the maddening siren call. And this frustrated the great monster. So it sent its minions after him, and more appeared, and they began climbing the sheer walls in their hundreds looking like giant lice clambering up a body in search of a drop of blood.

As the crab-creatures rose, the beast loomed up over Alex's HAWCs, and Alex felt its desire for the food, and for their memories.

He fired again and again, and then the mind-tearing screech got louder in his head. The more he resisted and fought back, the more insistent and painful it got.

In another few seconds, his eyes began to blur, and the dagger of pain finally reached the center of his mind – the deep, dark place where a different sort of beast strained against its mental chains and roared its own anger at the intrusion.

Alex knew he was losing the battle; his walls of resistance were coming down. Soon he, too, would be standing on the rock platform, waiting for the monstrous creature to slam down on top of him and his team and devour them alive.

As Alex was brought to his knees, he knew there was one last thing he needed to do. He sent a mental message to Tor.

And then he collapsed as his mind shut down.

CHAPTER 44

420 million years into the future, the giant German shepherd Torben sprang to its feet. It hadn't eaten in days, or moved an inch, but now it stood staring straight ahead.

If Jack Hammerson had looked into the bone-white eyes that were fixed on a place in the Earth's distant history, he might have seen something there that froze his blood.

Or he might not have approached at all. Because Torben's gums were pulled back from his huge, white teeth, and a rumbling growl emanated from deep within his chest. There was frustration and barely contained fury there.

* * *

The android canine's sensors became fully alert.

It immediately saw the danger its leader was in and understood the message. Then, like a blur of gunmetal-hued steel, it gathered up all the nuclear packages, all of them, and sped toward Alex Hunter's location.

* * *

Almost immediately the body of Alex Hunter got to its feet.

But it wasn't Alex anymore. It was the Other, and where the blinding pain and mind-tearing intrusion had overwhelmed Alex, the Other was born from pain and agony and absorbed it. And was fueled by it.

It balled its fists, threw its head back and roared long and loud in the cave. Its face was a contorted mask of rage as it stared down at the monster.

"*You dare?*" it seethed.

The Other drew both of the tanto-edge HAWC blades, one long and one short, and stepped to the edge of the cliff. He saw the rising beast, its clutch of red eyes now fixed on the humans as its huge maw lowered over them.

Alex could only watch now through The Other's eyes and scream his frustration at his own helplessness.

He had not been able to act.

But the Other could.

It lifted both blades. And leaped.

* * *

The massive beast, the slumberer from below, the invader of dreams, only became aware of Alex Hunter's body at the last moment, and its huge head lifted, bunches of red eyes staring at the small human plummeting toward it.

Alex was a hostage inside the Other who now controlled his body, and he could only watch as he flew down to land on the face of the monstrous being, his arms outstretched and a blade in each fist, and dug in. One blade sank into one of the manhole-sized central eyes, deep, which immediately gushed a burning red fluid.

The screech into Alex's mind reached him even where he was locked away, bringing with it a furious tornado of pain and anger, but Alex's body ignored it and held on.

He drew one blade out and plunged it again into the center of one of the smaller eyes, which was still a foot across. He immediately dragged the other blade out and crawled across the leathery face, seeking another of the vulnerable eyes.

The tentacles that had been hanging like a mottled, coiling beard exploded in activity, trying to reach him, and one monstrous arm lifted to swipe down over the being's face, seeking to wipe him away.

But the Other was ready for it, and while he battled the beast, Alex saw that the thing was now only focused on him and had forgotten the other humans. And that meant his HAWCs were released from their mental chains.

Casey was the first to regain her full senses. She saw the threat coming and grabbed the thick ropes binding the HAWCs that was attached to the metal ring set in the stone. She pulled with her robotic arm, straining, screaming her fury, as the ring was slowly tugged free like a bad tooth.

She fell back but was quickly on her feet. "HAW-*WW-WC*s." Casey's war cry filled the cavern. "Free fire."

Casey, Brandt, Gonzalez, Ito, and Cooper drew their remaining weapons and fired continually into the monster. Though their bullets were individually insignificant, together they were an added torment and distraction.

As soon as they noticed that the humans were no longer docile, the huge crustaceans in the side caves and crawling down the walls attacked.

Casey's robotic arm easily broke the rope around her neck and Brandt's, and then she used it like a battering ram on the crustacean monstrosities, shattering their carapaces as if they were made of porcelain. The huge Brandt joined her, but even with his great size and strength, without his HAWC armor he could not match the power of the nine-foot-tall beings.

Behind them the Other avoided another of the monster's car-sized claws, and scurried further over its face, using the blades in its hands to hook on as the creature roared and thrashed. He soon made it back to another of the biggest central eyes.

The Other stared into it, his face a death's head rictus, and this time just used one of his fists to batter at the membrane covering the eye, twice, three times, and then he punctured it. And this time he must have reached a nerve center, because he got a massive response as the monster pulled back and smashed into a wall, shaking down huge stones.

It swung again into another of the walls, catching the Other between its bulk and the rock face. Alex's body was crushed and shaken off. But the massive creature withdrew, submerging into the dark lake.

Alex fell and landed in the water. He came to the surface and screamed in agony as his bones began to pop back into place, his ribs re-knitting inside his bruised and battered body. He swam to the dark water's edge and when he emerged, it was him again, released from the Other's hold over his mind after the battle had been decided.

He dragged himself out and rolled, coughing, onto his back, gasping for air. He felt drained, broken, and just wanted to lie there and regain his strength. But turning on his side, he saw his team being overwhelmed.

Alex got slowly to his feet, then picked up speed, sprinting into their center to join the fight.

CHAPTER 45

They were coming for him.

Sam faced straight ahead, with the dirty rag still tied over his eye sockets. His great frame was ripped with scars, bruises, and dried blood, but he cared not.

The festival for their great deity, Dagon, had been running for days and was set to culminate this evening with his sacrifice as the ultimate gift to their decrepit god.

Animals had been slaughtered and hundreds of slaves brutalized, thrown to wild animals, or torn apart, and he had heard their cries, heard them begging for freedom, forgiveness, or mercy. All had gone unanswered. He imagined the Saran and his vile cadre of elite, sipping wine, smiling as they savored the cruel spectacle.

And then he would be sacrificed. He had found out he was to be bound between the pillars underpinning the giant god statue, and which the entire stone stadium rested. He was to be stabbed, burned, and then dismembered, slowly, in front of the roaring crowd, and beneath the gaze of the brutal, false god.

Sam half-smiled in his darkness. If his jailers saw him doing it, they would have whipped him mercilessly. But he knew now he would get what he desired – there was one thing that all HAWCs wanted, and that was to go out fighting and on their own terms.

His bearded mouth curved up at the corners. That's what he would do.

When it was his time to die, the colosseum would be crowded with all the barbaric Philistines – their royalty, their rich and elite, and their generals. They would be hoping to break him, and make him beg, and all the time they'd be screaming for his blood and for his torment and suffering.

Well, he would give them blood – rivers of it – but it would be their own.

* * *

Hammerson paced in the background, stopping occasionally to watch the scientists and the young woman before pacing on.

"He'll be confused and may not recognize you at first," Quartermain said softly.

Alyssa's large brown eyes were wide as she listened. Her mouth was pressed into a tight, colorless line, her nervousness warranted.

"Alyssa. *Alyssa.*" Quartermain waited until her eyes slid to him. "Remember, he's been trapped there for over ten years."

She crushed her eyes shut, but after a moment opened them and stared straight ahead. "It doesn't matter, he'll know me."

Hanley stepped forward. "I hope he does. But we don't know what state he is in, mentally or physically. We think he might have been lost in the twelfth century BC, 3200 years ago, and for ten years, eight months and two days."

Hammerson felt fury boil away in his gut and clenched his jaws to stop cursing the scientists out loud.

"Oh God," she said in a tiny breath. Her brown skin seemed to pale and her eyes watered.

Rashid sighed. "And he may be hurt. You need to be ready for anything you see and hear, and not flinch or hesitate. You'll only have mere seconds. Time will be everything." He crouched in front of the woman. "Alyssa, you'll have one shot at this. The time paradoxes create unbreakable rules for us. Once you have been to a time period, that slice becomes unavailable to us again. You cannot return to that exact point of points, as there can't be two of you existing in the same place at the same time."

Alyssa tilted her head back and exhaled a wretched sigh. "So I'll have seconds. And I can't go back twice?" She looked up. "And he might be . . . sick."

"That's right," Hanley said. "One shot, and one shot only."

"If I fail, then I can't go back again," she confirmed.

Hanley and Rashid looked to Hammerson, who just stared back through half-lidded eyes. But it was Pinchella who stepped forward and laid a hand on the woman's shoulder.

"We, and you, don't need to worry about that. Because you *won't* fail. You will succeed." She squeezed. "I know it."

Alyssa looked up. "But if something is really wrong, and I can't bring him back," she said softly, "could I stay with him? Whatever that would mean?"

"No," Hammerson said. "The program will bring you back automatically." He stepped closer. "All you need to do is grab him – and hold on. You won't fail."

Alyssa nodded. "What do I need to do, and when?"

"Now. Right now," Hanley replied. "Because right now, we can pinpoint exactly where he is. The signal is weak, but we've got him. If everything goes to plan, you'll be there and back, with Sam, in the blink of an eye."

Alyssa stood up. "Then I'm ready."

Pinchella straightened and smiled. "Of course you are."

Hanley stepped back and clapped his hands. "Team Janus, we are *go*."

Their technical team flew into action to prepare the time bridge, and Alyssa was led into the tachyon chamber.

They had given her a special suit, a little like the HAWCs' Kevlar skinsuits, but this one was designed to increase the tachyon power and remove the need for an implant. The suit was a shimmering, reflective white for high tachyon particle absorption.

Strapped to Alyssa's chest was a powerful tachyon magnifier that would construct an envelope over herself and the huge body of Sam Reid. It was all theoretical and untested, so they prayed it had enough power to identify them, hold them, and then bring them back together.

Hammerson began to pace again. All Alyssa needed to do was grab Sam. And hold him. Janus would do the rest.

In five more minutes they were ready. Alyssa stood in the chamber, her mouth dry and eyes glassy with fear. Her legs shook and she looked tiny, but her expression was resolute.

Pinchella gave her a thumbs-up, and Quartermain nodded to her.

"Initiating bridge," Rashid said.

The blue beam shot out and touched on the small woman. It soon enveloped her, and in her white reflective suit she glowed like a miniature sun for a second – and then she was gone.

No one spoke. No one seemed to breathe or even blink.

Hammerson sucked in a huge breath. Ten seconds was all they were going to give her.

He heard Quartermain whisper: *Get him, Alyssa. Please get him.*

He had the same prayer.

CHAPTER 46

Ito was shielding Cooper as best he could, but his blade was little more than a tool to parry the arthropod creatures' blows, as it could never cut their bodies.

Just as Ito was forced down onto one knee, Alex came in fast, lowered a shoulder and smashed into the thing from the side, crushing its carapace.

He didn't wait to see if it got back up, but instead moved among the swarm of shelled bodies, ripping jointed limbs from multiple shoulders, and punching right through armored shell.

As fast as he was and as furious his decimation of the horde, there were always far too many, and he knew his team could not prevail against the hundreds of what he assumed were the minions of the monster from below.

More and more poured into the lake cave; it was just a matter of time until they were worn down and beaten. Then he bet that Dagon would rise again. And this time none of them would have the strength to fight back.

"Gotta get to that exit." Casey pointed to the huge steps leading to the carved cave mouth on the other side of the water.

As the team was now being pushed back to the dark water's edge, their choices were rapidly vanishing.

Then Alex felt the approach of a presence, a welcome one, and looked up. Without slowing a fraction, the android dog burst from the high cave mouth they had entered and launched itself into the air. Even though it was encumbered with ten heavy nuclear packages, it landed safely and skidded to a stop between the HAWCs and the crustacean beings.

"*Defend*," Alex yelled.

Immediately the robotic animal went into defensive guardian mode. Combat armor slid over it, and multiple barrels extended from its front. Then lasers, grenades, and bullets shot out in a furious artillery barrage, obliterating the front line of crab beings and pushing back those that weren't destroyed.

Alex rushed to Tor and pulled the packs from its body. He knew that even though the huge monster from below had retreated, it would be back. Over the hundreds of millions of years until humanity's rise, it would grow, consume, and be waiting for them when they returned.

Unless he changed the game.

"Gonna seal it in," he said. "Sink this damn place."

"*Yeah*, burn and bury it!" Casey responded with a gore-spattered, raised fist.

Alex knew the staggered detonations going off every hundred years would create long term corruption to the environment. But a single mega blast would create a wound that would quickly heal.

He armed every one of the bombs and changed their century long timer to be set to sixty minutes. He turned. "We've got one hour," he said grimly, then tossed all the packages into the dark water and watched them sink. "Let's go," he yelled.

Without a second thought about what might be lurking below, he and his team dived into the dark water and swam across it, leaving Tor to generate his wall of fire between them and their attackers. Even Alex felt vulnerable as he swam over the black water, knowing that somewhere down there the beast was waiting. And maybe watching.

When they arrived at the other side, they all climbed hurriedly out, and Alex pointed. "Get up there, *run*."

The HAWCs and Cooper moved fast, scaling the colossal steps and making their way up to a massive stone archway. He saw that Tor had obliterated hundreds of the things and they lay in a burned and broken wall around it. But the android's armaments were being depleted and it was down to just the field laser. There was no more they could do – their job was done.

"*Tor*," he yelled, and then Alex, too, turned to run.

The android animal spun away and, rather than enter the water, it put on a burst of lightning speed, actually running up the sheer vertical cliff face until it got to Alex. Without even thinking about it, Alex lowered his hand and lay it gently on the metal dog's head for a second or two.

Then, together, they ran up and out through the massive doorway.

The HAWCs didn't stop, sprinting all the way to the shoreline, with Alex out front, using his body like a battering ram to smash a hole through the jungle. They then went south along the coast until they came to where they had left their boat, with Tor running backwards and cutting down any of the crustacean beings if they got too close.

At the beach, Alex remembered their boat was submerged a few dozen feet offshore. He cursed himself for only allowing sixty minutes until the massive detonation, but it was too late to change that now.

He powered ahead of the group, dived in and swam at speed to the waiting boat. As he dived down the ten feet to find it, he was buffeted by a large eel-like creature that had a flat, shovel-shaped head full of needle teeth. It obviously didn't think he was edible and swam off into the gloom.

Alex found the boat, pulled himself in, and started the engine. Then he brought it to the surface. They'd need to stay there now that they no longer had their HAWC aquatic suits, which wasn't great as the combined nuclear detonation might engulf them. Being below the waterline might have given them some insulation.

The group jumped in, with Tor boarding last and acting as a rear gunner, cutting down anything that tried to follow them into the water. Alex handed over the controls to Ito, who sped them away.

"Where to?" Ito called.

Alex wasn't sure. He turned to Cooper. "We're done. What now?"

Cooper checked her wristwatch. "It's almost time for pull-out." She shook her head. "Any minute now. It doesn't matter where we are; the tachyon drive should find us and pull us back over the bridge."

Alex nodded. "I hope it's before the detonation." He turned away. "If not, it's gonna get real hot here soon. Let's just get as far away as possible."

Ito kept the engines at maximum speed and the land quickly shrank behind them.

Alex checked his watch. Minutes mattered now.

He exhaled, feeling his frustration. They should be ten miles away, and bunkered down to try and get underneath the blast's shockwave, which would be like a brick wall moving at 500 miles per hour.

He checked his watch again. Time was up.

He'd failed. They weren't nearly far enough away.

"*Don't look at it,*" he warned.

Alex crushed his eyes shut for a moment as the incendiary flash of the multiple bombs heralded the titanic explosion that came from somewhere deep down in the earth. And then, as soon as the light receded, he opened his eyes again and looked back to see the massive bubble of heat, light, and blast plasma rising into the upper atmosphere.

Seconds later they could see the shockwave coming across the water. They didn't need to worry about the nuclear fallout, the sun-hot temperature, or the toxic debris cloud. The shockwave alone would be so powerful it would blow them into pieces, and nothing bigger than a postage stamp would remain.

He half-smiled as his mind started to drift. He remembered the faces of Aimee and Joshua. Did he really have anything to go back to? Why not join them now?

"Let it happen," he whispered.

CHAPTER 47

Phillip Hanley couldn't even blink as he watched the old-style analogue clock on the wall in their main laboratory as it counted down the seconds.

Time seemed to have slowed down, but then he heard the tachyon generators start up again and the bridge chamber began to glow its familiar soft blue.

The man prayed; first prize, they brought back Sam Reid and Alyssa. Second prize, he at least brought the woman home.

He could feel Pinchella's glare. The damn woman scared the shit out of him. Just like that damn colonel, who reminded him of a bulldog with a military crew cut, and with the pale, unblinking eyes of a killer. What was it about the HAWCs that the people they employed were so damn frightening?

He drew in a deep breath – they only had this one shot, and it had to work. Alyssa either grabbed up Sam Reid, or he was stuck there forever.

And another thing – they were sending Alyssa back for just ten seconds. But the time distortion might mean she was there for anything from two seconds to a week.

Hanley sighed. Everything was so complex, and they didn't fully understand the technical things they were working with. And he was supposed to be the expert.

"Initiating," Rashid said softly.

And then . . .

"Got something. I don't know what." Rashid looked up just as the tachyon chamber lit with its usual blinding blue flash.

* * *

It took twenty Philistines using stout ropes to drag Sam to the center of the arena. He heard their bloodthirsty cries: *Death to the mighty Samson.*

He fought them a little, for show, but really, he let them take him.

After the heat of the day, he now felt the coolness of evening coming on. The ground beneath him was crusted with blood and littered with what he thought might be viscera and the remains of dead animals and humans. He could smell the charnel house stink rising from the still-warm sand.

This is a horrible civilization, he thought. *It doesn't deserve to exist anymore.*

He tried not to dwell on the death that was to be his fate – it was going to be a gruesome spectacle; a massacre. They still feared him, so his restraints would not come off. They wanted him to die slowly and in agony. They wanted him humbled and begging for death.

He could smell the hot coals and the heating of irons. He knew what that meant – they were going to prolong his agony, by hacking into him, and then heat-searing the wounds with the glowing metal. Pain upon more pain.

How long would it last? he wondered. How long would it take him to die?

His huge body and toughened mentality had an ability to absorb punishment. It might fight death, even as he desired it.

He knew he had one chance – he would be bound between the two mighty pillars that the hundred-foot-high stone statue of their corrupt idol rested upon.

Let them do it, he thought. *Your god against mine.*

Before this day was done, if he prevailed, none would survive.

* * *

Sam felt the cool rock of the massive pillars against his hands. He was chained between them now, and he heard raised voices. When he turned his head he could feel the force of the crowd's jeers. The Saran's entire retinue, the nobles and high born, the army generals, and many hundreds of the cruelest of the Philistines were gathered here, drunk now on wine and bloodlust.

Good, he thought.

He heard the Saran's voice as he addressed the crowd. He taunted Sam, Samson, and promised the crowd he would die slowly and painfully.

Sam lowered his head and said a soft prayer.

This is where it ends, he thought. *My torment is nearly over.*

He rested his hands against the cool stone and flexed his fingers, testing it.

A drunken jeer rang out from the crowd. "The mighty Samson, now mad as a goat tied in the sun." More laughter as more and more voices heckled him.

The first arrow struck him in the chest. It pierced the flesh, and the pain was intense, but the MECH armor beneath his skin protected his heart. It could never be penetrated by a mere arrow.

Another struck his shoulder. Then another. The pain was intense, and the blood flowed.

He couldn't allow them to bleed him out, drain him of his strength. Not yet.

He lifted his head, his teeth bared.

"Go to Hell," he roared in English. "All of you."

"He speaks in mad tongues," he heard someone yell in response to this unknown language, and then the crowd roared with laughter.

Of course they could not understand his words. But they would soon understand his actions.

He spread his fingers, feeling the stone, feeling its weight.

Another arrow struck him, this time in the meat of his thigh.

Sam moved into HAWC mode and took himself outside of the pain as more and more arrows struck.

Then he heard someone give the command to approach him, and knew he had little time left before they began to hack at him with their long, machete-like swords. Already the blood loss was making his breathing labored and his heart work harder than it should.

He braced his hands and roared: "Let it be upon your foul heads."

He pushed.

Pushed harder.

Sam threw his head back and felt the internal machinery within him begin to fully engage. It was time to wake it after so many years of little use.

Laughter rang around the arena. Another arrow struck him, and he heard the slide of swords from scabbards. The soldiers were close now.

Screaming with exertion, he pushed with the combined strength of his own body and his internal chassis. His roars almost drowned out the derisive laughter.

And then . . . the mighty column to his left moved.

The laughter faded to a few nervous titters.

He pushed again, and this time the stone shifted several inches and he felt dust rain down.

The laughter stopped completely.

"Cut him down," the Saran yelled.

Sam heard the soldiers charge at him, and he pushed with all his remaining strength. The column to his left tumbled out and began to fall like a mighty redwood trunk to roll down the steps. There were screams of abject horror, and he could tell the soldiers had been crushed like bugs. But he didn't stop, turning immediately to the column on the right and giving it all his attention.

It shifted now too. In a few seconds it began to move.

Sam knew that when this one was gone, the colossal stone statue resting upon it, weighing hundreds of tons, would fall on the arena, bringing it down and crushing everything inside.

"*Cut him down!*" The Saran's scream was so high-pitched it could even be heard above the shifting rock.

Sam gave one last push, and the column began to fall away. He stood there then, lifting his arms wide, waiting for the crush of stone.

Sam could not see what happened. But just as the thousands of tons of rock bore down on him, a blue light engulfed him.

A glowing woman appeared, all in blinding white. She looked at nothing but Sam, put her arms around him, and then in another flash of blue, she and Sam were gone.

* * *

As the arena came down the Saran stood, holding his goblet of gold and rubies in a shaking hand. Around him the crowd descended into chaos as they were crushed alive. "Even the angels come for you," he said, raising his goblet in a toast. "To you and your God, mighty Samson."

The arena collapsed, burying everything and everyone within it.

The only thing that remained was a legend.

CHAPTER 48

Casey Franks grinned at the shockwave coming at them followed by a tsunami that was at least 100 feet high. "Fucking surf's up," she shouted.

"*Cowabunga*," Brandt yelled, and threw his head back to laugh loudly at the sky.

Cooper just lowered her head, maybe praying, and Gonzalez and Ito remained impassive, simply watching the wall of force as it came.

Alex's stomach began to tingle as the mile-high shock blast came at them, but he continued to smile, his feeling of calm never leaving him – five, four . . .

The HAWCs began to glow blue.

Three, two . . .

The shockwave hit, and the boat exploded into a million tiny pieces.

* * *

"I'm losing them, I'm losing them," Rashid yelled as the tachyon chamber glowed but refused to materialize its target.

"Don't you fucking dare," Hammerson warned.

Hanley was working a different console, reading the data, and shaking his head. "Oh god. It's suddenly locked on to multiple targets but it's trying to bring them all back at the same time. In the same place." He gritted his teeth. "Multiple bridge streams converging. It's not designed to handle that. We can't rematerialize them all into the same spot. The analytic engine knows that and it's getting confused."

"What happens then?" Quartermain asked. "If they come back into the same spot?"

"A body might rematerialize inside another body." Hanley looked up. "It won't be pretty."

"The HAWCs die, I wouldn't want to be you," Pinchella growled as she stared at the man from under lowered brows.

"Yeah, thanks, like I really need that pressure right now," Hanley complained, and refused to even look at Hammerson.

Quartermain put a hand on her arm. "Let him work."

"Isolate them, split them up," Hanley yelled.

"I'm trying," Rashid said. "I need to suspend one of them. But I have no idea which one it will be. Or whether they'll still be there after I finish . . ." He turned to Hanley.

Hanley turned to Hammerson, who gave him an almost imperceptible nod.

"Do it," Hanley said.

Rashid spun back and his hands flew over the keyboard.

The tachyon chamber flared and those without protective goggles shut their eyes or turned away.

When the blinding light faded, the HAWCs were there – Alex Hunter, Bernadette Cooper, Ito Yamada, Eric Gonzalez, Casey Franks, and Bill Brandt.

"*Yes*," Hammerson yelled.

They were sitting in a two-row formation, but a few had their arms thrown up as if to ward off a potential blow.

They blinked and then looked around.

Brandt whooped. "We're back, baby."

He reached forward to grab Casey and shook her. She grinsneered, but still jerked an elbow back into his chest, hard, making him *oof*.

"I've still got them," Rashid said loudly, with eyes almost bulging in his concentration.

"It's gotta be Sam Reid," Hanley yelled back. "Release the suspension."

Rashid nodded once. "Incoming – ten seconds – *clear the chamber, clear the chamber.*"

"*Out*," Alex roared, helping Cooper up and then pushing the others toward the exit. Tor's metallic feet skittered on the floor to keep up.

No sooner were they out of the chamber, than the door was closed, and Rashid set to finishing his retrieval program.

* * *

Alex Hunter squinted as the blue light grew to blinding luminescence.

"Coming in . . . *now*," Rashid shouted.

Hammerson had his arms folded across his barrel chest but briefly held a forearm up over his eyes.

The chamber flared once again, and this time when the light dissipated, there were just two figures, holding each other tight. One was Alyssa, and in her arms was the giant form of Sam Reid.

"Oh my God," Quartermain said softly.

Alex sucked in a breath as Sam collapsed with a thump. His huge body was emaciated, and he was punctured by at least ten arrows. Also a filthy rag was tied over his grimy and blood-streaked upper face. He lay deathly still as Hammerson hollered for the med team.

"What did they fucking do to him?" As always, Casey was

first in, yanking the chamber door open and rushing to her huge friend. Alex was right behind her.

Casey got down and gently removed the rag from Sam's face, her eyes widening when she saw the two empty eye sockets, although she said nothing. However, she bared her teeth in fury and made a small noise in her throat.

Alex went to his knees beside his big friend. "Sam," he whispered.

"Brother," Sam gasped softly.

Casey held his upper arm, just looking down at him. Sam reached out one huge log-like arm and placed it on her shoulder. "Casey?"

She nodded.

"Am I really home?" Sam asked in a voice a little louder than a breath.

Casey nodded again, but realizing he couldn't see her, she just rubbed his arm possibly not trusting herself to speak yet. For the first time in Alex's life, he thought he might have even seen the tough, female HAWC's eyes water.

"You're home, buddy. You're safe now," Alex said.

"The others?" His voice rose. "The team?"

"We're all here, safe and sound. We're right with you." Casey said.

"Mission completed, soldier," Alex added.

"Good, good." Sam then seemed to relax a bit. "How long . . .?" he asked.

"How long were you gone?" Alex looked at Sam's starved form and noticed a few grey streaks at his temples. "Days, just days, my friend."

"It seemed . . . *longer*." He groaned. "I really. Bought it. This time." He winced.

"Fucking pinpricks, man." Casey's chin trembled just a little. "You've had worse."

Sam nodded, and then his head slumped back to the floor. Quartermain already had an emergency medical kit and began to treat his wounds. "Blood and saline, *now*. And ready the chopper," he said as he worked.

Hammerson looked across to Alyssa, who stood now with hands clasped, staring down at Sam. Her face was streaked with tears.

"You're one hell of a brave woman." He nodded. "Thank you."

Quartermain shone a small light into Sam's empty eye sockets. "Okay, okay, good, the nerve endings are desiccated, but still there. I can work with those."

"We need to get him to a hospital." Alyssa wept openly now as she dropped to kneel beside them.

Quartermain reached out to take her arm. "Do you trust me?"

It took a second or two, but she nodded.

"Good," he replied, and went back to working on Sam. "We need to get him to my lab. I'll take care of him." He then used a pair of shears to cut the arrow shafts off close to Sam's body, and then covered him with a silver sheet.

Two of Quartermain's waiting medical technicians tried to lift the huge man onto a gurney but couldn't. Alex and Brandt helped and then with Quartermain and Alyssa beside them, the med team wheeled him to the door.

Alex put an arm around Alyssa as she headed up to accompany Sam to the incoming chopper on the roof. "Thank you, and well done. You saved him."

"Will he be blind?" she cried, clinging to the unconscious man.

"Leave him to Dr. Quartermain. He's the best there is." Alex handed her gently over to someone behind him and stood back as she and the medical team entered the elevator.

Alex called to Quartermain, "Look after my brother."

"You bet," Quartermain replied. "Just give me a week." And then the elevator doors closed.

Alex stood staring at the silver doors for a moment longer, finally feeling the adrenaline start to leak from his system. He then turned to head back into the laboratory, where his HAWCs stood talking to Colonel Hammerson. They parted as he approached.

Pinchella came to attention. "Welcome back, sir." She grinned and bumped fists with him, before going to join the other HAWCs.

"Choppers inbound," Hammerson said. "On the roof in five minutes. Reid and Alyssa are out first. You and the mission team next." He stuck out a hand. "Good to have you back, son."

"Good to be home," Alex replied. "Close call. We nearly nuked ourselves."

"Mission status?" Hammerson asked.

"Threat extinguished. In fact, multiple threats extinguished." Alex closed his eyes for a moment, drew in a breath and let it out slowly. "Large, non-terrestrial, aggressive lifeform, also extinguished."

"Repeat that, Arcadian?" Hammerson frowned.

Alex half smiled. "It'll all be in my report, sir."

"Okay, I look forward to reading it. Good job," Hammerson said softly. "And I've got some news you'll be happy to hear. The Janus team has perfected short-term jumps. You've got a date with a Russian shooter."

Alex's expression dropped and he stared straight ahead, his eyes burning silver momentarily. After another moment he blinked away the shock of what that could mean.

Hammerson stood closer. "Be ready to go back . . ."

"I'm ready now," Alex cut in.

CHAPTER 49

The Silurian period – unidentified landmass in the Paleo-Tethys Ocean

The multiple nuclear packages all detonated at once with an explosive force of fifty kilotons, more than three times the size of the Hiroshima blast. And they exploded deep, having traveled many miles below the surface in the bottomless lake.

The heat and percussive power melted the island's bedrock base, devastating the land's foundation so much that it sank below the sea surface. The geography of the time period was then brought back into line with what modern geological predictive analysts thought it was like.

The massive beast, Dagon, had already fled. The dark lake was the opening to a gravity well that was a corridor that traveled deep below the Earth, and all the way to a vast and hidden underground sea.

Dagon's burns would heal. Its damaged eyes would be restored. But the massive creature was now sealed deep beneath the earth. However, time meant nothing to it, and it could slumber until it was released to the surface world again.

It had read the minds of the small but intelligent bipeds, and it liked what it had seen. When they rose from the mire to rule the Earth, it would be ready and waiting. Time was always on its side.

CHAPTER 50

Today – The Janus Institute, Landsdowne Street, Cambridge, Massachusetts

It was just twenty-four hours later that they were ready, and Jack Hammerson reached up to place a hand on Alex Hunter's shoulder, grip it, and stare into his face. He thought the man looked strong and in control. His eyes were as intense as ever, but still haunted.

Sure, he had just come off a perilous and arduous mission, but physically, his body could heal itself in hours if not minutes. His complex mind was different. The problem plaguing Alex was purely psychological. And the potential remedy was right here, right now.

"You will have ten minutes to locate your shooter, and stop him. If you have time, find out who sent him. But the main game is to stop him. Because if you miss, you can't go back to that moment in time – ever." Hammerson gripped his shoulder a little harder. "It's critical that you stop him then and there, or nothing will change. Is that clear?"

Alex just glared at something only his mind could see.

"*Clear?*" Hammerson repeated, louder.

Alex pulled on a pair of black rubber gloves. "Crystal."

Alex's eyes burned with caged fury. Hammerson smiled grimly. He'd hate to be the guy that Alex was going after, and just wished he could see the look on the shooter's face when this monster stepped out of thin air.

Hammerson let go of his shoulder. "Good hunting, son."

Alex nodded, but his eyes were once again on somewhere far away. Or perhaps simply long ago.

Alex stepped into the tachyon chamber. He was dressed in civilian clothing and carried no weapons. He didn't need any.

Hammerson turned to Rashid and nodded, and the man started up the cycle. Alex clicked a timer on his wristwatch and then stood straight and tall, and now so still, he could have been carved from stone.

The light intensified, and Hammerson shut his eyes for a moment until he registered the darkness against his eyelids again. When he opened them Alex was gone.

"And he's gone back to Saturday 12th, 0750 hours. Approximately ten minutes before the, ah, assassination," Hanley said. "Return stream set for exactly nine minutes, fifty-one seconds and counting."

Hammerson continued to stare in at the empty chamber. It reminded him of something – that movie where a killer robot was sent from the future to assassinate someone.

He smiled cruelly. "I'll be back."

* * *

There was a flash in the hallway of a building half a mile away from Alex's house, on the third floor, just outside apartment 4.

When the light faded, Alex Hunter stood there.

He quickly checked his watch, noting the countdown, and then turned to the door – it was the right one. And he didn't waste a second. He grabbed the handle, found it locked as expected, and then crushed it, splintering the surrounding wood.

Alex pushed the door open and took everything in within the blink of an eye – the two dead occupants, the scattered food containers that were evidence that the assassin had been hiding out for days, waiting, waiting for the best kill shot on him and his family.

Those thoughts made the anger and fury explode within him. And then the assassin appeared. "You. *How?*"

The man was older than Alex expected. But he was still big and fit, and had clearly recognized Alex as one of his targets.

In his hand he held the Russian high-powered sniper rifle Alex knew he planned to use against his family. He was a professional and he wasn't frozen in shock by Alex's appearance, but instead brought the gun barrel up and in a smooth motion, fired.

But Alex wasn't where he had been a second ago. He moved so fast that before the professional shooter could even readjust his stance or even bring the barrel around, Alex was beside him, with his hand on the gun barrel. And by then it was all over.

Alex ripped the gun from his hands so violently, the man's trigger finger was torn right off his hand, spraying blood, and accompanied by a howl of pain.

Alex bent the barrel as if it were a piece of rubber, knowing the gloves he wore would leave no prints or DNA trace. He then grabbed up the television set's electrical cord and ripped it from the wall. He used it to tie the man's wrists together.

He checked his watch again – he now had six minutes, and he wanted to use them all.

Alex dragged the man to a chair and pushed him into it. He then leaned forward.

"Let's understand each other. You're already dead. But how you die, and how painful it is, is up to you. Do you understand?"

The man just stared and uttered not a word, as he was still sucking it in from the pain of his lost finger.

Alex looked down at the stump, and then back into the man's face. "That's nothing compared to what's coming. Do you understand?" he repeated.

The man clamped his jaws and shut his eyes.

"Okay." Alex reached down and ripped the trigger finger off his other hand – there would be no more shooting from either hand ever again.

The man howled again, and Alex ignored his wailing. The Other inside him wanted blood. He wanted to pulverize him down to ground beef. But Alex needed information first.

Alex leaned in close to his face again. "Who sent you? Give me a name."

The man cursed loudly in Russian, and then spat angrily into Alex's face.

In turn, Alex took two more fingers.

He straightened. "You have six more fingers, ten toes, two ears, a nose, and a penis." He stared, his eyes glowing silver in the darkened room. "I guarantee you, before I have taken all of them, you will have told me everything and be begging for death." He grinned like a death's head. "And I'm in no hurry," Alex lied.

It took Alex four more minutes, four more fingers and an ear, and just as his time was running out, the man gave him a name: *Grigory Villinov*. And a place: *Belarus*.

Alex felt the familiar tingle in his belly and knew his time was about up. He quickly reached out, grabbed the Russian's head, and twisted it so fast and hard that the crack of his vertebrae snapping was like a gunshot.

The man slumped in the chair.

Alex straightened, staring at the corpse with half-lidded eyes.

And then vanished.

* * *

Hammerson waited with arms folded as the blue ball of blinding light dissipated. When it was gone Alex Hunter stood in the chamber, head bowed, with blood up to his elbows.

He slowly lifted his head and opened his eyes. He took off his gloves, dropped them, and then left the chamber.

"Is it done?" Hammerson asked.

"Nearly," Alex replied. "I need to get to Belarus. A loose thread needs to be tied off."

"Good." Hammerson expected it. "Suit up. Chopper will pick you up in an hour."

CHAPTER 51

USSTRATCOM, Nebraska – Recovery ward,
Sub Level 4

In the USSTRATCOM recovery ward, Sam Reid held Alyssa's hand as they unwrapped the bandages around his head.

"I feel like a schoolkid, counting down to spring break," he said through his grin.

All his wounds were stitched, although it would take at least another few weeks for them to fully knit closed. But the serum Quartermain had given him was a derivative of the Arcadian treatment and used for rapid healing. It meant his wounds wouldn't just be misshapen scars by then, but full new flesh with only a small line indicting that there had ever been a puncture wound there.

And there was something else he was trying out.

"Just be patient," Quartermain said. "It's new tech, so I'm expecting you'll have improved vision, across a few spectrums that will be beyond standard 20/20. But . . ."

"Yeah, there's always a *but*." Sam's grin dropped a little.

"*But*, it'll be different vision from what you used to have," the scientist replied.

The bandages were off and then Quartermain removed the two round pads over Sam's eyes. He gently pressed around the eyes. "Good. Swelling has gone down considerably." He took his hands away. "Open."

Sam opened his eyes. He blinked twice. The light hurt him, but only for a moment as the lenses corrected the light sensitivity for him. Then things came into focus quickly.

Sam saw Alyssa standing there with her hands clasped together under her chin. She was grinning wildly and bouncing up and down like a kid.

Quartermain nodded and smiled. "Try them out. See what they can do – they have full neural connection. Think it, and the eyes will do it. Just like your own eyes used to."

Sam held up a hand, concentrated on it, and then he saw through the skin to the muscles. Then to the bones, and also to the MECH armor's endoskeletal structure. He pulled back and amplified the vision so he could examine a single strand of hair on Alyssa's head.

"*Whoa,*" he said under his breath.

Quartermain handed Sam a small mirror and he hesitated for a few moments before lifting it to look at his reflection.

His eyes. Looked. Exactly the same.

No, almost, but not quite.

He then saw that the pupils screwed open and closed like small camera lenses. But the color of the iris was the same, and the white of the sclera even had a few small veins; it looked perfect.

He smiled and reached out a hand to Alyssa. "Good to see you again, baby."

She took his large hand in both of hers and kissed it. "Welcome home."

"Can I get you anything?" Quartermain asked.

Sam kept looking at his beautiful Alyssa. "I've got everything I need right here." He then turned. "No, wait, there is something . . ."

"Name it," Quartermain asked.

"Lock the door and let no one disturb me for an hour." He kept smiling at Alyssa.

Quartermain smiled and began to back out of the room.

"Wait." Alyssa turned to him. "Make it two hours."

Quartermain nodded and opened the door, leaving quietly, and Sam saw Pinchella through the doorway, waiting for the scientist. She winked at him, and then the door closed on the pair.

Sam turned back to Alyssa, and he watched her as she stepped back, and, taking her time, dropped one shoulder of her dress. And then the other. She stood there looking at him with a sultry steam in her eyes.

"Oh God, I missed you," he said softly.

He thought he'd never be with her, smell her, and certainly never see her again. But here she was. The pain, the torture, the degradation, and the lost time, all meant nothing. Right now, he knew he was the luckiest man alive.

He held out his arms to her, his desire rising. "Hey, take it easy on an old man, will you?"

Alyssa quickly crossed to him and looked down along his body. She then looked back into his eyes and smiled. "You don't look so old to me." She reached down to grip him, and then bent forward to kiss his lips, hard.

Suddenly, Sam knew that two hours wasn't going to be nearly enough time.

CHAPTER 52

Grigory Villinov was ex-Russian military and a middle-ranking head of an assassination bureau working out of Belarus. By the time Alex and a HAWC team dropped in from the stealth chopper and opened his door, the man was already dead.

Alex stood over the cold body and stared.

"He's dead," he said with barely contained fury into his throat mic. "How did they know?"

Hammerson grunted. "Maybe you killing the assassin alerted them. Or maybe he had other enemies. Doesn't matter. Mission is over. Pull out."

Alex didn't move but instead continued to stare at the body. "You bastard. You needed to talk."

His chest rose and fell faster as his anger boiled over. After another moment he lunged forward and pulled the corpse close to his face. "Damn you. I'm not done with you yet. I'll find out who ordered the hit. And when I do, I promise you, I'll fucking tear them apart."

He threw the body against the wall so hard the sound of bones breaking was loud in the room. The other two black-clad HAWCs eased back to just watch from the shadows.

Alex then waved a hand in the air.

Thirty seconds later, the HAWCs were already on their way home.

CHAPTER 53

Alex headed straight home from the base and knew something had changed, had been reorganized, or reset – he felt it. And he prayed it was what he was waiting for.

He pulled up out the front of his house and put his hand on the car doorhandle, but then hesitated. For the first time in years, he felt a gnawing fear in the pit of his stomach.

What if nothing had changed? What if the house was still empty?

His hand eased back from the handle. *Then I truly am a ghost with nothing to live for*, he answered.

Alex shut his eyes, calming himself. He needed to let go of the depression, the rage, let go of the hunger for revenge. If what was inside that house was what he most desired, then he would be content forever.

"Please be there," he whispered, grabbed his kit bag, then shouldered open the car door and started running up his front lawn. But then he stopped as the outer screen door opened.

He slowly went to his knees.

"Hey Dad," Joshua said. "Guess what we're having for dinner tonight? Our favorite."

"*Burgers*," Alex said under his breath.

"Burgers!" Joshua said, and approached, grinning from ear to ear.

Alex stood and grabbed Joshua under his arm just as Aimee came out on the front porch. She was in her tight black jeans and an old, stretched-out t-shirt. She looked beautiful, radiant, and her electric-blue eyes shone brighter than ever.

"Good, you're back. That didn't take long." She smiled. "And yay, you remembered the ground beef."

Alex looked down at his hand in confusion. He wasn't holding his kit bag anymore, but a shopping bag.

When did . . .? He began to think, but she took the bag from him, and instead he pulled her in under his other arm and hugged them both, so close they squeaked and giggled.

He inhaled their smells, and then pulled back, looking at each of them. "I was only gone 420 million years, give or take a day." He grinned, ignoring the lump in his throat.

"Hey, Dad, are you crying?" Joshua's brows creased.

"Who, me? Never." He shook his head. "Everything is fine. Everything is just fine now."

He looked up at the first-floor window and saw the huge dog staring down at him. An image formed in his mind: *I was there*, it imparted.

I know. Thank you. Alex smiled, and the dog vanished back inside somewhere.

"I'm starving," Joshua said.

"Me too," said Aimee.

"Me three." Alex lifted Joshua up over his shoulder, spun him once, and then headed up to the house.

He couldn't stop smiling and sucked in a deep breath. He knew Jack Hammerson had made this happen. He'd had conflicting feelings about the Hammer over the years, but now he knew, he owed that man everything.

CHAPTER 54

Colonel Jack "the Hammer" Hammerson had watched the HAWC Belarus incursion through the small cameras embedded in the insertion team's suits.

He saw the body of Villinov lying cold and dead.

Good, he thought.

He then saw Alex lift the corpse, snarl something into its waxen face, and then throw it at a wall like a rag doll.

And then they were gone.

He picked up the phone and called a direct and secure line to his counterpart in Russia. It answered immediately.

"It's over," he said.

"Of course it is. The intermediary has been removed." General Bulgakov sounded like he exhaled through his nose, in and out for a moment or two. "He was a valuable man. You owe me." More breathing. "But you play a dangerous game, my friend."

Hammerson took a big sip of bourbon and grimaced as the heat hit the coldness in his belly. "Being a lion means more than just having a taste for blood."

Bulgakov exhaled again. "I underestimated you, Jack. You had his entire family killed, threw him to the wolves. You are more ruthless than I thought. Are you sure you are not developing a taste for that blood?"

Hammerson grunted. "This is the Arcadian; you throw him to the wolves, and he'll return leading the pack."

"This man. This Arcadian. I have heard of him. You make sure he never leads his pack to my door. I do not think that monster would show me mercy. Or you, if he knew what you had done, my friend."

"We're not friends," Hammerson replied. "And don't worry, no loose ends, General. You have my word; he'll never touch you." Hammerson hung up.

CHAPTER 55

It was a hot evening and General Bulgakov sat at his desk signing documents from a pile that seemed to never end.

His office was in the Kremlin complex, one of the most secure pieces of real estate on Earth – it had a garrison for 5000 troops, heavy-calibre machine guns and antiaircraft batteries on the roof, and the Moskva River running past it had submarine netting and intelligent mines. The Kremlin lived up to the meaning of its name: *the fortress within a city.*

Bulgakov dropped the pen, flexed his aching fingers, and luxuriated in the slight breeze coming in through the open window. The Kremlin was a fortress, but with poor air-conditioning, he mused.

He couldn't help his mind wandering back to the recent conversation he'd had with the American colonel, Jack Hammerson. He knew of this near-indestructible super-soldier called the Arcadian. He was supposedly as brutal and fearless as he was powerful. He was said to be the man who couldn't be killed.

Bulgakov leaned back in his chair, his hands clasped on his belly. Something about what Jack Hammerson had said nagged at him.

You have my word, he'll never touch you, he had said.

He'll never touch you.

He'll.

The sparrow-sized drone glided silently in through the window. It was little more than a flying eye with a powerful sting.

Bulgakov's eyes became alert. *You cunning bastard*, he thought as he leaped to his feet.

The drone identified its target, darted forward, and attached itself to the back of the man's neck. Bulgakov cried out and reached up for it – just as the few ounces of HMX crystals detonated. The small and super-powerful chemical mix erupted with a velocity of 25,000 feet per second and an oversized 39 gigapascals of explosive pressure.

The general's head was blown from his body to smash into the roof, and his torso was torn down the middle.

* * *

Watching the tiny drone's camera feed, Jack Hammerson saw the device dart toward the general's neck, and then the screen whited out, meaning detonation had successfully occurred.

He sat back and sipped his bourbon again. *Sorry, General, but no loose ends means no loose ends.*

The small earbud buzzed, and he lifted it from his desktop and plugged it into his ear.

"Hammer," he said.

"NK helo inbound," the man's emotionless voice said.

"Strike is authorized," he replied automatically.

"Roger that," came the reply.

Another loose end about to be tied off, he thought, and sipped again.

* * *

The F-22 Raptor came in over New Mexico's Gila National Forest low and fast. One klick out, its bay doors whined open to reveal a single AMRAAM missile positioned in the cradle.

The pilot could see the North Korean helicopter on his instrumentation panel long before he made visual contact. He didn't know it was carrying the NKs' only working tachyon drive, or the scientists who could operate it.

It didn't matter to him, because he had one job – destruction of his designated target.

Just as the helicopter was about to touch down on the dry scrubby land, he pressed the small button on the stick.

"Foxtrot one."

The AMRAAM was a sleek spear that weighed 340 pounds and used an advanced solid-fuel rocket motor. It could achieve a speed of Mach 4, but it didn't need that now; it had been selected for its targeting ability and detonation punch.

The missile took seconds to arrive, and it struck the North Korean helicopter just as it settled on the ground.

For several seconds the helicopter was turned into a miniature sun, reaching thousands of degrees instantaneously and with such explosive force it would leave nothing behind bigger than a melted beer can.

"Confirmed kill," the pilot intoned. "Coming home."

The deadly bird swung away and was over the horizon in seconds.

* * *

Hammerson took the bud from his ear.

He already had covert operatives inside North Korea who would track down anyone who had touched or even seen the Janus time travel technology. In a few days they'd all cease to exist.

He nodded to his reflection in the dark glass of the large window, and then leaned forward to lift his phone. There was one last piece of clean-up to do.

* * *

"Hey, what the hell?" Phillip Hanley jumped to his feet as the team of stern-looking men and women came in through the front doors. Rashid and the rest of their team just stared with open mouths.

"Who let you in? Who are you?" Hanley demanded.

And then it became clear, as in came Andrew Quartermain with the fearsome-looking female HAWC, Pinchella, right on his shoulder.

Quartermain stood with legs braced in the center of the room, as Hanley, Rashid, and the technicians were gathered together.

"Ladies and gentlemen," he began. "By order of the US Government, this facility is being closed down due to the risk to the sovereign power of the United States of America. All data, records, and assets, will be seized."

"*No!*" Hanley marched forward, but stopped dead when the female HAWC stepped in front of Quartermain and looked at Hanley from under lowered brows with a grim smile. He could tell she would not hesitate to smash him.

Rashid shook his head. "So this was why you spent that time with us learning our technology?" he said to Quartermain. "Because you want it."

The HAWC scientist shared a flat smile. "I like you. Both of you. But you and your technology nearly caused the destruction of the United States as we know it. You have proven you are not capable of controlling such power."

"And the US military is?" Hanley scoffed.

"It's a WMD," Pinchella replied. "It's going where weapons of this caliber should go."

"She's right," Quartermain said. "Assist us in the process, and you will be well compensated."

"And if we don't?" Hanley lifted his chin.

Pinchella smiled. "Then you'll be just another loose end to be tied off."

Quartermain sighed. "Phillip, it is important you know what that means." His eyes were unblinking as they bored into those of the chief Janus scientist. "Do you?"

"I – we – do," Rashid said softly. He turned to his colleague. "Phillip, it's time we retired."

Quartermain nodded. "There'll be a standard non-disclosure agreement for you all to sign, and then you can enjoy the rest of your life. Doing something else, somewhere else."

Pinchella stepped back and held the door open. "Good day, gentlemen."

EPILOGUE

Jack Hammerson turned to the large window, thinking about the things he needed to do to keep the world safe. The NKs had been put back in their box, the Janus technology had been absorbed into the USSTRATCOM labs, and he had successfully brought the Arcadian back into the fold.

He refused to let any form of regret or guilt enter his mind about what he had done to the man. As far as he was concerned, the world was a safer place with Alex Hunter fighting for it.

He looked out over the night-time fields of the USSTRATCOM base. He had learned a few things over the years, and one of them was that the world doesn't need more heroes, it needs monsters.

He sipped his bourbon again, but this time it just gave him a sick feeling in his gut, and his very soul felt as black as a lump of coal.

"A monster to fight monsters," he said softly as he raised the glass to his reflection. "There will be no place in heaven for me."

AUTHOR'S NOTES

Many readers ask me about the background of my novels – is the science real or imagined? Where do I get the situations, equipment, characters, and their expertize from, and just how much of it has a basis in fact?

As a fiction writer I certainly create things to support my stories. But mostly, I'll do extensive research on the science behind my tale, and I nearly always find something that fits!

Regarding my novel *The Silurian Bridge*, I begin my tale with a time travel event. Could time travel be real, now or one day? Maybe.

But if it did exist, how would we know? Because if you controlled time travel, you would certainly not want people to know. Or at least people from the past. And if you had the ability to travel back and forth, then don't bother looking for evidence, as the time travelers could simply go back and recover it or erase it (I touched on this in my time travel short story, *The Fossil*).

This novel also allowed me to explore further what I wrote about in the Center of the Earth series. Many of my readers of those novels asked about the massive creature I placed in the core of the Earth's underground sea called Dagon – where did it come from, how old was it? In *The Silurian Bridge*, we now have an explanation.

Read on for more interesting facts that came out of my research on Samson, Dagon, and the Silurian period of Earth's distant past.

Regards, *Greig Beck*

DAGON

Dagon was real. At least as far as the Sumerians, Babylonians, Syrians, Mesopotamians, and many other ancient civilizations believed. It was a god that had been worshipped for over 5000 years.

There were many references to it being everything from a half-man/half-fish god to the god of harvest and fertility, and even to it being the father of all gods. Human sacrifices were often made to appease this monstrous being.

Dagon also appeared in the Bible (The Book of Judges) in reference to the Philistines. And this is where I was able to weave in the HAWC, Sam Reid.

However, one of the most recent representations, and the one most of us are familiar with, is that of the great beast from the writing of H.P. Lovecraft in a story simply called *Dagon*, written in 1917.

From a young age, Lovecraft had a keen interest in actual archaeological discoveries and later used some of these in his writings. In his research he may have at some time come across this ancient god and decided to use it.

Lovecraft's story, *Dagon*, told of a sailor who finds himself stranded on a slimy expanse of hellish black mire – a region putrid with the carcasses of decaying fish and less describable things. He believes the miasmic area was formerly a portion of the ocean floor thrown to the surface by volcanic activity and exposing regions which for innumerable millions of years had lain hidden under unfathomable watery depths.

The sailor describes Dagon rising from the sea like this: "*With only a slight churning to mark its rise to the surface, the thing slid into view above the dark waters. Vast, Polyphemus-like, and loathsome – a stupendous monster of nightmares (with) gigantic scaly arms, and hideous head.*"

Lovecraft even had an idea where these great old gods came from, and the quote I used in the opening of my novel, drawn from Lovecraft's *The Call of Cthulhu and Other Dark Tales*, is one of my favorites. Here's the extended version: "*The Great Old Ones who lived ages before there were any men, and who came to the young world out of the sky. Those Old Ones are gone now, inside the Earth and under the sea; but their dead bodies had told their secrets in dreams to the first men, who formed a cult which had never died.*"

Lovecraft's works have been influential on many creatives such as authors Neil Gaiman and Stephen King, and directors John Carpenter and Guillermo del Toro. And, of course, me!

THE LEGEND OF SAMSON

Many ancient civilizations had mighty and mythical warriors as their heroes such as Hercules, Beowulf, Thor, Achilles, Samson, Gilgamesh, Perseus, and many others. These characters tended to be physical giants or had the strength of many.

The biblical account of Samson said he was a Nazarite who had immense strength which he used against his enemies, and which also allowed him to perform superhuman feats such as the slaying of a lion with his bare hands and massacring an entire army of Philistines.

Samson was betrayed and handed over to his Philistine enemies, who gouged out his eyes and forced the blinded giant to grind grain in a mill in Gaza for many years. When the Philistines finally took Samson into their temple of Dagon for his sacrifice, he was ready. His great strength allowed him to bring down the temple columns, collapsing the arena and killing himself as well as all of the Philistines.

Was Samson real? We'll never know for sure. But Joan Comay, co-author of *Who's Who in the Bible: The Old Testament and the Apocrypha, The New Testament*, believes that the biblical story of Samson was so specific concerning time and place that Samson was undoubtedly a real person.

SUPER ISLANDS OF THE SILURIAN

If you have ever seen those cool time-lapse motion graphics that show the evolution of the planet's morphology over the hundreds of millions of years of its existence, you'll be amazed at the malleability of the Earth's surface.

The plate tectonic cycle begins a billion years ago when the primitive Earth's atmosphere was dominated by gases like methane and ammonia. At that time there was a single mega-continent balanced on a super ocean. This oldest super continent is known as Rodinia, and it formed between about one billion and 800 million years ago. It fragmented around 750 million years ago.

Then, after sliding around for 200 million years, those massive fragments collided to form Gondwana, which existed about 510 million years ago. Then that too broke apart to later form Pangaea, our most recent super continent, which assembled about 335 million years ago.

Our story takes place just as Pangaea was forming. In the Silurian period, the super island or mini continent known as Laurussia (also known as Euramerica) was about to collide with the continents Laurentia (modern-day North America) and Baltica (modern-day northern and eastern Europe).

At that time, the west coast of Laurussia was a hot, humid land with near endless coastal waters, deep silty embayments, river deltas, and estuaries, plus significant volcanic activity.

Fragmented fossil evidence shows that the first significant life on dry land occurred around that time, when free-sporing vascular plants began to spread across the land, forming extensive forests which covered the continents. However, most of the dry land was still dominated by various forms of lichens, fungi, and towering prototaxites, the tree-like fungus that grew to thirty feet and looked like hairy powerline poles.

Life was beginning to explode and was dominated by the arthropod groups of myriapods, arachnids, and hexapods. The placoderms (armored prehistoric fish) began dominating almost every known aquatic environment. The ancestors of all four-limbed vertebrates (tetrapods) began adapting to walk on land, as their strong pectoral and pelvic fins gradually evolved into legs, and the first primitive sharks began to appear.

The further back we travel, the less is known about the former species that inhabited that time. But right now, more species are being found in fossils, and just in the last twelve months new species of fish, freshwater arthropods, and trilobites, have been discovered. It seems the more we look, the more we find.

Time tries to hide its wonders and its secrets, but it leaves us clues, and sometimes patience and persistence lead to wondrous discoveries.

FROM THE CUTTING ROOM FLOOR – THE JANUS RAT TESTS

In the early part of the book I have Phillip Hanley and Rashid Jamal being interrogated by Jack Hammerson after their first time jumps. We briefly see two live test runs they perform on rats, Bert and Ernie. To keep the story moving, I tightened those scenes considerably. However, for those who are interested in what happened to them, I include them here for your interest – enjoy!

July 25, The Janus Institute – first animal test of new device

Phillip Hanley paced like a caged animal on the raised management level of the Janus laboratory as he watched his team make the final preparations.

He stopped to stare again at the pedestal and what was on its top – a sealed, toughened glass case, inside of which was a black laboratory rat named Bert.

Bert was in a harness rendering him immobile. There were sensors attached to his head and body, measuring his heart rate and brain waves to gauge the effects of the time displacement on his system. Every scrap of data mattered now.

Jimmy's process was to be duplicated, but this time the camera included with Bert had a small tracking device. Even if something happened to the animal, the camera would be retrieved automatically.

Hanley watched as Doreen checked over the test animal and then the camera. Then she bent to wave a hand in front of the lens, and checked the playback to ensure that the data was being captured. She typed information into a computer tablet she held, and then waited patiently inside the tachyon chamber for Rashid to give her the go-ahead to turn the device on and begin recording.

Rashid seemed to mumble to himself, and he typed so fast the sound was a waterfall of clicking. The man was still devastated by the loss of Jimmy, understandably, and Hanley just hoped that he wasn't permanently broken by the event.

Maybe they could take a trip afterwards. Go to some tropical island and sip mai tais on a sunny, golden beach somewhere.

He smiled at the thought, but knew they were most at home and comfortable in a lab drinking lukewarm coffee, and not on some sandy beach somewhere.

They had been grossly impatient. This was what the first living being trip should have been; not sending a reckless adventurer like Jimmy. And they had gained nothing from his doomed voyage. Under normal circumstances failure was expected, and usually proved to be just valuable education – they gathered more data, learned more, adjusted the device, process, or code, and then tried again. But in Jimmy's case, the sensors and cameras had been obliterated, and nothing had come back but his mutilated remains.

Hanley grimaced at the memory and squeezed his eyes shut until it dissipated. Then he looked up; this time they planned to perform at least six more trips with live animals to stress-test their data. Along the way they'd progress the size of the creature, finishing with a goat.

Then, Hanley guessed, it was volunteer time. Again.

Who will go this time? he wondered. *One of our team, or a paid test pilot?*

Certainly not him.

Rashid finished typing and sat back. His eyes darted quickly over the lines of code he had just entered and then he looked toward Hanley. His mouth curved up on one side into a not-quite smile. "Say the word."

Hanley nodded. "Make it happen." He pulled his goggles down over his eyes and then folded his arms.

Rashid turned to Doreen Peng and nodded. The Korean woman reached forward and clicked on the camera and information feeds from Bert's body monitors, and then exited the spherical chamber.

She pulled back to her position with the other technicians and ensured her team's goggles were over their eyes.

"Commencing," Rashid said, and pressed a button on the console.

Once again the soft blue glow appeared around the spherical device. "Selecting bridge stream. Opening portal." Rashid moved a lever and the device's glow began to increase as it built up its displacement charge.

He continued to watch his screen. "Identifying object."

"Bert, the world's second chrononaut," Hanley whispered, and though he continued to smile he felt the fluttering of nerves in his belly all over again.

A blue ball of light then began to form around Bert on the pedestal. Rashid rested his finger on a small button.

"And . . ." He drew in a breath. "Sending." He pressed the button.

The ball of light glowed brighter and brighter for a second or two until it became blinding. And when it winked out, the case and the rat were gone.

"Good luck, little Bertie," Rashid whispered.

The only sound in the laboratory was the soft hum of the displacement device. Rashid watched the small digital clock count down from thirty seconds. At five seconds remaining, he pulled his goggles down again, and the flash of blue light immediately followed.

He looked up.

The package had returned. But the glass case was empty. He stood and Hanley came down the steps from the upper floor and walked closer.

"Oh my God. Again?" Rashid frowned. "Was it attacked?"

Hanley shook his head. "I don't think so. The box is intact. Unopened." He turned to Doreen Peng. "Get the camera. I want to see what happened."

* * *

While Rashid was uploading the data from the latest jump, Hanley had the small case taken to one of the side laboratories set up with a medical-grade stainless steel benchtop and other surgical equipment. He only had on a gown, gloves, and mask, as he didn't think there would have been any contaminants within the sealed case.

He opened it and slid out the small sled that the rat's harness had been fixed to. When it was fully in the light, he saw that everything inside the box was as it had been. Except there was a fine layer of powder or dust in there with it.

He used a scalpel to scoop some up, and gently poured it into a small plastic tube. He added some distilled water and sealed it and then took it to the spectrometer.

He inserted it, started the machine, and almost immediately the screen started to fill with peaks and troughs as it detected and analyzed the different elements. Hanley's eyes moved down the list.

Carbon 23%
Calcium 1.4%
Phosphorous 1.1%
Potassium .20%
Sodium .14%
Chlorine .12%
Magnesium .027%
Silicon .026%
Iron .006%
Copper .0001%
Aluminum .00008%
Manganese .00002%
Iodine .00002%
Molybdenum .000007%
Cobalt .000004%

He half-smiled. He bet there had also been traces of hydrogen, nitrogen, and fluorine, but they had probably totally denatured and/or escaped as gas when he opened the box.

Yeah, they were all there; the elements of a once living creature. Hanley got down on his elbows to peer in at the powder in the glass box. "Hello, Bert."

* * *

Phillip Hanley arrived back on the main lab floor just as they had loaded up the film and it was ready to play. He already suspected what they would see but was curious as to how it would unfold.

He broadened his stance as the images began the same they had in previous runs, with the traveler seeming to drop into a vortex of swirling colors before the camera stopped and refocused. Once again the pristine, white-tiled laboratory had vanished, and they were in a primordial, swampy jungle.

Bert's nose twitched and his legs skittered. Perhaps he wanted to escape into the foliage, but he was held tight, and then before he could do anything else, after his allotted thirty seconds, they auto-initiated the return.

And that's when things got strange.

The camera was focused on Bert and as soon as they entered the return stream, he vanished.

"*Stop*," Hanley said abruptly.

Rashid halted the film. "He just disappeared," he remarked.

"No, he didn't." Hanley narrowed his eyes and craned forward. "Rewind. Slow it down."

Rashid did as asked, and took the film back to the image of the black rat.

He restarted it at half-speed – again, the rat vanished.

"Again, slower," Hanley demanded.

Then one-tenth speed – the rat still vanished.

"*Dammit,*" Hanley sighed. "Frame by frame."

Rashid started again, in a glacially slow, frame-by-frame progression. As they brought it forward they only caught a glimpse of what happened in three frames – one frame, Bert-rat was his usual glossy, black self. Then in the next there was nothing but slumped bones. And then in the third, he was gone.

"Poor Bert." Hanley leaned back, the video confirming what he suspected. "He aged." He steepled his fingers. "Why?"

Rashid shook his head. "But the camera didn't. The containment box didn't. Just Bert did." The man's brows were deeply creased. "Only the biological component."

"Somehow Bert wasn't protected by the portal envelope. Oddly, Jimmy's remains weren't aged. So whatever software changes you made, did this." Hanley rose to his feet. "Unless we can resolve this issue, all we have is a device that would send people on a one-way trip. And then kill them when we tried to bring them back." He spoke over his shoulder. "Meeting in five minutes."

Later, the group sat around a large table in the central laboratory. In the center was the empty glass box, with the powdered remains of Bert in a sample vial. They stared at nothing, or at the box, or at the powder in the vial. But most sat in silence, and it reminded Hanley of some sort of scientific séance, where they were all trying to conjure the ghost of a solution from the remains of a dead rat.

"The tachyons," Rashid whispered.

"Yes?" Hanley looked up.

"We program a place and a time, and the tachyons organize themselves into a highway beyond time and space and take us along for the ride. It creates a bridge between the dual time events, folding the two chronological dimensions together. But the tachyons, they're unaffected by the process, and for whatever reason, somehow they have excluded the flesh from the stream." Rashid tilted his head.

"But we haven't fully controlled them or understood their effects on the flesh. We only think we have," Hanley replied.

"This time, the tachyons bouncing around in the containment chamber are not insulating the cells." Rashid frowned. "Atoms are atoms, cells are cells. What's different? What happened?"

Hanley pinched his chin for a moment, and then held a finger up. "Consider this: you are traveling in a car, safe and sound. But you have left a beach towel tied to the roof. You accelerate up to 460 miles per hour – yeah, it's a very fast car – and inside the car, you are fine. But outside, the temperature on the towel has reached body temperature, around 98 degrees." He looked at each of the faces of his team members. "But if I were able to accelerate to 3000 miles per hour, the friction-borne temperature on the skin of the car would be enough to incinerate the towel completely.

"But inside, you are still fine." Rashid began to nod.

"Correct, and I think that is what happened to poor Bert. He was incinerated, as it were, by time itself. The tachyon stream didn't know that he was supposed to be part of the package. It was as if he was left riding outside the car." Hanley looked back at Rashid. "We need to define everything that we are sending, and we need to better describe the flesh to the software. And that, sir, is a programming problem."

"I take it back. Maybe atoms are not just atoms." Rashid's expression suddenly opened up. "I need to define the bones, the skin, the blood, the cells, everything. I need to tell it why Bert wasn't a camera, or a box. He was so much more."

Rashid rose from his seat, his mind already having departed their meeting. Doreen and several of the technicians also stood up.

Hanley nodded to Doreen and she smiled back at him, as if telling him she approved of his logic. She turned and followed Rashid from the meeting room, taking the tech team with her.

Hanley sat back and put his hands behind his head. "And now, the hounds are on the scent."

* * *

"Test forty-five," Rashid said, and glanced at the pedestal in the control room.

He had never felt so nervous and excited in his life. He had worked almost around the clock to include another half-million lines of code. This time he had sampled the rat's DNA, and fed the strand information into the computer so the algorithms would be able to recognize its total form. They included genetic makeup, skeletal design, and mineral composition, plus cellular analysis, brain electrical activity and function, and Rashid had included details right down to hair strand mechanics.

The work was time-consuming and complex. But it forced him to focus and forget about all their past *mistakes.*

"This time," Hanley said, and lowered his goggles.

Rashid nodded and looked back to the new rat. "Good luck, Ernie. Come back to us."

He pressed the initiation switch, and the blue glow began to form around the spherical device in its sealed chamber, then homed in around the glass case on the pedestal.

"Go," Rashid whispered.

In a blink, the rat was gone. And just as the glow was receding, it brightened again, and the case returned.

The light died away. And then a cheer went up.

Ernie was still there. Alive, and by the look of him, unharmed.

"*Yes.*" Hanley fist-pumped the air. "Well done, everyone. I knew we could do it." He grinned at Rashid. "Well done."

Rashid gave his colleague and friends a small salute.

Hanley began to leave the room. "Continue with the examination. I want to know everything that went on, and is going on, inside that animal."

Rashid nodded and then turned back to the rat to smile sadly. "Sorry, Ernie. Your reward for being the world's first successful chrononaut is death and dissection." He looked up, trying to find Doreen Peng, but she had already left the room.

Odd, he thought. At this important time.

He waved one of the other bio-technicians over. "Take Ernie into the surgical laboratory and prepare him for a full autopsy. I want to know everything, right down to the chemical, skeletal, and cellular level, about what effects that jump just had on his system."

Rashid then looked back at the tachyon device and shook his head, smiling dreamily. His voice was soft, and he spoke mostly to himself. "Ladies and gentlemen, we just perfected the world's first time machine."

Milton Keynes UK
Ingram Content Group UK Ltd.
UKHW010643080724
445166UK00001B/48